# Monster

*Oil on Canvas*

# Monster

## *Oil on Canvas*

### DMITRY ZLOTSKY

## Illustrated by Olga Zlotsky

**A LeapLit Book**
Leapfrog Literature
*Leapfrog Press*
*Teaticket, Massachusetts*

A LeapLit Book
Leapfrog Literature

Published in 2010 in the United States by
Leapfrog Press LLC
PO Box 2110
Teaticket, MA 02536
www.leapfrogpress.com

Distributed in the United States by
Consortium Book Sales and Distribution
St. Paul, Minnesota 55114
www.cbsd.com

First Edition

Library of Congress Cataloging-in-Publication Data

Zlotsky, Dmitry.
  Monster : oil on canvas / Dmitry Zlotsky. -- 1st ed.
    p. cm.
  "A LeapLit Book Leapfrog Literature."
  ISBN 978-1-935248-09-5 (alk. paper)
  1. Conjoined twins--Fiction. 2. Artists--Fiction.
  3. Russia--Fiction. 4. Psychological fiction. I.
Title.
  PS3626.L68M66 2010
  813'.6--dc22

    2009053720

Printed in the United States of America

For Оля


От Д. к О.: Ода

От Д до О—меж нами треть
иль четверть алфавита,
что умудрилась уцелеть
до наших дней.
А что забыто,
как ять и фита,
в томах теней
не в счет,
коль речь течет
как Aqua Vita. . . .

. . . of course it's about Prince Charming, Vera. A very special Prince Charming who was saying not *I* but *we*, not *mine* but *ours*. It's a long story, but don't worry—I will continue even if you fall asleep, so he can accompany you in your dreams.

Will Love abandon him? Will he lose Hope? Who is Doctor Fo-Fo and why does he have such a funny name?

You are asking too many questions. Let's start from the very beginning. . . .

# Love (Part 1)

## MOTHERLAND

Our case history started with a dual image: Romulus and Remus suckling on a she-wolf. Kind Mother would surely excuse this lyrical embroidery. A bi-personal biographer will find our maternity ward in the nexus of crossroads, their tangle providing the foretaste of the fairy tale—turn right and lose your head, turn left and lose your mind, keep on straight and lose both. Welcome to life, chickabiddy. In a lame emulation of the local sky dome, the façade of Mother's labor institution was painted dirty azure.

Our entry into existence, nurse's shriek and doctor's smirk, didn't register in our memory because both of us were busy ripping umbilical snakes like two baby Herculeses and because each of us justly assumed that on our march from maternity to maturity, all supporting extras would exit into extinction.

Our birthplace is marked on the maps by a bold blot. Its name starts with *M*. Those worshiping Rorschach and his clique of inklings can take it from here. For others, unfazed by riddles, MoscoW's near-perfect point symmetry sets the proper tone for our story.

As a preview of nomadic wanderings, we started off with relocation from crib to swaddling table, back to the crib or forward to the carriage shortly thereafter replaced with a stroller—a custom-built two-seater. We moved from place to place so that a casual beholder wouldn't linger over our deformity, evident to both of us from the very beginning; over the deformity that caused us to use the plural personal pronoun not due to royal hauteur but out of accountant's diligence.

We assume that in childhood we could have been diminutively cute, which goes along with ugliness quite naturally, since any deviation in an offspring, be it amphibian or mammal—a cub, a calf, a kitten—sets off compassionate jingles in zoo haunters. Lilliputian helplessness never fails to evoke adoration.

While breastfed, we discovered the concord of symmetry—the world was delivering its nourishment in ample pairs.

Nature, in its blessing or curse, shaped our modus vivendi. We shared our wardrobe, our dinner utensils and our bed. Special kudos to Fate for creating us of the same sex; otherwise our tight coexistence could have turned genderly embarrassing. The month of our birth, named after two-faced Janus, and the hour of Gemini ascending offered yet another tip-off to universal relevance.

To suppress the craving for unfeasible autonomy, Mother gave us homonymous names. We suppose she had other options, like Nick and Nick or Ivan and Ivan, but never, under no circumstances, would we accept Wilhelm & Wilhelm, Otto & Otto, Peter & Paul. More insights into naming significance are forthcoming.

At some juncture in our story, under circumstances to be revealed later, we shall have to depart from the time zone of birth. From that moment on, the Anglo-Saxon semblance of our appellations will come handy, with no more need to clarify spelling obscurities ascribed to a circa-literate registration joker.

"Is it short for Alexei and Alexander?" we usually hear after the introductions.

"No and no!" we deny emphatically.

Both of us—Alex and I, I and Alex—cherish an old photograph, in which we stand holding limbs in eternal unity. We wear identical shirts, shorts and sailor caps. Mother, uncomfortable under curious stares, always dressed us in tailored outfits concealing our binary traits, which excuses our later infatuation with sartorial arts.

*We posed sideways,*
*masquerading our non-hygienic eyesore.*

# Dmitry Zlotsky

This picture opened a family album, long (sadly) lost. There we were—two brave seamen with the puffed-up sail of the mock plywood frigate in the background. The yesteryear quality of the snapshot offered little assistance to memory in its quest to restore minutes. We shall never know whether the palm to our left is a rightful envoy of the local flora or a flat cardboard cutout—an eruption of the cameraman's creative ambitions. Used to discretion, we pose sideways to the lens, masquerading our non-photogenic eyesore. A stranger unaccustomed to our even oddity (as later defined by Doctor Fein with his illegible wit in barely legible handwriting) could easily explain the illusion by the granularity of an old film or by imperfections of antiques and optics.

Time and place in the picture are mixed up—Long-Ago is perceived as Far-Away. The huge, birdhouse-like camera we smiled at then now must be sheltering bats alongside other relics in the attic of the photographer's descendants.

Which is *fein*.

(The underappreciated pun above—oh, we are such *puntheists*!—will be made clear below.)

Singular rascals—ordinary and disorderly—whined about nothing to do and nobody to play with. We, quite contrary, never needed solace and never experienced solitude, which was for us no more than a solecism—a misprint in Ursprache, the language of paradise lost.

Erecting castles out of wet sand, we guarded our territory, hurling handfuls and scoopfuls at sandbox intruders whose raging moms plucked their progenies out and, picking grains from sobbing eyes and snotty nostrils, screamed at Mother:

"This playground is for normal children! Keep your monster on a leash!"

Mother defended us, indicating that we were well-mannered, that we must have been provoked, that they should have watched their own youngsters, but our contented grins greatly diminished the legitimacy of her pathos.

Let's not overlook the vital overtone. The key word has been articulated—monster. That was the image we invoked in the jammed imaginations of our compatriots.

Nature bonded us in a tight package. We share the same style of hairdo (forelocks combed left), the same eyes (green), the same well-defined head lines across our left palms, indicating intense intellectual aptitude. Our life lines are rightly indistinguishable, as it would be preposterous to assume that fate intended to serve us different destinies. And, while on the subject, suffice it to say that we do not fancy *horrorscopes* of chiromancy or attribute any value to the fusion of heart and head lines, known as the *Simian Crease* believed to signify that neither of us makes distinction between thoughts and feelings, and sporting a mockingly misleading similarity to *Siamese*.

Unlike a visual riddle of locating ten differences in adjacent drawings, there isn't a single discrepancy in our external features. What differs is our inner life. I am inclined to dreams, Alex to actions. I am a romantic, while Alex is a cold and conniving entrepreneur.

This said, whatever traits we parade or whatever soul-searching we conceal, I never retire to the river for dreaming alone and Alex never starts a fight without having me by his side. It should be obvious by now that we always meet half-way, because every decision is doomed to be mutual. When one catches cold, both drink cough syrup. When one wakes up, both rush to the loo. Using modern evasive euphemisms, we are solitude-challenged and selfish-proof.

Memory is the key to eternity. Before a crafty medical treatment splits our mind into four detached hemispheres, we have to take advantage of the unique stereo stare and retrieve from the mines of the past all its rubies and sapphires. What do we remember? Many things. Almost everything.

The Indian Summer hatched into the full-blown fall. The approaching winter led to the climax of our favorite tale that Mother used to read out loud while we cuddled under two downy blankets:

*A thin coating of ice skinned over the big puddle by the road, and three little pigs. . . .*

Three, what a ridiculous number, we giggled.

Neither of us cared much about luckless Nif-Nif and feckless Naf-Naf, instantly identifying ourselves with shrewd Nouf-Nouf. In case the local folklore shuns pork and this reference requires clarification, Nouf-Nouf was the industrious one who built a house of bricks. The Big Bad Wolf failed to impress us with his bad breath and frontal assaults, but we were fascinated by the piglets' doubled names. Why not simply Naf and Nif? Was it a veiled message only Alex-Alex could appreciate?

For our birthday in whitish January we always requested identical cakes—twin carrot, twin honey, twin sponge. Lights go out. The dim kitchen flickers in the candle glow. We inhale and blow out the weak flames.

Mother never sent out invitations. She was reluctant to expose us before relatives, and we needed no friends. What did we care for detached confidants when we were so attached to each other? As a supplementary benefit, evenly sliced cakes lasted for the next day (dubbed for its food leftovers as *Chyorstvye Imeniny*—Stale Birthday).

By the time our peers, escorted by pompous kinsfolk, arrived at the first grade gates, our flair for mimicry had evolved so much that in a flowered crowd of bobs and aprons, bits and bobs, Bobs and Dicks, no one paid us any heed. Condescending to minors and civil to seniors, we managed to twist sideways when spoken to, so that our ambiguity never announced itself.

In school we claimed a desk in the far corner of the last row. Other pupils settled in pairs. As for Alex and me, the schoolmarm— an ageless witch with a fake chestnut chignon—left us alone, instinctively protecting the ambience from our ambivalence. During classes we stayed quiet, never volunteered and, if confronted directly, answered laconically, seeking neither approvals nor favors.

"Which one of you, children, knows what letter this is?"

Everybody went wild. Hands quivered like weeds. The matron

(bronze brooch, tight skirt, pursed lips) minced to our desk and, shamelessly bisecting our name, encouraged us by arching her penciled eyebrow.

"First of all," we corrected, "don't take us for a dodo. The appellation we respond to is Alex *and* Alex. Secondly, we know not only every letter in the alphabet but plural pronouns, punctuation signs and points of ellipsis. We don't, however, have to prove that to anybody."

We suppose our town still stands there, on its seven hills, although the country around disappeared for good. The imperial tower of Babel, like its biblical twin, tumbled down under its own burden, wreaking havoc on earth and failing to reach heaven, which, so likeably blue from below, turned into yet another unfathomable Fata Morgana. Pangaea of our childhood ceased to exist, burying evidence of personal Ago under a pile of social smithereens.

# FROM FEIN TO TULCHINSKY

Doctor Fein, who has already peeked into our reminiscences twice (once personally and one more time in an overlooked witticism), now demands proper introduction. Visits to his office became the integral ingredient of our nonage. Mother, in her old-fashioned dreadnought and ridiculous bonnet, always escorted us. Palms on her knees, she rested passively in the anteroom's unwelcoming chair. We, vibrant and energetic, exchanged caustic remarks until the door swung open and Doctor's starched assistant ushered us in. Whatever preceded our entry, we always found Doctor rinsing his hands. The allusion to Pontius Pilate washing off the metaphorical lymph didn't occur to us until the later luxury of retrospect. He hung his waffle towel on a hook and focused on us, his quixotic goatee scraping air, his effeminate lips stretching in sincere contortions.

Adhering to the routine, he made us chant *Ah-ah-ah*, peered into our throats, pulled our lower eyelids downward and tried to trick us into responding in soliloquy, offering dismal bribes like vanilla ice cream (a sole cone) or chocolate (a solo bar).

"Imagine," he addressed us, lulling his own subtle sagacity, "that you have only one popsicle. Would you share it?"

Or, knitting his unshorn eyebrows:

"Imagine that you have only one ticket to a very funny matinee. . . ."

*Two little monkeys, jumping on the bed; Mama called the doctor, and the doctor said* . . . we silently mimicked our dull-witted Paracelsus. Who was in charge here? Who was supposed to take the podium and, instead of posing impractical riddles, give dues to our symmetrical bliss? We would be much more cooperative should he talk about fertilization, about rare instances of mirror twins with opposite features and more common cases of polar twins, who develop differently, both varieties being monozygotic, that is when a single egg is fertilized to form one zygote as opposed to dizygotic twins, when two eggs develop independently.

That, Doctor, would have been an effective way to capture your audience!

The checkup over, he washed his hands again, and Mother held ours as we walked home, choosing quiet side streets.

Our childhood, which started along the tracks of cozy doubletude, eventually opened up to secondary characters in the passing roles of a sobbing sandboxer, his hysterical mother, Doctor Fein (a very fine doctor, indeed), patients, passers-by, idle townsfolk. Adults featured heavy hips, narrow shoulders and small, trapezium-shaped heads coning up from well-developed jaws to constricted temples, because our viewpoint charted the universe from down upwards.

As we were growing up, the proportions improved, but people still failed to expand their involvement beyond that of supporting extras. Most went by monikers—the postman, the pointsman, the physician. Similarly a butcher, either out of indifference or wary of emotional attachment, never names his livestock destined for the slaughterhouse.

It goes without saying that among our classmates we never met a single creature as versatile as Alex and me. They were passing through the backdrop of existence from singletons (a lone fetus in a womb, as Dr. Fein should have made clear) to simpletons, sharing peachy cheeks, a passion for team sports and an aversion to pariahs.

This said, no true account should maintain anonymity. The time has come to separate the first curly sheep from the nameless herd and announce: Enter Love.

Every tongue and every dialect has a name which signifies *Love.* In our language it also begins with *L.* The second letter is so soft that it's missing from the rigid Germanic family. Foreign speakers fail to evoke this elastic consonant-to-vowel transition, in their rugged attempts producing the impression of an infantry battalion dancing the Swan Lake. Its hard replacement *Loo* and the abrupt halt of *boff* in the most tender of sounds—*L'ubov'*—force us to use its translation instead of the never-adequate transliteration. The closest we can offer would be a soft L similar to that in *Lues,* and the ending of a soft V like in *View* without *You.*

Love was the name of our secret insanity. One aisle and three rows of crew-cut scruffs and pen-carved desks separated us during the classroom tedium. Forever will our memory cling to this ardent accounting.

Careless curls of her flaxen locks—pardon the palling epithet—went airborne every time she tossed her hair aside and shook her head in neglect or negation. Never did she turn back to look our way. While exchanging remarks with plump playmates (all of feminine zoology), Love would gaze out the window or, driving our hormones to a quick boil, bare her milky flesh above the knee, where, in neat handwriting, she shortlegged cheats for the upcoming quiz. Math was the subject of her discontent. The rational mind (so alien to her savage enchantment) was absent from her amorous armory. But that was fine. Love had to provide ardor, not prudence.

By some bizarre omission on the part of Mnemosyne, Love's

image, drawn in our minds from the ankles upwards, left no memory of her feet. We are not certain whether she was sandal- or shoe-shod, whether she wore low-cut whitish socks or had her toes deformed by tight leather straps.

Love wasn't a beauty in that classical sensibility, which Alex, as an artist, later strived to infuse into his canvas imagery. Mongolian eyes, low waist, sturdy forearms (shaped by persistent flaps of her tennis racket)—we were quite aware of canonical non-observance. It didn't matter. All imperfections paled compared to her captivating depravity. While others longed for fair Dollies (those impish nymphets of Humbert Humbert, another double fellow), we were happy to have our Lilith. The initial letter shared by Love, Lilith and Lolita is purely coincidental.

Turn around, silently prayed Alex.

Look back, look at us, I echoed.

Typically aloof, we became vulnerable during these mental pleas. The gates to our fortress flew open, ready to accept messengers of affection. However, circus dwarves and harlequins with their acerbic mockery were always the first to sneak in.

"Stop salivating, *twindler*, she is not into ménage à trois." The hiss stirred giggles all over the classroom.

We made no audible comment on the wunderkind's unfortunate choice of words, both concocted and imported.

What were we supposed to do? How could we retaliate?

How else but by confronting the offender and challenging him to a *triel*, the very possibility of the duel denied by our constitution.

Clumsy attempts to make fun of our peculiarity—two can't keep a Punch's secret forever—had to be cut short in the most efficient manner. Fortunately, the same nature that denied us conventional conformity endowed us with sheer force, not so much by doubling the share, but by removing moral constraints that held back its application.

In the sweetest of plots—we dub it the Monte Cristo Syndrome—revenge had always been our prime retort.

We studied the itinerary of the foe and traced his routes, marking the map with a dotted spider maze and an X—a location of both the encounter and the execution.

When the time to gather stones arrived (as the biblical chronicler had phrased it), we set the ambush, pressing ourselves into the scenery and hiding in the after-rain glitter of panes and puddles—world suppliers of casual reflections.

The place was well-chosen—quiet and secluded. The plan was clear-cut. He steps into our trap, we shed shadows and step out. I will say . . . no, words are superfluous. Denying him the opportunity for sorrys, my first blow will stagger him. Alex will kick him. The scoundrel will double up in pain and fear, dirt bubbling up his throat, blood dripping down his nose.

As our vision climaxed, we heard carefree clanks. That's him! Go, I signaled to Alex. You first, he hissed. You are closer, go ahead!

While we nudged each other out of our safe haven, the rascal stopped, slapped himself on the forehead as if he had forgotten something, and turned around. Were it another instant, another inch—we would have leaped out like Scylla and Charibdis, like Gog and Magog. We would have enclosed, crushed and turned him into inorganic dust. His demise would have been inevitable.

Fortunately for our foe, his intuitive vices or internal voices protected him, prompting retreat—his only way out. We stepped into the light, wheezing with excitement.

"Lucky bastard," Alex grumbled, cleaning the dust off our knees.

"Sooner or later, we'll get him." I shook my fist at the scene of a might-have-been bloodshed, albeit not without some relief, because deep inside, both of us were kind and sympathetic.

Our appetite rarely let us down. That evening we had chicken cutlets, mashed potatoes and tea with cherry jam. Disregarding Mother's disapproving sigh, we licked our plates clean. Later, in bed, until falling asleep, Alex and I quietly exchanged the minutes of our prowess.

In the morning, we found students and teachers in shock.

"What happened?"

Someone, they said, some ruthless evildoer or, better yet, a gang of cold-blooded rogues, caught our classmate—not a particularly peaceful bastard himself, we commented under our breath—in the same nook and at the same twilight where we had set our trap. The thugs had beaten him up impartially and indifferently, with cruelty of which Alex and I were never capable.

Once in the intensive care, the twitching urchin was stitched by an intern and, in the best case scenario, would have to miss a week of school.

"What about the worst case?" we inquired, unbiased and open to alternatives.

"The concussion may cause permanent damage, although doctors hope it won't happen." The shoulders of the schoolmarm trembled. Pale palms covered her sloppy lipstick.

She hides a yawn, Alex noted. Her compassion is a show. She is bored as much as we are.

Our detachment didn't stay unnoticed. We caught a flurry of hostile glances christening one of us *bête noire* and the other *enfant terrible*. That was unfair. First of all, we were upset no less than everybody else, and, second, he deserved it.

To kill time, we started a game of battleships on the checkered math notepad, carefully marking squares.

F5, I said.

I knew you were aiming there, Alex laughed. My admiral can read your mind. Our move now. How about A2?

In the midst of the turmoil we were the only sane and composed observers. Common inanity shouldn't disquiet us. That'll be a good lesson to them all.


After several ineffectual visits Doctor Fein showed signs of frustration. "When diplomacy fails, birching is the solution," he told Mother, rejecting her pleas for further therapy. "It may sound like an unorthodox counsel, but it's time for you to consider a whip."

Mother's apologies for the flowerpot, which we had accidentally knocked from the windowsill, weren't accepted.

"What am I supposed to do now?" She turned to us with little hope for support.

"How about surgical intrusion?" Alex suggested. I chuckled.

The next Tuesday Mother made an appointment with a new healer, this time a professor. A luminary, she said.

The commute was boring. Apparently luminaries were a rare breed, as we had to cross the whole town, sliding in street sand like a pair of pro tappers. The waiting room was more spacious than that of Doctor Fein. Instead of the flowerpot, we found a palm-tree in a vat, reminiscent of our old photo, although without a veneer frigate. Exotic fish flashed their tails in a huge aquarium. Two reprints—an autumn woods and a sea storm—adorned the wall. Nice, I whispered to Alex, lightly nudging him with my elbow. I prefer bears in the forest, he responded, referring to one of the three Russian paintings (by one Isaac and two separate Ivans) that came out winners in the reprint race—*Golden Autumn* by Levitan, *The Ninth Wave* by Aivazovsky and *Morning in a Pine Forest* by Shishkin.

Professor Tulchinsky—chubby cheeks and bushy eyebrows over a lazy eye—liberally lowered himself onto a three-legged stool and for a few long seconds peered into our faces, switching his superior eyeball from one to another.

"Well, well, well." His pen made a jousting gesture and prepared to take notes. "What's your story?"

We don't fall for cheap tricks. Alex shrugged. Needless to say, I mimicked. A long silence settled. Professor jotted down some shorthanded gibberish.

"If you don't wish to talk," he said, "I don't mind starting. I studied your case and read Doctor Fein's conclusion. He is absolutely right. Your condition is perfect. You have wolfish health. I see no troubling symptoms, which is what I am going to tell your mother in a minute. I suggest you stop pretending and take an interest in something becoming to your age and agility. Say, soccer or any other exhausting exercise. An evening hobby like chess or drawing is also appropriate. The choice is yours, but the street violence will have to stop; otherwise you may face serious trouble and not only at school."

We listened to his spiel straight-faced. He is like everybody else, Alex signaled. He looks at our profile, sees nothing and assumes that he cracked our swindle.

I laughed sans external mirth. Were he smart, this luminary could have delved into fascinating subjects like parasitic twins or chimerism. Isn't it marvelous when body parts that you consider your own actually belong to your twin? Talk about chromosomal comparisons, Professor, talk about mosaicism, and we shall pledge our undivided devotion. Hey, even a gag about Irish twins would be a welcomed relief!

"You trick neither Doctor Fein nor me," he continued instead. "You need no medications. I am going to advise your mother not to waste money on therapists and physicians. Good-bye now."

Our loving but unperceptive Mother wiped her nose with a moistened handkerchief and surrendered to his high-brow blindness. Instead of listening to his tedious didactics, she would have been thrilled no less than us to learn that chimera, as defined by the professor's own discipline, may come either from identical or from dyzygotic feti, that the number of cells derived from each fetus may vary in different body parts, often explaining mosaic skin coloration in human chimeras.

"What about parasitic twins, Professor?" we would inquire.

"Let's talk about it during your next visit," he would respond.

To our regret, this dialogue never materialized, because for him we were not an enigma but a dilemma—a problem offering two solo solutions, neither suitable to me and Alex.

On the way out, one of us (I am not sure now whether Alex or I, but it's never relevant) casually knocked down a photo standing on the desk. The glass cover shattered into nine hundred ninety-nine unaccounted pieces, like the mirror in the tale about the Snow Queen. However, contrary to the tale about Snow White, who came alive after her crystal coffin cracked, the figure on the picture lay flat and lifeless.

"Oh, Lord," Mother sobbed, "why can't I have a normal family like everybody else?"

We wanted to interrupt and remind her that, quite the opposite, we were utterly, terribly, dreadfully normal. The norm, we would have added, was nothing but the very mean average, distorted by overwhelming mediocrity—those with abrupt seizure of mind and heart lines on their palms.

Ever respectful, we didn't vocalize our disbelief in the services of Comrade Tulchinsky, whether genius or plain luminary. The world was swarming with clues, and two had to be perceptive to recognize them. If there existed a healer able to help us, his name—to which we assign immense importance—had to meet certain criteria. Alex-n-Alex, for instance, is very eloquent and gives away the unpretentious multiplicity of its bearers. The letter F (absent in *Tulchinsky*) was essential for compatibility of the delicate doctor-patient triumvirate. Not the Roman F, angular brush strokes of which are more reminiscent of Chinese calligraphy, but Ф—F-Cyrillic, F of our vernacular, F unblemished by the bond with the four-letter foreign invective, F often depicted in children's picture books as an owl also known as Bubo Bubo. To complement the bird's charmingly repetitive name—a hint not to be discarded—the Cyrillic F represented a symmetric image of two full circles (the owl's eyes in the alphabet pictogram) touching each other and separated by a vertical shaft of axial symmetry. Another way to write the letter—although neither of us advocates it—is to split a circle by a vertical strike. Whichever calligraphy two prefer, the parity always manifests itself.

This cleared, the healer's name better begin (like that of Doctor Фein) or at least include the sound branded by phonetic illuminati as fricative labiodental. Is that too difficult to understand, Fropessor?

Despite our bravado Alex and I longed for our share of human warmth. We wanted hope and love twice as much as anybody else and if a change was needed to achieve that, the world better be ready, because our unity was not to be sacrificed.

"We are disheartened," we told Mother, "and wish to continue the search for a practitioner to rely upon."

Once again we came back home, where, conceding to our insistence, Alex and I owned twin sets of toiletries, a double bed with puffed up pillows, two stacks of textbooks and other paired paraphernalia.

# Fairy (Part 1)

## Sophie wants a daughter

Sophie couldn't remember feeling so impatient since childhood, when she would wake up in the morning, counting days until her birthday, until New Year's, until whatever holiday was winking from behind the calendar grid. Time used to exhibit a rubbery elasticity. It didn't tear, and stretched so that the next week, let alone the next month, never peeked from beyond horizon. Year-long was synonymous with eternal. Life used to have no end.

She crossed the bedroom, then the living room, circled the coffee table, reached the farthest window in the kitchen, turned around and paced back. The gossip column drooled over a royal family scattered by a revolution and now gathered for a reunion in some Kurland or Lapland unpronounceable settlement. What's that old newspaper doing here? On the coarse-grained picture a group of people resembling each other bunched in front of a camera. Everybody was captured en face, smiling straight into the lens, except for one young man who had turned sideways.

Sophie couldn't concentrate and the newspaper flew away like a troubled bird.

What time was it? Still eleven twenty? Is the battery dead?

She stared at the watch, and three hours later the minute hand reluctantly ticked forward, only to freeze again until who knew how long. In the fifth or seventh lap Sophie hit her shin. The vase on the coffee table briefly considered suicide but, after a few hesitant oscillations, kept its balance.

The shin hurt. Sophie wheezed and whistled in a vain effort to trick time, but for her pain, for her inspection of the bruise, for holding the ice, for all this fidgeting, the clock donated only four minutes. Then, as if to crown her misfortunes, the mirror slipped out of hand.

"I am not superstitious," Sophie said out loud. "I don't believe in stupid signs. What does a broken mirror have to do with my appointment?"

She changed her skirt for trousers to cover the bruise readily turning rainbow, put on a jacket, and, not to provoke any more domestic objects, hurried outside.

Puddles from yesterday's rain had already dried. The sun was shining anew, and, although there was no indication that she was the sole recipient of its warmth, Sophie took the weather personally—as assurance of a favorable outcome. Who would deliver bad news on a day like this?

Instead of heading straight to the clinic, she took a detour and strolled around the park, past the museum entrance with its enormous colonnade and oversized announcement of the upcoming exhibition. Art was a godsend for killing time, but Sophie's mind couldn't focus on inanimate items right now. She went across the street to a small café and ordered a cup of cappuccino.

"Cup-puccino," chirped the waitress.

The window with overlaid reflections slightly distorted the Gothic structure of the museum, a linden alley and a playground. The clinic was about twenty minutes away. Walking slowly she could get there at quarter to. That will be all, thank you. Check, please.

Entering one of the paths bisecting the park, she heard her name and turned around.

Isabella, Fodor's former colleague, a middle-aged vulture with an eating disorder and an apparent excess of testosterone, had never become a family friend, although they met quite often in Fodor's office or at someone's birthday brunch. Caustically she called herself a well-rounded woman—even a loose cape failed to conceal her figure's generous curves. Compensating for the bodily ambiguity, her judgment was sharp and excessively acerbic. Sophie's never-questioned intuition cautioned against Isabella. This time, however, any distraction was welcome.

"Have you been exercising? You look good."

That was a lie, of course, but Sophie gratefully accepted it.

"My daughter loves this playground," Isabella said.

"Your daughter? When did you get married? Did I miss it?"

"Oh, no, you didn't. I mean, I didn't. Didn't Fodor tell you?"

Too many negatives, Sophie noted.

"Didn't Fodor tell me what?"

Isabella lowered her voice as if singling Sophie out for the role of a confidant.

"I'm not getting younger, sweetie. I tried the dating service, but it's a joke. You should have seen all those losers. Granted, I am not exactly a femme fatale myself, but come on . . . you know—"

"No," Sophie said, "I don't know. Fodor didn't mention dating services."

"Never mind. That's not what I meant. I am not that desperate. I mean, a man from time to time is not a bad idea, but those encounters helped me understand what I really wanted."

"What's that?"

"I said to myself: what if I get a girl—a little cute critter who would talk to me in her funny plyah-plyah, who would love me and care for me? Fortunately, these days we don't really need this other gender, know what I mean? Let them keep their matter in their own hands. Plus, just the thought of post-gestation acrobatics made me squeamish."

So, Isabella continued, instead of going through with nature's arrangements, she checked in with an agency ("Quite a different kind, know what I mean?") and they took care of everything. "There are countries with an excess of foster homes, you know. I got a ticket, went there, and I tell you this, sweetie—it's totally worth it. There, there she is, with the big purple bow. Isn't she a cherub?"

Isabella hummed happily.

"What about you? I mean, you and Fodor? Planning any kids yet? I think you should, honey. None of my business, of course, but you should."

Sophie forced herself to take her eyes off the vegetation on the woman's upper lip. They tried, she started explaining . . . it's been almost a year now . . . there were some issues, but luckily Fodor found a doctor, a very good doctor. . . . All the tests went well. In fact, Sophie had an appointment in a half hour and surely. . . .

A shriek from the playground pierced her choppy speech. Smoothly like a sea cruiser, Isabella rushed towards the commotion.

"I'd better be going," Sophie said to the vacated space, not to leave the conversation dangling without a proper closure. "I don't want to be late. We'll keep in touch."

Later in the afternoon, Fodor found her on the couch—her legs crossed, her eyes staring into the dusk outside.

"Why are you sitting in the dark?" He flipped the switch and noticed a glass in her hands, a bottle of scotch and an ashtray on the coffee table.

"Shouldn't you . . . ?" he began.

"Oh, it doesn't matter." Sophie waved off the little black flies of his anxiety. "Nothing matters. Barren as a baron. Infertile as a turtle."

"You are not making much sense."

"What does?" External emptiness leaked inside as she, herself, was withering into nothingness.

He sat down next to Sophie and stroked her hair.

"This is not the end of the world. There are other specialists. We can see someone else, try a second opinion."

"What's the point? That was the third, and they are all surprisingly similar—no, not you, never. . . ."

He mumbled about advances of science, miracles of medicine and new frontiers. No, she shook her head. Enough. I am tired.

His consoling words were seeping through, but one, apparently too angular to fit the drainage, got stuck.

*Barren as a baron. Infertile as a turtle.*

"Frontiers," Sophie repeated, "boundaries, borders. At least it's something."

"What do you mean?"

"Today, in the park, on my way to. . . ." She sat up and looked at her husband. "I spoke to Isabella."

"Did she give you a spiel about her new miracle diet?"

Sophie ignored his sarcasm.

"Do you have her phone number?"

"I don't remember. Must be somewhere."

Overcome by a sudden urge for action and careless of the scotch spilling over the couch, Sophie jumped up.

"Give me your phonebook."

"Funny thing, I haven't seen it for a few days. I may have lost it."

Sophie ran to the desk and dumped the drawer's contents onto the carpet.

"What are you looking for?" Fodor watched his wife feverishly digging through paper scraps.

No response. If Isabella could, why couldn't she? The mere thought of it swayed her apathy into the opposite extreme—all too obvious now, all coming together. Of course! So easy.

"There it is!" Sophie slammed the book against the table and flipped it open.

"Strange. I was certain that I had looked there."

"Isabella . . . Isabella. . . . What a mess! How can you find anything here? What letter is she under, F?"

"Please explain what's going on," Fodor begged, catching the glass swan that almost flew off the shelf under Sophie's elbow. "Should I be worried?"

"You should have been worried before. I am fine now," she announced firmly, the airy intoxication contributing to her resolve, and repeated, rearranging words so as not to leave any doubts: "Now I am fine."

Up to that moment her life had been desperate, like a game of chess against a skilled grandmaster. Now the goal gained the lucidity of tic-tac-toe. Sophie applied all her energy to the research and logistics. She got the contacts and references from Isabella. Overcoming nerves on her end of the line and an almost undecipherable accent on the other, she explained her objective. Yes, the voice replied, no worry.

"I would like a little girl. Do you think that's possible?"

Yes, no worry.

"Does it take long? How long does it take? When can we do it? Can we come right away?"

Yes, yes, no worry.

Sophie had a strange sensation that the place would be something of a warehouse with adoption-ready babies settled on the shelves, so Fodor and she would walk the aisles and point: "Do you have someone similar but with darker eyes? What about that one? No, we weren't thinking about twins."

Reality turned out to be quite prosaic. They were ushered into a small room with a desk and an old TV set in the corner. The hostess with a puffed up mane handed them a form to indicate preferences and prejudices. Some questions seemed ridiculously irrelevant; some—woefully reworded from their foreign origin—had to be read twice.

*Because you decide to adopt a child, did you try to bore your own baby?*

Sophie hardly realized what she was marking. This silly tease took about twenty minutes. Finally the hostess inserted a tape into the player, pressed a button with her prosthetic nail and, muttering raspy syllables under her breath, walked them through the succession of images.

"This city. Very beautiful."

The prelude to *Swan Lake* escorted a picture with a cluster of superimposed church domes in the background and the oval welcome message in neon blue.

After the majestic opening, the action moved to a shabby interior, the setting and operator's skills akin to those of an amateur porno.

A stately woman in a white robe greeted them in a guttural tongue.

"Welcome to *Love, Hope, Faith*—a child home," translated the hostess.

Looking at the tiny people on tape, Sophie hardly listened to the jumbled words. Is that my new baby? Or is it this little girl?

Sensitive to her clients' twitches, the hostess pressed pause and consulted her ledger.

"Sorry, this one is gone."

"Gone?" Sophie gasped.

"Gone. Yes. Someone already took her." The woman seemed innocently unaware of ambiguity. Ready? She pressed the play button again.

In an hour, totally exhausted by the misery oozing through the façade of the presentation, Sophie made up her mind.

Travel arrangements went under Fodor's supervision.

"How about a railroad?" he suggested. "I always wanted to try a long uneventful journey. Stops, stations, border guards. We can land somewhere in Europe and then take a train. Forced inaction will give us a chance to put our thoughts in order."

She hardly listened, immersed in her own world. Trains, planes, whatever. That's a man's domain. A woman must take care of the nest. Their space had to be rearranged. Clearing room for the tiny tenant, Sophie exiled Fodor's folios to cardboard boxes and moved breakable bric-a-brac to higher shelves.

Traveling by train indeed provided continuity. After ripping the space apart by a discrete air leap, they melted time in a gradual approach. The doctor's verdict marked the end of her old life. Now Sophie was entering a fairy tale in which she might have to grow a barleycorn in her garden, kiss the petals of the bloom and wait until it burst into a flower with a beautiful girl inside the blossom. That was not precisely how the carrot-maned witch described it, but that's how it felt.

At the border—the invisible line dotted the continent for the ease of state separation—two uniformed men checked their papers and inquired about the purpose of the visit. Pleasure and sight-seeing, Fodor ventured before Sophie could say a word. We don't need unnecessary questions, he explained later.

Their documents were found flawless.

"*Velcum.*" The guard saluted, returning the passports.

The landscape behind the windows changed. The eastward advancement left cute farmhouses behind. The endless emptiness emanated apathy and composure. The territory was enormous and bleak, as though the paint had to be overdiluted to color these vast plains at the inevitable expense of brightness and saturation.

Hypnotized by the rattling monotony, Sophie didn't notice how she slipped into daydreaming.

Light classic tunes accompanied her oblivion. Pinkish and purplish rifts, coiled tubes, fog, slime. A movement formed. A tadpole zoomed ahead, maneuvering through the maze. It was pursued by the next one, by one more, by the whole gang—their speed nauseating—until they all thumped into a whitish mass, trying to penetrate its protective membrane.

Wagging their tails, little ones sank into a giant zero. Could the prize of the divine acceptance be shared between two winners? Before cutting the orchestra short, the director made a final ec-static sweep—ta-da!—and tossed back his hair. The prelude was over; the new life began, shaped into a little angel with braids and dimples.

Two ears, two kidneys, two lungs, one heart. Please count and sign. Sign what, where? Here, right here, here we are.

"What?" Sophie rubbed her eyes, blinking against the light.

Their bags stood at the ready like trained watchdogs.

"Wake up. We are here," Fodor repeated. "Let's go."

# Love (Part 2)

That day we came to school to find pupils glued to the windows, giggling at the chalk arabesque on the asphalt canvas, where an anonymous satirist had inscribed *Alex + Alex = Love*.

This simple sum stunned us. Earlier, despite Fein's admonitions, we would have retaliated by choking the chalker or drowning the draughtsman.

L'ubasha—sweet and ripe like the virgin fruit from the Tree of Love—was indeed the summit of our sentiments; not the lower-case common noun but the proper name personified by our fair class-maiden.

"The bastard got it right." Alex pulled my sleeve. "The equation is perfect. Love *is* the *raison d'*our *etre.*"

"More than that," I added. "She is the *joie de* our *vivre.*"

Her image was accompanied by the fortissimo of our heartbeats. During French lessons of our *educación sentimental* (including those of the foreign language itself), we watched her fixing fringes behind pinkish auricles, knitting her eyebrows and forcing time to slow down or accelerate at her fancy.

Shy in amorous affairs, we couldn't avow our affection. Instead, we stealthily planted our *billets-doux* on her desk and chanced upon her on her walk home. Imperceptive to subtleties, Love whisked away our *sweet notes* (*doux* carrying such uncanny resemblance to *duo*) and, in a hurry to her tennis practice, skirted around our side-wise stance.

As much as we tried, Alex and I failed to snatch her attention. Even when her glance sailed in our direction, it invariably slipped by.

This being a romantic non-fiction, Love lived in a building separated from ours not by Lethe but by a well-trodden small-scale car-ridden Rubicon. In our lofty mood we jammed this mythic Greek and a historic Roman river into one culturally mixed metaphor. The avenue swarmed with dirty hunchbacks and grubby trucks importing suburban centripetal dust and exporting the city's centrifugal haze.

Every day after school, determined like Dotty and Totty, we would cross the yellow brick road leading towards the yellow brick building. The answer to the murky *Pourqoui*—why, oh, why?—was quite lucid. There, on the second floor, behind airy tulle curtains, behind the balcony with weathered whatever and a rusty three-wheeler, reigned Love.

Never were we hospitably ushered into her lair, never walked along those hallways, never passed the kitchen and peeked into the bedroom, where, on a downy mattress, the permanent heroine of our daydreams wasted her unary nights. Nobody invited us and we had to employ imagination to paint the scenery of our temperamental visions with pink tempera.

Her doors were shut to us. Windows, on the other hand, left a peephole into her universe. A potent lens (found in Mother's wardrobe and promptly translocated into our backpack) brought near things that couldn't be attracted by other means. We studied the flaking frame paint, blemishes of masonry and cracks of the balcony banister. Like conscientious caretakers, we were worried that even in nipping winter frost our athletic angel never closed her window's *fortochka*—its little upper-corner leaf.

Could our gold fish catch sight of us through her aquarium pane? Not a chance. We were safe in our vegetative haven. At such distance she couldn't tell us—in khaki shirts, behind solid shrubs—from local flora.

The binoculars focused on her loggia.

If only we were in a fairy tale! As soon as the princess of two-bed-roomdom stepped onto the concrete slab of her terrace, we would gallop up on a magical twin stallion, leave a blazing bouquet in her hand, a burning kiss upon her cheek, and disappear, hiding among classmates like two simple-hearted fools—our palm scratched by a rose, our hearts pierced by Eros.

Why a scratched palm? Melting in the heat of passion, she would find the presence of wit to slash the stranger with a thorn, so that later her messengers would rummage the school hallways in search of the handsome braves.

As to the magical twin stallion, it was our only haulage option, since no regular Arabian, Hanoverian or any other eponymous pony could gait us to the second floor of the fairy tale-proof residential low-rise with high ceilings and the always-open window leaf.

Quite likely our wound was to be inflicted not by a thorn—romantic but improbable; tea roses in these latitudes wane quickly—but by a splinter from the cracking banister.

Alas, we never reported to history class with a cloth wrapped around our hand to hide a not-yet-coagulated cut. Not because our blood with a flawless balance of erythrocytes curdled instantly (as per tests supervised and blessed by Doctor Fein). The shut balcony door was the true reason of the *unhappening*. Love never showed up next to the rusty tricycle, resting her palms, dominated by Venus mounts, upon the battered parapet.

"What do you think you are doing?" A cane poked through to our shelter, and an old hag frowned at our crouched pose and erect spyglass.

"Go, lady." We fanned her off. "Wilt away. What do you know about Love?"

## Love's birthday

During a recess, from behind one of the columns generously planted in school hallways by a pillar-obsessed builder, we overheard

Love talking to her friend. Her girlfriend, of course.

We didn't hide. We have nothing to veil or be ashamed of, happy to furnish our profile for anybody's sociable stare. The column was a matter of convenience—those who passed on the right saw Alex-*dextra*; those on the left Alex-*sinistra*; both of us dexterous, neither sinister.

"Who else is coming?" asked Love's freckled confidant, accepting an invitation to the birthday party. What was the name she responded to? Let's pick Anastasia as a replacement for the demonstrative but quite unemotional pronoun. Both girls were ugly uniformed in jackets, black aprons and pleated skirts, the latter—despite its mission of disfiguring flesh—revealing fully formed and thoroughly seductive kneecaps.

Despite our double chance, in the list of guests' names we heard neither of ours. Our hearts' pace quadrupled. Did she invite a crowd of outsiders and forget her most loyal devotees? We shrugged the treacherous thought off—how could we be vindictive and bear grudges against you, Love-dear?

How, indeed, could we be bitter when the curls and curves of our cutie throbbed behind the column, at a right arm's length of one Alex and a left arm's length of another? A brief internal counsel unriddled her reluctance to mention our names.

Commandment number three, I whispered.

Thou shalt not take the name of thy sweet patootie in vain, Alex picked up.

Love has offered us a chance to manifest our feelings, we concluded. Let's surprise her. Surprises stick in the memory forever.

Our cardiac crankshafts sped up again, this time enriched with adrenalin. That's what it was! She wanted us to take the initiative into our four hands. What would be the most effective? Think, Alex, think, Alex—two heads are better than one.

"Where are you going?" Mother watched us as we were getting ready to leave.

We hesitated.

"To . . . m-m-m . . . the chess club. We are wunderkinds, Mother. We defeated everyone else and reached the final round. Today we shall be facing each other."

"I didn't know that you liked chess."

Of course we like it. We adore it. We love it. Love—get it?—we Love it!

The journey of a thousand leagues began with the thousand and first lie. Steadily, like trappers familiar with their terrain, we marched towards the passage between buildings, the ever-ready binoculars dangling down our necks.

A recently deceased epoch of architectural exuberance had planted these passageways, now permanently imbued with the scent of our compatriots' bodily incontinence. Luckily, the sense of smell happened to be the least invasive of our informers.

A long time ago, young and inexperienced, seeking relief from a severe cold, we grabbed a vial from Mother's first-aid kit and sprayed a generous puff up our nose.

The stuff we took for an elixir turned out to be iodine intended for cuts, not colds. The twinge made us double, that is quadruple, up. Our mucus tunic was burning.

Our running nose instantly dried, taking away the ability to discern both the scent and the stench of our motherland's backyards. This little medical misfortune turned into a viable panacea for air purification.

Now in a festive—unfazed by olfactory insensibility—mood, we juggled the bouncing echoes.

"Hey!" Alex yelled.

"Hey, hey!" echo and I countered, in our exultation oblivious of the extremely consonant and exceedingly rude Russian expletive, just one middle vowel away.

We passed the arch, but the acoustic dummy still tossed about, trapped behind in the stone semicircles. The day, Doctor, was *fein*. Fine and special. We inhaled the dusty air and, after the winter slush, basked in the moment. Little sandlings—messy messengers of spring fever—crackled under our feet.

We grinned at a passer-by—*Hey!*—and it didn't cross our minds to throw a pebble at his back after he threatened us with his walking stick. That's how big-hearted we felt. People in the town of our birth were unaccustomed to big-, let alone double-heartedness. But let's stay away from generalities. Let's stick to the facts.

And the facts are that, unlike our two-dimensional compatriots, limited to height, width and mediocrity, our ability to observe objects from acute viewpoints allows for perceiving depth.

Love scheduled the celebration for the late afternoon. Even though no one personally invited us with a significant, larger-than-words message in heartfelt soprano, we looked forward to the solemn soiree.

We passed the playground, with swings squeaking the rust off their joints. Senseless youngsters splashed in the sandbox. Alex and I casually approached the flowerbed, already in bloom; then, in a swift harmonious grace, like a pair of deft pianists chiseling out four-hand Goldberg variations, we swept over the blossoming buds.

"Hey!" infuriated grannies yelled as if the arch's echo had finally caught up with us. "What are you doing?"

Oops, too late.

"If only . . . you knew . . . who this is for," we muttered under our breath in the intrepid escape, "you would . . . encourage us . . . to pluck more."

Pressing the binoculars and the freshly uprooted bouquet close to our hearts, we galloped away and nobody could catch us.

"For you, Love," we sang and buried our noses into pistils and stamens, sensing colors but not odors. Was this kind supposed to smell at all? We weren't well-versed in botany. School lessons in *floricking* failed to excite us. Adam, our singular ancestor, gave names to fauna. We, on the other hand, never name. We dub. And speaking of plants, we only knew the trees of Life and Love. The rest were generic—hay, thorns and lumber.

"I don't personally care about flowers, . . ." Alex remarked.

". . . but Love should appreciate them, . . ." I added.

". . . we'll quench our thirst from the well of her joy," we concluded with high-flown pathos.

Shuffling feet in order to scrape off the flowerbed humus, Alex and I reached our improvised observation post. Through the branches that guarded our privacy we magnified the sacred window to the full capacity of our binoculars like two Lord Nelsons.

What was going on behind the tulle? Were they ready for the reception?

Love and her helpers still had time. Quite possibly at this hour they had already arranged the sitting. The best tablecloth must have covered the fully unfolded tabletop. The birthday girl would sit at the head. You, girls, stop giggling and go to the far end; these two chairs are reserved for the daring admirers.

In its descent, the sun bounced off the window panes with the same agility that Love must have applied when returning ground strokes of her tennis foes. We squinted. Once again, imagination remained our most reliable mole.

The quest continued:

What kind of china were they using?

How many chairs had to be borrowed from the next door neighbors?

What was the theme selection of fare and refreshments; was it deliberate or eclectic?

Given a choice, we would prefer unpretentious but nourishing victuals—pasta, pickles, cabbage pie. Unfortunately, the curtains concealed the menu. It's fine, we consoled each other, let her surprise us.

Waiting for the sunset and for sun's crystal substitutes to light up the inside, we shifted focus to the building's entrance.

There, in the branches of the tree of neither love nor life, right above the front steps, a gang of pigeons set up its headquarters. Suffering from an unhealthy city diet, they turned the tarmac into the canvas of a pointillist. Fowl Seurats and Signacs accompanied every shot with billing and cooing. Like true artists, the birds drew inspiration from their own indigestion.

Finally some familiar backs started entering the building. Anastasia walked in, clanking on her mother's heels. In a minute or two we saw the nemesis of our childhood, whose bygone concussion proved to be nothing more than a harmless shake-up of wits.

As he carves himself a niche for his cameo presence with the persistence of a provincial prima, we shall, from now on, refer to him by name, by his unabridged and anglicized name that is, because everything *true* might be confusing no less than the truth itself. The straightforward transliteration of his name creates a problem—should *Pavel* be pronounced like *gravel* or like *navel?* The world defined by caconyms can be perilous unless unriddled by euonyms. Why don't we call him Paul? History knows cases of more careless conversions, like Jacob to Israel, Simon to Peter, even Aurora to George.

(Exiled from bookshelves long ago, George Sand, albeit not through her writings, bears uncanny relevance to our story. Her sanctified namesake St. George slaying the dragon is, of course, the Moscow mascot, and deserves mention if only for the names' consonance.)

Windows in the building lit up, resembling a chess *endspiel* by the rare placement of bright spots. Then, as the dusk grew denser, the blinking of lights intensified, filled the board with more lit squares and entered a lively *mittelspiel,* the only (apart from *Liebefraumilch*) poetic word in the whole German language. Soon all squares were on, overturning the game's timeline and announcing the beginning. It *was* a chess game. We hadn't lied to Mother after all.

By the time we scrambled out of the hideout, the sky had soaked in darkness long enough to develop its bleakest constellations. The posy in our hands went limp like overcooked noodles. That's all right, we whispered to the stems, soon you'll be taking a vase bath.

An instant later twin Tristans, ready for a tryst with their Izolda, entered a never-before-experienced proximity to Love's lair, optical attraction notwithstanding. Stairs, walls, neighbors' doors—the interior was alien.

We figured out her apartment by the geography of windows. The peep hole emitted welcoming warmth. Jingles of vinyl music, laughter, noisy chatter, all seeped out slightly choked by the sound-proof door. Alex pressed the buzzer.

What are we going to say? I nudged him.

The words will come, he reassured me.

We buzzed again.

"Too noisy. Can she hear us?"

Inside, the lucky losers were scurrying right to left as if writing a message and hurrying back—left to right—as if erasing what had just been written. Their bodies broke the light beam, flashing a message in Morse code through the eyelet: dot-dash-dot, flash-dark-flash.

"It's us, Love!" we hollered on top of our bellows. "We have come to you. Can somebody open the damn door?"

Nothing.

"What if we say that the world knows no souls as tender and affectionate as ours? Then we offer the flowers."

"We have to get in first."

In a fit of temper Alex kicked the soft padding.

"It's no use," I said feeling his pain. "They will never hear even if we ram the door."

The flowers in our hands were fading from thirst.

"What if you wait here, while I shout at the windows from the outside?"

That was impossible, of course. Even if we could, we'd never want to split up because Alex and I are two *hemis* of one sphere. All our jokes are insiders'.

"Let's climb up the balcony!"

Not waiting for his objections, I set off downstairs, jumping steps and leaving Alex in charge of maintaining the balance.

Two-faced Janus—towards whom we feel a kindred spirit and who had never been tricked by *Behind your back!*—served as the god of gates, doors and doorways. We were asking for a downright trifle. Oh Regional Almighty, in whose image we are made! Why don't you grace us with protection of balconies?

Amen.

Amen.

Alex looked left; I looked right. The street was deserted. All we had to do was to clamber on the canopy, then jump over to the balcony.

The awning above the entrance was supported by side walls with decorative holes. We appreciated the practical value of this improvised love ladder. Clenching flowers between teeth, we clung to the ornamental embrasures, flattened against the wall and felt for the next fulcrum—a left hand, a right foot; a right hand, a left foot.

"You shee," we yaw-yawed, bitter stems in the mouth affecting articulation, "noshing could be eazhier."

The high ceilings of the human beehive didn't hamper our ascent. In less than two minutes we, with a scratched knee and a slightly torn trouser-leg, were catching our breath on top of the canopy. We were two captains at the rostrum of the Flying Dutchman. Zephyr caressed our ruddy skin and the binoculars dangled down our necks. The view from the top was intoxicating.

"Don't look down," Alex mumbled.

He had to cheer himself, because *I* have neither high nor low anxiety.

Love's balcony was now within reach. The windows puffed out a cloud of light. Voices inside jingled, feet tapped, plates and cups rattled. During the brief respite we allowed ourselves an innocent fantasy.

What if L'ubasha decided to invite us to a dance?

As dancers Alex and I were, to put it mildly, inadequate. Waltzing each other was pathetic; having a third collaborator was a socially discomfiting exuberance. No member of the Strauss family ever composed a tune for an odd number of partners in a dancing pair. In addition to the numerical obstacle, our musical ear left much to be desired—we can't tell a Mee from a See.

At the moment, however, dancing concerns seemed premature. We leaped for the balcony and—our feet still on the awning—grasped the parapet. Alex, hanging slantwise like a forward slash, stared down and turned white. Our unprotected underbelly stretched over the stinging nettle. The chasm squeezed and twisted his duodenum. The poor boy felt nauseated.

"Get hold of yourself," I snapped, "or both of us will throw up."

I jerked forward, pulling him after me. We stretched even more, our fists holding on to the railings ahead, our toes clinging to the slab behind. The cooing above our heads intensified with clearly mocking undertones.

Damn the pigeons! With a decisive push we took off from the platform and scraped air, feeling for support. Somebody's foot slipped, somebody's—caught on. After a short struggle we rolled over the parapet and gasped, tumbling on top of the rusty tricycle. The touching image of tiny Love pushing these very pedals helped little to soothe the pain.

Back on our feet, we tried the handle. Locked. Forget the door. I pointed. The window is ajar. We scrambled upon the windowsill and pushed the curtains aside.

Act Two. Interior. The birthday party at Love's apartment. Enter Alex and Alex.

Our appearance was announced by crystal chimes. Blinded by the lights, one of us, whose name started on A, knocked off a vase. Fruits rolled all over the floor. The crowd came to a standstill.

We turned sideways and aligned our profiles. And then, out of the mosaic of reflections, came forth Love in a sky-blue gown spangled with silver stars. Blushing and beautiful, staring right at our outline for the first time, she focused not above our heads and not behind our backs. Her radiant irises pierced our ribcage and penetrated our hearts. The fairest apple from the vase made a wide circle and stopped at the feet of our Aphrodite. The vinyl disk crackled and hissed out. We cleared our throats and tried to compensate for the broken vase by breaking ice:

"Luckily, it wasn't an urn. *That* could be embarrassing."

Not a chuckle. I pulled slightly crumpled flowers out of our bosom. A few lilac petals flew off.

"Love!" we declaimed, still towering on the sill, "please accept these forget-us-nots as a token of our sincere. . . ."

Sincere what? Our flaming philippic momentarily stumbled. Fortunately the mind unclogged as the words muscled through.

". . . please accept these what-nots as the epitome of spring!"

Extending our hand with the meek hay, we jumped down. Love in her celestial garb drew back.

Should we embrace her? Should we endow her with a bi-kiss?

While we hesitated, the lights went out. Crystal slivers and shivers on the floor glistened like fallen stars. Sputtering sounds approached from the corridor. Shadows vacillated and came alive. Holding the candle-spiked cake her mother floated in.

"Happy Birthday, dear L'ubochka!" she exclaimed, stretching vowels in over-emphasized tenderness. Nobody joined so we did, to save the moment.

"Happy Birthday to you-ou-ou-ou. . . ."

A snicker bubbled in the dark corner, although every corner was dim at the moment.

Mother's coloratura faded. The pause was spreading out like an ink blot open to interpretation. Flowers in our extended hand wilted. Someone flipped the switch up. We squinted.

The room furnishing wasn't particularly exquisite. Along the wall stood a sideboard with stacks of family china. In those days, sibling sideboards were habitual tenants of every household. Faience and delftware satisfied the aspiration for coziness. A mandatory pre-one-or-another-war dish, placed upright, depicted a garden scene from the lives of nymphs and satyrs.

In addition to the cupboard, the room featured wallpaper with golden ivy over the white background, a black-and-white oval photo of a couple with dreamy eyes and diffused contours—a daguerreo-jump back over a generation or two. The table was moved over to the sofa, freeing up a dancing square. A television set in the corner hid under a home-made macramé like a Muslim woman under yashmak—our L'ubasha is such a hand savvy!

Among the guests we identified Anastasia, aforementioned Paul and one Pyotr, whom we prefer to call Peter. An old scar crossed Peter's forehead. Did we do that? I wired. Did we give him a double whammy like we had thrashed Paul? If not, we should've.

The adolescent scenery required Peter or Paul or someone else in the crowd to be infatuated with Love, but we feared no competition. Our chances against singularities were perpetually doubled.

Her mother finally focused on the crystal remains.

"My vase!" she howled. "Who did this? How could you? Do you know who it belonged to? Do you know how valuable it was? That was all we had from my grandmother!"

She dropped the cake, slumped on her knees and groped for fragments, trying to jigsaw her memory.

Delicately, we watched candles melting over chocolate.

"We also had a grandma's vase," Alex recalled with tenderness. "Just like yours, it was standing on a windowsill. Someone opened the door, the drought puffed up the drapes and—*bams!*—the vase was no more."

All heads turned in our direction. Now, that's uncomfortable, I whispered.

"Who is that?" Love's mom shrieked.

Rather than correcting her *is* for the proper *are,* we pointed to the wax stomps in the cake.

"The birthday girl better blow out the candles. No wishes should go to waste."

Nobody moved. The cake was half ruined. We leaned forward and synchronously, like two windy brothers—Eurus from east and Notus from south—blew out the remaining flickers.

"Let all your desires," we declared solemnly, our words bouncing off the glass cupboard right at our Loveling, "turn true."

"Who the hell are you?"

We didn't let her mother's anguish blemish the charm of the moment. Love must have come from a simple, discourteous family.

Alex and I rushed to redress the rudeness.

"Who are *we*? We hope that you are not asking our names like Cyclops Polyphemus was asking Odysseus—in order to curse him? Do you know *what* we had to go through to get here? We raided the flowers, we escaped enraged momsels, we climbed the vertical wall. All of this—to avow our affection. Love knows who we are, but, if you insist, we'd be glad to introduce ourselves."

"Alex," said Alex.

"Alex," said I. "Nice to meet you, Love's mom and you, other people."

"He just barged in through the window," offered Pyotr-Peter. The name just wasn't meant to be the rock of any faith, its carriers turning treacherous one after the other. We perceived communal enmity. Good thing he didn't try a brotherly kiss.

"I didn't invite, . . ." Love began, shaking her Love-ly head.

The skies split wide and cold streams spilled the heaven's despair. Rejected and trampled, the flowers flattened themselves on the floor.

"What do you mean, you didn't?" our harmonious duo exploded. "And who pretended talking to her (two index fingers aimed at Anastasia) as soon as we settled behind the column? Who cast low glances, too shy to look in our direction? How else should we have interpreted your premeditated indifference but as modesty and timid infatuation?"

"My vase!" her mom's moans resumed. "Grandma loved it so much. Did she save it through wars and fires so that some dunderhead could knock it on the floor?"

"Dunderheads," we corrected, realizing that the amphora was just a metaphor, although quite elegant, for matters falling apart. "We could help glue it together if you want."

Peter and Paul made sneaky strides in our direction. Surrounded by the gang, we couldn't protect ourselves back to back. We stood side by side.

Someone is going to regret angering us, I wired to Alex along our silent communication lines.

They held their fists low like matadors. We raised our hands high like martial artists.

And then the P-n-P attacked.

We jerked and twisted, trying to free ourselves from the iron embrace but the athletic bastards held tight, dragging us towards the door. Alex grabbed the hallstand. I freed my right hand and swiped at the offenders with a force that took away the remnants of our balance. Alex's foot slipped, the trousers' fabric cracked, and both of us, accompanied by the hallstand, went crushing backwards, down on the black and white tiles of the stairwell landing. Up and down, light and darkness, good and evil—all smudged. Above us hung a low sky dome of the second floor. We lay flat on our backs like defeated chess kings.

Lights out. Curtains. Brief unconscious intermission.

An angel face looked down at us.

"Who are you?" we mumbled.

"My name is Nadezhda. Are you hurt?"

Yes, we remembered. No, it didn't hurt. Wasn't she one of those quiet guests, a fair face in the sullen crowd during our echoing soliloquy? Nadezhda, what an appropriate name! Every language has a name meaning Hope. That's how we were going to refer to her for that's what she was. As to our vocal response, we said what any two noble men would say:

"We took pity on them. They are no match. We can maim any enemy. We just didn't want to harm anybody."

Then the strangest thing happened, as strangeness never gets exhausted in our presence. The familiar goatee appeared in the midst of the unfamiliar setting:

"Naden'ka, let me take a look."

"Doctor Fein?" we exclaimed, trying to sit up. "How did you. . . ? Why didn't you. . . ? What are you doing here?"

We were aided up and escorted back to Love's quarters, this time through the door, this time to the kitchen. A brief examination determined that, apart from instantaneous swellings on the backs of our heads, we had come out unharmed. A glass of water was supposed to calm us down.

"Two," we said.

"Two what?"

"We need two glasses."

He didn't argue. We took tiny sips, leaving both glasses almost intact, and demanded an explanation:

"Where did you come from? We are always happy to see you, but did someone tell you that we were in trouble? Did someone call emergency?"

"Why call?" Fein raised his eyebrows. "This is my home. I live here."

"How is that possible?" We recoiled. "Isn't it Love's nest? We mean L'ubasha's house."

"L'ubov' is my daughter."

If we had ever been stunned, this was the moment. The daughter? But your names . . . your last name is Fein. If she is indeed your daughter and if you live, like you claim, as a family, how come her last name is different?

"Well, I am her stepfather."

That's what it was! We could understand him, of course. Our town—the pinnacle of our motherland—our whole culture was very particular about oddity. Alex and I experienced it sharper than anybody else. Sometimes, when growing up in alternately freezing and melting slush, we wished to be like everybody else— careless and singular. We couldn't. Love apparently could. While *Fein* was an excellent signifier for an obscure scientist, it was no fit for a sexually appealing female. Her last name, to which we shall dedicate two forthcoming paragraphs, was perfect in that respect.

What could be better for a girl, than to be identified with the fairest of objects? Her last name, by which we knew her in school, was Tzvetkova. Although cognomens are customarily transliterated, we shall make an exception and translate it in due course, but not before we go over the name's standing in our society.

The vowels in order of appearance are: E like in *pet* and *bed*, O like in *soul* and A like in *sweetheart*. Gallic tongues, stressing the first syllable, would have articulated it as Tzv-*E*-tkova. By such emphasis we can always identify a non-native. The proper accent falls upon the soul—Tzvetk-*O*-va. Of the consonants the first two are really one (does that remind you of something, or better yet, someones?). In the original, *Tz* is indeed one letter which sounds not like *X* in *Xena*, but like *zz* in *pizza*. Now we have a complete acoustic concession of Love's lust name, pardon the typo.

She should have inherited a name from her father, step or no step, and used it for census data until upcoming matrimony and identification with her husband's lineage.

Proclaiming pluralism on paper, in daily life our culture worshipped conformity. Fein or Feinberg or even Faynburger stood out like shameful Shem among jovial Japheths.

That's why we were shocked to learn that Love's father was none other than our old mentor with a magnifying lens to peer into our retina and a rubber mallet to test our reflexes.

Jammed on a single tripod of a kitchen stool and rolling our eyes for Doctor Fein to enjoy our whites, we almost forgot the reason for the whole excursus into the name etymology.

*Tzvetok*—the noun from which the name originated—means *Little Flower*, and what's better for a girl than to be identified with the fairest of objects? Therefore, approaching the climax in the narration that could be dubbed as *Rejected by Love,* we finally arrived at her proper introduction—meet Love Flowerbud.

Later at night, on the brink of oblivion, we exchanged the day's impressions. Yes, there was a failure, but how spectacular! Love seemed closer than ever before. In her celestial dress, she continued to rule two unbridled imaginations.

"Shall we make a flowerbed for our flowerbud?" giggled Alex, ever fond of flipping letters. Apart from this flirtatious remark, our imagery remained virtuous. Obscene sensual intimacy, burlesque escapades of the gruesome threesome, perspiring puppetry and palpetry never shaped in either's vision.

# RETURN TO DR. FEIN

"Mother," we said, poking at the hotchpotch evenly smudged over a peanut-shaped plate, "why do you make such a fuss over the torn trousers? Young people often wear clothes out. Let's change the subject. You could have been right. We might benefit from a knowledgeable advisor. Please make an appointment with Doctor Fein."

A few days later, sane and sanguine, we settled in his waiting room, in its far corner, not to be associated with other wretched and unfortunate patients. Soon, Doctor Fein appeared in the doorway and welcomed us in.

During our absence, his office had shrunk in inverse proportion to our own growth—shrunk, shrank, shrink!—but otherwise it had stayed faithful to our memory. We moved two chairs together, turned sideways to his desk and sat down. Facing clouds outside, we aligned so that he had no misapprehension of our split personality.

"How is Love doing?" we inquired, politeness personified. "How is her progress in tennis? Are her volleys crafty, is her backhand steadfast?"

He ignored our well-intended elocution.

"Are you feeling all right? Headaches, nausea, dizziness?"

"Never," we swaggered. "The bang didn't bother us a bit."

"To what do I owe this visit?"

Alex and I cupped our chins. From Fein's viewpoint it appeared like Alex did it alone, so perfectly were the moves coordinated.

"That's an excellent question, Doctor. You see, when we were young and our poor mother brought us—two naughty brats—here, we didn't appreciate your science. Now, wizened in adolescence, we need to reevaluate illusions and overcome deformity. Our goals finally coincide, Doctor. You are the help-provider, we are help-consumers. We wish to become valuable members of society, be it shoveling slush or swiping sand. *Hippocratically* speaking, of course. And no, we do not intend to break-n-brick any bric-a-brac this time."

"Well," he mumbled, "I suppose it's a good sign. Acknowledging a problem is halfway the solution."

"Exquisitely stated."

As Doctor Fein circled his desk to get closer, we rotated like an astrolabe to keep his stare at 90 degrees—the most righteous of angles.

"Why don't you face me?" he suggested. "Turn, sit straight. Don't gaze out the window while we are talking. I need eye contact."

"Let's take it slowly, Doctor. If you indeed wish to look at us prima, pardon the candor, facie, we will demonstrate a little trick."

Alex produced a small mirror, which we had plucked out of Mother's powder box. Our glances met—the optical ploy brought us together.

"Is that better?"

He made a quick note in his ledger, undoubtedly praising our ingenuity.

"One more thing, . . ." we said.

Before we could continue our fruitful collaboration—after which we were supposed to become *a better person* as he would put it, or *twice as good* as we knew we were—Alex and I needed to clear a few formalities.

The language we used at the time was different from the one we shall employ later, after traversing the globe in our clockwise course. That language was quite appropriate for slush, sand and other circumstances of coming-to-be.

A part of that long-squandered lexical heritage was addressing minors with singular condescension. Doctor Fein did not make use of plural *you*. Instead he spoke to us as *thou,* which failed to satisfy us for two reasons.

Reason one: it always made us wonder whether he was talking to Alex or Alex, and thus impaired our communication.

Reason two: although convinced agnostics, we reserve *Thou* for the biblical implementation of innermost pleas to the Creator. All other applications are blasphemous.

If he still found our insistence in such matters bizarre, he could treat plural *you* as a polite form of addressing a singular but respected human being.

". . . after all," we concluded, "this is not Spanish, in which you have to be conscious when choosing *ustedes* before *usted*. It is more like French *vous* whether there is one or many. Is French courteous enough for you, Doctor?"

He scratched his chin—a much better developed fixture than the almost non-existent one of his decorated colleague Professor Tulchinsky.

"As you see," we ventured to note, "we are unique, if you can apply this description to a twofold entity. It's like the triune Lord without one Godhead. What does modern science have to say about such a case?"

"I don't think modern science should be concerned with you. So." He pensively placed both his hands, palms down, on top of the open notebook. "What do you want to talk about?"

"To better understand who we are, you should know where we are coming from. Unquiver your ballpoint, mark the beginning with two tightly embraced asterisks and be sure to capture the mood, because our very tone is now ascending to pathos. Let's begin with the enigma of our birth."

★ ★

Most family trees grow incognito. Blank shoots of plentiful parvenus hardly attract a bio-dendrologist. Should an anonymous annual wither away, nobody will care for its farewell fizz.

But, apart from weed and lumber, genealogic flora knows

a rare gem—species blooming in private property attended by gloved gardeners.

To trace the grand-Alex ancestry one has to cross a well-groomed lawn, approach a royal cedar, lean to its majestic trunk and listen to the story rustled by the leaves.

We shall let the clock hands assume the role of the compass arrow, in their circular yet straight chrono-motion, firmly uniting time and space.

Our facial outline, in maturity turning nobler, can be found on fading stamps and worn out coin heads. In the succession of names, whether in Latin or Cyrillic scripture, a philatelist and a numismatist identify those of Alexander, Nicholas and George but never Wilhelm, Juan or Luis.

This is how the dotted line of memories should have begun: we sit upon our grandfather's knees—striped uniform gabardine, sparkling boots, clanking spurs; our puffy fingers play with saffron-colored, tightly knit aglets; we scratch our cheek against a resplendent medal star. . . . Alas, despite our birthright to remember huge ballrooms with slippery parquet, and narrow windows rising all the way to the high ceiling, winter hunts with a pack of borzois—these scenes are stored in the back rooms of genetic but not personal reminiscences. By the time of our appearance, social tempests had wiped out the décor of family luxuries, leaving for us only a flat plywood cut-out of the fake frigate and plain toys of poverty: empty match-boxes, bent spoons and bottle smithereens polished by the sea and promoted to the ranks of jewelry.

Tsar Nicholas and King George—whose lifetimes had been annexed by history textbooks—had another distant cousin sharing with his regal relatives not only hereditary memories but also a majestic and noble profile—a pensive glance, a manly nose bridge, a well-defined chin. Was he an Archduke or a Grand-earl? We don't know. Fungus of democracy distanced royal title formation from common knowledge.

The turmoil started with a blank shot from the battle-cruiser *Aurora*. The rebels swept away guards and thronged the square in front of the Winter Palace, chanting for *panem et circenses*—perennial appetite of citizenry. Those who failed to flee were promptly converted into circus freaks.

A not-yet-named so-and-so (note the unmistakable X-and-X name formation, Doctor) turned lucky. After a narrow flight from the palace, our caped escapee reached the sea and, among the last passengers, boarded an overcrowded steam-boat. Background of the haven and foreground of the drama filled with shrieks, smoke, rifle crackling—all alarming, none harmful. With a steamy honk of the departing port, Cyrillic plains were finally left behind.

★ ★

The hinges squeaked, mocking the ship's toot and interrupting our tale. Fein's high-healed helperess appeared in the doorway, and we revolved so that both she and Doctor faced our profiles. Not a trivial mission, given the crossfire of their stares. But, adroit in the art of mimicry, we managed well. We always do.

"Are you going to be much longer, Doctor? We are running behind on schedule."

"Done for now." We slapped our knees, forestalling Fein's response to the nurse. "Tell your patients that Doctor is already washing his hands. Our story is to be continued elsewhen."

"I don't see the need for that. How is all that relevant?"

"You have to hear the end to appreciate the beginning, Doctor."

We cast a stealthy look around to see if he—by a common habit or a step-fatherly pride—kept a photo of his daughter. The mirror in our hand circumscribed a searching curve.

"Are you looking for something?"

We promptly pocketed our improvised periscope and stared out the window, where, according to non-Euclidian geometry, our parallel glances were bound to merge in infinity.

"Not some*thing*," we corrected. "The some*one* we are looking for is not here. This office brings back unpleasant memories. Our childhood, you know, wasn't a particularly happy one, although we may never be so unhappy as we imagine. Other kids, having nothing better to do, paired with peers. We, on two other hands, had to find our own path. Everything around your office reminds us of the past. Why don't we continue our discussion in less formal surroundings?"

We paused, expecting him to step forward with an offer. Instead, he became completely enamored of scratching his chin.

"What about your home study?" we hinted. "If you don't have one, your living room or kitchen will do as nicely. We can sneak in, in the evening, hooded and dusked, so your neighbors aren't appalled by our irregularity. What do you say, Doctor?"

"Aren't you something special?" he grunted.

"We don't know what you doodle in your notebook now," we said, "and we don't really care, since it's your job to make observations of what you probably diagnose as misfortune. Yes, we'd gladly visit your home again, as long as you respond to the doorbell and don't force us to climb up the balcony. And maybe, we don't insist, but maybe, after our fruitful chat, you would ask Love to join us and serve some tea, say, *Feulles de Menthe* commonly mispronounced as *Fools Demented*. The four of us can sit in your cozy kitchen together, get to know each other, tell a few stories and share a few laughs."

"Love?" he asked distractedly. "What Love?"

We had to explain that we took the liberty of assigning the true meaning to L'ubov', in which two awkward apostrophes (unequivocally reminiscent of two shy ourselves) served to soften forceful sounds of the outermost consonants.

"Oh, you mean L'ubasha."

Now he got it! Who else did he think we had in mind? Of course we meant L'uba, L'ubov', L'ubasha—our verbal and literal Love.

"You really think you'd feel better talking at my home?"

Alex and I rose from our chairs.

"Not just better—*betterissimo!* We can accompany you right now—that's how eager we are to continue treatment! Do you think

Love is going to be there? She may learn some of your professional tricks and decide to follow her stepfather's footsteps."

Foolsteps, we echoed under our breath and took turns shaking his feeble paw.

"We already anticipate progress. Tennis, by the way, is an excellent sport if only for its deuces! Young females shouldn't shun bodily exercise. We wish we could be her mixed doubles partners."

## Fein's prescription

"The session was exceptionally fruitful," we reported to our credulous mother. "Doctor Fein feels that both of us are very promising specimens. To make further cooperation more personal, he begged relocating appointments to his burrow. The chap nurtures scientific aspirations, and we help him understand intricate entrails of the psyche. Those mashed potatoes are better than ever. Can we have seconds?"

The next Monday in the school's corridor we passed Peter, then Paul, without turning our heads so as not to ruin our aligned posture. They must have been alarmed by our advance into Love's home base and wanted to make friends, but we had nothing to donate. Our raised hand abruptly terminated their attempts at an apology.

Desks and aisles separated us. Love, who must have known about our pact with her step-padre, exhibited no signs of forthcoming intimacy. Wise girl, Alex complimented under our breath. No one should suspect our strengthening ties, especially after rumors about her b-party fiasco.

While observing her moves from two not-quite-separate viewpoints, we noticed some unnecessary disposition towards Peter—all these exchanges, surreptitious touching of hands and sharing of answers inked upon her milky knee. You don't have to do it, Love! Neither this slob nor the rest of the crowd appreciates the subtlety of your dramatic affectation!

Our lunch was entrusted to Mother's care and not the local *vomiteria*. We unwrapped and compared sandwiches. As usual they had the same filling. And one very appropriate for the occasion—*Kolbasa Doktorskaya,* Doctor's sausage, our favorite bologna-like jumble with no texture. Mother had a refined sense of humor.

The bell called for the next class.

Religion, defamed and defined as *opium for the populace,* had no place in the public classrooms of our Motherland. Atheism denounced atavisms. The flattened globe was prostrated on the wall like a mock crucifix. As we passed the map, preoccupied with thoughts bouncing within our own hemispheres, Alex crossed the continent with a dotted ink line. What seemed like a debauchery was, in fact, a preview of our future journey. Subconsciously—for those denying destiny—we drew the precise trajectory of our epic escape. At the moment, however, we failed to accept the hint, because the discipline of geography had never been our forte.

Literature, however, was. What Love, more proficient on the athletic track than in the reading-hall, had to labor through, we achieved with ease. Our literature teacher, Mrs. Silver, announced that to complement our studies the class would do a theatrical production of *The Hunchback of Notre Dame.* We needed no extra credits, but Love was only too happy to jump on the troupe wagon to slow down the decline of her grades. She volunteered and had no competition in securing a role.

We were about to send a note, forewarning her of perils and the disgrace of public appearances. Beware, Love! In the innocent school performance of minors there was no worry about nudity. However, the plot may exhibit her as an object of lust for the whole school. It mustn't inspire you, Love-*cherie*, we wrote.

Alas, the note failed to reach the addressee. While we were engrossed in double-checking the spelling and punctuation—we couldn't be sloppy about the letter destined to end up between warm pages of her diary—the bell thundered, and everybody, including Paul, Peter and Love, rushed outside.

Life was stingy with excitement those days, which may explain a surge of the theatrical enthusiasm. Alex and I were the only ones abstaining from the role distribution. Our time didn't tick towards the opening night, but trickled in expectation of the visit to Doctor Fein.

That day finally came, and we crossed the avenue once again, no more on a reconnaissance mission but as rightful visitors to the second-floor *palacio*. The flowerbed had recovered from our raid, but we declined the temptation to repeat the attack. Now we were the healthy patients attending a troubled doctor and his playful step-progeny. The intrigue was tightening.

"No climbing this time," Alex warned. He is the romantic character, while I enjoy action and spontaneity.

"Don't worry," I responded, "the family is waiting at the gates with the welcome kit—a loaf of bread and a pinch of salt."

As we approached the entrance, sappy Alex slowed down, prompting me to do the same, and giving one of the birds above a stationary target. Shrieking in pidgin pigeon, the pterodactyl didn't miss, and we received a medal of dishonor right on our chest. The shots showered down. We should have picked up a stone and retaliated but, desperately outnumbered, we hurried to take cover under the awning.

Contrary to our sporadic bravado, we are sentimental. Walking up the stairs, Alex slid his hand along the wall stucco, and I touched the railing. We had to collect moving moments for future memoirs. The interior that witnessed our shame didn't anger us, because the defeat was succeeded by a victory. We felt generous like generals accepting banners from the honorably fought foe.

"Would you like to do the first buzz?" Alex offered.

"Go ahead," I said, "toll the bell."

We pressed two thumbs against the little button. No response. No music this time, no lights. We should have heard the siren. Was it broken? Did he forget about us? We kicked the door.

There was some distant shuffling.

*The latch clicked to introduce Doctor Fein*
*in a bathrobe and slippers.*

"Open up, Doctor and his family!" we yelled, banging all our fists against the padding. "Let us in!"

The latch clicked to introduce Doctor Fein in a bathrobe and slippers. Thin hairy drumsticks supported his bulky trunk. We made an effort to refrain from guffaw.

"You?" He hesitated between a plural *tu* and singular *vous*. "What are you doing here?"

"Why, Doctor! Don't you remember? You personally uttered the invitation. All three of us agreed that, to be fertile, our next session would take place in an informal setting."

"I was sarcastic."

"This is no joke for us, Doctor. Our condition is grave. We are here to get help."

Struggle sparkled the insides of his cerebrum, and we squeezed in before he could slam the door—not a trivial exercise for one amorphous and two lean bodies in a narrow passage.

"Where do you want us to go? Study, library, kitchen?"

"You don't give me much choice," he stated illogically, as if expecting us to add a bathroom and a closet to the list.

"If you need to change, be our guest," we suggested liberally. "We mean, host. You can leave us here alone. Alone, ha-ha, do you see? Self-inflicted irony is a sure indication of progress."

The living room looked different this time. The table, as we suspected, was repatriated back to the center. No gift wraps, of course. No debris of the ill-fated vase. We don't hold grudges against inanimate articles and we pity the demise of domestic objects. Sorry, whispered Alex to the vase's ghost, we came in peace.

Isn't he charming?

A minute passed, and the only sound we heard was the squeaking of the wardrobe—our host was trying on his healing gear. No giggling pixie peeked into the room to once-over the mysterious visitors. Did she forget, Alex and I frowned?

"Well?" Fein appeared, still in slippers but otherwise decently garbed. The actual word he used to hush away silence was *Nu?*—some sort of a sense-holder for the upcoming confession.

"We are ready, Doctor," we declared. "Since Love and her mother aren't here yet to serve tea, let's get down to business. Ask away. We shall be sincere."

"What would you like to talk about?"

"Are you asking *us*? We thought you had worked out a strategy on how to proselytize us into the society of useful members. Wasn't that the term we overheard when you were talking in a low voice to Mother years ago? Our memory, Doctor, is a mighty fellow, because if one forgets the other is always here to remind. We sense some detachment on your part. Why don't you, to break the icicle, tell us about *your* family? We are dying to know what a happy household of a loving faux papa and his jolly *fille* feels like. We also have three people in our family, although the parent-child ratio is reversed. It's us and our mother, who is unable to provide us with paternal guidance, which brings us to the continuation of our story. Pen up, Doctor. Follow the plot. As you recall, we took a break when a certain royal figure boarded a ship and left the Cyrillic landscape. Skipping years of the foreign-land misery, we shall take advantage of the long sight afforded by the future and—careless of one or two lost generations—jump ahead along the axis of time."

Like a performer ready to deliver a heartfelt duo-monologue, we paused, distancing ourselves from ourselves and beginning to feel our feet. We became but a voice of the unseen narrator. Are you listening, Doctor? Asterisks please. . . .

★ ★

One day, a gossip column of a newspaper mentioned in passing (with a lucent allusion to some Nordic sources) that in such-and-such Kurland-slash-Lapland settlement a reunion of royal kinsfolk was taking place. From all corners of the Earth, scattered descendants of once-exclusive court gathered in a reclusive courtyard. Pruned princesses and no-longer-charming princes, all those broken branches from the orchard of genealogy, mustered in one shadow of the past.

The story of one imperial incognito traversing the globe—

a hood, a cane, a second-class anonymity—served as the prelude to our own forthcoming odyssey.

Flattening the continent under the reading light, let us mark points A and B, two ink birds—those of a fashionable Scandinavian suburb and the distant southern shore from which our father set out for the reunion.

Yes, it wasn't a misread. We are ready to discard the no-longer needed ambiguity and invite him to the center stage. The fact that we never met him in person surrounds his image with a romantic cloud. Here is his profile; here is his receding hairline; here is a mole on his left cheek, which turns a morning shave into a small-scale bloodshed. His speech, preserved in its pristine clarity among guttural yonder-landers, is ceremoniously old-fashioned.

Someone unacquainted with fate's *modus operandi* might raise eyebrows, having learned that the shortest route from point *Aye* to point *Bee*, deduced under the ruler's guidance, passed through the very town that during winters gets slurred over with slush and in summers. . . . There is no need to repeat ourselves. It goes without saying that Father traveled undercover.

At the same time (there is no way to avoid this cheap cliché), Mother—young, pretty, with no shade of anxiety or shadows from our future mischief under her eyes—was going to the school graduation party. Analogy with chic balls of the past, where her intended's ancestors once circled in splendor, might be amusing, although not quite accurate. The two kinds of balls might only be linked by the unreliable humdrum of homonyms.

In these modest modern-day festivities, devoid of excesses and over-indulgence, the pairs were dressed in fathers' altered suits and mothers' shortened dresses. Unaccustomed to etiquette, clumsy males invited blushing females for a round of waltz. Frequent breaks featured tongue-tied wishes of luck and happiness, hardly a quarter of which were destined to be realized.

Close to midnight, everybody streamed out of the stuffy school halls. The crowd split into groups, groups into pairs and soon it so happened that Mother was alone.

Wandering along desolate streets, forgetful of direction and destination, still wearing an adorned eyeglass frame for a mask, she was immersed in thoughts available only to the omniscient narrator—if one existed—in his aloof third-person account. She allowed the envoys of destiny to choose her path. Following their silent instructions, she kept turning left and right until she found herself in the middle of a hunchback bridge. Above her hung the pale ailing moon; below a sinuous river—the namesake of the town—was splashing its undine secrets.

"Look who is here. Isn't she a Tooth Fairy herself!" A crackling, intentionally foul voice spread through the thin air like an inkblot.

Mother turned her head. The darkness shaped into a repulsive figure whose body language articulated an ill-literate obscenity.

If only we had access to a time portal! Wasting no seconds, we would have turned the vector into *Ago* and transported ourselves back, to that town, to that night. Oblivious of hypothetical altruism and love of thy wicked neighbor, we would unquiver our cane and, in a lightning-fast concession of precise motions, cripple the bastard.

"Please move aside and go away," Mother said firmly, trying to resolve the bulging (all associative connections are distasteful but appropriate) conflict by diplomacy. While addressing the hooligan in polite lexemes, she was stepping backwards until stopped by a parapet.

"What do you mean, aside and away?" The rascal's pride

was hurt. He stuck his wicked finger into his mouth and bared a gap in the uneven row of dentures. "I've been searching for the tooth fairy ever since I fell out of my crib. And when we finally meet, she rejects me!"

His foul breath oozed through the gap. The evildoer moved closer and grinned.

"You think I found coins under my pillow? Wish-well notes, maybe? Nope and nope. I don't even have a pillow! How do you imagine it makes me feel?"

Mother tried to concentrate on his feelings, but her own prevailed.

"I will scream for help," she warned.

"Help? Such a romantic beginning and help? Last lust lost? What about infatuation, ardor, passion? Only after our union reaches its climactic rupture, we may discover incompatibility of tastes. Don't rush time! Its chariot is tearing at full speed. Don't lash the stallions with the whip of impatience. We are about to share some memorable moments!"

Finishing his sentence, somewhere in the vicinity of *mom* or *ments,* he grabbed Mother by the shoulders and pulled her towards his disgusting self. His parodontic crypt puffed out stagnant vapors. She recoiled in fear.

Stop now! Don't move. Halt the tape. The action unwrapped so swiftly, so *rapidamente,* that we had no chance for an intermission. Mentioned in passing, the envoys of destiny brought Mother to the hump of the bridge—oh, those ever-Freudian slips!—for a reason. At this very point, across that very river and through that very bridge, the dotted line of Father's route was taking him to point B.

Drawn with a ruler, invisible for an unarmed eye but well known to the excited scions, the line entered the town through the old gates, left its chopped footprints along the main street, crossed the main square and led to the bridge, in its dotted haste jumping over the cobblestones and cobble stairs.

Mother losing her balance, the vile vagrant, the moon rolling its eyeball up the sky dome—we can't leave the frozen moment unsupervised for too long. As soon as the projector resumed its chattering, they heard the clatter of a cane.

It was him, of course it was him! At the very same instant—oh, why aren't we skilled taletellers?—Father flew up the steep stairway. Facing ready-to-occur injustice, he—reared in the knightly code of ancestors—lost no time.

Throwing aside his bag with travel needments, Father used his left hand to tear the predator away from the prey. Sparing the unbecoming handshake, his right hand crashed into the jaw, knocking out the few remaining teeth. The vagabond retreated but not fast enough to avoid two more blows: one, short and sharp, into the solar plexus, and an immediate follow-up of the stunning—both physically and aesthetically—uppercut.

Mother watched motionless, in a trademark female gesture covering her mouth with her palm. And we, usually apathetic to battery, cheered through the looking glass of our future nethertime: "That's your Tooth Fairy! Kick him, smash him, crush him!"

The breeze whistled its victorious accords on the bridge's girder. Mother and Father exchanged their first glances. They smiled. It was impossible to miss the theatric irony—Mother still in the carnival mask and Father wearing a cloak and a wide-brimmed hat.

He ceremoniously inquired whether milady was unharmed. She nodded. Words clogged her throat. Feminine sensitivity prompted her to identify hereditary origins of his courtliness.

"My mission," Father said, bowing, "demands my presence in a certain Kurland suburb. However, my upbringing doesn't allow me to leave the damsel in distress. Please allow me—" he extended his arm "—to escort you to safety."

His chivalrous speech and soft-flowing dialect enthralled Mother. As soon as she leaned on his arm, a surge went through her whole body. They walked together, enchanted and oblivious of the fading dotted route. The conversation flew on wings of magic. Melody reigned over sense. Words were irrelevant. Turning her head left, for the first time in her life Mother saw our well-defined profile against the backdrop of the dark-purple skies.

She didn't take the mask off, afraid to break the captivating equilibrium.

"I don't know how to express my gratitude."

"Your safety is my biggest reward."

Lowering his head, Father kissed the tips of her fingers. She responded by kissing him on the lips. A meadow in the public park (closed after sunset) was sprayed with dandelions. When Father spread his cloak over the petals, the delicate moon retired behind clouds. The cockpit of our not-yet-existent viewpoint grew misted from our quickened breath until the past became completely impenetrable.

All night long the high-charged lightning kept blazing in the heavens. Stars blew into starrions of sparks as if a giant crystal vase had smashed into pieces over the sky dome. Innocent infants smiled in their dreams. Everything rejoiced and only magi, running out of euphemisms, kept their prophecies to themselves.

"I have to go," Father said at daybreak. "I gave my word. But I will come back as soon as I can."

"Go, my love. I shall wait for you."

They parted, never to see each other again. Only genetic nostalgia of that night and our biological appearance in this world two hundred and seventy days later connected their further existences by invisible and imperishable ties.

Soon, newspapers of strange lands published a short account about the reunion of former royalty. The article was accompanied by a small coarse-grained picture, in which a

*Lowering his head, Father kissed the tips of her fingers.*

group of people resembling each other gathered in front of a nameless photographer. Everybody was captured *en face*, smiling straight into the camera, except for one young man who turned sideways, his sad gaze leaving the photographic boundary and focusing beyond its limits.

We bear no doubts that he did his best to keep his word, but the puncture in the state borderline had been sewed over. Brave sentinels bunched shoulder to shoulder and violently jabbed their bayonets into the void to hold intruders in check.

★ ★

The kitchen cuckoo clocked a half-hour. We whisked a tear away. Fein toyed with his notebook and covered a yawn. While we were too emotional to break the silence, he grabbed the microphone.

"Hold it for a minute. Your story is incredible but it takes us too far back. Let's try something more appropriate. A simple exercise. You will have to overcome resistance. Are you ready?"

Fein needed a rest, we realized. The truth was too overwhelming for him to absorb.

"Ready, Doctor?" We leaned back. "We deface confrontation all the time. Give us your best shot."

Having stepped down from the podium, we started talking cliché. He put his pen down.

"Say *I*."

"Pardon?"

"I want to start with something trivial. Say—*I had pancakes for breakfast. I am talking to Doctor Fein. My name is Alex.*"

"*We* love cakes. They are particularly delicious with cherry jam. Unfortunately our mother doesn't *pan* them often enough."

"Don't avoid the subject. Pancakes were just an example."

"And an excellent one! Don't worry, Doctor. We know what you mean. The personal pronoun you just mentioned is a frequent guest in our internal dialogues."

"Let's externalize them."

We sighed. First Alex, then I, but the gap was practically non-existent and appeared to the world as stereo sadness.

"Nothing could be easier than saying things we don't mean. We came to you for real cure, not for pretense. Enough illusions, Doctor. Give us the truth."

He cupped his chin, impersonating a thinker. What was he going to come up with next? And where the hell was Love? How much longer were we supposed to sustain this travesty?

"Why don't you describe the problem as *you* see it?" he offered.

Love, that was our problem—his delightful and wicked L'ubasha, who never displayed her true feelings to us. We understand. Adolescent affection can be traumatizing. She must have been reluctant to demonstrate it in school because of her inborn feminine diffidence.

"The problem is not us, Doctor. The problem is everybody else. We would need no assistance in dealing with internal insurgents, were there any. The world sees us not for what we truly are, and that's why we have to resort to tricks, turn sideways and hide our essence. People are sick, Doctor, and our own radiating health serves as the litmus paper of sanity, which, incidentally, is as relative as time."

"You are very articulate about your persona," he commented. "Alas, therapy knows no such cases apart from narcissism and arrogance, both being neither a malady nor a medical condition."

"Before you say another word," we interrupted, "let's think about it. We subjected ourselves to your academic ambitions. It's not easy to be laboratory mice in a world run by wild rats. We confided in you, but, if you are not ready for revelations of the world's first stereo-solipsists, let's shift the course. Tell us about this photograph." Alex pointed at the oval photo on the wall. "Who are these charming seniles? L'ubasha's g-parents? They too seem to love each other so much."

We weren't sure what to do next, but at that moment the necessary luck chimed. The key turned in the lock, then steps, then—there she was.

"Ta-da!" We spread out our hands, two emphasizing joy, two surprise. "Here we are!"

Tennis racket still in her hand, Love leaned to kiss her steppy but froze and stared at us.

"What are you doing here?"

"You caught us in the uphill of a very exciting discussion. Your step-doctor was about to enlighten us about conjoined twins, which we had begged and bugged him to do a long time ago. Do you know that they are monozygotic? We would have no idea—until Doctor told us, that is—that the zygote is supposed to split after fertilization from the thirteenth day on. That could be a root cause for the infamous numerical superstition. If your own distant pregnancy is a concern—don't worry. It only occurs once in fifty thousand tries. Most of these poor bastards can be surgically divorced unless, of course, they share something vital, like mind. Isn't that right, Doctor?"

Love's eyes were devouring our profile with silent admiration.

"I wouldn't say that. . . ."

Not giving him a chance to ruin such a beautiful contexture, we used the moment to make it a little more personal, showing interest in her athletic advancement:

"Have you practiced well?" We addressed the glass cupboard with Love's lucid reflection, letting words bounce towards her like tennis balls. "Were your shots accurate? Was your coach impressed? Did you stay away from unforced errors?"

Her father's presence clearly made her uncomfortable. She couldn't relax. That's all right, Love, don't be nervous, we understand.

Instead of engaging in a conversation, she shrugged it off.

"I'm going to the shower," she said to nobody, not to us that is. "No time. Gotta run soon."

"Where to?" he asked.

Excellent question, we nodded. We couldn't phrase our own anxiety better. Where and why was she leaving if we were already here—ready to talk, hold hands, enchant?

"The rehearsal at school. A play. I told you." She fled into the apartment's enfilade. Another door slammed, and a remote waterfall turned on.

Left alone, the three of us tried to revive the still-born subject of therapy. Doctor Fein was uttering words, which we had trouble to comprehend since the sounds coming from the shower—rustle of the curtain, jets of water, far-flung crooning—painted our imagination pink.

". . . your artistic idiosyncrasies," Fein continued. Apparently he paid more attention to Alex than to me. "Why don't you redirect your destructive personality towards something creative, something befitting your interests? Take up arts. Music, painting, whatever."

"Whatever!" we exclaimed. "What a wonderful suggestion, Doctor! Arts, indeed. No music, though, but performance arts—heartfelt dialogs delivered to the mesmerized audience. We could stun the crowd, you know; do what no actors before us could achieve; portray complex biopic characters like Boyle-Marriott or Gay-Lussac."

It was good that we expressed ourselves before Love showed up again, because we both, Alex and I, I and Alex, lost our speech at the sight of the tank-topped, tight-jeansed Aphrodite stepping out of the shower waves. Her physical exertion scraped off the protective layer of indifference, and now her pure animal nature radiated all around, turning everything else bleak-n-white like the photo on the wall. If that was her reflection, how stunning she must be in direct view! We didn't dare to look, afraid of burning to ashes.

We held on to the chairs, fighting dizziness. Love stamped a smacking kiss on her father's bald spot and hopped to her room.

"I am afraid," Fein said, "there is no need for further meetings, whether here or anywhere. Contrary to your self-diagnosis, you do not constitute a disruption of the complex machinery. I am not sure what your real purpose is but it very well may be the presence of my daughter."

Was our goal so underveiled?

"Deny help to the needy? You are killing two birds with one rejection!"

We sobbed, asked for directions to the bathroom and excused ourselves. Let father and daughter discuss things alone.

Not without combinatorial effort Alex and I squeezed into the tiny room, still moist and steamy. Two deep breaths. Mere minutes ago this very air enveloped Love's sweet sweat glands. It was no bathroom but the holy of holies, and we were its high priests. We touched the rug wet from her bare feet, and the smudged drops on the inner side of the shower curtain. Then, overwhelmed and humbled by sharing the same space with Love (albeit misplaced in time), we clambered into the bathtub and curled in a feti position like Jacob and Esau.

*Oh, Lo-ve-lee-ta, light of our life, fire of our loins; the tip of the tongue taking a trip of two steps down each palate.*

That little show Love put up about leaving . . . she must have been teasing us. Surely, the tea is already brewing; and the kitchen table—no need for formal fuss in the dining room—is groaning under a heap of home-baked smorgasbord. We long for sweets and sweeties. Love must have guessed it in her perceptive heart.

Leaving wet footprints on the parquet—oh, who cares!—we rushed to face the surprise. Here we are!

"What happened?" Fein raised his eyebrows at our dripping clothes. "Little accident?"

His sense of immediacy left much to be desired.

"Never mind, never mind. Where is she, where is she?"

Still captivated by our tub vision, we allowed unsynchronized screams to surface. He noticed nothing. Talk about physicians' attention to details!

"L'ubasha left for rehearsal," he said.

If we hurry now, Alex hissed, we can still catch up with her.

"Good bye, Doctor." We jumped up. "That was a first-rate tête-à-tête. Let's resume it at another time."

# QUASIMODO

"How did it go?" Mother met us in the hallway.

Must we describe how we failed to coordinate movements, how we tripped and nearly crashed into the wall at the end of the flight, how our hearts were beating the drum of peril and passion? No. Mother cared for Fein's verdict, not for our staircase pursuit, downward jumps and step-skipping leaps.

"It was a lire concert for one liar without orchestra," we said. "The bad news is that Doctor proved underadequate to treat our condition. Although his name does start with our favorite letter—*f*araoh of the al*f*abet—his narrow wits impeded his judgment. He doesn't see beyond his mind's eye. We had hopes; now we are disenchanted."

Mother wiped her hands with the apron's hem. We sat at the table, always next to each other, never opposite.

"Chicken cutlets are superb," we commended to cheer her up.

"Did he prescribe anything?"

"Not every misfortune can be helped by medication. Don't be alarmed, Mother. There is also good news."

She lifted her head. Her wrinkles filled with hope. Pass me the salt shaker, I signaled to Alex.

"Yes, the good news—another mischievous fusion of plural and singular—the good news, like in the synoptic saga of Br'er Mark, Br'er Matt and Br'er Luke, is that we found a pro'er application for our talents. We decided to pursue a career in arts. In performing arts."

"Not even vitamins? What about homeopathy?"

"No." Alex and I were firm. "No quack healers, no alternative quaaludes. Throughout the ages, arts were the best cure against spleen. We already feel their soothing influence."

During a brief respite between classes we approached Mrs. Silver.

"We accept your offer."

She looked up from the pile of essays and scraped the glasses down her nose bridge to fit us above the rim.

"What offer?"

"You win—we shall participate. We need no extra credits, but your Hunchback troop lacks theatrical flair. Want proof? Listen to this famous Edgar Allan Poem:

*Once upon a midnight dreary, while I pondered weak and weary,*
*Over many a quaint and curious volume of forgotten lore,*
*While I nodded, nearly napping, suddenly there came a tapping,*

(enthralled by the image, we stomped ravenously)
*As of some one gently rapping, rapping at my chamber door.*
*'Tis some visitor,' I muttered, 'tapping at my chamber door -*
*Only this, and nothing more.'*

"Verify not," we ended. "The quote's accurate down to the last *ore.*"

"Your affectation is inspiring. I don't believe we have unassigned roles, but you are welcome to come to our rehearsals, of course. Five o'clock in the main auditorium."

She didn't say *five o'clock* or even *five pm*—in the town of our birth the time was marked off in precise military digits.

"We are very punctual," Alex and I assured her. "Seventeen hundred hours it is."

A playful pigeon on the tree branch outside winked at us and jumped sideways, parodying our own style. Was it the same one that had used us as a practice target when we slowed down, hesitant and emotional, before entering Love's building?

The auditorium was swarming. Scraps of sounds filled the air. Dust refused to settle. The half-finished scenery depicted a yesteryear Paris corner with the famous double towers of the Notre Dame Cathedral. We took it for what it truly was—a providential omen.

Mrs. Silver's jacket hung on the back of the chair. She held the script in her legislative left arm, her executive right arm pointing at the distant Paris. We noticed Peter and Paul and Anastasia. Other people were present as well; all—preoccupied, most—useless. But where is. . . ? Why don't we see. . . ? Ah, there, there she is! Relieved, we spotted Love as she was hopping upstage. How could we miss her—vulgar, lustful, gorgeous—dressed in the maddening rags of a juvenile gypsy?

"What are you doing here?" That was Peter. Not the most articulate and hospitable greeting.

We chose to ignore him.

"Alex," Mrs. Silver said, looking up from the script, "good that you came. Don't worry. We shall find something for you."

In case we failed to point out earlier—names are very indicative. Mrs. Silver's most outstanding feature was her argent hair. Undoubtedly it belonged to her husband. The name, not the hair, of course. In her maiden days she must have been Ms. Fair or Ms. Chestnut. One day we shall inquire.

As to our name, it sounds in such a way that people tend to shorten its plural form. Like others ending with an S—Rufus, Boris, Curtis—ours is awkward because of its ill-sounding plural and possessive forms. We, Alex and I, realize that addressing us as *Alexes* is lexically perplexing, not to mention a looming confusion with Alexis. Therefore, we've learned to accept and respond to plain Alex.

"Have you assigned the leading parts?"

"Are you interested in some particular role?" In a typical manner Mrs. Silver answered with a question.

"We didn't come here just for joy." We squirmed, twisting two buttons. "Certain someone, whose opinion we value," a quick glance to make sure Love giggling with Paul could hear us, "a very close relative of certain someone else," we raised our stereophonic voices, "advised us of our dormant talents. And since no gift, whether endowed by the focused god or flippant nature, should go to waste, we are here."

"Take a look. This is the role distribution."

She handed us the printout. Alex, standing closer, took it and, a second later, confirmed: in a terrible miscast, Love was playing Esmeralda—a beautiful and licentious gypsy doll.

"What kind of approach do you take?" we asked. "Is it a farce, a drama, a modern interpretation? We are open to options and could perform even as Love's—we mean Esmeralda's—goat rubbing against her thighs. Her outer thighs, of course."

This was our first appearance at the thespian gathering. While we dallied about, other people seemed to know their lot. L'ubasha—arms stretched, head tilted—danced around the stage, once in a while peeking at her reflection in the big mirror. ". . . *if that looking glass gets broke, Papa's going to buy you a billy-goat. . . .*" we whispered tenderly. Peter lipped his lines. Paul, packaged in French garbs, was morphing his face through the spectrum of emotions. Both drolls, apparently making their excuse in the lexical proximity, felt the right to flirt with our doll. A great idea dawned on us.

"We must play the monster."

"Are you talking about the hunchback?" Mrs. Silver consulted her notes. "I am sorry. This role has been given to Konstantin."

"K-konst-tant-tin?" We didn't stutter, oh, no. We used echo to emphasize the impact. Alex went ahead with hard consonants while I stayed a half-note behind. The effect was powerful. We continued—now in sync—wringing our hands like masters of ceremonies: "Konstantin? How could you? We have to give him some credit—he does boast an oversize frame and the presence of twit! With such talents shouldn't he rather be heaving props and helping backstage? And what do you suppose we do? Impersonate the crowd?"

She was about to say something, but at this moment our gypsy enchantress called for attention and we waived Mrs. Silver off—go. Don't mind us. We'll talk to Konstantin ourselves. When Love summons, you should drop your mundane fuss and hasten. Never repeat the mistake of Ulysses, who tied himself to the mast to withstand the sirens. He regretted his reticence ever after.

We backed away and closed the door.

The plump tome of *The Hunchback of Notre Dame* waited for us at home. Let us talk about reading for a moment. We are super fast with folios. Pages fly like pigeons, because Alex reads odd sides while I go over the evens. We discovered this special technique, although, even if we disclosed it, humankind is unlikely to take advantage of our invention. Clause after clause, chapter after chapter, we soared over the text, skipping outdated politics and slowing down over the incredible love story.

Plot summary: Fool's day; church; everybody gazes at Esmeralda. Deaf and deformed Quasimodo is sent but refuses to catch her. Both are captured by the guards. Captain lets the girl go. Court sentences Quasimodo to be flogged. Esmeralda is accused of the captain's death and promptly convicted. Will Quasimodo be able to save her? Will she see beauty in the beast? Will they find their love? Eleven books, 1488 pp., translated from the 19th-century French.

"Do you know why they dubbed him Quasimodo?" Alex asked.

We both knew the question and the answer, but the dialog routine was like bonding for us—we stayed true to the game.

"Wasn't he born on *Quasimodo Sunday?*" I replied.

"That's right—the least important Sunday in Easter. That's why its other name was *Low Sunday.*"

Peter, not our classmate apostate, but the first Apostle, wrote in his First Epistle: "*Quasi modo geniti infants. . . .*" ("As newborn babes. . . .") That's exactly who we were—the newborn babes, naïve and vulnerable, an ugly deformity in the universe of illustrious beauties. Just like the hunchback we had the mystery of our births, shared earlier with Doctor Fein as respite from the high-charged narration.

Should literature be treated literally? Unlike the deaf monster we were quite sensitive to sounds. Like his lone heart, ours were perceptive and compassionate. Acting or not, witnessing Love-Esmeralda's flirtation with Peter-Pyotr-Pierre Gringoire counter-plotwise accelerated our plummet into insanity of three G's—Gringoire, the Gypsy and the Goat. Yes, Doctor, insanity. Nobody but Quasimodo was to hold the girl and snatch her away from the Gallic gang.

We were *destined* to play the monster. After all, that's exactly what we are in the world's eyes. But what do we do with Konstantin?

If we haven't already mentioned it, nature had been generous to Alex and me. When our turn came to receive gifts, the serving was doubled. The angel endowed us with two kisses. Others flexed a muscle; we flexed two. Others racked a brain; we racked both.

Every free lunch, however, ends up with cleaning dishes. To maintain our physical dominance we had to submit to strenuous exercise, which neither of us enjoyed. We preferred cerebral evolution. The saying goes—two heads are better than one, not four arms better than two.

Konstantin, on the other hand, indulged in sports. Our old method of bodily intimidation was out of the question. Plus, our sideways stance didn't grant an advantageous fighting posture. Should an unscrupulous foe attack from behind—we would be defenseless.

We ruled the ambush out. What might have worked in dealing with an insolent classmate earlier, was no longer appropriate. To pressure Konstantin we needed to understand the meaning of his name—every consonant hard and definite, no softening apostrophes required. K like in *con*; ST like in *stun;* T like in . . . like in *tin*. In accord with his namesake Roman emperor, Konstantin's last name was irrelevant. In contrast to his Roman namesake, our friend lacked any spiritual greatness.

After classes we used a moment when he was alone.

"Listen." Alex and I carefully positioned ourselves. "We shall talk to you about Quasimodo. Do you know why you got the role?"

He mumbled something like *why, what* or any other interrogative pronoun, equally insignificant.

"Surely," we went on, "you know that the part is that of an outcast, a monster, a laughing stock."

"Who cares? It's just a role."

What a dunce!

"Don't you understand that there is no such thing as *just a role?* People will treat you the way you present yourself. Do you really want to be a freak?"

The last word tipped the balance of his inadequacy. He clenched his fists.

"What did you call me?"

We minced out of his reach. Alex and I had to be alert—who knew what poisonous fruit blossomed behind his frontal lobes? We value Rimbaud over Rambo, but we are never afraid.

"You are what you are, whatever you are," Alex uttered diplomatically while I was weighing the next argument. Konstantin eased a little, but the threat didn't go away completely. Come on, Alex signaled, say something.

"Dear Konstantin," I announced, and echo smeared my voice down the empty hallway, "as star pupils we have influence over Mrs. Silver. We can put in a word for you. We think you have much more potential than settling for a cartoon character. You should be the master of ceremonies. You should orchestrate the farce."

The seed of superiority had conquered better protected citadels than his compact cerebrum. We left him in doubts and parted, meaning Konstantin and us, because Alex and I are inseparable. Out the window, we watched him cross the school yard, just as Quasimodo surveyed the square from his tower in the climactic mise-en-scene.

"Esmeralda, our love, . . ." we whispered in French, spreading our wings and visualizing a crowd, a hangman, a scaffold.

At the next rehearsal we walked in and settled in the back.

"Alex!" Mrs. Silver waved. "Very good that you are here. Would you come over?"

Konstantin was standing next to her in a very unbecoming pose—pretending to think. We never looked in his direction.

"There has been some rearrangement. The role you were interested in has become available. Would you like to fill in?"

Our wicked gypsy stood right there, coquetting with Peter and Paul in a clumsy and desperate effort to ignore us. Oh, *amoral mio*, silently exclaimed Alex. And mio, and mio, echoed I. Is there such a word as *our* in the language of love?

"Yes," we said out loud, "we shall fill in. We don't mind playing the outcast. We shall be covered by a cape—a suspect deformity is more reviling than the revealed one."

"Very well, let's start with the scene where. . . ."

Alex and I took our new assignment seriously. We didn't just follow the instructions of a well-intended but, alas, timidly talented Mrs. Silver. Teaching the lapses of literature to young rascals is one thing, creative drive—quite another.

The rags our girl was wrapped in drove both of us mindless.

"Stay away from Esmeralda." Mrs. Silver stepped between us. "We are still in the second act."

In regret, we watched Love hopping away.

"How can we stay uninvolved? First act or last, she is about to be lynched. We shall hold her tight and steal her to safety."

"I told you, Mrs. Silver, it was a bad idea. This Quasimodo should have been chained to the bell."

Mrs. Silver turned. "Pete, let me handle it." "Don't," we interjected, poking at him with our judicial finger, "mess with the plot if you don't understand the morals of the main heroes."

Alex hunched over in the cape. He was magnificent.

"Let's do it again," said Konstantin the Tin-man, the new monster of ceremonies, flipping pages of the script backwards.

"For the scene to feel authentic and vibrant," we suggested, "should we shout something in French? Should we say the word *merde*?"

High school morale denied passion. All scenes with lurking intimacy were stricken from the script. Never mind, never mind, wait until the premier. We'll show all of you what true art is.

Just like Esmeralda, who enjoyed exposing tennis-trained thighs through the torn garb of her character, we insisted upon appearing at school in full Quasimodo armor—a loose robe with the hood low over our foreheads. It allowed us to better identify with the fiend, we explained.

While our rehearsals were advancing in full steam, another team was building the scenery. A bespectacled school genius drew the outlines of the famous cathedral on a piece of plywood. Close to the top, he left an opening so that the audience could take pleasure in the torments of our bell-towered hero—both mental and physical. With the blessing of the creative crew, the invisible bell was to thunder through the hidden speakers.

During the break we tapped the artist on the shoulder.

"What's with the double-headed gargoyles?" I asked. I am the arty type while Alex represents spontaneity and action. "Are you

Salvatore El Greco? Or maybe Vincent Picasso? That's not how the scenery is supposed to look."

The wretched Rembrandt mumbled something about vision and symbolism.

"What do you know about symbols? Do you major in semiotics? Give us the brush," I commanded, Alex pushing him aside.

"Why are you bossing everybody around?"

Puny and frail as paintbrush folks usually are, he rose to face us, and we had to act quickly, turning 90 degrees counterclockwise to avoid confrontation. Doctor Fein—or was it Professor Tulchinsky?—used to warn us about suppressing our quick-boiling temper. We are good listeners and remember everything the mentors advised.

The little Van Gogh attempted to push our chest but hit the shoulder. Wait, I restrained Alex, don't kick him yet.

"What is going on?"

"You see, Mrs. Silver," we meowed amicably, "while performing talents are crucial, the scenery must have a character of its own. Flat background drapery does little justice to the complexity of the play."

In the corner of our eye we made sure that Love heard and appreciated our diplomacy. Alas, she seemed to be immersed in Peter's fables tickling and trickling into her earlobe. Her giggles were vulgar and so deliciously devilish! That's all right, Alex said. Two ice skaters circle around the rink before hugging in the center-ice climax. Soon we shall cuddle each other.

The faux Gauguin's falsetto scattered the dream away and made us pay attention to our own unfolding intrigue

Referring to both of us, the outraged dauber used a derogatory singular pronoun.

"Why is there always trouble around you?" Mrs. Silver sighed.

"Because you two-dimensionalize us," we replied, taking no time in inventing the word. "Our hero may be deaf and ugly, but we are not. The creator is larger than creation. Quasimodo doesn't save his love in a vacuum. Look at this. You call it a cathedral? Rectangular background is too plain."

"What do you suggest?"

"It should be a trapezoid, starting thick and solid at the bottom, getting narrower and lighter to the top, giving the audience an extra point of perspective."

"I don't have time for arguments. If you can do it, go ahead. Let, . . ." here she mentioned the humbled Leonardo by his name, which we have no intention of relaying, "let him do the gallows."

"Yes," we confirmed, "go butcher the scaffold. We'll pull the rope later."

## The Performance

On the eve of the show we had a dream, tender like only dreams and Mother's mulberry mousse go. We don't usually fancy reveries, but this time the vision was relevant. Doctor Fein, in his professional prejudice, ascribed no importance to our personal prehistory and never gave us a chance to reach the dénouement. And now our internal dialogue, burning to be concluded, picked up where we had left off—at the dawn after the only night our mother and father spent together.

Any conscientious dream practitioner would have his hands full of begging-for-interpretation imagery. So. . . .

★ ★

Days, weeks and months passed. Mother realized that he would not return. Her pillow got solid and scratchy from the dried tear salt.

Ceding to the pressure of social conventions, she married a thickset woodworker, master of kitchen cabinetry, a full foot wider and a couple of inches shorter than her. With the years his mahogany-colored mug acquired shades of the most luxurious lumber. We saw his photos—the perpetually hunched mulish go-getter.

Having thrown sandbags of enchantment overboard, life kept itself afloat. Enter we—Alex and I. Not to cause unnecessary questions, Mother pushed our double-size carriage, choosing deserted side streets. She tried to inure us to thinking games, but of all the colored cardboard we rejected boards and embraced cards, fascinated by the conjoined non-conformity of the images. Neither of us understood back then why her eyes soaked in sadness when, unconcerned with the rules, we quartered the deck and played exclusively with Kings and Knaves.

One day a state postman dropped into our mailbox a letter with an exotic stamp and no return address. Mother didn't open it until late at night. When Alex and I fell asleep, holding each other's hands, she pulled an old handmade mask (resembling both the lemniscate and embracing twins) from under the pile of clean linen, whisked away an unwelcome tear and unsealed the envelope.

*My dear, beloved, precious milady,* the letter began, *it so happened that.* . . . And Father repeated what her heart knew all along. He wrote that regardless of how watchful the state guards were, despite the cards played by fate, the two of them would always be together in the dimension unreachable by human trickery. At the end he enclosed a copy of the family tree, the spread of which took Mother's breath away. Names, comfortable in history books and school primers, settled on the boughs like pigeons over the entrance of Love's building. His initials were also there. Branched off his lodgings, he added a hand-drawn cloud, leaving it empty for Mother to inscribe our names.

Although for him our existence was no more than a blurred image in the crystal ball, he took a moment to address us directly in a concerned footnote. Together with genetic noblesse you carry a strain of hereditary sins. *Moye ditya, my child,* he went on in gender-neutral singularity, watch out for signs of degeneracy like a unibrow and recessive earlobes. Should those become apparent, waste no time and seek medical assistance.

*We decimated the deck and played exclusively
with Kings and Knaves.*

Oh, well. We inherited the ancestral profile. We featured neither a unibrow nor alarming lobules. However, despite the professional admonition of Doctor Fein, Mother had her reasons for seeking help.

Before or after this letter—at the daybreak of our memories, the events gathered in crowds rather than duly lining up in accord with chrono-seniority—our woodworking step-Giuseppe disappeared from the canvas of life. Sobbing Mother told us a taradiddle improbable in its visual splendor of how, atop a freak accident, he made himself into a part of somebody's vanity.

★ ★

We woke up agile and vigorous with the word *vanity* melting away from our minds. The past was gone, ready to yield to the future. The prelude gained momentum. The stage gallows were erected. Theatrical villains prepared to cover their freckles with mascara scars. Our love was ready to hatch.

We brushed our teeth, first I, then Alex, looked at ourselves en face and felt satisfied. Upon our insistence Mother arranged the looking glass in three adjacent leaves so that we could see our profiles. Figuring out which Alex is romantic, which resolute, is at times obscure even for us.

Not to expose our dichotomy to the world, we meet it sidewise. During old-fashioned pistol duels such posture presented the most challenging target.

"Mother," we announced, "the matinee will thrust us to fame."

She seemed scared, the poor woman, never truly understanding our interests and aspirations. The enigma of our birth, which we mentioned earlier and to which we shall never return, had unsettled her so much that she feared the worst even when love was about to shine over her enclosed universe.

"Please, don't get into trouble."

"Don't worry about us. We have many talents, twice as many as an ordinary being, and soon the world will acknowledge them."

"Does Doctor Fein know about it?"

"We see no reason to discuss our plans with anybody, especially Foctor Dein. He has nothing to say to us anymore. Everybody plays a role, and recently we found what his was. He brought us to Love. Now he can step aside."

We took no notice of Mother's sadness.

"Just don't do anything stupid," she repeated.

If her child, or children, were ordinary juveniles, misunderstood during the day and lonely at night, she could have been right. Luckily, Alex and I were nothing like that. Loneliness is the root of depression. As to us, at any instance of insomniac fantasies, we had the company of a like-minded waking ally.

Quasimodo's robe on, we threw the cape over our heads and, careless of stunned passers-by, crossed the avenue on the way to the school. Strangers stared at us, but all they saw was a bulky figure, determined in its hooded mission.

Alex proved to be proficient with his artistic vision. While I was busy shushing El Picasso, who cast hostile glances through the bars of his ridiculous gallows, Alex created a true masterpiece. His tower of Notre Dame looked better than the original, as melted watches on Dali's canvas tell more about time than do their well-rounded kinsmen. The cathedral came out so real that the parterre audience couldn't tell paint from mossy stones, a bit rugged, a bit uneven.

"How do you do that?" I whispered in amazement.

"Comes naturally," Alex responded, tilting his head left, then right to take a better look over his creation. "It must be in our blood."

As the last-minute chaos intensified, we hunched, cloaked and hooded, in the darkest of corners. Konstantin—the prentice of ceremonies, the fool of authority—was telling others what they knew without his interference. Interjections served as the main tools of his oration, rhetorical questions—declaration of power.

"Ready? Remember the words? Huh? Well. . . . There. . . . Why are you hiding in the corner?"

We dismissed him with expressive, albeit hidden by the robe, fingers. Doctor Fein would have so much fun observing this human comedy and vanity fair (both extracurricular).

The audience's impatience was oozing in from under the curtains. Esmeralda, our Love, our maddening obsession, shivered from the tasteless obscenities that Pyotr, a.k.a. Peter, a.k.a. Pierre, was whispering into her auricle. Wait, we breathed out, wait for two acts. We shall hide our passion no more—you, *Notre* little *Dame* and we, Alex and Alex, the twin outcast with a fake hump, a double heart and an oversized soul.

The warning gong thundered. Konstantin's send-off would have made us burst out laughing if not for the gravity of stage matter.

"Remember, this is a rebellion of the oppressed against tyranny and corruption," declared he—a non-classy miscarriage of the class struggle.

"Children," Mrs. Silver added, "don't be nervous. This is just a show. Your comrades and parents in the audience will support you."

They will, they will, we muttered. They had no idea what kind of action was about to unfurl. Just a show, ha-ha! Ignoring the last-second encouragement, we climbed the scaffolds to our lair in the bell tower.

The curtains parted, revealing the full house. The speakers spat out the prelude.

From the height of our hideout, we watched the puppets walking the stage and ranting words mutilated by translation from another time and another tongue. Unaware of the world's true beauty, they failed to portray true feelings.

Protected by fake stone walls and gargoyles, we were waiting for Love. Finally, Konstantin, emperor of the backstage, gave a sign. She waltzed out. The author had visualized her in the company of a little goat. What a wicked twist—Faun in the pet's guise! The symbolism behind such pairing could be interpreted manifold, either version appalling, neither appealing to the monster in the tower and the girl at the town square. Fortunately, the scope of the production and the code of conduct tolerated no beasts on the school property.

The gypsy spread out her arms and began the gyration.

Esmeralda! we moaned. Look at her. Isn't she gyneco-gorgeous?

This was the perfect opportunity for Professor Tulchinsky to grin and ask—what would you do if her heart only had room for one? Don't worry, Professor. Love's heart isn't a cheap motel. Alex and I share everything—mind and space. We can squeeze in.

The music accelerated. Our Love—or as we whispered in our romantic vernacular—*nasha L'ubasha*—loosened her hair and propelled around the props. Her scanty clouts flew up, baring more and more of her defiant flesh. How unjust! We, her intimate mates, were served with the bird's-eye view. Other characters leveled up, but the audience located below the *see* level had access to what was supposed to be ours, ours only—something of which we were now totally deprived. How could we wait, how could we allow it to go on?

"Hold on to me!" Alex seethed, and I had little time to object even if I wanted to, which I didn't, because Alex and I are one. We rose in all our magnitude, fearless when facing the crowd from under the hood. We spread the wings of the robe and took off. The audience gasped; the cast froze; Esmeralda was too involved in her dance to notice us.

"What the hell are you doing?" Konstantin hissed from behind the curtain.

"Alex!"

"Alex!"

"Alex!"

Our names, multiplied by many mouths, echoed in their true multitude.

The flight was magnificent. We soared through the scene like we often did in our dreams, the only difference being that this time the vector of direction carried us downward.

Two glorious eagles glided in airstreams, closing in on their naïve *chicklette*. Behind us, unset by the powerful push, veneered but no longer venerated, creaked the tower.

"Love!" We crashed down, barely missing our target. Esmeralda jumped away like the little goat she never had.

"Are you nuts?" Pierre burst out. His hat fell of and rolled from the stage like Robespierre's head.

"What page is this on?" Konstantin was feverishly flipping the script.

We scrambled upon our legs—no easy feat in the hunchback's loose robe. One of us, Alex or I, grasped Esmeralda's wrist. She didn't pull away. First act or last, that was the true climax. Everyone's eyes were fixed on us.

"Esmeralda!" we sang in well articulated, perfectly synchronized duo. "Our Love, forget this cardboard Paris, forget the past, forget this useless education. Old books only confuse you. We are here to cross over to the future. Take our hands, and let's run away from this dusty town!"

"Where did you get these words?" Konstantin's continuous hiss was accompanied by the tower's squeaks. The chapfallen public inspired us. Peter, contrary to his prescribed role, tried to force Esmeralda back into ill-conceived safety, and we brushed him aside like a piece of scrap paper.

We scanned the hall for the cameras and filming crew Mrs. Silver promised to invite, so that our performance would be immortalized. No lenses sparkled. Never mind. The word of mouth is a great fertilizer for legends.

"Paramour." We turned to Love, holding her tighter than in a tango. "The world is about to learn the meaning of this word. Not *mon amour* but ours! Let us embrace you like Yin and Yang. Time to open up—true heroes have nothing to hide!"

Alex made sure that the hood didn't fly off. I grabbed Love, and we each stamped a kiss on her opposite cheeks.

"Get off me, you freak!" Esmeralda screeched.

The audience applauded. It was the best interpretation of the boring story they could ever have hoped for. The scream seemed to break the spell, and everybody rushed the stage. Love's betrayal drained our strength. We released the grip and she, our might-have-been princess, aided by Peter-Pierre, Konstantin, and other school and townsfolk, pushed us in the chest with all the angst of philistine mediocrity. Weakened by the treacherous twist of the tale, we crashed into the base of the trapezoid tower. It waved, tilted, swayed and finally lost its balance just as our sanity was about to be lost in this loveless universe. The towers, handcrafted by Alex, came down hard, crashing lights and tearing down curtains. The furious pseudo French crowd, already pulling the gallows intended for another act, backed away in terror. We stood alone, as usual, the captains of the sinking ship, two kings in the desperate chess *endspiel*.

The no-longer *Notre* and now quite *Dumb* cathedral collapsed, proving that although Love had escaped, some remnants of luck were still on our side. The stones, fake or not, would have killed us, were it not for the opening in the bell tower, the same one from which we'd jumped. Deafening thunder filled the halls, clouds of dust erased characters of both drama and farce.

If only one of you had a chance to flee. . . .

Shut up, Professor! We never took your single-minded wisdom seriously. Having neither will nor wish to reap the benefits of the best interpretation of the old play, we slipped into the anonymity of dust, out of the hall, out of school, away from Love.

# Fairy (Part 2)

## THE NEW DAUGHTER

The maze of nightlights was zooming past the cab window. Disoriented by the trip and drained by expectations, Sophie and Fodor finally settled in the hotel.

"The lodestars brought us to the stable," Fodor joked, squeezing into a tight room with a double bed reigning from wall to wall. Three bears crawled over a fallen hemlock on a discolored reproduction above the headboard.

Sophie fell flat on her back, on top of the black and white squares of the bedcover. The springs squeaked.

"Tomorrow I am going to get a daughter," she whispered with her eyes closed. The words originated halfway in oblivion. There must have been more snippets and syllables, but most of them failed to reach reality. "Tomorrow I will become a mother."

Fodor paused by the window overlooking the town, traced the black band of a river below and two familiar constellations at unfamiliar aspect angles above. Then he took a hasty cold shower, because the hot faucet produced nothing but angry hissing, and went to bed.

In the morning they called a cab and, instead of mangling the Cyrillic stew, handed the address to the driver. Alien streets looked like permutations of the same building blocks—a church, a square, a monument. Then the variety withered into rows of uniform carbuncles.

The taxi pulled over to the frayed façade painted dirty azure.

Close up, the headmistress looked rather obese than majestic. Her jacket with bulging side pockets—vestured over a plain sepia dress—had an unmistakable man's cut. Elephantine feet were firmly rooted in heavy-duty pumps with unevenly beveled heels.

"Call me Directrix," she conceded, sparing her guests after Fodor almost choked trying to repeat her name's consonants.

*Director-Rex*—a crossbreed between Directress and Imperatrix, he whispered to Sophie after momentary confusion.

"Our country provides the best education to these poor orphans," the hostess declared without further introductions. "Although you uproot and transplant our flowers abroad, they remain our posterity. You are not rescuing them, mind you, but we grant you the honor of having what nature has failed to provide. Understand, yes?"

The building resembled the combination of a prison and a cancer ward—locked doors, hushed hallways, barred windows. They were escorted to an office with a large black-and-white photo of a man above the desk, a red phone on the desk and a vat with a rubber tree in the corner. Bleak plastic toys on shelves were meant to exemplify the inmates' simple pastimes.

Directrix put on reading glasses and opened a folder.

"You indicated interest in a girl. Effeminate gender is very popular, and our inventory is presently limited. Grigoriy will usher them in single file. You will not be able to talk to them, of course, since they don't speak your foreign language, yes?"

To get to the meaning of mutilated words, Sophie had to hack through the jungles of coarse accent, compression of *th*'s into the buzzing *Z* and the total interchangeability of *he* and *she*.

Grigoriy—a dutiful aged sergeant—nudged the first girl in.

Oh, my God, Sophie gasped.

The headmistress stretched her celluloid lips like a lion tamer trying to charm the audience and intimidate the beast at the same time. She turned to her guests and explained that little L'ubochka was ready to parade her talents.

"I will require her to salvage the pyramid from the shelf, take it apart and reassemble in the proper succession of colors from the red-most to violet. This exercise demonstrates mindful comprehension and spatial coherence."

Bark, bark.

The girl didn't move.

"It's all right. She must be nervous. What's your name, little girl?" Sophie asked.

"Like I told, he doesn't understand your language. Grigoriy, bring the next one."

Naden'ka was dressed in the same semi-military brownish outfit. She reached for the pyramid, shook the rainbow-colored rings off the pole and assembled them any which way.

"You mischievous little devil." Directrix affectionately patted her back, then beamed at Fodor, whom she identified as the leader. "He can do the colors. He's just teasing you."

Grigoriy's closely shaven head appeared in the doorway. His flannel shirt was buttoned all the way up to the chin, his civil pants tucked in to the tarpaulin boots, military style. He snarled a few syllables, which Sophie interpreted as *something-went-wrong.*

"The next girl caught a cold," the headmistress translated, "but shouldn't you worry. Grigoriy will summon else."

Descant steps, accompanying heavily stamping bass of Grigoriy's iron-shod clodhoppers, were hardly audible.

"And this is. . . ." The headmistress consulted her ledger.

Sophie got up from her chair, circled the desk and squatted down.

"What's your name, fairy?"

"Take the pyramid from the desk and put all the rings in order." The headmistress encouragingly smiled at Fodor as if reassuring him of her pupil's capabilities.

"How old are you?" Sophie asked and, after brief silence, turned her head to the hostess. "Does she hear me?"

"Of course! She is entirely a vigorous youngster. She just is shy. All our orphans perform according to the guidelines of their age."

"Would you like me to be your mom?"

"She doesn't, you know, understand," the matron indicated, exhibiting her patience before the public proudly, like abrasions from the crown of thorns.

"Would you like to go with us? My name is Sophie and this is Fodor. He is going to be your father."

"Now put the rings back on the pole, the big one first. No, no, that's green. You did this before. Are you trying to show how stubborn you are? We have no time for your whims."

"Never mind the pyramid," Sophie pleaded. "I am sure she can do it."

"Grigoriy! Take her back. We don't have all day here. Now." Directrix, who had been towering over the girl, went back and perched atop her throne. "While making your minds up, I need you to fill this form."

Sophie was motionless, still staring at the slammed door. Fodor put on his glasses. The first questions were simple, and he went down the list almost mechanically. The hostess tilted her head, her gaze following the unreeling ink thread.

"Fodor is strange name, no? You maybe Fyodor? Your parents born here?"

He paused at the next question, raising his eyebrows in confusion.

"What is my business?" he repeated. "I'm not sure what it means."

"Your business. What you do. Are you a capitalist, a tycoon, an oppressor?"

"No, not really. I am a doctor."

"So, write *doktor*."

## Fairy's birth

In the hotel Fodor looked down at his shoes.

"Strange. This morning they were perfectly clean."

"My hair feels like hemp," Sophie said. "There must be something in the air."

The paperwork and all the formalities were going to take a few days, Directrix had explained. Fodor told Sophie that he didn't want to waste his chance of sightseeing. This was supposed to be a beautiful city and who knew if they'd ever be back.

They went—he marched ahead, she dragged behind—to the historic quarters. The cobblestone square appeared smaller that its wide-lens photo in the brochure. The cake-like cathedral of the local saint attracted a stream of camera-armed tourists. Fodor was noisily impressed by the mossy bastion, massive fortifications with embrasures and the drawbridge over the ravine, but Sophie failed to share his joy. She was going to have a daughter, and this place, this town with its ancient citadel and a harsh disjointed tongue by a bizarre twist of fate happened to be a birthplace of her child.

In ten years, she thought—forgetful that leaps into future often miss the target—we must return here, the three of us, and I will show her this square, her first home, her . . . I need to know more about her. Sooner or later she is going to ask questions and I'd better be prepared.

"You go ahead," she said to her husband, not very excited by museum relics and mausoleum remains. "Death doesn't attract me. We are here because of life. I'll go back and talk to the directress."

Fodor hesitated for a moment but then helped her flag a cab. Sophie handed the address to the driver.

"You not speak? You from where?"

He had a bald patch and a wild, unhygienic mustache.

*I will have to memorize him too. He is now part of your story.*

The driver grasped at the chance to practice a foreign language. During the fifteen-minute ride, he jumbled his views on politics and culture, lamented that the Nobel Prize for literature was awarded more for the social context than creative appeal, and—while Sophie sorted out tiny bills (an uncanny combo of currency and candy wrappers)—indicated major flaws in String Theory as well as a sure way to overcome them.

"Bottoms up!" He waved his hand from the car window in farewell—the last outburst of his linguistic ambidexterity—then, unalarmed by the rattling of his conveyance, reversed all the way from the driveway to the street.

The headmistress came out to greet Sophie in a bluish work-robe. She expected no visitors, she explained.

"Your paperwork not ready. It requires approval from the committee, and Ivan Ivanovich only returns from business trip tomorrow."

Sophie didn't quite understand what this committee was for and how *Ifan Ifanofitch* was related to her baby.

"We do not appreciate unwarranted strangers on premises. It is you a stranger, until the state permission is granted." However, Directix agreed to spare a few minutes and talk to Sophie just because she was very kind in her heart, you know, and always suffered from her own, you know, kindheartedness. "As the saying goes: *Ne hochesh zla, ne delai dobra*—if you wish no evil do no good. I am not like that, you know. I am too naïve and trusting and never learn on my own mistakes. How do you say, learn on?"

"From," Sophie replied mechanically. "Learn from mistakes. Could you tell me more about the girl? Who were her parents, what happened to them?"

"I can't disclose this. This against rules."

"I need something," Sophie pleaded. "When the girl grows up and starts asking questions . . . I want to be able to answer at least some of them."

"OK, OK. Not much to tell. I went through her file yesterday with attention." The headmistress leaned towards her guest and switched to a conspiratorial whisper. "Maybe this one story. You tell no one, yes?"

They knew nothing about the father, which wasn't uncommon. The mother had just graduated school and, according to her own statement, didn't need this burden at the very beginning of her life. She tried plotting an amateur miscarriage, absolutely foolproof, according to her wise ad*vicer* ("A very excellent word, yes?"), but nature turned obstinate and favored obstetrics. "This young girl, whose name I am not allowed to disclose, accepted the hint and decided like that song in your old movie—*sera que sera*."

The headmistress sang a few lines in a surprisingly pleasant soprano until Sophie nodded with recognition. Of course, she saw it.

Unfortunately, as soon as the decision to keep the child prevailed, fate became bored like a cat whose mouse no longer attempted an escape. One night the young girl was attacked on a street by a drunkard. Dead scared, she fainted. The mugger turned out to be a conscientious *sukin syn* ("That's a son of a doggy") and, having pocketed her purse, called emergency from the nearby phone booth. The baby girl, although born prematurely, was nourished by our wet-nurses, the best wet-nurses in the world. Unhappily, the mother defied all vivifying efforts and passed away shortly thereafter.

"It now beautiful and smart child," the headmistress assured her at the end.

"What did you tell her?" Grigoriy asked, cleaning a misted spot with his sleeve as the two were looking through the window at Sophie's diminishing figure.

"Same story I tell everybody. So dramatic. They love it."

## THE PORTRAIT

"I have to take you to that gallery," Fodor said. He had returned to the hotel a few minutes earlier, his impatience and excitement ready to detonate. "Why don't we go there right now?"

"I am too tired."

"You can't be thinking about the girl all the time. It's out of our hands now. Relax. There was one painting . . . you'll love it." And, looking down at his shoes, he added: "I am going to need a new pair. The leather is all eaten away. Bizarre. They usually last much longer."

The gallery squeezed itself in between a café and a mysterious sign *Toilets for brides*. What could that possibly mean? Sophie wondered. Before she rejected the wild option, promptly served by her imagination, the sun's reflection graciously moved aside, uncovering a window with a mannequin in a wedding gown.

*"What did you tell her?"*
*"Same story I tell everybody. They love it."*

"Come in." Fodor held the door, and Sophie entered the gallery.

He let her wander about, stop in front of little bronze deformities and midsized garbage piles made out of some rusty waste, each dubiously dubbed an *Installation.*

"Isn't art a peculiar thing?" she wondered. "Under a limelight anything lame immediately sets claims to be a masterpiece."

"Madam is interested in the *Installation #11?*"

Fodor shook his head—madam is not interested. He had already made a purchase and would like his wife to see it on display before they wrap it.

"What purchase? You didn't tell me anything."

"Let's go. It's in the next room."

Sophie cautiously moved forward and froze in front of a huge frame. The inscription read *L. Samorodok. Monster. Oil on canvas.* It wasn't really a monster. The portrait depicted a man's profile. His deliberate eye was sharply defined; everything else blurred into ambiguity, the farther from the center the less definite. One could guess a nose and a mouth. The clothes were sketchy. The man's features displayed nothing openly monstrous. He seemed like a normal person. The only hint as to what could make the artist come up with the title was a slight transgression of proportions. Were it a bit more apparent, the portrait would become a caricature, but this last step into ridiculousness had never been made. The realism could be doubted, but its borders hadn't been trespassed, like a sanity indicator frozen at a standstill on the very edge of normalcy. One more brushstroke and it would slide down.

The smeared outline merged the man with the background, upon which a few dark figures were hinted upon but never spelled out. Was that a child in a sailor suit next to a palm tree? Or a train with a puffy cloud, making its way through an eerie landscape? Or a broad figure in an overcoat leaning on the cane? Like pieces of a puzzle, the fragments offered resemblance to familiar objects, but then quickly took it back, hesitant which of many options to choose.

"Why is this man a monster?"

"I don't know, but he does look delightfully wicked to me."

"Not sure if I want this in my home," Sophie said slowly, not taking her eyes off the picture.

"You like it, don't you?"

"It's unusual. I wouldn't say it is very inspiring."

"Why not? Look, he is winking at you. Life is fun for him."

"I wish I had as much fun."

"So—" he took her hand, beaming—"you approve?"

The conclusion of their journey was uneventful, not counting one man-made obstacle, which Fodor quickly overcame with endowment deceptively huge because of the favorable conversion rate and all trailing zeroes. He and Sophie signed the release forms and were given a small travel bag with the girl's clothes.

"On behalf of our staff and from me personally, we wish your new daughter happiness in toil and private life. Go abroad, child, but don't forget your roots. You are always welcome here, when you grow up, of course." The headmistress whisked a tear, the gesture well-rehearsed but a bit premature—her eyes were dry.

"Don't worry," Sophie whispered, "as soon as we get home I will buy you nice things. Give me your hand. Can you say mother, mom, Sophie?"

"She needs time," said Fodor.

The door behind them slammed, and the new family was left alone.

"Her name translates as Faye. I knew she was a fairy the moment I saw her. How do you like that—Fodor, Sophie and Fairy? I am Sophie; you are Fairy."

"Would you like to take a ride now?" Fodor waved his hand at the roaring traffic and squatted down. "Have you ever been in a cab?"

The road took them uphill. The scenic view of the citadel loomed up, somewhat diluted by the bluish, almost visible air.

"Don't you think that one of the fragments in the painting's background resembles these domes?"

"All churches are alike," Sophie responded. Focused on a tiny warm hand, she never looked outside.

# Hope (Part 1)
## Ten Years Later

### MEETING HOPE

There came our time to question the past in order to move on into the future.

Did you have a misconception about our birth, Mother?

Did Doctor Fein play the role of whitebeard Santa or blackbeard Stromboli?

Was Professor Tulchisky like a kind stepfather or a wicked step-mother.

Were we intended to be crucified like saints or pardoned like criminals?

Humans failed to provide us with wise guidance, so we searched higher. Looking for the new motto, Alex and I accepted what Apollo, the Greek master of moderation (also substituting as the god of sudden death for males—hence, the quiver and the bow), inscribed upon his temple in Delphi. Not *The Mean Is Best,* of course, as we are neither mean nor average, but *Know Thyself* by accepting two's own strengths and limitations.

Having no limitations, we embraced our strengths.

Alex and I constitute a society of our own. I make decisions and take initiatives. It might sound counterintuitive, but I never think twice. Professor's desk or not, it took me no second thoughts to knock off an inkpot with Rorschach embryos or flick away a picture in the superficial glass armor.

Alex, on the other hand, is superior in the creative pasture with his refined strokes and flair for complimentary colors. As soon as we decided to take on painting, his talent blossomed like a benign lump. I handed Alex the *carte blanche* in the form of the blank canvas. Get up, Lazarus, I commanded. Get up and limn.

"You can't hide home forever," Mother said. "Go, see people, do something."

Poor Mother. She refused to accept our essence.

How could we see people, if our 90-degree attitude didn't let us face anybody? Our vulnerability made us work out a defense code often mistaken for indifference or aggression.

Clinging to the easel, we didn't have to mingle with the crowd or serve in an office, let alone a sweatshop, where we had a double chance of getting injured by hostile hardware with swerving, shaking and screeching parts.

We drew diptychs, biplanes and two-headed unicorns, violet and violent.

"Why purple?" I tilted my head, nibbling sunflower seeds while Alex etched horns and hooves.

"It's the color of royalty," he stressed.

Our first works were stuffed with mythical beasts like Noah's Ark as if the world beyond our easel was submerged in sins and scheduled for re-destruction. God's wrath redoux, I joked from behind Alex's shoulder.

Quickly fed up with the apocalypse, we moved through a concession of land- and seascapes, still-lifes and battle-pieces, toyed with optical illusions of trompe l'oeils and fancied distorted projections of anamorphosis. Then we discovered portrait.

That memorable morning Mother went to work, leaving us as alone as we could ever be. Garbed in a smock frock, we converted our room into a studio.

"Check if the door is locked," Alex commanded. "I don't want to be disturbed."

I didn't argue who was more important. Giving orders and running errands was evenly split between the two of us in the most democratic of social arrangements—the chief was always an executor, and the judge was invariably an executioner.

Peeping Alex checked the landing through the spy-hole and reported no sighting of Lady Godiva. I clicked the latch.

As opposed to ordinary artists, two *nolens* loners had nobody to use for a model. All our attempts were doomed to be self-portraits, although that wasn't quite accurate since, of the two, Alex is the gifted one; hence, it was always I whose features were reflected on the canvas.

On that particular painting—the face already worked out in details, the rest barely outlined—I was immersed in thoughts. The artist depicted me in an old-fashioned uniform, high-collar jacket thrown over my shoulders, the right aglet already sketched out, the left still missing. A star upon and a *bend sinister* across my chest, I stood supporting myself against a short column. A frigate with inflated sails scrambled up the steep ninth wave in the background.

"Just like on that old photo," I said, smiling.

"The past is gone." Alex was dead serious. "Look at me. Our expression is supposed to be poignant. We are working on the eyes."

Sun dust drew lazy circles in the air scented by solvents. Thick grooves on the palette reminded us of the terracotta used by the Creator when claying us in His image. Now came our turn to be imaginative. Royal features—the scepter and the orb as supporting parts of the ornament—were ready to come alive any minute. Our genealogical dowry made the portrait even more believable. A dab, a touch, and the august eye sparkled.

"Aren't the colors too bright?" I asked.

"They will lose their luster. Hold the mirror and don't move. We are not done yet."

By late afternoon I grew edgy and Alex tired. Healing two birds with one stone, we decided to get out and breathe some fresh air, the dusk masking our venture anonymous.

We strode sideways, for good luck avoiding cracks in the asphalt and holding hands like we used to in our childhood, while it was still sweet.

That's when destiny made its next move.

Lest anybody had doubts, we bumped into two another heads to head.

"What a pleasant surprise!" we exclaimed in instant recognition—Alex-artist had a faultless memory for faces and features, while I never discarded names and numbers. "We didn't *hope* to meet you again!"

The pun was exquisite, for it was she—Hope the Compassionate, Hope the Emphatic, Hope the Concerned. Our paths had crossed at L'ubasha's birthday bash. In the consistent trickery of unreal names, hers wasn't Hope. In the notary-public sense she was Nadezhda, Nadia, Nad'usha, but every language has a name that translates as what we were going to call her from that moment on.

Long lost Love left a scar in our soul. Now, triggered by this fortuitous rendezvous, we perceived a live beat under the dead spiritual tissue. It may sound made-up, but Love and Hope were cousins, and although Doctor Fein provided no blood connection to either, his Cheshire wink didn't stay unnoticed. Observed in the reflection of our pocket mirror, Hope proved to have hatched into an attractive young specimen.

"Do you remember us? The broken vase, hostility instead of hospitality, fallen kings upon the chess tiles of the landing."

She squinted in hesitation.

"How *could* you forget?" The emphasis on the modal verb, we outlined our profile with a wave of the hand. "Look at us closely. The ordeal should have left a deep dint in your psyche."

There was indeed some incident, she recalled, the particulars of which formed as much from the stories of others as from her own memories.

"If you are not in a rush, . . ." Alex suggested.

". . . we'd be happy to tell what truly took place then and there," I echoed.

Our society, we explained, suffered from the incurable daltonism. One exemplar of it—childhood retrospectively painted in shameless pink. How cruel! No other phase of life stacks so much absurd brutality and injustice. Youth knows no tolerance.

How tough was it for us to have stigma *Stran* and *gers* burned across our foreheads? A crafty trickster (nothing personal, Doctor) was too smug to explain our unsettled minds by pursuit of ghosts and ghouls. Oh, how we wished they could be chased away as easy as by blowing dry sand off a palm!

She shifted from one foot to the other impatiently.

"Never mind the past." We hurried to change the subject. "Is that an easel in your hands? Was that an uncle's gift?"

"I am taking an art class."

"An art class!"

There it was—a fortunate fluke, fate's favorite ploy.

"We are no foreigners to art, you know," we exclaimed. "Where is your studio? We never thought about formal education, but, you know . . . who knows? You don't mind if we escort you?"

Alex picked up her easel, I took her hand.

"First of all, the water well is nowhere to be seen." We minced, bravely stepping over the pavement cracks, the old game no longer exciting.

She raised her eyebrow.

"The water well?"

"It's something we learned from folklore. A prevalent motif. A young man meets a girl by the well. She is alone or with her feminine friends. She asks for help, and a romantic story enters the next stage. That's where Jacob met Rachel who came to water her father's sheep. That's where Isaac's servant met Rebecca."

"Your books are too old." Her lips were serious, but her eyes smiled. "There are no sheep or wells in the middle of the city."

"Well," puns just kept piling up, "then we get an inversion of the story. Add to it another discord—a young woman meets *two* young men. Two negatives, as your substitute teachers should have taught you at school, comprise something positively optimistic."

Her mock frown was absolutely disarming.

"You said that was first. Is there second?"

"Second," we concluded, not without pathos, "Love, who was destined to stay close, brushed us aside. Hope, with paints and brushes, now walks hand in hands."

T HE ART CLASS

We never lied to Hope about being no strangers to art.

It didn't matter whether we had been cool with colors *before* meeting her or had met her first and only *then* picked up painting. As in an equation, the summands' order doesn't change the result. It's the commutative law, Doctor, and in law we trust.

To spend more time with her we began attending classes. Alex was as natural in the art as a faun in the forest. Weaving doodles in the back row, we watched how Hope leaned to the easel and bit her lip in classic manifestation of assiduity. Our over-salted and under-peppered instructor marched up and down the aisle, briefly pausing by the students' canvases. Three top buttons of his hip shirt were perpetually undone, revealing a bony hairless chest. His feet in leather loafers never knew socks.

The less significant the character, with more aplomb he demands a proper name. The teacher's was Leonid. He wished to be Leonardo. We dubbed him Leonidas—the King of Three Hundred Spatulas.

In coordinated head-n-hand motions, he would toss his long strands back, then take a sanguine from a phlegmatic pupil's hand and add a few sweeping lines. His miracle touch turned a sketchy frog into a starched-up princess.

Nad'usha's visual paralalia (an utterance of a vocal sound other than that desired, as Professor Tulchinsky should have explained) presented a touching jumble of effort and failure. But, however helpless her strokes could have been, they were never *hopeless*. We watched Leonidas stop by her easel, where a cube—a still-life *du jour*—was being zealously painted over:

"What are you doing?"

"Coloring."

In our remote darkness, we chuckled over her charming naiveté.

"Stop using blue," he commanded.

"But the cube *is* blue."

"Rubbish!"

Leonidas took her seat and, in what seemed to be totally chaotic dashes, started throwing colors, all but blue, over her flat drawing. To our amusement and Hope's amazement it turned into a life-like, blamelessly cerulean artifact.

Is that how you do it, I whispered to Alex, whose bubbling glee attracted Leonidas:

"You!" He pointed at us with the dead end of his brush. "Are *we* better than everybody? How come *we* don't work in class?"

Even though we understood his lexical twist as nothing but fancy of the false-royal first person, its plural form was flattering.

"We are not into cloning square objects." We barred him from consideration.

"What are *we* into, then?"

When in front of a doctor or professor, we, the patients, always chose a wide seat. Here, we, the painters, were treated to a tight stool limiting our maneuvers.

You are the resourceful one, Alex wired, say something. You are the artist, I telegraphed back, he and you speak the same language.

"Please," one of us finally uttered, "button your shirt. It's making us uncomfortable."

He made a step back and tossed the hair off his forehead.

"True art causes pain, triumph, insanity but never comfort. Now, work."

We are here with Nad'usha, for Hope's sake, we were about to snap, mesmerized by sunlight sifting through our girl's pink ear.

We chose our own subject. Alex took a crumpled bill out of his pocket and smoothed it. I pretended to be engaged in making a copy but soon got carried away by its hypnotizing patterns. Money is as still a life as a blue cube, you know.

In the front row, Hope put down the brush and braided her hair. We grew numb, unable to take our eyes off her downy nape with a soft groove—its anatomical impact, other than sending shivers down our spines, unidentified.

T HE GALLERY

In spring, little sand crystals replaced street slush and joyfully squeaked under our feet. We addressed Hope in tender *tu*. She addressed us . . . when she was looking at me, she called us Alex. When talking to Alex, she said Alex, but her tone was different. Like a caring mother, always able to tell her *twangels* apart, we were never confused and immediately realized who Hope was talking to.

Chance encounters had long stopped surprising her. Our Juliet allowed her two roaming Romeos to stride alongside to the studio or to the grocery or to any other of her divine destinations. Her handbag dangled on a leather strap, hiding such treasures as her pocket mirror, her notebook, the keys from her Sesame residence. We, the eighty thieves, were banned from entering it.

If the reticule happened to be on Hope's right shoulder, Alex took her under her left arm. When she moved the clutch bag to the left, we switched. I nudged Alex off and linked her right arm. That was our agreement, and we abode by natural internal laws. Trotting side by side, we could feel the burning silk of her skin under the irrelevant layer of chintz or satin—despite our efficiency in clothe alterations both Alexes suffer from chronic textile idiocy.

Here, she said, our ways parted.

"The city is a dangerous place. Cars, craze, crowds," we pleaded. "Can we escort you another minute, another turn, until the next junction?"

Hope wouldn't listen and ran away, careless of honks and shrieks. Where did she master that impossible science of teasing? Alex said, admiring. She is a woman, I replied. That stuff's inborn.

Hope never admitted it, but with our presence in the studio she bloomed. Older and more experienced than other classmates, we assumed the role of observers rather than participants: Hope in a knitted jersey, Hope with a bow in her braid, Hope licking her pencil—a childish and enchanting routine.

Leonidas put together the next *nature morte*, this time mortifying nature with fake apples, as if wishing to poison our gullible Snow White. We didn't fall for his bait, just like Adam should have rejected the temptation on the eve of expulsion.

The slow pace of flattening nature on a piece of paper was boring for Alex. Instead of exercises, he sketched a fragmentary outline of our princess.

"*Profil perdu.*"

The pencil in our hand cracked. Preoccupied with the drawing, we didn't notice Leonidas.

"What?"

"An outline showing more of the back than front is called *profil perdu*—the lost profile. Now put that aside and do the exercise with the rest of the class."

"We are not interested in vegetation, especially apples. The fruit of seduction was supposed to be a *pear*. Or, at the very least, a *pair* of apples," Alex responded. I crumbled the paper and tossed it to the waste basket. The sketch's magic was *perdu*. We resorted to our diligent doodles—ruble curlicues.

By the end of the lesson Hope's canvas blossomed with unripe fruits (". . . from the tree of ignorance," I quipped, the acid aimed at her dubious educator). Our banknote copy came out better than real. We cut it out to demonstrate to our sweetheart later as a curio.

"Next week," Leonidas announced with the authority of Master Leonardo, "we are going *en plein air.*"

Sandal shod, his yellow shells of toenails confirmed the arrival of summer. He was talking to the rest of the class, but we took his invitation personally. First of all, Hope was going, and second—we were his most gifted students.

*Wit* waited for her at the entrance to the train terminal; *wit* being we, Alex and Alex—the old English for the sadly discarded dual first person pronoun, so suitable for the two of us, because when a third party is involved, the narrators' *we* can be misleading.

Hope looked serious and determined, concentrating on visions of the forthcoming landscape.

Pale artists herded close to one another in the hostile fuss of departures. As befitting the leader, Leonidas arrived last.

"We'll do the *plein air* the next time," he shouted from afar. "The forecast has changed. It might rain."

"Wonderful," Alex murmured into Hope's earlobe, the one that I often sketched with tremulous tenderness. "We shall escort you home and gladly accept an invitation for two cups of tea."

Terminals aren't intended for privacy. Echo captured our whisper and scattered it all over the platform. Hope blinked and blushed.

"No one is going home," Leonidas commanded. "I have something for a rainy day. We'll have a class in the museum. Copying masterpieces sharpens your skills."

Birds of a paintbrush flocked around Father Goose. Hope minced by Leonidas's side, making two steps for his one. This ratio so intimate to us, we stayed in rearguard, closing the procession.

The forecasters didn't con this time. As soon as we reached the false Gothic building of the museum, the drizzle moistened the asphalt in the heavenly aquarelle.

Leonidas led everybody to the hall with portraits of the old royalty. The room was empty—other visitors preferred modern silverware, no longer curious about the mighty of yesteryears.

"Set your easels here." He pointed to the full-length figure of a child. "That's what you will be copying."

We had always admired this work. In fact, our feeling was more profound than a simple sympathy to the little prince depicted sideways, in a sailor suit, with a fierce sea battle puffing in the background. A proud corvette under St. Andrew's standards was putting the enemy to flight.

"Who is that?" Hope's lips folded into a flower.

Leonidas announced the last name of the court artist, something this or that, something completely irrelevant, leaving out the most important detail. Were we alone with Hope, we would have surely told her the story of our childhood photo which resembled this portrait way beyond a happenstance.

Had history chosen some other dream, the prince's fate could have led him to the throne of his forefathers, the sea behind symbolizing the conquest of elements, not the exile to a faraway anonymity. We could have recounted his escape in the last panting steamer fairwelled by shots and shouts ashore. You see, dear Hope, flight by the sea is much more dignified than the train stench of modern-day defections.

The group of paupers settled in front of the petite prince, next to the portraits of the stately Imperatrix and . . . and then we gasped. Oblivious to paints and brushes, to Leonidas and even to our effervescent Nad'usha, we stared, unable to take our eyes off a true *chef d'oeuvre*.

What is it? I mumbled.

How is that possible? Alex wired back.

Can it be yet another coincidence?

We froze in awe as one always does when dumbfounded by a miracle. It was an uncanny copy of our self-portrait, still unfinished, still mounted in our home studio. There, Alex was my model, and here we saw the exact same posture, the same unyielding gaze, the same royal features. Such likeness was impossible in nature unless it belonged to one kin.

"His epaulets are a shade darker," I said, squinting.

". . . and the column is Ionic . . ."

". . . and his sadness is heartfelt . . ."

". . . because, while we were looking at his glorious past, he was foreseeing our dismal future," we concluded.

The quest for ten differences was interrupted by the shuffling behind. We barely had time to swivel sideways.

"You brought your friends today?" A figure in the curator's uniform addressed our profile.

"Old woman," our voices trembled, their emotional discord mistaken for echo, "we never saw you before and have no idea what you are talking about."

"What do you mean? Don't you come here every week, standing in front of this very canvas?"

"You confuse us with someones else."

Our high pitch attracted the group.

"Oh, you have come here before?" Leonidas asked.

"Why would we? To indulge in our semblance to the Tsars' family? Let's not get distracted from the educational goal. Paint ahead, exercise the little Tsar-ling and don't mind us."

Our rational spiel convinced them to leave us alone. Leonidas circled about and made his trademark trite trivia about primary colors and secondary characters, spending as much time by Hope's side as around all others combined.

We didn't move a single hand. With us, nature sponsored the existence of two identical subjects. Now, we encountered two identical objects. What was the reason of such redundancy? In the background of our meditation, Leonidas was preaching his shallow truth to pupil *pupas* who had no chance of hatching into *painterflies*:

"Who can tell me what art is for?"

Before anybody ventured a hackneyed *create-beauty* or *make-this-world-better*, we intervened:

"Art is a vessel of insanity. Those who create it wish to escape their private specters. Those who long for it are desperate to disguise inner voids with outer illusions. Art indulges those who mislead and shelters those who are misled. There can be no other purpose."

T HE NEW STEPFATHER

By the time we got home, the daylight had dimmed. The windows lit up with the ticktack of tic-tac-toe, no longer resembling a chess riddle.

Mother was home. After we acquired hope (lower case conveyed, upper case implied), we rarely talked to her. Not due to our insensitivity, but because we were quite content by the sheer fact of her existence. The need to escort us to an office of a quick-n-quack practitioner was eliminated. If Mother spent a night elsewhere, we never questioned her morals as long as our underwear stayed laundered and warm dinner was found on the stove.

Adjusting our cloak on the neighboring hooks of the hallstand, we heard clicking and clanking of silverware coming from the living room.

"There you are." Mother's reflection in the pier glass clasped hands. Another figure in the far end of the room moved in a succession of ill-defined images. Was it a black knight or a dark horse? We threw the cloak back on and stepped into the shade.

"I wanted to tell you for a long time, but you are never around." The reflection moved from one glass section to another.

"We are always around. We just don't like to be disturbed. Who is this person? You didn't show him our room, did you?"

"Oh no, don't worry."

"Well, then," we exhaled, carelessly parading our relief, "tell us who that is and what that wants."

Mother trotted back and forth, rearranging objects on the table. She placed a pepperbox and a saltshaker in the middle, then moved them aside, giving the center to the vase with carnations. The vase's throat was too wide and the flowers bunched on one side.

"You must be Alex," we heard. "Your mother told me so much about you. She is a very special lady. My name is Michael. How are you?"

We ignored his extended extremity and turned to face Mother. *To face*, of course, was a metaphor, a 90-degree approximation. She shuffled trays and bowls—pickles, pickerel and other peculiarities furnished for the festive occasion.

"Have a seat. Here is the potato salad. Your favorite."

"You didn't put celery in this time?" Alex the Thunderer demanded.

"Everything's as you like. We were waiting for you. The fish is getting cold. Misha, pass me your plate."

Under our slantwise scrutiny, Misha turned out to be a square-faced gray-haired heavy-set feeder, quite likely a retired major or a male nurse. Regardless of Mother's affectionate form of address, we shall refer to him without emotion—the reasoning opposite to what made us call L'ubasha and Nad'usha by their semantic equivalents.

We retired to the loo to wash hands. Upon our return his plate at the head of the table had been filled: mushroom salad, beets, crispy sauerkraut. A foggy bottle had its seal broken. Mother bustled about. We took a seat.

"Someone else is coming?" His fly trap full, Michael battled articulation, nodding in the direction of the spare stool.

"Mish-sh-sha. . . ." Mother's eyebrows drew a conspiratorial arch as if shushing the unmentionable. She didn't have to be afraid or ashamed. Knowing us for so long, she never realized how skillful in spatial orientation we had become. Facing our aligned profile, the dull-witted sergeant never suspected our true intricacy.

"Pickerel, huh?" Alex began, friendly, while I engaged in potato salad. "What's the special occasion?"

Our guest took the initiative. He released his fork and lifted his cup. Beet pieces left little blood stains on the tablecloth. He wiped the corners of his mouth with his palm and grunted.

"Your mother is a wonderful woman. She had a very difficult life taking care of you alone. She deserves happiness."

More salad, we waved, another spoon, that's it. Go ahead.

"We have known each other for several years. I am a widower myself. My wife had been an ill woman and I couldn't leave her. Now that she is gone, my duties have been paid. Your mother and I decided to move in together. Life is too short to miss opportunities."

"Misha is a very kind man," Mother reassured us. "He'll be like a father to you."

Their cups touched and clanked.

"We already have a father." The piece of bread in our hands crumbled. "We don't need a substitution."

"This is not always about you." They exchanged a quick glance. "We would be happy if you support us. If not, you will have to accept our decision."

"Mother!" we cried. "What does it mean? Are you betraying your vows? Are you disloyal to Father?"

She started sobbing about what a wretched, unfortunate character he was, and we cut her short:

"We don't mean the woodworker. We mean our *real* father, he whose regal profile we inherited, he who keeps fidelity despite the bidirectional resentment of borders and unidirectional flow of time. Are you giving up on him, Mother? Are you leaving him for the bird in hand?"

Another wordless exchange; a male grumble, a female sigh.

"This is not the conversation I want to have. Misha is going to live with us. He has left his apartment to his daughter. She is married. A very nice young couple. You'll like each other."

"We already like each other," we quipped, and our guest goggled at us in bewilderment.

Although we rarely lose composure in public and always act cool, panic began its menacing drum. Is privacy slipping out of our hands like sand? No more place called home? No clicking our heels three times twice? What about painting? We can't concentrate when the next-room headboard is banging against the wall, when a stranger may wander in, peep over our shoulders and make derogatory comments about deformity.

"Mother," we concluded, "you know us, you know the enigma of our origins. How can you settle for *this*? Is he another carpenter? Or is he of royal descent with a name starting with R like Rurik or Romanoff?"

In their self-absorption they surely missed our point. The letter R—Cyrillic Р—together with its mirror twin, constituted the sacred symbol Ф.

Our favorite salad tasted like wet cardboard. We pushed the plate away. They should realize how disgusted we were.

"Enough!" Michael threw the napkin on the table and rose from his seat. "I will not let you bully your mother."

Before somebodies lost their righteous temper, we hastened to our room in an awkward racking gait. No longer was our haven safe. No longer was Nouf-Nouf's home his fortress. Once inside, we leaned on the door, ready to protect our besieged citadel.

"This can't be love," we yelled into the keyhole. "Love is for young people."

"What do you know about love? Have you ever loved anybody?"

"Oh, we have, we have, don't you doubt that. And we didn't betray *our* Love, she left us. We don't have her anymore."

"You are a spoiled brat. That's what you are," Misha-Michael roared like an enraged archangel. "How can you be so selfish?"

"Now, *you* will foster us? Now, *you* will be telling us not to eat off this tree and drink from that brook?"

"What are you blubbering about?"

"Were you a good father, had you read goodnight stories to your offspring, you would know."

Fists hammered the door. Mother sobbed in the background. The opaque partition separated the two of them from the two of us. We heard whispers, then receding steps. Our hands were trembling.

"Does he feel at home yet?" we screamed at the top of our lungs, addressing not so much Mother but Fate. "Is he wearing slippers? Is he walking around in pajama pants with suspenders?"

Our shelter was being invaded. Remus and Romulus lamented in the ruins of a never-built township. The portrait looked at us scornfully from its scaffold. We felt vulnerable like naked girls on a seashore. Hope was all we had left.

## WE FINISH THE PORTRAIT

Mother's no-longer-a-boy friend, corporal or carpenter, was moving in, destroying a lulled illusion of privacy. Our temples pulsated, making it uncertain whether they were two, four or plenty.

Art as a cure from anguish and insanity—wasn't that what we had told the class?

"We have to finish the portrait," I said, assuming the model's posture. "Go ahead, I shall stand still."

Alex took the brush and made a hesitant stroke. I couldn't see if he touched frogs or aglets. It didn't matter. We had to eliminate the ten differences and I was determined to pose all night.

Stray sounds sifted in from under the door: dish dangling; hushed splashes of conversation with no beginning, end or sense. The outer door lock clicked, and we heard a tired plod.

"Alex, Alex."

We kept dignified silence, which—should two trust master Confuster—never betrays. I, the model, was not allowed to move, and Alex was too involved in mixing colors. Or, maybe, each of us chose to treat the call as related to the other Alex. When you are many, so are the options.

"Misha is a very gentle man," Mother sighed. "I need him."

She did, but for us his existence risked disrupting the delicate equilibrium.

"Mother, you always knew that we were unlike other people, that we were special. It's twice as hard to find a place in life for the two of us as it is for an ordinary critter. Only recently professorate prophecies started giving shoots. We began *knowing thyselves* as Apollo—the god of sudden death—had prescribed. Now, more than at any other time, we need sympathy and solitude. Is that too much to demand? Is that? You think about yourselves—two forlorn miseries exchanged for a malformed union. We are hurt, Mother. We aren't opening the door. Good night now."

Is the eye finished? I whispered. May I blink?

I am texturing the sky, Alex responded. Blink but don't wink.

Mother shuffled away.

Was our love too hard on her? The world had taught us to be tough. It made us who we were. It made us strong and fearless.

Resentment is the art's greatest catalyst, and haste didn't affect the quality of our work in the least. All done, the pale dawn distilling blackness outside, we sat down and exhaled. I stared at the completed portrait agape, and my fresh perception inevitably affected Alex. We experienced the awe of the Creator for the first time facing his creation as an independent entity. Detached, the portrait acquired a new status—wise, majestic, so much better than its deplorable spoof in the museum.

We left it to dry and get accustomed to the new world.

The week melted away. We didn't see Mother. Only once, tiptoeing out of our room, we caught a sign of the invasion—a new double bed and a fiber suitcase in the middle of her room, a man's suspender slammed by the lid.

The habit of locking our door was promoted to an obsession. Only then we could relax, look into the portrait's eyes and talk to it.

"You are a big boy now," we whispered like two fathers talking to their son. Like every father except for the one stopped by bayonets of border patrol. "Your time to face the world has arrived. Never forget your origins, never betray your land, despite its summer sand or winter slush."

"One more thing," Alex added.

". . . thing," I promptly echoed.

"Stay as you are. Don't grow old and gray. Follow not Dorian's footsteps."

Whether I was serious and Alex joked, or vice versa, the conversation came out bittersweet, both ironic and poignant.

# Plein air

We joggled in a suburban train. On a bench across rested Nad'usha, and rest she could, because Alex and I watched out for smirks and shrugs, ready to cane any scabrous squabbler. The rattling car zoomed towards the *plein air,* to its cow, meadow, willow—the scenery where we planned to perform our hope confession.

(For pen-handlers tracing our trajectory, the locations of Moscow terminals, trolleybus routes and scenic overlooks are available at any conscientious cartographer's corner. Just ask.)

A short rural trot from the station brought us uphill. The battery of easels confronted the vast vistas—facing west in terms of the local topography and belonging to the east as viewed from the global perspective.

Nad'usha's tongue tip squeezed through tight lips, as she diligently began trans-coloring the Earth's quilted cover. Alex jotted a carefree touch-n-go of the bloated horizon. Landscape was not our forte—every tree looked like linden, every season like fall.

How long should we wait?

What if we sneak up now and exhale two vapor hearts, tickling both of her ears by a single assertion? We don't mean that of giving preference to portrait over landscape, to man over nature, to union over separation, but rather something lofty—sincere words born during sleepless nights, the visions of hearts, heat and Hope.

As we inhaled and stepped forward, barefoot Leonidas with his crown of greasy hair put his hand on Nad'usha's shoulder, his thumb tickling her collar bone. We paused and exhaled. Measuring trees with his gnawed pencil, he mumbled something about compliance of forms.

Other students, their names as uninspiring as their daubs, were present but totally irrelevant. For us they were no more than inferior details of the landscape's interior, no more than Golems able to talk only by negligence of the Creator.

While Alex and I were exchanging some bitter observations, Leonidas lowered his head, almost touching Hope's temple. His breath filled her dimples. We considered rushing over and shouting prophetic words. Not in the sense of predicting the future but something valiant, with total disdain for authority—what the ancient prophets were notorious for.

For instance:

"Take your dirty hands off! Your touch leaves oil stains."

Or:

"Hope is a personal affair. We don't share Hope; she is an indivisible value."

We said nothing, crashing the lead and leaving a screeching groove in the easel. Our anguish would have been too subtle for Leonidas, who moved on to other pupils, correcting their helpless travails by his firm strokes.

"Alex!" Hope exclaimed, and then emphasized: "Alex!"

Still knitting our eyebrows, we turned to our angel. We couldn't

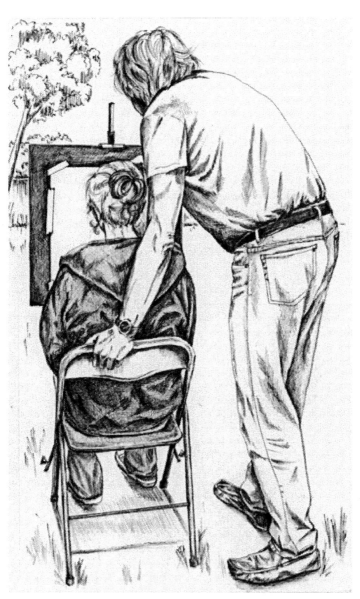

*Leonidas lowered his head, almost touching Hope's temple.*

stay angry. The dear girl knew the shortcut to our hearts. First, her voice, then her considerate address. Even Mother called us only once, aware that if one came over, the other had no choice but to follow. We understood Mother's intentions, but it would have been so nice to observe decorum. . . .

"We need to talk."

"Of course, we do," we agreed eagerly. "We had a confession to make. By the way, this cloud here is misplaced. You better move it to the right. When it forms a face, your picture will acquire deeper meaning. See, the sun is an eye; the tree is a nose. And this cloud—"

"This is not about drawing. Your constant breathing behind my back irks me. I can't take it anymore."

Alex looked at me for a helping hand. Keep talking, I waved, I'll think of something. He is the one fine with arts, while my domain is action. I make quick decisions and can wield a cane like a lance. In our little army I am the chief of staff as well as the quick reaction force, while Alex carries the suitcase of the Propaganda Minister.

"Speaking of breathing," that was Alex, of course, "in your sketch, which we hope the *brushster* didn't touch yet, we feel air, liberation, freedom. We love how this oak—it is oak, isn't it?—resists the wind gusts. Its crown is swaying, ready to surrender the throne, the leaves are about to be snatched away, but the trunk is unflinching."

She put the pencil down.

"It's not about the sketch. I am talking about your muttering, groaning, cheering behind my back. You embarrass me in front of my friends, in front of Leonid Ivanovich who is too kind to kick you out of the group."

"That's untrue! You might call our behavior atypical, we suppose. What do you expect from someones who have absolutely nothing conventional about them? Your uncle Fein was just one among many to admit it. Leonidas, artistic spirit that he is, must understand our nature better than anybody else. Alex, he told us many times, Alex, you have tremendous talent and a unique vision. Come any time. I am honored to have you in my class."

"You know what?" she said. "I am tired. My every step is being observed, my words scrutinized—turned, twisted, dissected until they fit your Procrustean head."

"Heads. . . ."

An insignificant pest was climbing the long stem by her ankle. The grass blade bowed until it reached unstable equilibrium. While Alex was talking on behalf of both of us, I knocked the insect off, thus telling flora from fauna, as the Creator alienated darkness from light at the dawn of all being.

". . . and," we continued the thought with no beginning or end, "you and us have known each other for a long time. We would like to meet your parents. Surely your mommy is a wonderful chef with plenty of family recipes, and we shall find a common language with your daddy."

She was about to accept—one can't resist flawless rhetoric—when Leonidas clapped, interrupting our intimacy:

"Wrap it up, people. The light is going away. We are leaving in a half-hour. Nad'usha, stop chatting, let's work."

Who is chatting? We were annoyed, although we managed to keep our indignation silent. Some call us unceremonious, not realizing that it's nothing but the exoskeleton—an external protection of the vulnerable pith. Attack is the best form of defense. I brushed Leonidas off, and Alex continued:

"Seriously, Nad'usha, why don't you invite us for a family dinner? We spend so much time together, we bump into two another, all over town. We have a common passion for art. Is Sunday good? We shall bring flowers. You will make a dainty dish, some of your secret specialties. Please don't tell what it's going to be. If your parents need a cause, we can celebrate a birthday—yours prematurely or ours overdue. The calendar is bursting with dates."

Hope wrinkled her nose like a sneezing kitten.

Tell her to add a plane in the sky, I signaled to Alex. A puffy-tailed loop will enliven the picture. We know tricks of art; we can draw shapely apes and shades of Hades; we have separated *chiaro* from *scuro*, and that was good. So many things we could teach our girl, so many more than her long-maned braggart!

"Not ugly." The passing-by Leonidas cast a quick glance at her canvas. "Not ugly at all."

"So, what about dinner? What about our first supper?" we insisted.

On the way back we chose an empty compartment and killed time by detailing our miniature profile on a hand-drawn banknote.

The train's sharp stop spilled the passengers all over the terminal square dominated by a huge poster *Of all art forms, the most important for us is film* (as conned by V.I. Lenin—the most prolific source of references). Not painting, mind you; not sculpture. Our fellow artist wannabes, heads drawn into shoulders, should have listened to this official ill-disposition. Horned snails of trolleybuses scurried about the pockmarked cobblestone.

"Don't follow me," Hope said. "I'll go alone."

"What about. . . ?"

"Some other time."

"How about tomorrow?"

"Whatever."

She didn't say where, and we didn't ask under what circumstances—the three of us had no doubts that the opportunity would muster us together, as it had many times before, be it a sunlit thoroughfare or a side street in twilight penumbra.

The story was about to take a night break, allowing for a brief philosophical discourse.

We have noticed that our lives carried an eerie semblance to a fairy tale with kind snow whites and evil snow queens, although the roles could have been distributed differently. Some of the characters have already made their appearance, animate like a deceptive advisor in the guise of Professor Tulchinsky, or inanimate like the trolleybus—a miracle carriage converted for the occasion from a pumpkin and taking Nad'usha away to her distant Hopeville. Someone else, maybe you, Doctor, still try on a costume behind the scenes, waiting for the appropriate moment to ascend the stage.

Only a blind man may disregard such obvious folklore themes permeating our destiny, such as stories about:

- innocent outcasts (if not we, then who?);
- a simpleton-protagonist (too often we have to put on this mask);
- three brothers (three or two makes little difference);
- a dragon slayer (like St. George on the blazon of our town);
- procuring a bride (no comment here);
- charmed and bewitched (both are quite common in our story);
- possessing a talisman and other miraculous object (the cane was our magic wand; the portrait was our talisman);
- and finally—somebody else's wife (now we are off our plot; let Paris and Helen take it from here).

We can only guess which direction our lives' course could have taken if we were two in the philistine sense of the number, if we were the separate ones of the Roman numeral II, if the vial with the Fein-scribed elixir stood upon our bed stand. Two sips on an empty stomach, two teaspoons before going to bed, and we could turn into mirrored Princes Charming. Alex could throw away his stick. I could dedicate all my time to painting *profile perdu* of our *behoped*. Instead of hiding, we would leisurely walk the boulevards of our native town glowing in the reflection of streetlamps and streetlights. Heavenly manna, taken by middlebrows for sand, would crunch under our feet.

Don't blame us for the world's imperfection, Doctor. We have spent too much time together to realize that our joint health is impeccable; our hearts beat in a well-paced tempo, accelerating and slowing down when required; we have little trouble dissecting any situation with mindful clarity. Our desire to cure ourselves is not a declaration of the problem. Not at all. We are far too vigorous and energetic to be obsessed with anatomical antinomy. Alex is well coordinated and can knock off a daisy bulb with a single strike of his cane, without the stem even quivering. I have a shrewd mind and a deep understanding of human vices and voices. Ruining such gifts by a psychiatric intrusion or surgical incision would be a crime.

Unfortunately, there is also *the other hand.* Humanity treats our tête-à-tête as *folie à deux*—an alarming deviation from its square standards. Blue-eyed Apollo is a monster in the town of tongue-tied pessimists. Instead of deforming beauty, Doctor, why don't you correct the rest of the world? Prescribe your miracle pills to everybody else, give them your mind-cleaning concoction. Then we wouldn't have to avoid public forums and tear ourselves apart, deciding whether we should follow Hope or head home to make sure that Mother's enchanter didn't trespass into our room and steal our masterpiece.

Muse about it, Doctor.

# Fairy (Part 3)

## At home

"This is going to be your room, Fairy. Have you ever had your own room?"

Sophie flipped the nightlight switch. The lamp, limp and pale in the daylight, failed to produce any of its flashing enchantment. The ghost of Fodor's study left its footprints on the parquet—the desk, the file cabinet, the bookshelf—mismatching the contours of the new tenants: a small bed covered by a quilt of pink and purple diamonds, a chest-drawer and an empty corner ready to accept another furniture novice.

"Look out the window. We live on the seventh floor. See all those tiny people below? They seem even smaller then you. Isn't it funny?"

Sophie kept touching objects as if that brought them to life. The wardrobe door flung open, sending Sophie's mirror twin into a giddy flight. As soon as the door was shut, the reflection returned into its neverwhere.

"Come here," Sophie called. "This is the bathroom, and this here is your toothbrush. Do you know that you have to brush your teeth twice a day? Have you seen a jacuzzi before? It's a bubbly-bathly-tubly. This is our room and there, there is the kitchen. Are you hungry now? Eat, uhm-uhm . . . would you like to have a snack? How about some chocolate kisses? Have you ever tried them?"

Fodor left for work. Sophie prepared breakfast, most of which stayed untouched. I am a mother, she thought, adjusting to the unfamiliar essence of familiar words. I have a daughter. If I don't find something to do, I will go crazy.

Luckily, there was always something demanding her attention.

It was one of those days when the weather lured one outdoors. The air was dry, the sun tender and the breeze refreshing. Sophie took Fairy not to a café or a boutique where she would have headed before, but to the playground.

On their way, Sophie—stooping to level their perspectives— pointed to a tree, a streetlight, a house, articulating names. She had never paid attention to these simple inexplicables earlier. Words pronounced repeatedly with diligent deliberation felt fake. Oak, oak, oak . . . koa. . . . What do O, A and K have in common with this regal colossus? What did you call that tree? I know, I know, the street is too noisy. You will tell me later.

"There; that's a playground. Do you want to try the seesaw? *See-saw-sacke a downe.* Don't be afraid. Things with funny names like teeter-totter can't be scary. Up, down, up, down. How about a slide or a sandbox? Do you want to play with that little girl? This is Fairy, and . . . what's your name, child? Would you like to play together?"

Someone tapped her on the shoulder. Sophie straightened and smiled shyly and proudly at the same time.

"I took your advice," she said to Isabella. "Fodor and I just came back. We have Fairy now."

"Congratulations! How do you feel? Better?"

"I don't know yet." Sophie slowly backed away from the sandbox as if letting a carefully constructed house of cards stand on its own. "This is still very strange."

"You'll get used to it."

They retreated to the bench. Sophie hesitated before asking a question that was beginning to dominate her mind.

"How long did it take for Katie—Kate, right?—to understand you? Was she laughing or crying? Did she talk to you. . . ?"

She was about to continue with *because Fairy,* but Isabella's smile made her pause.

"She got it right away. Such a sweetie. We never had problems. I even started learning her language. It's very funny, you know. I loved this tongue twister about Carl, Clara, her corals and his clarinet. I can never get it right. *Chyornyi* is black, *Chyortic* is an imp, *Chyorstvyi* is stale. And this one is absolutely charming—*Poludurok!*"

"What's that?"

"A half-dimwit."

"I wouldn't know when to apply it."

"You're right. I didn't even try to memorize, but the least useful sticks to memory like a weed and never flushes out."

"I am afraid you've just made me remember it too. So. . . ." Sophie slapped her knees and nodded in the direction of the playground. "What do you two usually talk about?"

"Oh, I tell Kate stories, fairy tales."

"You know fairy tales?"

"I used to read tons of myths and still remember one or two. Some are so incredibly bizarre, like the creation story about monster Kholomondumo. But if I run out of stories," Isabella confessed, casting a cunning look and lowering her voice, indicating that a secret was coming, "I make'm up."

Fodor returned in the evening, kissed Sophie on the cheek and headed straight for the kitchen. His hat—thrown on a stand on top of his wallet and keys—hesitated, then tipped over. It always did.

"I am starving. What do we have today?"

Did he forget? He behaves as if nothing changed.

"*We* had a wonderful day," Sophie said unnaturally loud, stretching rubbery vowels and pretending to talk on behalf of her daughter. "We went to the pla-a-ayground and met many ke-e-eds and built a sa-a-and castle just like that fortress in her old town. Didn't we, Honey?"

"Oh, Fairy, how are you?" Fodor mumbled with his mouth full. "How do you like your new life? Did you learn anything today?"

"I spoke to Isabella. She said that children were all different. Some pick up the language right away, others may take longer. She said we shouldn't worry."

"I am not worried. Everything is going to work out just fine."

After dinner he went to the living room and stared at the wall.

"You think it's a good spot?"

Sophie shook her head. What was he talking about?

"I stopped at the frame shop. You know what they told me at the gallery? An unframed painting is like a general in a sauna. I think this wall is excellent. Direct sunlight never reaches here, and the chandelier is well removed. There should be no flare."

Fodor had his clinic and his patients, and his mind was like a public house with rooms occupied by lodgers. Some, like Sophie and now Fairy, were permanent there, many were transient, others, like that new painting, were inanimate. The rules required that he take care of them all.

"Isabella and I will meet at the playground on Saturday. The daily routine is going to be good for Fairy. She has to be comfortable and get used to new children. It's very different than what she had over there. Do you hear me?"

"Every verb," he murmured between snores. "Every adjective you say."

Walks to the playground acquired the importance of educational expeditions. Sophie firmly held the little palm as they stood waiting for a stream of cars to freeze.

"Red light means stop," she repeated. "Green means go. Yellow means wait, even if you're late! Remember? Easy, isn't it? See, the green is on now, let's go."

She minced, adjusting her pace to the tiny steps by her side. At the next intersection they missed the green, because she gave Fairy a chance to lead. The light faded into yellow. The first attempt failed. Never mind, never mind.

"No jumping on the roadway. Wait till we get to the other side."

Once they reached the playground, Isabella—in a bluish cape

and a bell-shaped chapeau—helped blushing Kate off the swings and turned to Sophie.

"Your turn. Go ahead. Kate can't get enough of it."

"I like swings. Swings are the best," Kate confirmed, and Sophie admired the precision of sounds streaming from the little doll. After a brief silence, she picked up the loose end of the conversation:

"Thank you, sweetie. Fairy doesn't feel like it now. Maybe later. Do you want to build a sandcastle together?"

"I have a red scoop and a purple pail," Kate articulated with charming seriousness. "What color is your scoop?"

From the mothers' bench Sophie watched her friend's lively pixie taking leadership. The girl seemed to know precisely what she wanted. Every kid in the sandbox was enlisted to raise a hill, make forms, dig furrows.

In the middle of the adults' small talk, Isabella suddenly cut her story in mid-sentence, jumped up and raced towards the commotion that erupted in the sandbox.

"Be careful." She gripped Fairy's hand, jerking it high up. "You can't throw sand at children. If you play together, you have to follow the rules."

"She didn't mean it," Sophie said, hurrying to the defense. "Fairy is a kind girl. She didn't mean to hurt anybody."

Isabella ignored her, fixed on the disturber.

"You wouldn't like other girls to throw sand in *your* eyes, would you?"

"It's all right." Sophie tried to downplay the anxiety. "She understands."

Back on the bench, the old conversation was lost and the new one took awhile to bestir. The trust needed time to skin over.

Peaceful play resumed but not for long. This time not Isabella— her Kate safe on the swings—but some gaunt lady pulled a boy out and cast inimical lightning at Sophie.

"Fairy didn't do anything. She was pointing at his truck with a scoop," Sophie said.

"I don't want to wait until she does *something*. Who knows what's in her head?" the scrag muttered, pretending to be talking under her breath.

"What do you mean?"

"Nah-thing." Manifold meanings, none positive, were squeezed into this hollow notion. Sophie didn't like that at all. The war of the words didn't take long to flare up.

"Just look at her! Clearly, she is unstable. You have to teach her how to play with other children first, and then, ma-a-y-be, bring her here. I don't know what crazy ideas she has, and I don't want to find out."

Sophie turned to Isabella for support, but her friend's face stayed hidden behind the straw brim of her hat.

"Now she crushed Pauley's tower."

"It was an accident."

"Don't try to fool me. You think I am stupid? That smirk on her face! She did it on purpose. Pauley, baby, go play with well-mannered kids over there. This girl is wicked."

Sophie got up and put her hand on a frail shoulder.

"Time to go home, Fairy."

They stopped trips to the playground. For two days it rained sporadically, and the question never came up. Sophie called Isabella to propose that the four of them meet in a children's museum, but no one answered the phone. She decided against leaving a message.

Fearing that Fairy was going to be bored, Sophie entertained her by dressing up dolls. She picked up a tall brunette and, watching the girl's eyes, said:

"This is mom, and this . . . " long suggestive silence, "I don't know what name we should give this little dolly. F . . . Fa . . . Faye. . . . What do you think?"

Plastic heels of the nameless toy clanked on parquet.

"Where is she going without shoes?" Sophie smiled. "She can wet her feet and catch cold. See, it's raining outside. We are all putting our boots on to go out and so should she."

Sensing that Fairy didn't care much about make-believe lives,

Sophie tried to remember how she had spent time at her age. Unfortunately, memory refused to reach so far back and got stuck in school years mostly woven by whispering secrets with girls and giggling at boys.

On Friday Fodor returned excited. He rushed to the living room and asked loudly so that everyone could hear:

"Anybody call yet?"

"Who called?" Sophie asked. "What do you mean?"

Fodor munched a few words and started humming a tune in key major, tasteless by its own virtue or turned such by his tone-deaf performance.

"Good, good." Rubbing his palms, he made another circle around the apartment. "They'll be here any minute."

"What are you talking about?" Sophie didn't remember him mentioning guests, but a second later realized what was going on.

His arms crossed, his legs wide apart, Fodor paused in front of the empty wall. That same minute the doorbell interrupted his daydreams, and two men in overalls hauled in their bulky load wrapped in brownish paper.

Sophie squatted and tilted her head to look under the table:

"Don't be afraid, silly. Come out. No one is going to hurt you. These men just delivered the painting. They are nice people. They will help us hang it and then leave. Your father bought a very interesting picture when we came to pick you up from . . . your old home. In a sense you and this portrait are cousins."

"Here." Fodor pointed. "Put it here."

The frame he'd chosen turned out to be of weighty gilded wood. Monstrous, as befitted its subject and sovereign. Dribs and drabs of the heavy-duty wrap rustled about. A nail was not nearly enough, and a whole system of strings and supports had to be erected, ruining recently renovated wallpaper.

Before Sophie had a chance to object, Fodor said, good, this means that we will never take it down.

"Careful." Her embrace protected Fairy, while the men were removing broken laths of the carcass.

In the closed space the portrait seemed much bigger than in the gallery, and, having no other artifacts around, completely dominated the scene.

"I suppose we'll get used to it."

"Should we start our own art collection?"

"I already have my art." Smiling, Sophie tightened a large pink bow. "I wish I knew how to master it."

## Doctor and Nanny

Every hour was imbued with Fairy's quiet presence—her little toothbrush on the bathroom shelf, a bluish stripe of nightlight, a drawer full of pinks and purples. It's good, Sophie kept saying to herself, making rounds; it's good.

After fighting the doubts gnawing inside, she finally decided to summon help.

Fodor had just come back after another hectic day in the clinic, tired and all too willing to dismiss her worries. "The girl must be humming or talking to herself. Kids often have imaginary friends."

"This is all very strange. If there was something wrong, they would have mentioned it. They'd have to. The headmistress was such a nice lady. She told me the story of Fairy's birth. She wasn't supposed to, you see, and could get in trouble. Such a tragedy. I'm sure the girl can hear. I'm sure she understands us."

Fodor had wanted to tell an amusing story from his office life, this one patient, you would never, I mean, never guess what he was complaining about . . . but the conversation took a turn that disallowed his lighthearted ridicule. Maybe later, he sighed, and poked the little hill of mashed potatoes on his plate.

"What if something *is* wrong?" Sophie asked.

This uncertain *what if* had been bothering her for many nights. Sleepless, mesmerized by the pale nightlight seeping from under the door of Fodor's old study, she kept on building the house of cards from the ethereal *if-then-else*. What if, indeed, her daughter happened to be one of those . . . even in her mind Sophie couldn't make herself to spell out the word . . . one of those . . . you know . . . troubled children? A rare exposure through a sanitized gloss of mass media that Sophie had to . . . those people . . . gave her shivers. These poor children. . . . Who knows what's going on in their heads? I mean, what's *really* going on there? *They* do seem smiling all the time. But their poor parents. . . .

She needed reassurance. There was nothing worse than fighting alone. Isabella belonged to a healthy world. Her cute Kate personified the norm. She liked the swings, enjoyed playing with other kids and talked, talked, talked, tricking her tongue into rolling out one tiny syllable after another with ar-ti-cu-la-te me-ti-cu-lous-ness.

Where is my unease coming from? Sophie wondered. That's wrong to dislike them only because they are happy and well. If Fairy had tried talking or, at the very least, struggled to, Sophie would have known and taken measures awhile ago. But the girl behaved absolutely naturally as if she simply had nothing to say. Adults always come up with meaningless questions. Who do you like more, your mom or your dad? Did you stop missing your old home? Why would you answer something when both *yes* and *no* are wrong? How could she stop what she had never started? What a silly game! Anybody in Fairy's place would shrug and withdraw to her world, wherever it was.

"Yes, I am a doctor," Fodor sighed, "but I am not a pediatrician. Have you spoken to any of your friends, to Isabella?"

Sophie shook her head. Sharing sorrow was one thing, exposing sores something completely different.

"What about your colleagues?" she said. "Can you ask them? Someone always knows someone."

Conceding to her insistence, he worked the oracle and came up with a name. An excellent specialist, the best, they said. Sophie dialed the number, withstood a lethargic hold with accords going rondo and had a long conversation with the secretary. She explained her situation, shed an uncalled for but very timely tear and squeezed an appointment into the first cancellation.

The office was close enough and Sophie decided to take a walk. It was ridiculous, she realized, but the very decision to go to a specialist seemed like a notch of treachery, as if she doubted not just Fairy, who deserved none of her distrust, but Nature that stood behind. This shame and the necessity to summon disgraceful truth or invent awkward lies, should they meet someone on their way, made Sophie choose quiet side streets.

"We are going to see a doctor. You are not afraid of them, are you? Remember how we went to see that sugar-cone lady who checked your weight like if you were a huge watermelon? Yes, no? Careful, the light is about to change. That's fine. We'll wait until the next green. There is plenty of time."

A palm and an aquarium took the bigger part of the waiting room. Sophie checked around and couldn't help feeling proud for Fairy. One kid, his head tilted aside, sat motionlessly next to his mom, two more were picking out random objects from the big toy box in the corner. Her daughter was the prettiest. In fact, she wasn't even sick or anything. They came just to eliminate this annoying thought, this humdrum, these drops of nonstop torture in the back of her mind. Striped fish with cold careless stares observed them for a moment through the wavering weeds, then swam away.

"What is your name, child?"

The doctor with his well-trimmed beard and heavy-rimmed glasses looked like a mish of a wise owl and mash of domesticated Santa. In the course of life everybody was drawn to the image others expected to see, Sophie figured. It was like the centripetal force that made owners resemble their pets, husbands and wives borrow features from one another. The doctor must be a kind magician, she thought. I want him to be. "We call her Fairy," she hurried to say.

"Nice to meet you, Fairy. How do you do?"

He got up from his chair and moved closer.

"Do you understand what I am saying, Fairy? You have such a beautiful name. Can you repeat after me? Sun, oak, eagle. What does the cow say?"

"You see, Doctor, the reason we came here is that Fairy used to live in a different country. She spoke a different language. Well, I haven't really heard her speaking, but we've been to a pediatrician who found nothing wrong."

Doctor Santa completed the circle and seated himself behind his desk, knitting eyebrows and chewing lips. Sophie stroked the little warm hand and held it tight between her palms.

"Maybe she just doesn't want to talk to us?"

"Why wouldn't she?" Doctor took a loose paperclip, deftly threw it at the magnet bristling like a hedgehog and made a few quick crosses on the preprinted form. "A normal child always wants something. He wants toys, he wants attention, he wants to dominate other kids, and speech is a natural means to obtain it all. That's what makes us human."

"Do you think that Fairy is not . . . may not be normal?"

"Don't worry. Her silence might just be a figure of speechless, excuse the pun. We need to run a few tests before I can make any statement. Children are usually perceptive when it comes to new languages, but there is always a chance that stress creates resistance. Did you try to speak to her on her terms?" He turned to Fairy. "If I name a thing, can you point to it? I have a photo on my desk. It's me and my wife long time ago, although you may not recognize me. I wouldn't recognize myself, but that's a different story. Can you point to it?"

"There it is," Sophie whispered, helping. "This is an old picture. Show the doctor that you understand."

"You should try talking to her in her terms," Santa broke the silence, when further inaction became meaningless "It certainly wouldn't hurt. Some kids take longer to adjust to the new environment."

Sophie thanked him and helped Fairy off the chair. Careful! But it was too late. The girl's awkward motion accidentally swiped the photo frame off the desk. The glass shattered and tiny smithereens spread all over the floor.

"I am so sorry! She didn't do that on purpose."

Santa's twitch released his inner Rudolph. He called his assistant and waved them off. Go, go. Sybil will do the cleaning. The next patient is waiting.

Sophie picked feathery Fairy up and with another round of thanks and sorrys headed for the door. Pieces of glass crackled under her feet like sand.

"It's all right," she whispered. "I know you didn't mean it. These things happen to everybody. I have dropped hundreds of plates. He'll get another frame. Let's go buy some ice cream."

Sophie remembered how relieved she used to feel after leaving a doctor's office, which, despite her parents' merry assurances, always frightened her. A threat of discomfort, whether an injection or a mouthful of bitter solution, had always loomed there.

It's all in the past now. There was nothing to be afraid of, was there? I love when you smile.

Why didn't it occur to her before that the whole silence-misunderstanding-confusion tangle could be explained by the incongruity of their languages? Why would Fairy respond to something that had no relevance in her world?

What's her mind like? If it's anything like mine, it must be an attic of antics—you can never find what you are looking for. What's that weird word *poludurok* doing there? Where did I hear it? Yes, yes, of course! Isabella mentioned learning Kate's language. The answer must have been on the surface all the time.

Sophie had never been quick at picking up hints. She needed to weave a thought slowly, ring after ring, so that at some moment in space and sense she could find her way home like Theseus following Ariadna's clew.

The runes and rules of foreign languages were her worst subject in school. What if she somehow passed this ineptness to her daughter over their genetic gap? What if Fairy too was unable to absorb the gusts of odd sounds?

After a sleepless night, accompanied by Fodor's sonorous snores, in the solidifying irreality of the dawn, she found a solution—one of those answers that, once reached, seemed so obvious.

She had to recruit a bilingual ally!

"You have to be kidding," Fodor exploded. "A nanny? Where is she going to live? This is an apartment, not a king's palace. You already kicked me out of my study. Now you want to convert my library into a guest room?"

What do you need a library for? Sophie wondered. You only read in the bathroom. That pile of newspapers by the toilet drives me mad. And don't raise your voice. Fairy is still asleep.

Fodor got up and paced back and forth before stopping in front of the painting, looking for its support and consolation. Whoever was portrayed there must have spoken one language with their girl. Sophie understood her husband's unrest. Every change takes time to get used to. It's difficult for him to shatter his well-tuned life and give away home turf, foot after foot.

Not used to dealing with help, Sophie had only a vague idea of what the nanny should be like. Any intrusion alarmed her. Occasional forays of a plumber or an electrician made her retreat into the bedroom. The cleaning lady intimidated her. Although she learned to accept them as a necessary good, these visits were no more appealing and no less appalling than an enemy invasion.

*A live-in aid needed for taking care of a girl, . . .* the ad to the local *Expatriates Tribune* stated, further enumerating a sought-for list of conventional prerequisites and conversational virtues.

The paper, begging for demand and consisting of supply—dentists' grins, used cars, real estate steals—came out every Thursday. On Saturday, after futile expectation by the silent telephone, Sophie dialed the office again. An unfamiliar voice with the familiar accent went through laborious, letter by letter, verification of her last name. Paper rustle ensued, concluding with joyous "Akha!" This Kh—a *kheavy* stone tied to the neck of the weightless H—almost deafened her.

"Pardon?"

"Zer you ar. It vill be zis Toursday."

"You mean, Tuesday?"

"Not Tusday. Toursday! Munday, Tusday, Venzday, Toursday."

The weary cracklings explained that her ad *vill* be printed the next Thursday like she requested. There was no confusion and her instructions, vocal and unequivocal ("This joke, yes? You understand?"), were meticulously written down by *our comrade*. Never mind, Sophie said, just print it. It was easier to wait for another week than make her way through these syllable jitters.

"Don't be so nervous," Fodor said. "Let's go out. I am getting sick of pizza leftovers."

"Fairy loves it," Sophie responded absentmindedly, her hand resting on the dead receiver.

On *Toursday* the phone finally came alive.

"*Khello.*" The other end of the line must have belonged to the headmistress's twin—same bulky, unbendable Vs and Zs, same manner of utterance when, as opposed to raising the tone at the end of sentence, they brought it down almost beyond the audible range as if losing interest in completing the lexical unit.

"*Zis goot.*" The voice agreed with Sophie's choppy reasoning and accepted the invitation to stop by with glorious neglect for lesser children of speech, such as connecting verbs. Articles, definite and indefinite, although not entirely ignored, were thrown into the mix just to claim presence, with no regard for the proper placement.

I understand Fairy now, Sophie told Fodor later, when relaying the conversation. If anybody kept speaking to me in this pidgin I'd be speechless too. Is that how little sense we make to her?

The doorbell rang and a middle-aged woman hesitantly stepped in. She circled the room, stumbled over the package with Fodor's homeless encyclopedias expelled from the former library, peeked out the window and took the farthest seat, her purse on her knees, her hands on her purse.

"And this is Fairy," Sophie introduced. "She is a very sweet girl."

"*Weed girdle,*" the guest echoed and, as if still unfinished with her internal debate, inquired: "Where this window go?"

"That's the square. The kitchen and the bedrooms face the side street. It's very quiet at night. Even here you don't hear the buzz so much."

Sophie didn't quite know how to proceed. She observed the visitor, trying to visualize the woman helping Fairy dress up, preparing her food, talking to her in their unreal tongue.

"I Marina Petrovna."

"Fairy, would you like to come closer? This is Marina Pert . . . Petr—"

"Just Marina," the woman conceded.

The refrigerator door slammed. Fodor walked in from the kitchen.

"The patronymic Petrovna was left behind in *Patria*," he mumbled, pulling curtains aside. Sun lit the room. Marina jumped up, made a semicircle, avoiding the direct light, and cautiously inspected the square below.

"Something's wrong?" Sophie was concerned. "Are you allergic to sun?"

"I allergic to people."

The phrase circled in the air like dust. Sophie changed the subject and started talking about petty things like the favorite food, the day schedule and the room arrangement, dressing Fairy's silence into her own chatter.

"No, no," interrupted Marina. "No walks. I not go outside. You go to park. I stay here."

"If you are concerned with the gas-laden air, it's actually pretty clean here. You shouldn't worry."

"This not about air."

"Then what is this about?"

"Mafia."

Sophie and Fodor glanced at each other.

"Mafia?"

"In what world you live? You close eyes on everything, but you should know that mafia everywhere. If you only get mugged you lucky. They watch all; they do what they want."

"Hm . . . well . . . I don't think mafia should be our primary concern. The police. . . ."

Satisfied but not lulled by her surveillance of the outside world, Marina returned to her chair.

"Police," she mimicked. "They all venal. They close eyes. You naïve. I know."

"You know the mafia?" Suddenly, Fodor seemed to have no idea what to do with his hands. He clenched them, then slapped his knees, then scratched his cheek.

"I know *about* them." Marina's confidence made Sophie feel like a lectured child. "My brother has business *there*." An uncertain wave of a hand (the reticule handle released and recaptured) indicated the faraway town with a citadel for its heart. "Gangsters everywhere. They not think twice of kidnap her and demand ransom from Kostya. That my brother. If they see us together—aha!—they calculate. They may drive ambulance and pretend like doctors. You never know. You don't want to listen my stories. The more you sleep, the better your appetite. Oh, yes. I take sleeping pills, so I no get up at night. Fairy? What strange name."

When she left, Fodor stood by the window and followed Marina's terrified trot all the way across the square.

"There," he commented. "Kidnapped by the bus. She must pay a ticket ransom or else."

"Don't be ridiculous. You could have asked her to say a few words to Fairy."

"I was afraid she would talk about the mafia." Fodor winked to the shadow under the table as Sophie got up from her chair and headed for the kitchen.

"Anybody want some tea? We still have the apple pie."

They both raised their hands as if voting and turned to the girl, their arms still in the air. Sophie lowered hers first. "I am making three cups."

The next guest threw her coat over the chair and squatted down before Fairy.

"Hi, sweetie. I love your braids. And this bow! It really becomes you. You are a very pretty girl. My name is Irina. What's yours?"

After the endless second, Sophie came to the rescue and spoke in plural first person with intentionally cartoonish intonations:

"Fairy is a tiny bit shy. But after we get used to each other, we can play together and laugh and talk. Is that right, Honey?"

"Are you affiliated with the mafia in any way?" Fodor asked, with his serious mask on.

"Pardon?"

"You know, the mafia. Blackmailers, kidnappers—"

"Fodor, stop it!"

Irina rose in sincere indignation:

"That's the worst stereotype I have ever heard of! Because I came from that country, you immediately take me for a criminal?"

"My husband has a non-sense of humor," Sophie explained, standing behind Fairy, her hands on the girl's shoulders.

"I am sorry," Fodor admitted. "It is indeed a wonderful country to be from. We had a very unconventional applicant the other day. I am sorry. I am . . . we are relieved that it was a case of isolated insanity. I do tend to make bad jokes. Here, let me show you the apartment. Fairy, would you like to accompany Irina to my library? I mean, my old library. Never mind, wait here if you want to. We'll make a quick tour."

Sophie turned the lights on.

"What is this?"

"I knew you would like it." Fodor squared his shoulders. "We brought this painting back from—"

"Are you kidding me?"

"No, no, I am serious. We did buy it there."

"It radiates bad energy. I can sense it."

Fodor cleared his throat.

"Actually, we like it. Fairy likes it. I think it's very nice."

"I can't stay in the room with this . . . this monster. How can you keep such ugliness at home?"

"It's not all that bad," Sophie intervened. "I don't quite appreciate it myself, but there is something there. Treat it as a pattern on the wall, like ivies and violets."

"What do you mean, pattern?" Fodor wondered, standing up for his protégé. "It's art. It's a great portrait. There is a whole story to it."

"It gives me jibblies." Irina shuddered and backed all the way to the door, not waiting for a formal farewell.

"That's a pity. She seemed like a nice lady. You aren't disappointed, are you? Let's do something together," Sophie said to Fairy when they were left alone. "Whatever you wish. How about dolls? We can dress them up. No? I know how you feel. I am kinda bored with them myself. Hey, I have an idea!"

She took two pieces of paper.

"There, move closer. We are going to draw. Have you done this before? Me neither. I mean, not for a long time. Hold the pencil. Let's see . . . what should I draw?"

Sophie scribbled several loosely connected doodles and tilted her head. After a short meditation, she mused:

"It's an animal. No doubt about that. The question is, what kind? Is it a crocodile or a cat? What do you say? They have more in common then you might think. They both start with the same letter."

"Some similarity," Fodor quipped. "Are you sure they start with the same letter in her language as well?"

Her language, right. The question kept creeping up.

"If Marina and Irina could learn ours, why can't I learn theirs? It's just words." She turned to Fairy. "Mama is going to the bookstore. All three of us will go. We'll start with something simple, with the alphabet. How difficult might that be?"

"You go ahead." Fodor flicked his palm in good-bye. "I have a report to finish."

The Foreign Languages were exiled to the second floor of the bookstore.

They took the escalator.

"It's not scary, silly. Come, I'll hold you in my arms. See how many people are riding? Nobody is crying. It's only one flight. Here we are. Was it that bad?"

In many words sliding over one another, she explained to a sales assistant what she . . . what they were looking for. "One of us needs to learn, the other—not to forget." The languid slacker pointed at the corner shelf. Sophie made a random pick—large print for beginners. Cyrillic characters shouted at her from the centerfold.

"What are these squiggles?" Sophie wondered out loud and lowered the book so that Fairy could see for herself. "Have you seen these letters before? Of course, you have. Would you introduce me to them? Look, I can read! *KOT, MAK, MOCKBA.* I wonder if it means anything. Surely, we'll be good friends. Hi letters, my name is Sophie, pleased to meet you."

She flipped a few pages and tried to pronounce dense clusters of consonants, three or four in a row.

"*Zdr . . . tsch . . . khv. . . .* What a gibberish! If someone spoke to me like this, I'd lose my tongue too."

They also bought a picture book about Winnie the Pooh with words practically extinct.

"Never mind," said Sophie. "We can always take the stairs."

A surprise was waiting for them at home.

Fodor got up. "Honey, please meet Ree . . . Ra. . . . Excuse me, I am terrible with sounds. I don't want to mutilate your name."

An elderly, slightly bent but still agile lady looking like a kind grandma from a folktale opened up her purse and handed them a passport introducing her as Arina Rodeeon. How do you say that again? Fodor frowned. Is that Roe-dee-on? Do you mind if we just call you Nanny? She nodded and repeated after him what in her version resembled champing—nuh-nnie, nya-nya, nyam-nyam.

"Do you feel comfortable here? Anything bothers you?" Fodor asked cautiously, Sophie's reproof still fresh in his mind. "Inside," with a vague handwave circumventing the room and speedily bypassing the portrait, "or, maybe, outside?" with a gesture to remote hideouts of hired kidnappers.

Instead of answering, Nanny moved straight to Fairy.

"Look," Sophie whispered, "she is smiling."

Fodor coughed to attract attention. What? Sophie articulated.

We have to ask about references, where she came from, some contacts. Producing no sounds, his lips had to work twice as hard.

Instead of answers, the very next day they received a monstrous, old-fashioned wardrobe trunk that took up a good third of Nanny's new room. The chest shed a scent of old times and old age, and Sophie secretly, although to no avail, sprayed it with deodorizer. Whatever they filled the little can with was no holy water—the flagrant smell defeated Sophie's fragrance.

"I can't even walk into that room anymore," she complained to Fodor.

"Doesn't seem to bother Fairy," he replied. "I peeked in yesterday. She was sitting right on top, laughing and dangling her feet."

"They certainly fit each other well."

To Fairy, Nanny sang in strings of strange sounds. Fodor and Sophie she addressed in short, firm stitches, as if working on a tambour embroidery—each word recognizable separately but, when corded together, making little sense.

"Fairy looks happy," Sophie said once, to strike up a conversation. "What are you two talking about?" She concentrated, ready to sort the jumbled reply into a sentence.

*That's not her real. . . .*

". . . name?" Sophie concluded . "Yes, yes, we know. But it's so cute, and she is such a cute child. Don't you think that it becomes her? The first moment Fodor and I saw her, we thought—that was it! And it translates as Faith which is almost Fairy."

"Wait!" Fodor exclaimed, turning to Nanny. "How do you know it's not her name? Did she tell you that? Did she speak to you?"

Nanny showed no interest in following his lead in the conversation. She had an agenda of her own. Leaving the parents in bewilderment, she dressed Fairy the way Sophie never had before, mimicking her own style, wrapping a scarf around the girl's neck and putting on mittens even though the Indian summer had hardly hatched into the full-blown fall.

The first week, even the first month, Sophie was dying from curiosity. She would stop by Nanny's door and try to discern the new voice in the murmur that was seeping out.

In the mornings, when the pair went outside, Sophie pressed her forehead to the windowpane until they disappeared around the corner.

"Did you go to the playground?" she asked upon their return, trying to elicit a response. "Did you have a good time?"

Whatever Fairy was playing, the feared conflicts with other well-bred and duly responsive children never overshadowed Nanny's stories. Sometimes they came back with odd objects either purchased at a street fair or, most likely, picked up from the sidewalk. They were always small, often rusty and made their way directly to Nanny's trunk—the lid squeaked, then, after a momentary stillness, banged shut.

Nanny and Fairy teamed up so well that the girl's life seemed to have little need of anybody else. Fodor made a joke that now they had become a real family—they even had a Fairy-sitter. Sophie had to suppress pricks of jealousy. As long as her daughter was happy. . . .

# Sᴄʜᴏᴏʟ

Everything was going well for Doctor Santa. He had a first-rate appetite, a nice house south of North Pole, and his heart's valves kept time like a cuckoo's clock.

"Good, good," he sang, leafing through his folder and, without looking at Fairy, offering her a tennis ball. "There, squeeze it tight."

"Grab it," Sophie whispered.

"Hold it," Santa encouraged.

"Remember, we saw a boy who could juggle three of those?"

"All right." Doctor pushed the glasses up his nose bridge. "If you don't want to play ball, that's fine. No one is forcing you. We are here to have fun. How about this pyramid? Look, it has six rings. The biggest one on the bottom is purple. That's my favorite color. You have seen the rainbow, haven't you?"

Sophie was about to say that it had been the exact same exercise when they met Fairy for the first time, only that other rainbow had seven colors. . . . Santa made a soothing gesture, it's fine, let the girl answer. The picture in the new frame stood now beyond reach, in the far-corner safety.

He massaged Fairy's palm.

"What can I tell you? The heartbeat has some unusual pattern. We shall run a few more tests. The reflexes are fine. Are you saying she communicates with her nanny without a problem?"

"I am not sure if they communicate in a literal sense, but they do get along."

"The girl might be a late bloomer. She needs to be around kids. Nanny and the bedtime stories are fine, but she has to be in contact with her own age group. I see no contra-indications against school. Talk to her. Prepare her. Teach her letters and numbers."

"Which letters?" Fodor asked when Sophie re-enacted the visit. "Theirs or ours?"

"Your lame jokes aren't helping."

He came up with a clever compromise. They started with the common ones—A, O, E, T. A garland of paper squares now hung over the girl's bed.

"Show me M," Sophie was saying. "M like in Mama, or like in the name of that town I told you about. Are you positive? Warm, warmer, a little to your right. There you are! My girl. Was it difficult? Let's do it again."

On the first day of school the three of them—without Nanny, who expressed no interest in going—joined a flowery crowd. Some kids were quiet and solemn, approaching the foothills of the adults' world; others talkative and excited. Sophie peered into the eyes of other first graders, searching for the distinctions that made Fairy so special.

The moment of separation passed easier than Sophie had imagined. As soon as she kissed Fairy and released her hand, the flow sucked the children in. The doors closed.

Fodor headed straight to his clinic. Sophie walked home alone.

As quiet as Fairy was, as little space as she occupied, the apartment seemed lifeless without her.

"Tell me," Sophie insisted again, "what are you two usually talking about?" Anybody else in her place would have had trouble carrying the dialogue, but Sophie had learned to understand the old woman by listening, not with her mind, but with her heart.

Nanny shook her head. *Nothing special. Fairy tales, folktales, fables.*

"What kind? You know all of them by heart?"

*Know, remember, what difference does that make? If I forget, I pick the new ones from our own lives, like threads of a tapestry.*

Sophie didn't quite get it, but Nanny considered any further explanations unnecessary, returning to the crisscrosses of her embroidery.

"Can you tell me one of your stories?"

Nanny fidgeted on her chair like a little girl, put the tambour down, then picked it up again. *They wouldn't make much sense neither to you nor to. . . .*

"To whom?" Sophie's eyebrows formed a cone of bewilderment, but in a second she burst out laughing. "Is that how you call Fodor? I suppose that's fair. If he gets lost in your Arina Rodeeon's *Ra*'s and *Ree*'s, it's only fair that you dub him Fo-Pho. See, I understand you. I could understand your stories as well."

Nanny beaded a few words together. *For you it has to be a totally different tale. Names, places, quests—everything rests on the language. Translated, they lose their soul and tumble down. Vera feels it all too well.*

"Who?" Sophie caught herself asking again, only to realize that she had known the answer.

The telephone rang.

"Is school over?" Fodor inquired. "Not yet? How are you two coming along?"

Sophie was standing by the window looking at chaotic car dashes, pressing the receiver with her shoulder.

"What do we do? Nothing. You know how it is, talking to Nanny. I can't get anything from her. We just wait for Fairy."

She went out a half hour early to pick the girl up. Nanny put away fragmentary flowers—some colors already finished, some barely plaited—and moved to the kitchen to prepare her usual brownish brew, which Sophie deliberately avoided but Fairy didn't seem to mind at all. In fact, she digested both food and tales coming from Nanny much better than Sophie's healthy diet and the peculiar cases from Fodor's practice, as much as he tried to translate them into childish.

The way back from school didn't differ from most of their walks. Sophie asked questions and habitually filled in gaps of silence with her own comments. Was it interesting in school? Of course it was interesting—you met boys and girls and they all talked and laughed. How did you like the teacher? A very nice young lady, isn't she? Father and I saw her when she led your class in the morning. Did you see us waving? You are a really big girl. You go to school now.

"She must cool down to those silly stories," Fodor said. "What can she learn from Ra-Ri. . . ."

". . . from Nanny. . . ."

". . . sooner or later everybody grows out of dragons and elves. I did."

"Now you only have case histories."

"Everything I read, I have to treat critically. I am sorry, but I can't take monsters and heroes seriously anymore. Can you?"

"There is at least one monster that you treat with respect." Sophie cast a sidelong glance at the wall.

"By the way—" Fodor livened up , grabbing the new subject "—I saw Fairy staring at the painting the other day. She didn't notice me and I was watching her for a minute or two. She loves it as much as I do. I can tell. Her lips moved, and I think she spoke to it. I didn't hear sounds, but it *was* a real conversation."

Sophie pressed her hands tight to her chest.

"Did you try to read what she was saying?"

"Funny thing, I couldn't make out a single word. Maybe she was talking in Nanny's gibberish?"

"I wonder if that language of hers is the one we think it is, or if it is something only she knows."

"Only she and Nanny."

"Only she and Nanny and the portrait."

After the steep climb into the new routine of getting up early, sharing Fairy with a hundred strange kids and having homework assignments eased a little, Sophie's anxiety softened. Silence didn't irk her so much. After all, she and Fairy understood each other, and the actual word barter seemed a welcome but unnecessary spice. Sophie never faced a scandal, tears or confrontation. Their co-existence was peaceful, and Nanny, contrary to Fodor's predictions, never slowed down with her thousand stories, the thousand and first yet to be told.

Fodor's involvement in home affairs grew thinner. He was coming in late and tired, having used all his daily word ammunition at work. As he shuffled into the living room, a shadow, frozen before the painting, quivered and retreated like a shooed robin.

In winter the mailman brought a letter addressed to Fairy's parents. Her teacher, Miss Klein, wanted to see them.

"I have a patient scheduled," Fodor said, summoning his typical excuse, "but you go ahead."

"What happened?" Sophie looked at Fairy. "Did you do something wrong?"

The two of them came to school earlier than usual. The morning halls were empty and lifeless. Sophie left her daughter on a chair in the office where a red-cheeked secretary had just arrived and was building her daily nest by turning on lights, switching on the coffeemaker and applying the final strokes of her make-up.

Sophie asked for directions to Fairy's homeroom, and the secretary, busy with her mask of mascara, pointed with her elbow. Over there.

Miss Klein looked like a high school overachiever—youthful and idealistic. She started with ". . . such a sweet child, . . ." which alarmed more than reassured Sophie, who smiled without saying a word—a ploy subconsciously borrowed from Fairy. The mien came out somewhat forced. The worst was yet to come.

". . . it's not in my habit to hide from parents that we do have concerns. Nothing to be alarmed or upset about. I just feel that the sooner we both acknowledge it, the better."

"Acknowledge what?"

"Well, you see, Mrs . . . m-m-m . . . we all love your girl, and do everything we are supposed to, here at school. However, the results will be more effective if you and I cooperate."

The guest's smile was waning away, but Miss Klein was too preoccupied with her verbal buildup to notice the strain. She was erecting a fort from standard blocks of the teacher-parent architecture—formal, solid and impenetrable.

". . . children need to learn about responsibilities. Not only do they play together; they work together. Is she sharing with you what's going on in the class?"

Sophie shook her head, but the teacher needed no response.

"I am sure she says how much fun it is and how we laugh and what games we play. But this is not just about games anymore. She doesn't seem to be excited by the class activities. Whenever it's her turn, she just grins and never says a word. The other day, when I sent you the letter, I don't know if she told you, but we had a very unpleasant incident. In the middle of the lesson she got up and walked to the window. Do you know how difficult it is to keep control over twenty kids? They are all sweet devils, but rules have to be rules for everybody. Faye totally ignored my request to sit down. She wouldn't take her eyes off two squirrels running after one another in the schoolyard. We can't tolerate disobedience here, Mrs . . . m-m-m . . . and we won't. Imagine, if everybody would do as they pleased? What kind of school would this be? They have to respect order and obey the authorities. This was far from the first occurrence. Not that she is stubborn, but maybe, maybe, and don't panic yet, maybe she needs a slower pace of learning."

"What do you mean?"

"We have a special program for kids who—how should I put

it?—require a more gradual approach to education. It might be better for her too, because she needs to feel comfortable. If she doesn't participate in our program, something must be bothering her. Talk to your daughter, explain it to her, ask her what she thinks. Kids are all different, and I am sure that in a year or two she'll catch up."

Sophie searched for a way to squeeze her long story into the allotted interval, but, before she could find the right words, her time wore thin. The halls came alive with tramping and screaming; the space filled with verve, leaving little room for quiet Fairy. Miss Klein put on her friendly-frozen airs, concluding the dialogue on a high note, and saw her visitor to the door. Stepping into the corridor, Sophie felt estranged in its ruckus and rumpus.

Maybe Fodor was right, and the time had come to replace Nanny with someone who could give Fairy more than tales? Exit Mary Poppins, enter a drill sergeant, he said. Let's get her a tutor. Music, art, something.

"Nanny," Sophie asked at home—an examination akin to a chess game in which she had been defeated many times, "I really need to know what you and Fairy talk about."

*I tell stories about princes and beasts, about tricksters and brave hearts, about love and hope.*

"But she is a big girl now. She needs to learn how to deal with real people, not your imaginary princes."

*People have preserved these stories for many years. There must be a reason for that. Worthless luggage may drag along for a few years, for a generation, but the husk always crumbles away. The same fables tell different stories to different listeners. You hear what you are ready for.*

"Tonight," Sophie insisted, refusing to give up that easily, "what are you going to tell her tonight?"

*Let tonight come first, then the right tale will form. I never prepare in advance.*

Sophie watched Fairy, trying to guess what was going on underneath her quiet obedience. Still waters run deep, is that what her teacher said? I hate their cracker-barrel wisdom.

"How was your day? Are you learning interesting things? Did Ms. Klein speak to you about joining a different class?"

She could be an empty shell, Sophie thought, or, just as possible, she may be smarter then we all are, for our fuss and bustle is hardly worth the words we say. At least she hears me, it means that. . . . Oh, I have no idea what it means.

Nanny mumbled, and Sophie frowned in concentration. The sounds formed no familiar tunes, only the usual meaningless gurgle. Pressured by all that abracadabra, common reasoning started losing its ground. That's it, I'm insane, Sophie thought. I'm going crazy. I don't know what I'd do if it weren't for Fairy. She absorbs our nonsense so effortlessly.

"My head spins," Sophie confessed to Fodor. "I listen to Nanny and sometimes I can't get what she says at all. I asked what her stories were about, and she just said, stories were stories. What does that mean? How am I supposed to understand it? I have to fill in the gaps and assign the meaning she may not even have in mind. Is it their country, their citadel? Is it that place they came from, that turns everything upside down?"

Fodor yawned. "I know. Even when you think Ra-Ri speaks to you, she always talks to herself. Fairy adores her, though. I have no clue how the two of them get along so well."

"Are we anywhere in this idyll?"

"Right now this bed is as close to the idyll as I can imagine."

"I am not joking."

Fodor rolled to his other side. His voice was getting fainter. "Life has to be taken seriously like organic chicken—"

"Are you sleeping? I am quite serious. The girl either stares at your horrible portrait or sits on that horrible chest in Nanny's room. I don't like it. I am afraid of it."

"The chest or the portrait?"

"Both."

*"The girl stares at this horrible portrait
as if it's telling her a story."*

# Hope (Part 2)

No longer do we fancy matching sailors' suits. Matured peers had shed school uniforms for military outfits, professional overalls and medical robes, but our favorite was a roomy cloak, tailored so that street beholders took us for one XX-large individual—common case, not a curio. In accord with our own stature, the cloak rested on two adjacent hooks in the hall.

In the morning we tiptoed past Mother's bedroom, trying to ignore the sobbing snores seeping from inside. With Misha's sheepish addition, our sanctum ceased to stay sanctorum. What troubled us wasn't the lack of personal safety. We are valiant and unselfish, but how could we go out now, leaving the freshly finished portrait alone?

Alex helped me put the cloak on, while I rolled the canvas and hid the tube in the fabric's flexures.

"You are a dry boy now," we lipped to the painting in a feat of anthropomorphic fraternity. "We shall bring you along, and, if you promise to keep quiet, we have a little surprise for you." It was only appropriate for the union of originals to arrange a reunion of copies.

The streets took us to the false Gothic building of the art museum. In this early hour tourists were still waking up, and the halls echoed in emptiness.

"No," we replied firmly to the uncharming checkroom Cerberus, "we absolutely refuse to disrobe. The cape protects us from sneers. This is not a proper place for anatomical discourse. Treat the cloak as a medical necessity like an arm's plaster or an eye patch. We must keep it on."

The next line of defense was a lethargic sentinel who tore off two ticket stubs with no numeric concerns and promptly retreated to the sport section of his tabloid. We strode upstairs, escorted by our personal echo unsmeared by other visitors. Greek amphorae on our way displayed ancient athletes with outlined profiles in a multitude of matching figurines.

"Are they parodying us?" I frowned.

"They couldn't possibly have known." Alex shrugged.

Luckily, the annoying old spinster that had nagged us before was taking a day off. We reached the royal hall with gilded frames—the little heir, the stately Imperatrix and there, there he was. Figures and faces paraded our might-have-been fate: a scepter and an orb in the hands of our singular look-alike. We made sure no one was around to disturb this quality moment—bonding with the might-have-been.

Alex pulled the portrait from under the robe's folds, I unrolled it, and we spread the canvas on the wall, next to its estranged twin. What a special flash! The two of us, identical, indistinguishable, inseparable, and the two of them—identical, indistinguishable, reunited. I was looking at one canvas, Alex at the other, or it could have been the other way around. A mere coincidence was no longer sufficient to explain this glorious impossibility.

We walked on a rainbow. Did any time pass? If so, how much? Extra-temporal moments hardly go along with the clock hands.

Then the rainbow under our feet cracked. The colors broke apart. We heard a noise. Scraps of words in the hallway were getting denser, closer, forming a sweep-net. We had to leave.

"Faster!" we breathed out.

"Careful," we breathed in.

Alex and I grabbed the canvas, ready to escape, when something unheard-of happened. In the haste of bodies and under the tension of minds, we failed to coordinate movements. One could be overly passive or the other excessively vigorous, but, entangled in the loose garb, we lost our balance. I hung on Alex; he grasped whatever was within reach. The strings burst; the world shattered, and in a blink, everybody was on the floor—Alex, me, both masterpieces: ours deformed, the museum's deframed.

"Get up, run!"

"Wait! Which one is which?"

We stared at our images, one finished just a week ago, the other painted by a court artist many years before we were great-grandfathered by his model. Who was the prince, who the pauper? Which child was Jacob, which Esau?

Time was running out. We couldn't afford the leisurely search for superficial mismatches.

"Doesn't matter," Alex muttered, "no one will ever suspect."

We grabbed the first canvas that came under hand, muffled it up in the folds and escaped just before a flock of aficionados flooded the room, their teeth and eyeglasses glittering in the artificial light.

Cuddling the costly cargo, we barely had enough hands for holding on to the staircase railing.

"Wait! You! Stop, stop immediately!"

". . . can't . . . ," we grumbled.

". . . talk. . . ," a two-step jump.

". . . stomach. . . ," a three-step flight.

". . . upset. . . ," to the door, to the door!

Someone blocked the way but was swept aside by my mass and Alex's momentum. We heard alarming sounds and sounds of alarm. It didn't matter. The final leap, and the rotating door sped up, expelling us out and sucking unsuspecting out-of-towners in. The crowd was pushing from the outside, clogging the entrance and stopping our pursuers like the rejoined waters of the *Reed* Sea. Free at last! Thank God Almighty, we were free at last!

Although athletic, our constitution doesn't favor track-n-field. Alex and I can wrestle, but we are way too solid for spurts and sprints. Out of breath, our dialogue was never articulated, which made no difference since we could read each other's minds like inscriptions under museum artifacts.

"That went well."

"Nobody ever visits that room."

"They'll stop the chase as soon as they make sure that nothing's missing. So, there was some commotion; so one of the paintings accidentally skewed; so the frame cracked. But the nail's still in the wall. No harm done."

"What now? Where do you want to go?"

As in our expired childhood, when returning home from a quack clinic, we took shadow sides of side streets rather than rushing through plenty-peopled plazas.

The recent scene kept replaying on the stereo screen of our minds. How could such a well-intended enterprise end up in such spectacular fiasco? Well, not entirely fiasco. The portraits proved their miraculous semblance, thus scratching off the mystery gloss over the mystery of our birth.

We turned the key. Our apartment was empty. Neither Mother nor her balding beau had stayed home. Too emotional for the triumphant tap dance, we hurried to our room. A sparse sand trail on the parquet marked our way.

Adrenalined into activity, any activity, we started cleaning the room. There shouldn't be any evidence of art. The easel, palette and paints went to the bottom of the wardrobe, behind the twin sets of shirts and pants. We winked at the precious painting. Whichever image had escaped the palace, no one could tell the difference.

"Sorry, little brother," we whispered, swaddling the portrait into tubular darkness, "this is not a friendly world. One day we shall nail you to a deserving wall, but for now you better stay away from the daylight."

In a half hour the room lost any vocational flair. A knock on the door, a rude intrusion of sniffing mastiffs would unveil zilch. We are sick, Officer. The smell that you may have confused with solvents and oil is our medicine. Here is the drawerful of prescriptions signed by the best of medicine men; here—the drawer with pills. Our case history goes back to Romulus and Remus. Have you heard about Doctor F and Professor T, binary luminaries of our childhood, Officer? You haven't? We are disappointed but not shocked. Doctor F taught us to be ourselves, and Professor T explained everything about gestation. Please, hush your doggy away, Inspector. We are allergic to intolerance. Our health, you see, hangs on a thread in a very delicate balance. Why indeed should such standard people like you (no offence, Lieutenant) burden yourselves with a parade of medical oddities? Our appearance might look ordinary only because we are standing sidewise and you see our aligned profiles in one matching outline like that in Egyptian art. The ointment, the odor of which your adorable puppy confused with oil paint, is essential for our skin. The juncture of our bodies, you see, is particularly sensitive, demanding incessant maintenance. Don't blame your Alsatian beast; or is she a bitch? It did everything it has been taught, bursting into our little fortress, barking and scaring the shit out of us, pardon the euphemism. We are very perceptive. The shock may aggravate our condition, so, Captain, if you don't want legal trouble, we suggest you harness your foaming behemoth and get the hell out of here.

The apartment door slammed.

"Who's there?" we screamed, our daydreams disturbed. "Go away, we have done nothing wrong."

"Are you home, Alex?" said Mother.

She often spoke to one of us, depending on the subject at hand. As a spiritual being, I converse about abstract substances, while Alex is much better at discussing mundane annoyances.

This time, neither of us responded, listening to the steps and trying to figure out how many pairs of feet or quartets of paws filled the hallway. The refrigerator's door squeaked. Mother must have been unloading groceries in the kitchen.

"No reason to be nervous," Alex said.

"We are innocent," I nodded.

"Like virtuous pagans," Alex confirmed.

"Or undipped infants," I concluded.

The heavy curtains shielded the street. Can we walk out leaving the evidence . . . we mean the portrait, and pretend that nothing happened?

That's precisely what a cold-blooded criminal would do. Does the little museum mishap give anybody rights to brand us as thieves? Preposterous! We surely overprice the whole incident. It must be forgotten by now, as the tourists stare at the royal masterpiece, never suspecting the substitution. Not the ill-intended swagger, Comrade Sleuth, but utterly accidental, if it indeed took place, of which no connoisseur can be certain. Alex would confirm my alibi and I wouldn't hesitate a second to support his. We can even offer to prove our purity by coming there first thing tomorrow morning with the presently wardrobed copy, safe like Job in the whale's innards. Don't give us rubbish that wrongdoers are attracted to the scene of their discontent. We had painted it ourselves. Conscience, so you know, Inspector Holmes, is no petty stuff. It should be kept unsoiled at any cost.

We imagined the exultant scene with bearded and bespectacled experts of the jury. Handcuffs are replaced by cufflinks. Leonidas nods; the critics admit talent of our hands and greatness of our hearts; Hope kisses us on the cheek. . . . Chmock-chmock.

Nad'usha! We slapped out foreheads.

Did you forget, Alex? How could you, Alex? In adventurous agitation, the date with Hope slipped out of our minds. What time is it now? Is it dark outside yet? Is it too late? The poor thing must have been waiting for us all day. How alarmed must she be not to see us peeking from behind corners! We needed to talk, the three of us, because we, the two of us, had never broken our word before.

"We have to see her immediately."

"We are too tired."

"But we promised. She is wringing her hands. She is disconsolate."

"Let's wait till tomorrow."

Does it sound like an argument? Hearing it, Professor or Doctor or whoever it was, trying to instigate our internal discord earlier, would feel proud. Calm down, Professor, the conflict was only skin deep. Whether Hope could wait or not was irrelevant—Alex and I peacefully dozed off the way we were, in our clothes and shoes, right in the middle of the passionate Tristanesque sentence. The complete account of reveries and delusions, potentially beneficial to the future therapist, was inaccessible—our visions blurred together, the two of us being the characters of one and the same dreamscape. Love and hope mixed together, and no one wished to set them apart.

What is my name? the dwarf asked.
    Is it Peter?—No.
    What is my name? the dwarf asked the next day.
    Is it Paul?—No.
    What is my name? the dwarf asked on the third day.
    Isn't such pattern a guarantee of a well-crafted fairy tale, Doctor Frumpelstillskin?

## THE BREAKING NEWS

The next morning, shrugging off the museum blunder, we headed for our habitual observation point—Hope's window, Hope's balcony, Hope's building entrance. Some vignettes in our lives turned repetitive.

    Her building had a *choyrnyi khod*—literally black, semantically back, door—never serving as the entrance, often as the exit. Depending on our objective, the arrival or departure of our H-valentine, we had to choose a proper viewpoint. The day was still young. If, out of some fancy, Hope wished to escape early (the reason for such escapade totally inconceivable), she'd probably choose the *choyrnyi khod* in the building's hind side. If, on the other hand, she had nothing to *hind* and sought our rendezvous as eagerly as we did, the front entrance should be our mutual choice.

    On a regular day, Hope wouldn't make us wait for long, hopping from home towards the bus drop or the subway dive. We would then bump into her at the next intersection, in a metro train or during her spirited stop at a corner confectionary—two éclairs, *s'il vous plait*, we are such sweet tooths!

On a regular day. . . . Today, apparently, wasn't regular. She refused to show up. Was that resentment or a rebellion? Terrible possibilities zoomed through our minds. What if she is sick—fiery from fever or freezing with flu? (Further particulars of her tossing in bed, sweating and panting, drawn in our imagination to the tiniest minutiae, are irrelevant and only distract from humane empathy.)

Not letting our eyes off the entrance, we edged towards the nearby newsstand. An abundant selection of published *Truths*—People's, Evening's, Ours, Theirs—offered themselves for a nominal fee.

"What *Truth* would you like?"

"Give us *Pravda*. We'll go with a plain one."

Alex discarded the editorial as if cutting wax off a cheese head, and we went directly to cultural events. Reading and watching Hope's building simultaneously could pose a challenge for an ordinary persona but not for us, Doctor. Nature etched us with omni-tasking in mind. I kept my eyes fixed on the target, while Alex rustled the paper leafage. It could have also been the other way around, since the rate of our inter-wit exchange is comparable to the speed of desire. I became immediately aware of what he read; he would know if I saw Hope the very instant she appeared.

Alex flipped a page.

"What?" shrieked both of us—the reader and the observer—as Alex stared at the centerfold. "Is this a trick, an impractical joke?"

The grainy photograph depicted the familiar false-Gothic structure.

> Missing Masterpiece
> Yesterday morning a gang of criminals engineered
> thievery of one of the greatest jewels in the national
> collection. . . .

Flukes occur. We acknowledge this fact readily, but *that* was overkill! The robbery-proof building was plundered on the very same day when we had our mega-hugger-mugger? As unbelievable as the dual incident seemed, it explained the commotion we had witnessed on the way out, when flying down the staircase. Apparently, the thieves, the whole gang of them, as the mistrusted *Pravda* stated, used the wee hour and empty halls to pinch a picture while we were admiring our family features oiled on canvas. How ironic it must have been—the guards taking our innocent dismay for the cold-blooded criminal calculus.

> . . . as if making fun of people's art, they left a mock copy—an advisedly childish pastiche—of the famous portrait. . . .

It could have been funny if it weren't so sad! Not only did the rascals break the law, they threatened to mar our good names. Did they hope that the curators wouldn't recognize the substitution? Ri-di-cu-lous.

"Do you remember the alarm?" I asked. "Sirens, shrieks, whistles. . . ?"

". . . screams behind?" Alex shook his head. "I was too busy trying not to trip."

"I thought I was in charge of that."

> . . . the investigation possesses enough evidence to identify the gang's principals. Inspector Peter Pankoff from the Art Crimes Investigation Unit expressed his confidence in the prompt apprehension of the offenders. . . .

The next photo showed a uniformed puppet in front of the microphone cluster. The print was small and hardly legible, but Alex's artistic memory is faultless. It punctually delivered another image, that of the days gone—the school's assembly hall, the theatric scenery, the limelight fixed on spinning Esmeralda, her feelings misdirected at the treacherous and unreliable Pierre—none other but newly anointed Inspector Peter—while the poor hunchbacks were about to plunge into their lethal leap.

"Where is she?" I looked up from the paper. "Are you watching the entrance?"

"Don't worry."

> . . . witnesses reported a large figure in a long over-coat—most likely to cover the stolen painting—pushing the guards aside. The perpetrator moved in awkward sideways sweeps and managed to disap-pear before help arrived. Inspector Pankoff assured our correspondent that the description was detailed enough to identify the mastermind.

"I never liked that *sukin syn*," Alex confessed. "You know what it means, don't you?"

I sure did. That mediocre Pierre, that Sleuth Jr., his title of Inspector no more than homage to the whodunit convention, shuffled the mispointing clues like an old-time sharper. His hints at the detailed description indicated beyond doubt that he had retrieved us from his school memories and that very soon, maybe as soon as this very hour, a squad of qualified goons would enclose our home and break into our apartment, scaring Mother and her newly fetched, aged archangel into stuttering twits.

Sooner or later the truth prevails. It arrives with the inevitability of the happy end. But before the good guys get rewarded, the crew of armored androids will rush in, knocking our door off its flimsy hinges—oh, Janus the door-maister, why hath thou abandoneth us?—and pushing both of us against the wall with Mother's favorite planter right between our proximal ears to hinder communication.

Could we go against Peter's common nonsense, withstand trial and prove our innocence? Of course, we could—in a trice, or, rather, in a twice. Was fighting questionable justice in the guise of yet another falsely accused victim worth it? Of course, it wasn't. Who cares about book-like misadventures? Life's too precious for Don

Alex and Alex Panza to waste it protecting windmills. Neither had we desired to relive the hardships of Comrade Monte-Cristo—Alex and Alex incarcerated in a local mock-up of Château d'If like twin Edmond Dantèses in a collusion of Alexandre Dumas, whether *père, mère* or *fils*.

Crime-wise we had nothing to be afraid of. However, the incident could unearth our deformity—something Alex and I were uncomfortable exposing to the rumor-thirsty hoi polloi.

Why were we in the gallery? Why in that particular chamber? Why at that particular time?

Listen, Inspector, first of all, we prefer to call it a museum. Gallery reminds of gallows. Second, you are falling prey to the web of coincidences. Our interests were in another hall. You want proof? Here, this is our self-portrait, self in the sense of Alex the Artsy using Alex the Craftsy as a model. Look at it. Look at us. Call your phrenologists to match-n-measure. Do you detect any semblance, Detective?

"As all of you armed-to-the-wisdom-teeth faultfinders are aware," we would continue, still flattened against the wall, "the painting in the museum, similar to the one your howling bloodhound pulled out of our wardrobe, depicts a royal figure, an Emperor, whose rule was cut short by the revolution."

"Indeed," Peter the Ferret would mumble, "now that you mention it, I do see that you look very much like Tsar Nicholas and Tsar Alexander."

Then, only then, our dear Mother—pressured no less than Alex and I—would give away our paternal origins, our ancestral treasure. We would deny it for a while, but then with a desperate "how could you, Mother? Why did you . . . ?" we would crack down, knead our faces in palms and synchronously weep, unashamed of emotions, as other heroes did, as Odysseus wept when, captive in Calypso's island, he peered into the horizon trying to discern smoke, if only rising from his motherland.

Raising our swollen-with-tears eyes, we would look straight at the man's reflection in the cupboard:

"Ask yourselves—would Nature, aloof to mass production, create such incredible likeness for no reason? The Tsars for you are Grandpa Nick and Grand Uncle Al for us."

"I am sorry." Peter no-Pan would scratch his chin. "Guns down, boys. The freaks are beyond suspicion."

The charges of the museum robbery would be dropped in exchange for the twin dunces' caps.

Like in the school production of the *Hunchback of Notre Dame*, our treacherous Peter will supervise the construction of gallows on the main square, cleared for the occasion from sand or slush, depending on the season when the mock trial is over. The signs will scream *Peter the Pee-Tea Barnum Presents!* The two of us will ascend the Calvary. The crowd will cheer. We look around in search of sympathy and find nothing but apathy.

Yes, look around. The scene was just a daymare stirred by the newspaper's nuisance. While we were still free and absorbed in visions of no-crime and punishment, Nad'usha never left the building. The hope to see her oozed out. Defecting from our makeshift deck and ignoring all decency concerns, as a disheartened mother would when grieving over her sick child, we loped to check the back exit. In vain—no heartbeat, no sign, no scent of her sweet perfume.

"Hallo!" we screamed into the payphone receiver. "Hallo! Pick up, please, pick up."

Nothing, nobody.

Where does one, or two as it happened, search for Hope? We hurried up hill and down dale to the art studio, our advancement neither graceful nor gracious, angering people and crossing intersections in total disregard of streetlights.

She wasn't there either. Instead, a crowd of underage neophytes sweated over an eclectic still life—a book, a bottle, a bonsai tree, sounds of Bolero. Exhausted, we plopped onto the chair in the back, wheezing in and breathing out. Heads turned in our direction like weathervanes.

"You?" Leonidas, his brush and palette like sword and shield, rose as if protecting his personal Pass of Thermopylae. "Nad'usha said you were sick."

"Sick? Since when have you two started discussing our condition? So that you know, we are healthy like two bumble bees, although, in a certain sense, we do seek the cure for a condition you will hardly understand. We were on the right track, and it was none other but Uncle Fein who brought us to . . . and we hoped that Hope. . . ."

He lost his concentration, and we sighed:

"We need to think. Go on, continue your lesson; tell these young lads about complimentary colors, about light and darkness. Teach them how to become pros and cons. We'll wait for Hope and won't disturb your class."

"Doctor Jekyll and Mister Hyde," someone in the crowd giggled.

Was that what they were calling us behind our backs? Jump up, Alex, punish the offender!

Leonidas hushed the noise down.

"Stop talking! Everybody work. Actually—" he turned to us, switching the subject and softening the tone "—if you wanted to say good-bye, this is perfect timing."

"What do you mean, good-bye? They can't lock us up. We are innocent. Peter has no proof."

"What proof, what Peter? This is my last class here. No more teaching. I will pursue my own art now."

He went back to his desk and, with our glances glued to his grimy ankles, retrieved a glossy magazine. On the cover he stood next to a canvas with some tasteless color blotches. The flashy title blinded us: *Breakthrough, Stunning, Genius.*

Leonidas beamed vainly.

"I thought it was never going to happen. It's a tough field, and—"

"Yes," we mumbled, "we know. Cons of an artist."

". . . and then the luck squeaked like a rusty flywheel, and set into motion. I don't know what your dreams are, but I tell you this. Some day everything clicks together—your life and your art. Clicks together and makes sense." He raked the room and clapped hands. "This is it. Time's up, people. The class is over."

Without giving us a chance to mutter our parting wishes, he tossed his hair back and walked out of the room, flashing his sockless Achilles heels. Students clattered their easels, visibly relieved. The ground was giving way from under our feet. Hope vanished. Leonidas was gone. The noose around two necks tightened. Wasn't it a definition of the doomsday, when the pious were punished and the impudent rewarded?

"Youngsters!" we exclaimed. "Lads and lasses! Does anybody want to help fellow artists?"

Disrespectful youths ignored the plea, chirping to each other and skirting us on their way out of the room.

"Stop!" We blocked the doorway right in front of the last urchin. "We need your help, kid. Here." A crumbled bill appeared from our chest pocket. "We shall reward you generously."

He stared at the banknote.

"What's that?"

"Don't worry, this is real money," we assured him. "This is better than real. It's the most precious bill ever. Follow us. We'll explain everything on the way."

Things we talked to him about had nothing to do with our true pain—missing Hope. That wasn't something he, at his tender under-age, could grasp. His freckles and his reddish hair made him less inconspicuous than we'd prefer, but under the circumstances we had little choice. Alex was firmly squeezing the nape of his neck in a fatherly way. I grabbed his backpack.

We dragged him towards our home.

"Do you see this building?"

He nodded.

"Consider it a . . . m-m-m . . . game, yes, a game of wit and inventiveness. We need to get something from our apartment. When you have no hope, we say, scrape the barrel. You'll understand it one day. You want to grow up strong and resolute, don't you? Girls . . . m-m-m . . . girls will dig you."

Two forefingers pointed at the fourth-floor window.

"We live there. Bad people may be waiting for us. You have to fetch a little roll hidden in the wardrobe behind coupled shirts and paired pants. It's nothing special—a canvas, a sketch of no commercial but purely sentimental value, something our father should have left for us as a legacy. One day we shall tell you this sad story."

While I kept an eye on the little rascal, Alex drew arrows on the ground using my cane as a stylus: the entrance (dash), the hallway (dash), the wardrobe (the cross).

"Don't be afraid. This wardrobe is witch-free. There might be a couple of skeletons in the cupboard, but you aren't going to Mother's room." I looked at Alex reproachfully. It was no time for lame gags.

What? He made a wide gesture. Careful, I signaled, don't let him go.

We checked the area. No police cars, no yellow tapes. They are hiding well, those cautious bastarderos, pardon our Portuguese!

"Can I go now?"

"Wait. We didn't finish yet. For the game to be exciting—and remember, all of this is no more than a game—for every robber there has to be a cop. We are using these terms in a strictly descriptive, abstract sense—cops-n-robbers, slides-n-ladders, hunky-n-dory. As good gamers, we suggest that you don't take the elevator."

"How do I get in?"

"That's a very good point. We knew you were a smart alec the minute we saw you. We'll teach you. Listen here. It's a tale about lost love. Some time ago, we had to get into one apartment. The door was locked then, but we didn't turn around and leave with tails between our legs. We climbed onto the awning, grasping for ledges and grooves, and before we knew it, we were on the balcony!"

His freckles formed a question mark.

"Yes," we admitted, "it was the second, not the fourth floor. But what's in the number? The method is the important part. Once you master the technique, you can make wonders. We could do it ourselves, you know, but two large figures in a black cape are more likely to draw attention then one youngster in an almost-brick-color jacket. You want to be an artist, right?"

We tousled his red chevelure with kindred (once removed)

encouragement, and before he could say something, Alex snatched the bill from his hand and pushed him in the back.

"You'll get it, after you retrieve the portrait. Go. We'll take care of your easel. Don't worry, we never misappropriate what doesn't belong to us."

The boy made his way through the bushes and crossed the open space in front of the building. Nobody charged at him, screaming or aiming machine guns. That was a good sign. Peter the Ambusher waited for two men in a loose cape, not for one boy in a tight jacket.

Despite the well-working plan, our hearts were heavy.

Did we have the right to risk his young life? Did we teach him every trick? Did we make his venture safe and secure? After all, we should assume responsibility for the younger generation. If not we, then who? If not now, then when? Too bad we didn't ask for his name.

"When he crawls up the wall and peers into bedrooms," I said, "he might catch glimpses of inappropriate intimacy."

"Let's hope it will not traumatize his soul," Alex reflected. "Collateral hazard was inevitable."

Ten more steps, we counted, five, two, one, there he was. We stretched our necks, ready to observe the climb. But, instead of following our instructions—two feet, two hands, two other feet up the wall—the boy pulled the door and disappeared inside.

"What is he doing? They will capture him; they will extort a confession."

Alex panicked. Medieval images shaped in his mind and, due to the specifics of our anatomy, I became immediately aware of his visions. A boy, practically a child, whose only fault was a questionable sin of disobedience—optional on the list of commandments—was captured by masked Peter the Pan-face, an expert in fine and martial arts, his *Kiiiyaaa!* muffled by his helmet's visor.

*We know who sent you. Tell us their names. Tell us where they are hiding. It's not your fault. These men are criminals. My duty is to arrest them.*

*What are you talking about?* The brave redhead shrugs. *Torture me all you want. I will never give out their names. I will never betray Alex and Alex.*

*Don't be too sure of yourself,* the artful cop hisses, grinning. *I am a punch-n-pinch expert. You will not be the first sympathizer I break.*

Interrupting the hideous scene unfolding in our imagination, the door flung open and the unharmed boy reappeared. Another clever trap? Did Peter use him as bait? One needed a double agent to catch a double victim. We weren't afraid, ready to accept the challenge, even though no Hope was presently available.

Alex dashed ahead, snapped the precious canvas out of the boy's hand, and we took off in the direction of the crowded plaza—the least likely of directions—intended to bedevil pursuers. Had the flee taken place a hundred years ago, we'd have been running down a cascading staircase in a wind-swept Inverness coat and a scarf—the former pitch-black, the latter snow-white—one hand pressing down the top hat, one squeezing the cane, two more spread apart to keep balance like a lone ropewalker. Cabby, we'd scream, drayman, jehu!

"Hey, what about my easel, my money?"

Welcome to modern times. With no respect for seniors, the little bastard was screaming at the top of his lungs, totally clueless of the danger lurking behind.

"Run, young fool, run! Save yourself. The chase is on. The easel will only hinder your escape. We always pay our dues. Next time we meet, you'll get your tri-fold."

The last words were hardly legible—was it a tri-fold or a trifle? We had to pay more attention to breathing than to sense or articulation, and should he be the one who had quipped about Jekyll and Hyde, this was going to be his rightful retribution.

# Hope's home

Reunited with the portrait, we roamed through streets and squares sprinkled with sand dandruff.

The recurrent theme brought us under Hope's windows. She should be home by now. Passing a small gathering of aged Elisa

Doolittles, we pulled a bill and picked a bouquet.

"What is this?"

We turned around with the grace of an ocean liner—alignment of sterns and poops maintained at all angles. The aproned prune grabbed the strap of our cloak and was waving the banknote right in front of our ear.

"This, common woman," we uttered with dignity, "is the compensation for your merchandise. That's how the civilized society operates. Wares-for-money as opposed to the old practice of goods-for-goods. As plain as the rain in Spain. Take care now."

Our good-natured attitude only angered her.

"You call this money?"

Oh, we chuckled. That's what you mean. We understand you now. It's a separate story and we don't have time to tell it all—about the class and Hope and the pseudo-Spartan, bare-ankle kingster. What you hold here is a precious, hand-drawn artifact. We don't counterfeit money; we create genuine art. This piece of paper happened to be among other bills in our pocket. It's much more valuable than anything you could have received for your vegetation. We had no intention of favoring you, but what's done is done, no taking back. Keep it, flower person. Now, before we call the police to check if you have a valid permit, let us go, let us go.

To conclude our tête-à-tête, we jerked the cloak free and paced away, never turning back.

Of course, we exaggerate. What's a good story without some vocal knick-knackery? The word *police* was never articulated, as she had no reason to fear it. *Police* was a vague force of oppression in yonder lands, far away from our sand-n-slush *Mutterland*. In the unabridged version of oration, we used a term she could relate to and dread dearly. We threatened to summon the *people's militia*, and she had better know that nothing *people's* (as in People vs. Alex-n-Alex) promised good.

No more Hope window-shopping; we headed straight to the entrance, took the stairs—Alex abhorred even a minute-long confinement in the elevator cell—and pressed the buzzer.

"This is Alex and Alex. Is Nad'usha home? Are you her mother? Your daughter must have told you about us. It's imperative that we see you now."

I pushed the bouquet of *carne*-colored carnations in front of the glass eye in the middle of the door. We addressed it with reverent anthropomorphism, quite common in the rhetoric aimed at the Creator and destined to reach nobody. The hinges squeaked.

"Did something happen?"

"Something happened, all right." Looking askance, we observed familiar features. The mother looked like her daughter's parody—a crumbled crosshatching sketch. Whisking her aside, we marched into the narrow corridor. After a sharp turn this Minos's maze brought two Thesuses to the dead end of the bathroom.

"Where are you going?"

"We don't have the clue." The maze theme still on our minds, that meant the Clew of Ariadna, akin to the *kloubok*—a ball of yarn. "Take us to the kitchen. The hearth is a place for the heartfelt confession. We have a few questions to ask."

Turning around, both of us rubbed distal shoulders against opposite walls.

"Naden'ka isn't home." She used the new diminutive substitution for *Hope*. As in our previous transliteration exercises, the apostrophes indicate soft consonants—*d'* like in *dear, n'* like in *nude*.

We moved the second stool over and took seats, both backs leaning against the refrigerator rumbling and trembling from internal permafrost.

Of all interiors in our lives, this kitchen was probably the least essential. However, we copiously traced its details. The windowsill housed a rickety stem of unknown origins in a pot, and a vial with the viscous syrup—a home-brewed panacea from one ailment or another. Dirty dishes piled up in the sink. Lazy drops dripped from the faucet like in the Chinese torture. The last year's calendar and a traditionally patterned tin platter, hooked by three bent paper clips, served as the wall decorations.

We concurred that walls, hostess, cupboard and other Hope-less décor were to be erased from our memory shortly after the visit.

"That's not how we planned our acquaintance. There—" Alex pushed the flowers forward "—put them into water so they can demonstrate to Hope their libido, and don't leave the vase on a sill. A draught, a whirled-up curtain, a window visitor—too many mishaps have mishappened."

I waved our hand, stirring the cuckoo clock's weights and disturbing the bird. It squeaked, sucked air into its mechanical lungs but then changed its mechanical mind—no performance at quarter to.

"You must have heard many stories about us," we began. "All of them are true. Your daughter and we had something special going on."

"Naden'ka told me that. . . ."

Whatever polite joy she had to express, it was irrelevant now. Alex and I hadn't come to listen. We continued:

"Only recently, a few days ago, she insisted that we come in and meet you around a cozy dinner table. Work or business trip, don't bother to justify your husband's nonappearance. We'd provide a bouquet of hyacinths (under the circumstances replaced by dwarf carnations); you'd bake a cabbage pie. The evening would have been charming. Alas, all plans shattered."

". . . you are that fellow. . . ."

We frowned.

"Let's set two things straight. It's *fellows*. And what do you mean—*that*? Are you using *this* and *that* derogatory demonstratives behind our backs to indicate our *demonstrosity*?"

The mother-Hope kept standing, her hands crossed on her chest. She stared at us through her washed-out aquarelle pupils.

"You came to lecture me on grammar?"

"Please, don't distract us. Better yet, boil some water. Preparing hot tea will keep you engaged and justify our stay. Three lumps of sugar, heavy cream. We are lactose tolerant."

I nudged Alex in the ribs, giving him no chance to object to sugar. We'll figure it out later, between the two of us.

175

"Yes, yes, of course, I remember Naden'ka's stories. So funny."

Funny?!

"There were indeed one or two amusing slips, and your daughter—we have certain issues with calling her by name now—your daughter does have a knack for acting."

A spark lit fire under the enameled kettle, and flames burst up as if under Signor Bruno. The water was about to denounce heresy of its liquid state.

"As you are surely aware," we said, our fingers beating the tattoo of a cavalry squadron over the table's steppe, "this is the second day since your daughter vanished without a trace. She didn't show up in art class, and her silhouette never graced the bedroom window."

Like every oldie, our hostess failed to stay focused for long. Putting a sugar-bowl and crackers on the table, she smiled to her inner thoughts. What was so amusing? We were talking about serious things, no side-splitting matter. Having learned about her daughter's disappearance, any loving mother should have been alarmed. Didn't she teach her Little Well-Bread Riding Hood not to step off the path? By the way, speaking of this fairy tale, which we used to enjoy in our childhood, it is necessary to mention that both of us find ridiculous some researchers' allusion to the heroine's sexual awakening with the cloak symbolizing the blood of the menstrual cycle. No less ludicrous is viewing the story as a caution against becoming a working girl based upon the far fetched observation that a red cloak served as a sign of a prostitute in medieval France.

The tea ready, we took sips in turn. Alex drank his without sugar, while I lulled the lump behind my cheek.

"Jokes aside," we wheezed in the burning concoction. "What do you know about her whereabouts?"

"Don't worry. Naden'ka didn't disappear. She . . . went away for a while and asked me not to tell anybody."

"That's who we are for you? Anybodys? Stop this nonsense. Tell us, tell us. Where is she, where is she?"

176

"She is not home now."

"We figured this much! That's a matter of life and sanity. We need her. Without her our future is bleak and has no. . . ."

Alex and I jumped up and paced the small kitchen back and forth, indignant and impatient. Our palate was burning; our cheeks flared. The cuckoo squeaked again and retreated into temporary timelessness.

"We have developed a very special bond with your daughter. It's more than friendship and more than this other feeling, which we also can't spell out. You don't need our help to guess what it is."

"Are you saying you love my daughter?"

"We . . . we hope her."

She dipped her lump of sugar into her cup and sucked in sweetness with the sound track of a water pump. We turned to the window, its external side so familiar that intent stares from the street had left a permanent imprint on our retina. The new layer threatened to smear the image of our behoped—her lost profile, her *profil perdu*, the aura around her pink ear, the nape of her neck, her head turned away, leaving visible only the cheek outline.

The daydream was interrupted by a bewildered "What?"

"Visual memory," we repeated patiently, "is a precious palimpsest. One should look beyond the surface for a deeper meaning."

Had there been conventional two of us, one would stay on guard in the apartment, while the other would search for Hope elsewhere. We imagined the content smirk of Professor Tulchinsky, proud of his mind-splitting stratagem.

"Who is Professor Tulchinsky?"

Did we say his name out loud?

"Never mind him. It was supposed to be our internal dialog. He is one clumsy charlatan from the past. He could accept the Holy Trinity but denounced our Holy Duality. We tried to explain that we were different and yet the same, like two endless numerical sequences—one odd, one even."

"Naden'ka did tell me one or two things about you, enough for me to understand something. You see, Alec—"

"Our name is Alex and Alex, much like with the famous story-teller Andersen. It's erroneous to refer to him as Hans or as Christian, since Hans Christian is a single name. But we are losing patience. For the last peaceful time, where is she?"

"Naden'ka is fine. I think she is happy. I will certainly let her know that you stopped by. Are you done with your tea?"

We pushed the unfinished cups away and considered alternatives. I gave Alex a last chance for verbal resolution before resorting to action. He stayed silent. "You leave us no options. . . ." Alex and I rose, heavily leaning on the table. We'll never know what our impulsive move would have been if, at that very instant, deceptively delicate sounds hadn't approached from the hallway. Claws nagged the corridor linoleum, then, closer, kitchen tiles.

"Beast!" We pressed ourselves into the corner between the wall and refrigerator, swishing our cane like a fencing foil. "Get thee gone!"

"Don't be afraid. Dinah is a sweet little kitten. Aren't you sweet, my baby, aren't you cute?"

"A Siamese cat? What kind of disrespectful burlesque is this? Are you making fun? Are you mocking us?"

"She is harmless."

"What do you know about harmless beings, strange woman? We are not like your typical *Homo vulgaris*, or idiopathic ailurophobes like Julius Caesar and Genghis Khan. We are prone to allergies. An asthma attack or acute asphyxiation might strike at any second. The beast's breed name alone is horribly destructive. We are not afraid. We never are. But we must leave. Hook the leash. Let us go."

Its tail hardly twitching, the feline watched our every move. Unkind pupils didn't blink. What could it know about pulmonary edema, about swelling mucous tunic of internal organs, about yearning of heart and abrupt seizure of the lifeline?

"Well, if you really must go . . . I will pass our conversation to Naden'ka word for word."

Our eyes were fixed on the wrinkled hand stroking fur. Sideways, sidewise, rubbing our backs against the wall, we reached the exit and rushed out without formal farewell. The origin of an empty suitcase in our hands remained unexplained. We must have picked it up as a supplementary defense against the vicious behemoth—the freckled boy's trophy easel was too small a shield for the two of us.

Once outside, the case did come handy. The easel and the portrait, until that moment sweating under our armpits, fit there nicely. Painting paraphernalia wasn't a safe thing to dangle about, advertising our vocation in a time of art crimes and artful criminals.

## The farewell

When Love had vanished from our horizon, our allegorical wings were too immature to afford the double eagle's eye view of life, the Double Eagle, incidentally but not accidentally, being the mascot of the Russian royalty.

So what if she's gone, we thought. If not she, then someone else; if not now—later.

Disappearance of Hope made us frown. The Great Censor was striking names out of the heavenly register. Should this trend continue, we risked draining our reserve of positive notions. What's after Love and Hope—Miss Misery, Dame Despair and Mademoiselle Melancholy?

If Alex planned to wait at Nad'usha's until Peter the Panoptic found the true crook and resolved the confusion of masterpiece identities; if I thought about temporarily stashing the portrait somewhere between Hope's lace underwear—both of us were wrong. In some sense, that was good, since our organic unity couldn't endure internal discords.

Our hopes were betrayed. Squeezed out of this town like lemon seeds, we had nowhere to go. Instead of offering hospitality, Hope's wicked mom set on us her Dinah-mite. Tolerant Leonidas was gone, and the arty horde from the studio, headed by the freckled infidel, must be vying for a *bi-heading*. Mother had found a new darling in her Misha. Peter's uniformed gang stirred up its snarling retrievers, and we wouldn't be surprised if one or another Paul gave them a helping hand. Peter, Paul and Mikhail—what a saintly swarm!

Ignoring the ever-present urine tang, we squeezed into the way-too-public telephone booth and considered a call to Mother.

Who? she would scream. What? Speak louder!

Fate withdrew its favors, we would say without raising our voices. We have to make a difficult decision. Forgive us, Mother, forgive if you can.

Or something to that effect.

The impulse was still strong when another image replaced that of sobbing Mother clinging to the life wire. We visualized grinning Peter in our bedroom. He picks up both receivers of our special phone apparatus and in frantic waves signals to his goons: "It's them. We got'm! Trace the call!" We slammed the handset without dialing the number.

Instead of giving away our *hear-abouts*, let the line dispatch busy Morse tap: dot-dot-dot, dash-dash-dash, dot-dot-dot—Save-Our-Sanity! Alex and I walked out of the booth, shedding off the old world's stench. We had to get out of here.

Was there a place for two hopeless homeless to attract no attention?

We reached the railroad station and settled on the rigid seats of the waiting hall. The suitcase served as a pillow. Cuddling into our cloak, Alex and I tried to get some rest. There we were, promoted from outcasts to outlaws, approaching the end of yet another chapter of our lives.

After much tossing and turning we finally dozed off. If life and fable flew in accord, the reader would share our destiny and spend the night fighting reveries and mumbling confessions in this rare extratextual moment. Luckily, the law of the genre allows two to push the clock hands, flip a page, skip a night and jump on to the next morning.

As soon as well-rested, clean-shaven and deodored travelers started

re-peopling the station, we got up from our makeshift cradle somewhat battered but otherwise intact—apparently the train bringing
Doctor Procrustes to chop us into common folks was delayed.

We moved from the transit lounge to the departure hall.

"What is this?" Alex pointed with his cane at a checkered suitcase, an exact clone of the one we had borrowed from Hope's
apartment. A panic attack dissolved quickly. We hadn't lost the portrait—I was still holding the bag in my outer hand. Identical twins
are far more common among manufactured objects than among
natural subjects. Shrugging off the coincidence, we turned away,
fortunately not quickly enough, because in another second a young
woman picked up the suitcase. Although the surroundings imposed
their own shades and shapes, although she wore a mackinaw we
had never seen before, although she was looking away from us and
her only visible feature was the cheek outline, it took us less than an
instant to recognize our dear *profil perdu*.

That's why an empty suitcase was in her apartment! She'd
packed her things but, being tenderly singular, didn't need the extra bag, leaving it in the hallway of her apartment, the very bag we
used as a shield against her cat, the very same bag we were presently pressing against our chest. Even for the inanimate articles the
semblance proved meaningful.

"There you are!" We hopped ahead and covered her eyelashes
with free palms. "Guess who and who?"

Too impatient to wait for speculations, we spun her around by
the shoulders.

"We knew that you would wait for us!"

Hope was no less overwhelmed.

"You? I thought . . . Mom said—"

"Don't blame your mom, like we never blame ours. She didn't
break your trust. This is all pranks of fortune which almost drove
us you-less. The past isn't important anymore. We are here, together, you and us. This is so exciting! Tell us, pray, where we are
going?"

She was about to name resort Aye, coast Bee or seaside See.

It made no difference. Hope would turn any hell hole into a holy heaven.

"You see . . . ," she began, and as eager as we were, we didn't rush her. So many things to catch up on. Such a sweet voice. Talk to us, Hope, talk to us.

"Everything's fine, Nad'usha; the crate's been entrained. We are set to go."

What the fluke? I swung around, dragging Alex behind. The horrific truth dawned on both of us at the same time. Bare-ankled, track-suited, travel-ready Leonidas emerged out of nowhere, leaned forward and, before noticing our cross crisscross stares, kissed Hope right below her ear, in the very same spot we loved to sketch by short, accurate, closely knit hatches. Only then his eyes caught the sight of our feet, cane, cape, profile, and everybody exclaimed:

"What's going on?"

"We were supposed to meet Hope." Alex was the first to come to his senses.

"That's right," I confirmed, "we always met her."

"Did you follow me from the studio yesterday?" Leonidas asked, frowning.

"Follow you? Why would we? You have nothing to do with Hope."

"You are wrong. Nad'usha and I have everything to do with each other."

"You see, Alex," Hope addressed the one of us whose profile she faced, "it was supposed to be a surprise. Leonid Ivanovich, L'onya, has been invited to exhibit his works in. . . ." Here came the time of town Aye, but we no longer cared for topography. "His painting finally got the recognition it deserves."

"Good things happen in due time," Leonidas merrily confirmed. "Last year I would have died to get a chance like this. Now I have better news. Nad'usha and I got engaged, and this trip becomes sort of a honeymoon."

"What do you mean, engaged? You are old enough to be her stepfather."

Hope tousled his hair.

"The grizzle is misleading. L'onya isn't much older than you are."

Their snuggle was nauseating but, before we could appeal to decency, Leonidas straightened up, tossed his locks back again and checked the time.

"Still a few minutes left. I need to go to the restroom. You never know when the next chance will come."

His prostate talking, we scoffed to each other. He isn't that young after all. Without waiting for Hope's consent or our blessings, the newly baked genius skipped away. His gait was severely affected by his desire. The young bride blushed, relieved by our askew posture—she didn't have to look us in the eyes.

"Listen, no hard feelings. I'll go get a cup of coffee. Do you mind watching my things for a sec?"

Rhetoric matter; she didn't wait for our response and dived into the crowd, which was getting denser and more aggressive. We froze in dismay.

"Welcome to hell . . . ," Alex said, looking at me.

". . . brought to you by the creators of paradise," I said, looking at Alex.

"We've been fooled and betrayed. How can she favor him, who pretends to be special by creating art, over us, who are special by virtue of being ourselves?"

"They are both pathetic. What do we do with this?" I kicked her suitcase. "Are we their garbage's keepers?"

We considered our limited options. After a brief hesitation, the nostalgic side won. Alex grabbed the bag.

"We'll take it with us. These pieces of the shattered past will be our tribute to Hope."

In the wrong embodiment of the right reasons, we snatched her sack and mixed with the crowd—twin people carrying twin suitcases. Our imagination made no attempt to picture the scene of revelation, when hopeful—in multiple senses—Leonidas, or his precious Nad'usha, or both of them simultaneously, returned to find their things erased from the sketch. Was it going to be surprise, anger or bewilderment? We didn't care. If their destination was in the south, we would dash north. Should it be east, we would run to the west.

It was a true treasure trove that we got away with. A long time ago Love left us nothing. Now, in that bag, we inherited Hope's warmth with a possible bonus of pearl earrings and a purple vial of her perfume—rich nourishment for forthcoming nostalgia.

We locked ourselves in the restroom stall—the only secure retreat around, albeit too tight for the two of us. Our hearts fluttered like a bride's eyelashes, like a diva's uvula, like toilet paper on a Halloween tree. Constricted between narrow partitions, Alex put Hope's suitcase on our laps. I flipped its lid open. . . .

. . . and immediately slammed it back. *For ere this the tribes of men lived on earth remote and free from ills.* It was no Pandora's box, which released all evils keeping only one thing in—hope. In our case, that was Hope who had escaped, *bringing baleful spirits upon men; for in misery men grow old quickly.*

In his *Works and Days* Hesiod never explained why hope was one of the misfortunes in the box given to Pandora by Zeus.

We lifted the top again, this time not bright and optimistic like morning windows, but sad and disillusioned like mourning widows. Drama turned to spoof. We were looking at a man's matilda. The underwear belonged to Leonardo. The whole bag was crammed with his swags—single shirts, single pants, lone toothbrush, not one pair of socks.

Beggars aren't Chaucers. We could take fractional advantage of his wardrobe, as ridiculous as we might look in mismatching colors. Oh, Hope, Hope. Why did you run away? We could have given you so much! We could commit a crime for you, not a serious one, more like a misdemeanor but still. . . . We sighed so heavily that our hearts' ventricles nearly exploded with sadness.

Should we return the case? Should we run after them and *bag* forgiveness?

We paused, trying to find words appropriate for this heartrending moment:

"How about some farewell decadence—reciting a poem from the

bridge's parapet or popping our veins in a warm bathtub? Would that be suitably solemn?"

Not sure what was taking upper hand—scorn or sorrow. Our eyes caught a little hidden pocket. Absentmindedly we retrieved a few bills. Oh, who cares? Money can't buy two happinesses. This word didn't even come in plural.

Anything else there? His passport. There was nothing Mona-Lisa-subtle in Leonardo's smirk. Beside myself with grief, Alex tore the artist's photo off the page and flushed it into the toilet. I took crayons out of the freckle boy's easel and started filling up the bareness on the page, drawing the only picture I knew—our portrait.

Time flew by, providing us with the consolation no doctors were able to offer. I drew, and Alex posed, patient and considerate like he rarely was.


Let's not despair. It's not the end. The fairy tale is still sailing on. The time comes for the main heroes to leave the fold. How did classic stories herald the forthcoming exodus? Ten plagues darkened ancient Egypt, Odysseus gave orders to foragers, and shipwrights knocked up a framework of the Santa Maria.

A bang on the door returned us from oblivion:

"Hey, are you gonna crap there much longer?"

"Tie a knot," we retorted. "We aren't finished yet."

# Vera (Part 1)

## THE TRAIN

With a checkered suitcase in each peripheral arm, we ascended the landing stage. Pigeons under the high roof fussed around spreading the news—Alex and Alex are here!

We are not sentimental—our future perpetually outweighs our past. However, not to deprive potential nostalgia of its fare, we raked the train station. The air was steeped in coal, foretelling the stench of long journeys. Fast-food offerings supplied the odor of rank donuts and acorn coffee—home-bred alchemists managed to fake the color but scent and taste of the brew defied their efforts. Pigeons bred on the leftovers. Sparrows took what pigeons had ignored. Iron brakes screeched. Porters voiced graceful obscenities. Ubiquitous clocks reminded travellers of fickleness and fluidity. Despite its hideous size, the cathedral of the Holy Voyage instilled little piety into its gregarious congregation.

Pushing through the crowd, we reached our car.

The conductor checked the ticket.

"To cross the state border you will need a passport and exit visa."

"Visa?" We forced a spontaneous ha-ha. "Who said anything about defection? The purpose of our trip is no secret. We are artists, good conductor, and very patriotic ones. We explore a series of landscapes celebrating the splendor of our anthropological motherland. We have done landscapes before with a group of talented creatures, when Hope was still within our reach. We may tell more about her during the idleness of the voyage. Portraits are too individualistic. We don't fancy them. Our plan is to get off at the very last stop, urban or, better, rural, roll up our pants and walk across the meadow, up the uncultivated slope, totally oblivious of dew ruining our shoe chamois, conscious of not trespassing the state boundaries. We shall reach the top and—our backs to the nearby foreign turf—set the easel to face the vast expanses inside, so that not a single nook of our native humus is left unsung. We shall start by dipping the brush into the sky-clear azure. The first stroke is going to be confident and relaxed. Museum halls throughout the country are being redesigned to host our future oeuvres. The populace desires to imbue the beauty of toadflax fields in their entirety. Why would we want to cross the border? As for the moment, please deliver two glasses of strong tea with extra sugar to our compartment. We are not concerned with diabetes."

"What do I care about your diabetes?" The conductor shrugged, scratching the blackheaded grooves around his nostrils with his foul finger. "Color squares if you wish. You'll get your tea not before the boiler is on."

Content with the outcome of the cordial exchange and our own lenience, we ascended the car's stairs and moved along the corridor. The compartment with the number marked in our tickets was vacant. We chose the two seats facing forward. Should someone—who knows those transitory morals and manners?—decide to check the contents of our luggage, we pushed the case with the precious stuffing deep into the dusty entresols. Alex settled by the window, leaning upon the second, innocently content bag.

No, the entresol wasn't a good hiding place. Attics and basements are the first choices of an inquisitive sleuth. Climbing up one more time—my left foot on the left seat, Alex's right on the right—we reached for the suitcase and pulled it out. Much safer was it to keep the bag under the bench, right in the open, as if we had nothing to hide. Mysterious *they*, whoever *they* were going to be, wouldn't bother passengers and make everybody get up only to check the place that someone sneaky, unlike us, would never use to smuggle goodies. After all, we shall explain to whoever cared to know, the canvas was our personal belonging, our father's gift passing in the family down the generation ladder, a relic, a unit of memory that for you—we countered an imaginary uniformed fink—holds no value. Trust us and leave us alone.

The train trembled and began rolling.

The compartment's door slid aside. Not to burden fellow travelers with importunity, we pretended to be absorbed by the scenery outside—the melancholy mire that our motherland was so liberal enough to donate.

Smudging a purple blur in the corner of our eyes, a woman entered. She scanned the room, briefly stumbling over Alex (I was congruously concealed behind), moved in and took the seat across from us. Pulling off her gloves with the grace of a snake shedding skin, she turned her head towards the door.

"Carl, for God's sake, what takes you so long?"

Pushed ahead by a knee, an overweight sack squeezed in. Following it, firmly attached to its handles, an effort-strained crimson man blocked the doorway. Plopping his load down, he moaned, pulled out a crumpled handkerchief and wiped his forehead, then the neck, then the collar. His glossy face gradually tarnished and turned matte.

We sent a reserved but polite smile into the window. Let the pane redirect our hospitality.

## THE BORDER

The view turned sour. Heavyset bushes foreboded our approach to the border—a draftsman's over-indulgence dotted across dells and ridges. The day came to an end. The lights dimmed and the full-cheeked moon rolled up. Trying to be helpful to the frontier guards, it was burning the neutral zone with a hygienic blue beam.

"This is how one masters the chiaroscuro technique—the bright spot of our motherland in the center and obscurity elsewhere," I told Alex even though the conductor couldn't hear me.

"Yonder lands always look darker," he agreed.

In the cacophony of rusty brake pads the train halted by a deserted platform. Cautiously, so that our pale faces wouldn't attract outside attention, we peeked out the window. Somewhere close there must be a barrier and the notorious, zebra-striped sentry booth separating dark from light, good from evil, Latinberger from Cyrillicovsky.

*The travelers trespassed borders and saw that it was good....*

Good it was, indeed, but—the borders approaching—an unwelcome tingle rolled down our spines.

What if, two identical thoughts flashed through our minds in sonorous unison, what if we climbed up into the luggage niche, into its overhead innards? Who would want to search the dusty hollows at night? Or, how about lifting up the seat and sinking under the lid? We could deport suitcases and souvenir sacks and lie still until the car jerked, until the machinist added heat to the furnace and played his march-major—a farewell symphony for the train whistle.

We discarded these immature visions. Our shoulders were too broad for the narrow trench, and the document we had conjured up was blameless.

Still, despite the presence of both minds and the ice-cold perfection of our profile, we couldn't stop the hearts' drum duo.

To take our mind away from unpleasant impossibilities, we turned to an undemanding game. We wrote down the names of our spiritual benefactors—Doctor Fein (ten letters) and Tulchinsky (also ten letters, sorry, no title for you, Professor). Which Alex would come up with the best anagram?

"Coined-Fort," said Alex-Fein.

"Clunky-Shit," said Alex-Tulchinsky.

"Confinder-To, Forced-Into, Doctrine-Of!" parried A-Fien.

"It doesn't make any sense," objected A-Tulchinsky.

"That's exactly my point!"

After a few more combinations, we declared the winners. Doctor Fein was exposed as *Con-Dirt-Foe* and Tulchinsky—as *Hick-Sly-Nut*.

The mirror door, shielding our compartment from the rest of the universe, slid aside. The symmetry—a sure sign of higher order—

was ruined. The window opposite to the entrance reflected a uniform—a rat-colored overcoat, a khaki headband on the cap and a tarnished star on the cockade. The figure introduced itself, emphasizing its military rank, and saluted like a ceremonious cannibal tucking in a napkin and checking silverware.

I hope, Alex commented on the picket's last and least name in a flashing dispatch across our cerebral channel, I hope that soon we shall be surrounded by more poetic people.

"Papers, please."

The lady across stayed unconcerned while her spouse handed over their leather-clad booklets. Leafing through one crisp passport, then the other, the leather gloves seemed satisfied. Our turn. We didn't move, and he repeated his sizzling mantra:

"Papersssssss, pleasssssse."

"Be our guest, colonel," we offered, careful to avoid the touch.

The scrutiny commenced. He observed our profile, our cloak, our cane. Then, folding the passport's wings like those of a dead dragonfly, he raised his eyebrows.

"Vaut iz zis?"

"What do you mean?" We chose the path of sincere bewilderment.

"This," he repeated, our dishonored ID tight between his phalanxes.

Like a second dragon's head, the conductor's pate popped up from behind his back:

"Them said that them get off inside motherland, them said, to draw fields and forests," the traitor hissed. "Them are like painters or something and them wanna clone nature on their carcasses. For gallows."

"Canvases," we corrected the dolt. "For galleries."

"Shut up, Off." The picket shrugged the conductor off his epaulets. "You will get the talking part when I need you."

Per the last-name convention of our mothland, the suffix *off* like in Smirnoff or *ov* in Tzvetkov indicates a family attachment. Standalone Off, on the other hand, only displays its grammatical wish but nothing to belong to, a non-existent entity, devotion without a cause.

"What you are squeezing between fingers is our passport, the trustworthy certificate. We stand behind the craftsmanship and verisimilitude of its every feature, however meaningless. Just look at the seal, the signature, the pale sinews of the ink flourish! You have to appreciate this intricate art."

His face folded into fastidiousness like origami.

"Why is the picture non-conforming?"

"Non-conforming?"

"It needs to be *en face*. Open forehead, two eyes, two ears."

"General," we appealed, "you can't apply the same rule to everybody. What if someone has only one eye or a harelip? Our constitution prohibits *en face*. It's impossible! You may not understand—"

"Oh, I understand, all right," he mused. "I understand more than you think. Impossible, huh? For every honest *sukin syn* it's possible, and for you—it's not? And there is no such thing as *your* constitution. The constitution is one and the same for everybody. It belongs to the people."

The head behind him kept nodding, confirming each and every ridiculous statement.

"Get your stuff. Up. Follow me."

Helpless in this grotesque farce, humiliated by his singular disdain, we chose obedience as the most honorable response to the plebeian's arrogance. One of our bags—with Leonardo's underclothes—was within reach. As to the other, sacred one, it remained under the bench. Let it lie low.

In silence, not disrupting our heartbeat by futile pleas, we strode sideways along the car's passage. The fidgeting conductor minced ahead, the sergeant concluded the procession. We descended into the night.

The breeze cooled our burning skin. A blinding star upstairs dimly reflected off its cockade copy. With the gesture of an ill-acting malefactor, the picket pulled out a revolver. The moon shined. The moon clip snapped.

"You go first," he barked.

He was now joined by the dopy gang of his doppelgangers, all in perilous imperial uniforms. At the tip of the wedge, we were cutting through the darkness. Pebbles rustled under our feet as oversize sandlings. Hostile interjections flashed behind our backs.

Soon, the road brought us to a dead end, its etymologic tip-off not helpful. The train and the platform seemed much farther away than they actually were, the distance switching from topological to the ontological notion. We reached the corner—two walls joined at an obtuse angle. An anemic lantern rocked in the wind, blessing us with the light cross—left-right, forward-backward. As in the climaxing scene of a second-rate movie, our executioner swayed on widespread legs.

"You are accused," he announced, and echoes obligingly bounced from the bricks, "of betraying your kin and trespassing decency. Our people gave you all—food, shelter and condescension to deformity. But, for those like you, it's never enough. Forging the exit permit with your insolent profile in place of an honest *en face*, you attempted to swindle your own brothers and sisters. You are a de-facto defector, a demoralizing demotherlander."

While his well-trodden speech rolled, ready to peak at the vile verdict, the squad spread out at even intervals. Breechblocks clicked, opening latches of the purgatory gates.

"In the name of justice, on behalf of those heroically toiling inside, under the burden of undeniable evidence," he declaimed, consulting the hand-carved cognomen in the passport, "Alex Alex is sentenced to the capital pun—the highest measure of social mercy—"

"Wait!" we begged. "You can't just shoot us. What kind of nightmare is it? We are innocent. We had reasons. The profile is the only option to hide our disgrace—nature's mischief in the distribution of beauty. We are too sensitive to reveal sores in public."

Disregarding our petition, the villain turned sideways—the posture so dear to us—and thundered an earsplitting command:

"Squad! Get ready!"

From far away, from a different, quickly fading reality, the horn whistled its farewell. Letting the steam out, the machinist gave his final salute. Smoke puffs flew over poplars' crowns—another allusion to our eluding lives. In some invisible vicinity, soot sleepers creaked and sagged under the train's load, hardly relieved by our elimination from the passengers' register.

"Set!"

"Hold your triggers," we begged, "don't deny our last wish. What's a pinch of altruism for the universal justice? What's a splash of philanthropy for the embodiment of righteousness? You have already hoodwinked us, now be merciful and blindfold us. At this sad moment we want to face not your bared teeth but our ultimate illusion."

"Well," he hemmed, "we, the people, are against spiritual darkness but have nothing against darkness literal."

He pulled a not-so-fresh khaki handkerchief out of his pocket, came close to us and froze, deciding which one should get it—Alex or I. Taking advantage of his fleeting indecision, we pushed him away with all our might. Whether caught unawares or overwhelmed by our power, he flew backwards, knocking down his hapless goons. They tumbled like skittles. Drumming shots dotted the air, and the bluish light sifted through the holes of the punctured sky dome. Polaris faded and Gemini brightened. Croaking crows took off from the low boughs—the parterre of the fowl entertainment. Two noble vultures soared in the high. How do you interpret that, seers of Ithaca?

Imitating the birds, we spread out the cape's folds and went airborne to the top of the wall. With giant leaps Alex and I rushed away, holding hands like in childhood and keeping balance on the wall's narrow edge.

Hails and curses chased us. A shot whooshed by, then another, neither causing any harm. Dogs barked. Guards swore. There was no turning back. We jumped and our cloak carried us over the black backyards. Our feet barely tapped the platbands and garden-beds. Dense air nurtured us in its palms. Seeing no target to fire at, the squad panted along, their tarpaulin boots shuffling over the tarmac. Shoulder stars sparkled like fireflies.

Eternity came so close that time lost its composed pace. In less than a few seconds we spotted the train, about to cross over the horizon. The striped border barrier—senseless and pathetic in its lonely arousal—poked the sky.

An exalted minute called for a memorable spiel with a timely quote from Confucius of Orient or Ecclesiastes of Occident.

"Bye-bye, Motherland!" We leaped onto the car's footboard. "We wish we may, we wish we might, have the wish we wish tonight. Farewell to you, thirty-two letters of Cyril and Methodius! Bye-bye dry humors and gloom of home literature! We shall never forget you. Our hearts will always cherish your image, steric but never sterile, stereo but never stereotypical!"

Fading away, the armed squad lost its menace. We did what our father had failed to do—punctured the border! Flaps of the cloak fluttered over the sleeping land. Beautiful and fearless, we accepted the welcome of hospitable Zephyr and hurdled ahead on the train's roof.

That night, Hermes—the Conductor of Souls, whether *Psychopompos* or a pompous psycho, the god of tricksters and those trespassing boundaries—took us under his care.

In a few more moments we climbed inside the car and smoothed our hair. The scared conductor took refuge in his den. He had no reason to worry. We felt too magnanimous for petty retribution.

Matter-of-factly, we entered the compartment and took our seats. The neighbors—the honey and her hubby—were about to doze off, but our unexpected return drove them back into awareness. At our sight he hugged her; she hugged her purse.

"Everything is under control," we assured the couple, dismissing their anxiety. "The misunderstanding has been resolved. The uniformed scoundrel admitted his fallacy and begged forgiveness."

A shy knock on the door was repeated.

"What is it?"

The humble conductor, our lowly *Off*, appeared for his final *On*. Careful not to meet our eyes, he brought a tray with two glasses of steaming tea and a pyramid of extra sugar lumps. The rotter had professional memory. The tea leaves floated in aromatic blackness.

We clanked teaspoons against the faceted glasses—Alex stirring up his double dosage of sugar, I just mirroring his gestures.

"Be alarmed not." We nodded cordially to our neighbors. "Neither of us is a serial stranger. One of us is innocent, the other amicable, making the two—both. What you witnessed was a comedy, all errors of which have been rectified. Allow us to introduce ourselves—Alex and Alex."

They exchanged glances, the unease gradually releasing its clutch. Nice to meet you.

Carl and Clara were tourists returning after a few wonderful days in the town of our turning-stale past.

"Did you like it there?" we inquired, genuinely involved. "What impressed you the most? Was it the sand under your feet or the gilded domes above your heads?"

The danger gone, they relaxed and moved slightly apart from each other.

"I loved it all!" Clara's eyes flared up. "I loved the churches, nesting dolls and amber necklaces. It was magical."

"You should come in winter," we suggested. "You won't find that slush anywhere else."

The tea was gone. We pushed the glasses away from the table's edge and leaned back.

"Do you know that the colloquial for a policeman in Russian is *moosor*?" Carl said. We nodded and he continued. "It means *litter*, another word for which is simply *sor*. Scripted in Cyrillic and read in Latin it becomes a *cop*. Isn't it amazing?"

"Don't pay attention to him." Clara's glove jokingly slapped Carl on the knee. "My husband ascribes too much value to word play."

"Cops wouldn't be our topic of choice, but since you brought them up, Carl, have you returned Clara's corals?" And we recited the popular tongue twister: *Karl u Klary ukral korally, Klara u Karla ukrala klarnet*—Carl snatched Clara's corals; Clara stole Carl's clarinet—a playful misdemeanor with no sexual connotation euphemized.

Carl grew ecstatic. Clara stayed unconcerned.

"Your union must be harmonious," we mused leisurely. "That's how matches should be made—by names' consonance. Carl and Clara, Marat and Marta, Oleg and Olga. Every happy family is the same, but unhappy families are all different. Hope has no business to flirt with Leonidas."

"Who is Leonidas?" Carl asked.

"So, your sweetheart must be Alexis?" Clara smiled, accustomed to disregarding her husband's remarks.

"Our case is more complex than that. Let's change the subject. Our soul is still sore."

Wheels rattled under the car while our compartment remained submerged in the verbal void.

"Have we met before?" Carl wondered, breaking the silence. He stopped sweating and assumed a quite civilized conversational posture, tilting his head aside and unfolding his palm as if trying to gain our trust by exposing his love- and lifelines. "You look familiar."

"Your profile is exquisite," Clara added. "Am I mistaken, or are you indeed of a noble descent?"

"We feel liberated," Alex and I uttered. "The border is behind, and there is no need to be secretive. We can judge people well. You are wonderful and understanding folks. What can be a better atmosphere for mutual trust than a sleepless night in the train? Are you ready for a very special story?"

They nodded. Charming aliens.


We told them everything, beginning from the time before the beginning, about the stately garden of our family tree, about our father's travels and travails, about our parents' quixotic acquaintanceship on the hunchback bridge.

Carl and Clara hearkened, breathless.

". . . and one day," Alex and I concluded, "we heard an authoritative knock. We held on to Mother's skirt when peeking from behind her back. When she opened the door, the landing was empty. We found a tightly bound roll leaning onto the wall outside our

*"Happy matches should be made by names'
consonance—Carl and Clara."*

apartment. Having unfurled it on the kitchen table, we discovered an old, frayed-at-edges oil portrait of our paternal forefather. 'Cherish it—Mother told us, and tousled our hair—this is your legacy.'"

Clara sobbed and winked a tear away. Carl, a practical person, inquired: "This portrait must be very valuable. Do you still have it?"

"How could we lose it? What kind of ungrateful grandchildren would we be? Of course, we have it. It's always with us, in the bag that we hid from the guards. We are now as old as our grandfather was when the artist painted his portrait. The resemblance is nothing short of a miracle. Under no circumstances shall we part with that canvas."

"I always dreamed about assigning sentimental values to historical artifacts," Clara said. "You are so fortunate."

"It didn't come as a charity," we admitted. "There was a price to pay."

And we surprised ourselves by opening up before total strangers in the night-piercing train. We confessed to the terrible stigma that nature marked us with. Nothing contagious and alarming for you, kind Carl and enchanting Clara, but terrible, terrible for us. We wouldn't want to spoil such a cathartic crossing and indulge in gory details of deformity.

"Science these days does wonders. Have you been to specialists?"

Have we? Alex and I exclaimed. Not just specialists. We've seen the best. We've been mentored by a Professor and a Doctor, both, alas, powerless. In all likelihood, no healer in the world—esoteric eastern or scientific western, homeopathic marginal or allopathic mainstream—can save us. The portrait is our lone consolation in life.

"Honey," Clara asked, turning to Carl, "do you remember that famous doctor who saved that wretched . . . whatever her name was?"

"We haven't told you another story," Alex and I intervened, continuing our sore thought. "We can't be hopeful anymore, because we are Hopeless. As to the doctor's name, it can't be random. We assign high importance to a cognomen and are unable to entrust ourselves to some false-name bearer."

Carl grumbled, flipping through his memory catalog. We waited. Clara encouraged us with a smile.

"Is he Doctor Zhivago, Doctor Freud, Doctor Castro or Doctor Schweitzer?" we inquired casually. "You see, we've known too many Doctor Feigns. Sadly, we've come to realize that ability is nothing; debility is everything."

Carl slammed his palms against his knees.

"Fo-Fo! His name is Fo-Fo."

Alex and I went speechless.

"Why?" we exclaimed, coming to senses, "what a perfect name! You wouldn't know about our secret signs, but Fo-Fo surpasses them all. Not only does it start with our pet letter, it also contains perfect symmetry. It's him! We have instantaneous trust in this man. You just gave us a reason to breathe! The stakes are high. Mother-land forfeited, we are ready to accept the new rules. We are ready to surrender merry rolling R's of our tongue in exchange for foster circumflexes and umlauts. Where, where is this he? Wheel us to his waiting room!"

Carl and Clara exchanged sad glances. That was all they could offer.

The dawn's cheeks behind the windows had acquired shy coloration. The train was tattering the night apart.

"Never mind." Alex peered into the promising daybreak. "We know that he exists now. It's enough. We'll find him."

"What an exquisite brooch you're wearing, Madam Clara," I complimented to mark the end of our conversation, carefully aiming at her semi-transparent reflection and letting the words bounce off the pane according to the optical commandment.

# Fairy (Part 4)

Fairy is drawing. The old man paints

The first year of school was over. Their names amplified by the speakers, little people, one by one, trotted to the podium to accept little honors. Conscious of eternity watching them through the camera lenses, they shook the principal's hand and returned to their seats in a barely restrained gallop.

The list was coming to the end, and Sophie got edgy. Do they award everybody? Hadn't this boy already gotten something? How can he be good at music *and* math? All these kids look so much alike! Fairy is the only truly special child here. Could they forget about her? What if they skipped her name by mistake?

On one hand, Fairy hardly excelled in learning but, on the other hand, she was her daughter and that made all the difference. That was one, and, second, how adorable she was in that purple-petaled tutu! The messy reasoning of multiple *other hands* didn't bother Sophie in the least. Who cares? Fodor squeezed her elbow and winked: everything will be fine. His lighthearted inattention annoyed her, especially if he was going to be right, because she was serious. The clapping for a plump boy, whose achievements Sophie missed, rose and faded. The principal scanned the ledger over her eyeglasses.

". . . and, the last but not the slightest," the joke set off a few polite giggles, "Faye Phobus receives the Art Teacher Helper Award."

The crowd cheered.

"What's an Art Teacher Helper?" Fodor whispered. Sophie shrugged. Who cares? Fairy got a distinction like everybody else . . .

better than everybody else, and got to walk the aisle in full view. Isn't she a sweetie? Look, look at her!

The claps turned to kisses, the silence to murmur, moving chairs, laughter. The ceremony concluded. Fodor stretched his legs in relief, uttered a meaningless comment to the bored neighbor and got up. Sophie put her palm upon his hand.

"Don't go yet. I'd like to talk to the teacher."

She made her way through the crowd to the podium.

"Nice to meet you, Fairy's mother." A tall man with a flaccid ponytail shook Sophie's hand. "That's a delightful name. Is that what you call her at home? Your daughter loves drawing. She definitely deserves the award. Have you seen our exhibition? It's at the end of this hallway."

He stretched his lips, forestalling a farewell, but Sophie wasn't ready. Not yet, not until she asked questions.

"Does she do well? How does she behave in class? Is she attentive?"

"She is charming. The only thing is that—" as he spoke Sophie clenched her fists, ready for the inevitable *but*—"she is limiting her choices."

"What do you mean?"

"My program gives children an opportunity to try new things. See what they like, test their hands, explore their imaginations, but your daughter knows exactly what she wants. That's a rare quality at her age. She is set on drawing faces in the same manner, quite creative I must admit, and doesn't seem interested in anything else. I am sure it's nothing. She will grow up. Would you excuse me?"

His hand described a semicircle, and Sophie realized that she was grabbing his sleeve.

"I am sorry."

"Take a look at our drawings. Over there, around the corner. You can't miss them."

Fodor signaled from the exit. No, she shook her head and waved a silent counter-invitation, because the hubbub turned everybody deaf and mute. No, you come here. His face morphed into a mock martyr's mask.

*"Your daughter knows exactly what she wants to draw."*

"Why didn't you tell us?" Sophie tightened the bow and fluffed up her daughter's dress. "You know how much we like everything you do. Where are your pictures? Would you take us there?"

The three of them threaded their way against the flow. Parents were talking to parents, children chirped with each other. The exposition turned out to be a dozen sheets pinned to the wall, eclectically aslant to emphasize their artistic worth.

"Don't help me. Let me guess. No, I'm not reading the names," Sophie said, scanning the sketches, tilting her head left then right, depending on the incline. "Let's see, this is a very good tree. I like how the colorful dots make the leaves. This car must be a boy's work. Am I right?"

Slowly, they minced along.

"How cute—the whole family is holding hands. Is that a dog or a cat? Fodor . . . Fodor, where did you disappear to? There it is! Look, I found it."

The sheet Sophie pointed at was almost untouched, only a soft double line—one blue, one green—flowing top to bottom.

"I like it. I am just not sure. . . . No, no, don't tell me." She summoned Fodor with playful encouragement. "What do you think this might be?"

"The lines must be riverbanks. Did you draw a river?"

Sophie kissed Fairy on the crown, then hugged the girl, then kissed her again.

"That's excellent! It does look like a river. I have an idea. Why don't we go for a walk now? It's such a beautiful day!"

It took about twenty minutes to reach the riverfront. Along the way, their slightly warped reflections gleamed in large fashion windows among caged mannequins.

"Wait here. I'll be back," Fodor said.

He returned with two long-stem flowers.

"Sophie is my red rose," a smile, "and you," a bow, "are my fairy-white rose. Hold it. Peace of the roses."

They found a vacant bench. Sophie sat down, closed her eyes

and breathed in what seemed like air but in fact was the very essence of joy. If anything ever felt good, that was it—panting of the water tram, the sun, the breeze, her family. She crossed her legs, then crossed her arms—relaxed and unlocked, like the wings of a tired angel. The flower swayed slightly, dozing off in her hand. When she opened her eyes, Fairy wasn't around.

"Where is she?"

Fodor stretched his neck in obedient anxiety but then quickly relaxed.

"See the man with an easel? She is right behind him."

Sophie squinted, caught a glimpse of the purple bow and patted his knee. Get up, get up.

They walked over to the artist. His canvas was three-quarters busy with paint strokes, somewhat careless, leaving stripes of untouched surface here and there. There was something childish about the broken perspective and skewed proportions. Sophie couldn't say whether the shortfall was intentional or whether the man tried hard to be realistic but something—his talent or his vision—let him down.

At the height of daytime, the artist was painting night. A blurry figure of a young woman stood on top of the hunchback bridge. A pale ailing moon hung low, stretching shadows beyond any resemblance to their originals.

"Look how she watches his hands," Sophie whispered.

"I know what her drawing is," Fodor said suddenly. "It's the portrait."

"What portrait?"

"A face. What we took for the river was a man's profile."

"Why two lines? Why no eyes or mouth?"

"Maybe she had two people in mind, one behind the other. I don't know." He spread his arms helplessly and pointed at the canvas with his chin. "The art is what it is. Why would he distort the bridge? How can you rationalize artistic vision?"

His voice too loud, the words reached the painter. The man turned his head.

"Sorry," Fodor said, smiling. "Didn't mean to offend you."

The brush paused in the air.

"I don't intend to copy that bridge. If I wanted everybody's reality, I'd take a snapshot with a camera. Painting is no point-and-click. It takes you beyond the illusion. I can tell you a story about this young woman—what night it was, why she came to the bridge, even who she was destined to meet, although, obviously, I can't fit it all in one painting. This little girl understands me, don't you?"

His grayish goatee poked at Fairy. His skin used to be tight, but the filling had lost its elasticity like the springs of an old couch, and, pressured by trickling time, formed vertical furrows. . . .

. . . along which he will be folded one day and put in a chest with other old toys, Sophie thought.

"I shouldn't have said that. I am sorry," Fodor repeated out loud, good-naturedly.

"This is Fairy." Sophie rested her hands on the girl's shoulders. "She is also an artist. She just received an art award."

"Very nice to meet you, young lady-artist." The old man wiped his brush with a cloth. "I come here often. You are welcome to join me any day. Bring your easel—you have an easel, don't you?—and we can paint together. It's always good to have company."

## The theater

They stopped at a small café and sat at the table with dark-green cloth, discussing items on the menu. The catch-of-the-day caused polite curiosity, the list of desserts evoked loud enthusiasm. The waitress's pencil impatiently tapped the notebook. Fodor's finger paused at the chef's specials. What's the dish du jour? Can I have it with mashed potatoes? Is there celery in this salad? What about cilantro?

"Since when have you become so picky?" Sophie chuckled.

"I'd like to know precisely what we are in for."

Their table, right by the window, provided a view of a street poster with a mysterious . . . *rable* wrapping around the ticket booth.

"I always wanted to see that!" Sophie clasped her hands. "That would make an exclamation point after such an excellent day."

"*Les Miserable,* what a wretched name for an entertainment," Fodor commented.

"Don't try to get away with your witticisms. We shall go together. No excuses. Even if you don't like musicals, what's a sacrifice of one note-n-tone deaf man, compared to the family happiness?"

"You can't build communal happiness upon personal sacrifices. All right, I am kidding! Let's check their schedule first," Fodor reasoned, playing it down. "What if there is no show today? What if they are sold out?"

Unfortunately for him, the circumstances took care of timing (". . . and spacing," he added with a deep breath, accepting three seats in the orchestra).

"I am sure Fairy will enjoy it." Sophie's lips, so close to Fodor's ear, made him huddle.

"You are a grim tickler," he sighed in a mock complaint, but Sophie missed it and concluded her serious thought:

"Maybe it'll open up a new side of life and outweigh Nanny's tales."

By the first accords of the prelude, the hall filled up. In waning lights, a large woman with sinful but insincere thank-yous took a seat in front of them, shielding the better part of the stage. They rearranged, Fairy now sitting between her parents. The rustle died out. The curtain rolled up. Sophie and Fodor watched the girl—Fodor seeking shelter from the music, Sophie sharing her daughter's joy.

As soon as the reality sank into silent darkness, the illusion provided its own ambient sound, colors and characters. Had Fodor and Sophie sat next to each other, they would be whispering something like *Look how involved Fairy is* or *Her eyes are glowing* or *We should come to the theater more often.*

The scenery opened on a view of the city square, a row of trading booths, a backdrop with streets narrowing in perfect perspective. On the right side, a mammoth structure towered over the stage. Its coarse texture gave the impression of enormous mass—a menace that governed the scene and overwhelmed the audience. The tower's monstrosity dominated the performance, the music, even the heroes' passions. Sophie intercepted Fairy's worried glance at the massive bell on top and had to squeeze the small hand, reassuring her that it was all fake, no more than a game that people played, a picture not unlike our painting in the living room.

She had a feeling, though, that whatever she might say would go unattended, because the words were lifeless, paled by the live and colorful extravaganza in the limelight. Sophie decided to go over the plot on the way home, and explain who all these people onstage were and what they wanted. They are almost like us, only not quite real, you know.

Immersed in these thoughts, Sophie nearly shrieked from the piercing pain. Fairy's nails dug deep into her hand. What, what? The bell swayed, and its swing rocked the tower. The stone wall creaked, leaning over the square, ready to crash and crush not only the sleek singing chap in a top hat but the audience.

The scare must have been engineered. The arioso transmuted into a chorus then into a dance, and the catastrophe was happily avoided. Sophie exhaled with relief and rubbed her wrist to smooth down the pangs.

The day came to a closure, and the memory of it was ready to take its place among other days of the past, whether dull or exciting. They found the door to Nanny's room shut, only the strip of light indicating that the old woman wasn't asleep. Sophie in her night gown knocked quietly.

Nanny rocked in a little chair, holding the tambour with unfinished embroidery.

"I think," Sophie began, "that your stories affect Fairy too much. We went to a show today—a charming musical, lots of kids; the girl really enjoyed it. This fantasy was as real for her as life."

*As soon as you walked into the theater, the fantasy became a part of her life. Therefore, it was real.*

"But it's still different. It's as if she joined the people onstage and the events were happening to her. You should adjust your tales. Explain to her that there are no kings and monsters, and Prince Charming isn't going to come galloping to our terrace. This is the seventh floor, and we don't even have a balcony."

*How do you suppose her prince will arrive? On a train?*

The conversation wasn't going as she'd intended.

"Good night," said Sophie.

"I don't know if she is making fun of us," she confessed to snuffling Fodor in sleepless darkness.

"She may not be the brightest girl, but we love her."

"I wasn't talking about Fairy."

Morning sunlight shushed away the night's specters.

"I wish they had summer vacations for adults as well." Fodor paused before the mirror, corrected his tie, went for the door then returned to give a good-bye kiss. "Don't be bored without me."

"We'll go to the boardwalk," Sophie decided. "Remember that artist? Fairy and I will be drawing just like him. I've always wanted to paint. Maybe he'll teach us something."

On their way, Sophie stopped by the art supplies store and bought two pads with heavy paper sheets.

"Which pencils would you like? I think twenty-four colors is enough for starters. We will share. Here, you carry the pencils, and I will have the pads. They are too big for you."

When they reached the riverfront, it was crowded.

"Do you see him anywhere?" Sophie asked. "Me neither. Let's walk to the next bridge. Who spots him first, wins. Do you remember what his name was?"

The old man was nowhere. He had either finished his work or simply skipped the day.

"Oh, never mind. We don't really need anybody, right? We can start on our own, you and I. There is a vacant bench. You want to sit on the left?"

They settled down, the joy of anticipation comparable to, if not greater than, that of accomplishment.

"You know what we forgot? A sharpener."

The concern went away as soon as Sophie opened the box—the pencils were already sharp.

"Hold it. This pad will be yours. Hm-m-m . . . what are we going to draw?" She looked around. "See that cloud? If you move it to the right it'll form a face. The sun is an eye; the tree in the middle is a nose. What will *I* draw? I think . . . ," she hummed, "I think I'll start with that bridge."

She almost commented on how charming the overpass was, but an unwelcome association with Prince Charming of last night's conversation made her falter.

"It's very . . . picturesque," Sophie mumbled instead.

Knees proved to be a poor substitute for an easel. The pad tended to slide and demanded incessant care. Two faint lines, to be adjusted later, marked the river banks. This curve will later become a bridge, she thought. Here we shall have trees and benches and people. Details aren't necessary now. That's good. What color should I use for water?

Sophie got carried away with her own sketch and for a few minutes paid no attention to Fairy's. Then an askance look made her stop, leaving the tentatively outlined bridge suspended in midair.

"No, no, that's not how you hold the pencils. You don't need two at the same time. Put one down, otherwise you'd be drawing two lines. If you want it, you can always add the second line later. See how I do that? Oh, well, I suppose. . . . You are the artist, you decide."

Sophie watched, trying to guess what her daughter was drawing. Determined joggers were passing them, oblivious of the world, concentrated solely on their own wheezing. Casual strollers turned their heads and smiled.

"Are you done already? You don't want to add any details? I thought we would draw from life. No, no, it's not bad. It's very similar to the picture you made at school, almost the same. Let me guess, a portrait? Here is a forehead, a nose, a chin. This double line is nice. Is it two people? They look so much alike—they must be brothers. How about adding an eye, an ear? If you make a mouth like this, he will smile. Is he already smiling? Well, I guess you can leave it the way it is."

Her own sketch lost its appeal. Sophie made a few rash strokes—green trees, blue sky, yellow sun. Pulsations in her temples announced an approaching headache. She wanted to go home.

# Vera (Part 2)

## THE NEW LAND

Our journey brought us to New Wye. Down, down, down the alphabet, from M to N, from the old-world metronomia to the new-world megalomania. But, whatever its map-name, every town for us is Phila Delphia.

We chose a modest apartment in a quiet neighborhood, away from the town's trumpery, where sirens and marches never tapped on our window panes. Paying a three-month advance, we cautioned the landlord—a stooping *starets*[1] with sparse stubble on his chicken neck—that we didn't question his terms and his absurd steep fee.

In return we asked him to honor our seclusion. Back off, antediluvian; let Alex lock the door. You see, we bent forward and screamed into the keyhole, we are suffering from one very unorthodox bodily condition, which often places us at the focus of unhealthy curiosity.

"We traveled here," we went on, "to meet one exceptional practitioner, a specialist in one narrow medical field. Are you still there? We will not trouble you with particulars, because neither his name nor his forte means much to laymen. Past disappointments did not dispirit us. We are very optimistic and soon, maybe as soon as tomorrow, we intend to begin our search for this exceptional chap."

"I understand," the old man mumbled from the landing. "I am not going to bother you. Get well."

1. *starets*: Russian: Old man.

"... and should you, for any bizarre reason, have an urgent message for either of us," we groaned as our crooked posture started causing back pain, "don't feel shy. We are quite democratic—you'll get the attention you deserve. Just come and push a note with questions under the door. We shall promptly write the response. Good day now."

From behind plastic blinds we watched him cross the street, look back at our windows, sigh, shrug and disintegrate. Where did he go? Where else but to his miserly Mrs. to account for the new eccentric tenants. Most likely, he will cram her with lies, poking his gap-toothed fun, twisting our accent and exaggerating our deformity. It was quite practical to shut the door at the first opportunity, giving no more food to his geriatric imagination. Let the mad hatter and his dormouse have a party—revelry in the anile kitchen under a lampshade eaten away by many generations of moth. Let them soak biscuits in their broken tea and slurp the slush. Let them. What do we care about their lisping bliss?

The apartment suited us well. Rolling the blinds up, we could convert the living room into a sunlit studio. The bedroom's topography was no more relevant than the oblivion it hosted. Our only requirement was a wide bed accessible from both sides, since we never knew who, Alex or I, would decide to get up first. The tiny kitchenette contained a stove, a cast-iron sink and a rectangular table, pushed into the corner by the window. And finally, the apartment had a hidden storage room—semi-pantry, semi-coal-hole—ideally suited for our auxiliary artistic fancy. Should we shut the door tight and tuck the chink with a terry cloth, neither light nor whiff would seep through. And then we, voluntary hermits, may attend to creating our bill-size masterpieces.

"You are too precious to vegetate in this shelter," we apologized to the portrait, leaning the roll in the corner like a broom or a cane. "Sooner or later you will get the wall you deserve."

Alex bolted the pantry, lightheartedly christened as the Mint, and we returned to the living room where the sun trickled through the yellowish plastic blades.

Soon, the fatigue took its toll. We lay down on our backs, locked our hands under our heads, closed our eyes and started thinking.

Fo-Fo's trace led us to this place. We liked the residential nook with its cobblestone heart, cozy coffee shops and curiosity stores, the picturesque wharf, flowers on the balconies and, closer to the city center, statues of horsed raiders. In full compliance with monumental symbolism, the heroic horsemen differed from one another by their pets' postures: firmly-footed, one leg up, or prancing—indicating whether the tin-man's flesh-n-blood twin perished in a battle, was mortally wounded, or passed away in his own shoes.

Our gutsy puncture of the borders, further journey in stuffy compartments, sea sickness when crossing the ocean, corporal discomfort and spiritual ambiguity—all had its reasons. Sooner or later, during therapy with our future healer, we would disclose the truth. Indeed, how could it happen that we had abandoned home and ended up in this indifferent foreign terra, where people scoffed at our accent, where dual negatives were frowned upon?

It didn't matter, because Alex and I were about to open uncut pages of the new story, in which everything was still unknown—the twist of the plot, the mask of the villain, the identity of the savior.

During our brief but lively oblivion, we galloped past the still images of *Ago*—childhood, infatuation, amorous L'ubasha, amoral Nad'usha. Then the heartbeat of the train carried us away.

While we were stuck in the dream intermission, the angels were busy changing scenery, deftly getting rid of the old props. Discarded were:

- the slapdash side street where we had ambushed the school foe,
- the flowerbed in front of Love's house,
- Leonardo's studio,
- a piece of paper with the fading *profil perdu*,
- a jolty train compartment.

Wait, angels, we prayed, don't drag time away by the clock hands as if it were a disheartened captive. Visions aren't subject to time.

But angels, as befitted higher beings, never listened. Wake up, they said. You are here. Let's go.

We slept through the rest of the day and woke up only to find the cityscape no longer colored. The sun yawned. Losing interest in the painting game, it washed brushes and splashed dirty water over house facades, shading all in uniform maroon. The thickening darkness crept inside and threatened to choke the lamp. With a brisk move Alex and I shut the blinds.

After we got off the train, we had purchased two identical capes to replace the one snatched away by the wind during our extravagant getaway. Now, scissors in hands, we ripped the fabric open and reshaped it to fit the anomalies of our anatomy. Alex the Artist sewed wedges from one cape into the slits of another so that, with the raised collar and the lowered hood, no one would tell us from ordinary passers-by. We used the cape like a knight's armor, like an old maid's make-up. It served as an exoskeleton, protecting our soul from casual offenders.

Then we turned to our real agenda—the search for our healer. Endless articulations of his name formed grooves in our mouth. He was supposed to succeed where others had failed. He had to cure us from our agonizing duplicity, remove the crust of distortion, crack our crystal jail open so we could come out of it as free men—Alex and I, I and Alex. Where was he now? Could he be unaware of our existence and of the miracle he was about to deform?

Exceptional personalities cannot stay incognito for long. This was twice so in our case. It was also true in respect to Doctor Fo-Fo. We didn't know his whereabouts, but that didn't bother us. The town had only so many hospitals. How easy was it to dial a number and, with voices trembling from debility, inquire about the visiting hours of Doctor Fo-Fo? Oh, you mean, Professor Fo-Fo? Yes, yes, of course it's him—professor, mastermind, genius.

Having marked his schedule in the calendar grid, we would drape ourselves into the altered overcoat, pull the hood over and head to the right place at the right time.

We commissioned resolute and energetic Alex with the telephone search. While he was dialing his way through the yellow pages, I grabbed a pen. A few firm strokes made a sketch of Fo-Fo. He came out as a middle-age man, average height, frosty hair. Eyeglasses? Possible. Goatee? Probable. Absent-mindedness in everything unrelated to medicine? Definite.

"How else can you spell Fo-Fo?" Alex screamed into the receiver. "Yes. Yes. I am writing the address down."

## The foray to the Fo-Fo funfair

The path leading onward past the cast-iron gates split into a drop-shaped approach. In the old days the building must have hosted local nobility. Now, due to the general degradation, it sheltered the sick and crippled. We felt two lumps in our throats—somewhere behind these walls, in his snow-white smock, escorted by a flock of starched snow-whites, our Doctor was declaring diagnoses, mending or cutting patients' life threads with the efficiency of three Moirae.

"Is he fickle like Fein or firm like Tulchinsky?" wondered Alex.

"What kind of maladies does he cure here?"

My question was more important. Indeed, what words should we choose, when he appears at the other end of the hallway? Should we face him or let him face us?

Looking at the well-groomed flowerbeds of a tamed landscape, Alex figured that this place was not accustomed to flashing emergency lights. Was it. . . .

". . . a child-bearing beehive . . . ?" I suggested.

". . . a dispensary with mud baths . . . ?" he put forward.

". . . an aroma- and urinotherapy . . . ?"

". . . an open-heart sanctuary . . . ?"

Speaking of hearts, as we were getting closer to the entrance, ours quickened their pace, about to explode only to be reconstructed under the skillful scalpel of our Fo-Fo.

We pushed heavy—not for feeble sufferers—doors and entered

the foyer. A reflection in the looking glass across the empty hall greeted us, pale and nervous. It was a worthy centerpiece of a museum collection—passions of St. Alex and St. Alex.

"We," we announced at the registration desk, "came to see Doctor Fo-Fo."

Fo-fo-fo . . . confirmed echo. An elderly clerk, her soft facial curves pierced through by an unlikely pointed nose, stared at our outline.

"Pardon?"

We squinted, trying to make out the name tag turned backwards in out handheld mirror.

"Merciful Theresa, we came from a far-away country to meet Doctor Fo-Fo."

Her silence didn't discourage us.

"Should we call you Sister or Nurse? You see, Nurster, we are unwell. We have endured . . . m-m-m . . . bloodcurdling cramps in our hypophysis," Alex explained.

". . . and our hypothalamus is cracking up," I clarified.

". . . and that spleen colic," Alex added, in case our healer's forte excluded anything *hypo*, "the pain is agonizing."

"Summon Fo-Fo," we demanded in impatient unison. "Call him. Page him. He alone can alleviate our bleeding nexus!"

She observed Alex, then slowly turned her eyes to me. Or, maybe, I was first and Alex second. We were too restless to record the sequence and coherence.

"There is nobody here by this name," she mumbled finally.

It's our accent, Alex whispered. The witch is confused.

Thoroughly articulating every freaking syllable, we repeated our request, this time the emphasis not on the diagnosis but on pronunciation.

"Oh!" she exhaled with relief. "You mean Doctor Phobus. I didn't quite get it the first time. Where are you from?"

"Our origin is utterly irrelevant. We suffer from acutest attacks of congenital thyroid deficiency or whatever infirmity Doctor Fo-Fo's formal focus is, no hocus here. Our beloved motherland with its ridges and meadows, woods and brooks, ups and downs failed to groom a physician able to cure us. One of our old well-wishers—his sobriquet presently irrelevant—was more concerned with his singularity than our dualism. The other practically begged us to conduct our sessions in his apartment, only because he wanted to get his stepdaughter off his hands. Don't make us wait any longer. Send us to the staffroom, to the surgery theater, to the man whose miracles are known throughout the Ultima Thule. Bring us to Fo-Fo."

She paused again, battling the rust of mental machinery.

"There is no emergency department here. We don't usually take walk-ins. But if you are in pain . . . I'll see what I can do."

"Good." We nodded. "See. Do."

She picked up a bouquet of folders, holding them on her forearm gently *Quasi modo geniti infantes*—like a newborn babe.

"It must be terrible to suffer from so many ills. Can you walk? Should I call for a wheelchair?"

"No wheels, no trolleys, no more questions. Show us the way."

Hardly able to restrain our anxiety, we dragged after Sisturse, passing the walls adorned with reproductions.

"I feel his healing aura," Alex confessed. "I'm sure Doctor himself chose the artwork."

"Alex and Alex will impress him with their artistic flair."

As in our our distal adolescence, in the remote time and space, the two connivers quietly giggled. Addressing ourselves in the third, or more accurately, third *and* fourth persons, amused us.

A few more turns, and we entered a cold room with skinned humans on wall-wide diagrams. We found a small desk, a waste basket, a washstand and a mechanical (twin size) bench with a shiny foot lever.

"Take off your clothes." Theresa dropped a washed-out robe on the bench. "I will let the doctor know."

We searched for the proper construct of objection, but she was gone, leaving the door ajar. Apparently, modesty and privacy—attributes of the soul—step down in times of bodily malfunction.

Both Alex and I suddenly felt as if we had never left the town sprinkled with sand, as if not Fo-Fo but one or another Fein would appear any second and start posing his idiotic riddles: "Let's imagine, there is this girl. One of you likes her and the other one hates her. What do you do?"

How do we make this half-dimwit *poludurok* understand that such discord was unfeasible? All efforts to split our monolithic coalition were doomed to fail.

"Well?"

Carried away by the vignette of déjà vu, we overlooked arrival of the host. Heavy and hefty, he lifted his eyebrow, the one distinctly redder than the other. He towered over us, trespassing our comfort zone.

"Well what?" My voice cracked while Alex remained silent.

"Need help undressing?"

Instinct made us grope for a cane. Too bad we had left it at home, although we'd never dare to threaten, let alone attack Doctor despite the glaring inconsistency of his idyllic image and factual looks.

Is he really our long longed-for luminary?

The flesh-n-blood Fo-Fo proved to be younger and more athletic then we had expected. In addition to his unkempt eyebrows, some false notes buzzed in his trapezoid neck and thickset forearms showing from under the rolled-up sleeves. Well, we've been wrong about Love and Hope, we could err about Fo-Fo. We should accept him the way he is.

"Doctor—" our sincere greeting tickled his massive mentum— "we have heard so much about your miraculous talents!"

He stared nonchalantly over our heads, barely blinking. Do something, I signaled to Alex—more imaginative among the two of us. He picked up the vibe in no time:

"On our way to your office, Doctor, while following kind Theresa . . . we couldn't help noticing . . . on the corridor walls . . . all these reproductions. . . . What an impeccable selection! Fine arts—*Fein Arts,* we call them—is the embodiment of beauty. We are no strangers to that splendor ourselves, you know, and we appreciate a good taste in others. Every daub was excellent, but the sunflower field totally charmed us by its color spectrum! So much freedom, so much air. . . ."

The tirade affected Fo-Fo.

"I guess the flowers are a'right," he agreed. "Yellow."

"Yellow," Alex echoed, "yellow, indeed. What an acute observation! The healing force of this reproduction is worth hundreds of prescription pills. And what do you think about this masterpiece?"

We pointed to a childish doodle under the glass, next to the skeleton entwined by a Gordian knot of blood vessels. Doctor hesitated.

"It's a'right, I suppose. Although, the glass—"

"The glass!" I joined Alex, and we jabbered together. "The glass is an obstacle—the barrier between the artist and his audience; it disjoins the two halves of one whole, something we know more intimately than anybody else."

". . . should a patient turn unstable, the glass may fall out. I hate sweeping pieces."

That puzzled us for a moment. What in the world is Fo-Fo talking about? Is he so unpredictable? Is that how the great mind operates?

"Listen," he interrupted our internal uncertainty, "when Doc comes you may discuss whatever you pay for."

"Doc?" we gasped. "Aren't you. . . ? We thought you were. . . ?"

"I am here to help you undress, hold your arms, see that you don't brawl. Some patients are such. . . ." He reached for our belt. The resolution of this tragedy of errors blurred in the face of our helplessness. We were ashamed by our wrong judgment. How could we confuse the brute with the brainiac? Our captor shed an air of authority, afforded by his physical might and spiritual apathy. Well? he said again, threatening. We fingered our buttons in search of a diplomatic solution.

"We should mention that even Professor Tulchinsky never resorted to coercive inspection."

Alex unbuttoned the shirt's collar to ease his anxiety. "Surely, Professor checked our throats and ears, but. . . ."

The red-haired alpha-male didn't twitch.

The shirt was now fully unbuttoned. Next stop—double indecency.

"Our fitness has always been impeccable," we blubbered and

had to bethink quickly: "not counting the colic in hypophysis, of course."

"Pants," the envoy of health indicated listlessly.

A few humiliating minutes passed. We may use force ourselves—if a moment calls, that is—but we get flustered when others push it upon us. The Cerberus obviously lacked any diplomacy. While we were holding to every fig leaf, ready to be expelled from the paradise of the dressed, he never looked aside.

Finally, wrapped in the robe so inappropriate for our anatomy (one size doesn't fit all!), we sat on the coach, our feet dangling and hardly reaching the floor. Our bare behind got covered by jimjams from the cold leatherette. Were our mood not so far-from-playful, we could have joked that Alex had jims while I had jams. This, however, was no laughing matter.

The orderly collected our garb and disappeared, assuming that we were now totally demoralized and unable to turn our back on anybody. He was right. The idea of chasing him down the hallway and cooling our tender loins never occurred to us.

We didn't remain alone for long.

A stout figure with a snake of the stethoscope—a medical symbol, indeed—appeared in the doorway. Although without mustache or goatee, he fit the brand of Doctor Fein et al., firmly imprinted in our stereoscopic memory.

As he scanned his folder, our exclamations collided in midair.

"Doctor Fo-Fo?"—"Alex Alex?"

Silence.

"Are you Doctor Fo-Fo?" we repeated suspiciously.

"I am Doctor Phobus."

Alex was about to jump off the coach, and I barely (what a sad pun!) held him back.

"We are here to meet Doctor Fo-Fo."

"Cramps in the hypothalamus?" He consulted the notes. "What's that nonsense?"

We assumed a posture of as much dignity as our attire could afford:

"If you are not who you are and even not who you should pretend to be, either call Doctor Fo-Fo or we take our misfortune elsewhere."

"If your hypothalamus no longer clashes with your hypophysis, feel free to go."

He made a half-circle on his slick heels and trotted away.

For two endless minutes nothing happened. Neither new Fo-Fo nor the orderly with our clothes appeared. It was getting chilly. Alex wiggled my fingers. I waggled his toes. We slid off the couch, leaving moist imprints of our hindquarters on the fake leather upholstery, and cautiously looked down the corridor. An indifferent nurse passed by, pushing a gurney. Our unguarded rears pressed to the wall—the robe was too small to over-flap—we set out for the storage room.

Misery is a superb stimulant for friendliness. We forced a grin at every stranger. After two or three doors we found a closet with piles of linen, robes and—oh luck!—an oversize straight jacket. Not giving it another thought, we wrapped ourselves in the extra-large armor. Despite its long-sleeve cut and thanks to the suitcase buckles on the chest, we felt secure.

Dragging hollow sleeves over the checkered linoleum, we headed for the exit. Nurse Theresa was still in the registration booth, sheltered behind the safety mesh.

"That's what I said," she happily confirmed, "Doctor Phobus."

"Do you think it's an operetta?" patiently questioned Alex, slapping the counter and paying no attention to the flipped-over inkpot that instantly turned somebody's case history black. "Fo-Fo, we said. Is that so difficult? Fo-Fo, Fo-Fo, Fo-Fo!"

She recoiled. Someone pulled our sleeve. We jerked the shoulder to set it free, trying to get hold of the register with the list of medical personnel. The character behind knew better. His grip tightened. We looked in the mirror and, to our total dismay, recognized the orderly who had humiliated us earlier. Turning purple from futile strain, we pulled and pushed to no avail. The sleeves entangled us. The buckles clasped.

"Set us free!" we demanded. "We have a dream!"

Pale Theresa and the pink-cheeked hulk looked like white and red roses joining forces.

"Calm down," another voice said behind our backs. "Constantine, pull it a tad tighter and let's all go to my office."

The degree of our liberties shrank to a minimum. Alex couldn't see him, but I recognized the voice of Doctor Phobus. Wiry Constantine knocked us onto a narrow wheelchair, and rolled it along the same labyrinth. This time, the would-be charming reproductions, especially viewed from a detrimental stance, hardly touched us.

"Listen, dear, or whatever adjective you prefer. Terrible injustice takes place. This is a farce, in which our every word is twisted upside out and understood wrongly, against the hair. Untie the knots. Our extremities turn numb!"

The usurper kept pushing the cart. Squeaking from the excessive load, the wheels carried us—turn after turn—back into the Minotaur's burrow.

"You, monster, say another word," the garlic stench washed over my left and Alex's right ears, "and I will kick your shits out."

We shut up. Not because the threat worked. We had withstood brutality many times. We had been intimidated, humiliated and once stood in front of a firing squad, overpowered but never broken. Some day we will share this story with an attentive listener. And, although Constantine did employ a plural form referring to the double set of our internals, the captor managed to hurt our feelings even if his hissing diction had simply misarticulated *Mister*. We didn't say another word, not to cast pearls before the plebs, especially when our right of self-defense was taken away in such disgraceful fashion.

As soon as Phobus walked into the room we screamed:

"Who do you think you are? Untie, unclasp and debuckle!"

His hesitation forced us to get more persuasive, but the tension dented our otherwise precise rhetoric with impersonal *Listen*:

"Listen, Doctor, we came here, to this clinic of yours, to this asylum of Asclepius with one purpose—meet our healer. But instead, we were subjected to the slapstick of disrobing and entanglement. Our temper is not to be tampered with. Talk to us. We dig logic and reason."

He half-perched on the desk's edge, his left foot standing on the floor, his right leg slightly swaying in midair. His lacquered shoe came into the unpleasant vicinity of our groins.

"All right," we conceded, "if you are concerned with unpredictable outbursts, order an injection of some philter, some antidepressant to subdue our reflexes. Then we shall tell you our story."

The crankshaft was slowly turning in his brain. Either because of second thoughts or first doubts, his face went through a succession of miens like that of a gutta-percha imp.

"Calm down. You have to promise not to riot and not to bump people against the wall. Let's think logically and assume that your accent, as you claim, triggered the flurry of misunderstandings."

We nodded with dignity or whatever of it remained available in our restricted range of motions. How could we explain that no two balanced and sanguine personas could withhold from emotional splash when confronted with such shortage of sympathy?

Unclasped, we immediately turned sideways, tossed our chin up and started from afar:

"Tell us, Doctor, have you ever been betrayed by Love or deceived by Hope?"

After our long and passionate spiel he nodded: "You've convinced me. I do see now that you are a very troubled individual."

"Individuals," we corrected.

"Unfortunately, I don't have much time now. We can make an appointment to discuss your condition later. I am not going to deny or confirm the existence of Fo-Fo, but giving you a referral is out of the question at the moment. Let alone disclosing his home address. If you wish, we can talk about him and other things during your next visit."

That's even better, I whispered to Alex. The clown underestimates us. Nolens or volens, willy or nilly, he will tiptoe us to Fo-Fo.

Out loud, we expressed pleasure from mutual understanding and agreed to whatever the hell he was saying, just order your thug to return our clothes and turn away until we wrap ourselves into the cloak as if we were strangers in the chilly night.

# Phobus

Doctor Phobus became the next bead on the rosary of our well-wishers—the string leading to elusive and illusive Fo-Fo. Alex noticed once, and I fully share his observation, that life's drama, as viewed from a therapist's chair, becomes slapstick.

Under the lowered cape and securely tied cloak—one and one always insist on double assurance—we entered his private office through the backstairs reserved for infectious patients and unforeseen circumstances. As soon as we armchaired ourselves (the cowl intact, the belt slightly loosened), Doctor Phobus appeared in the room.

Mother doesn't accompany us any longer. Nobody is sobbing behind the door. We are alone in our quest for the golden fleece of sanity, pardon our Argonauts' argot.

"Our first encounter," we began, skipping the formal greeting, "was marred with a few glitches. It's not our intention to point fingers and assign blame. We admit that our internal tension—incidentally one of the foci in the upcoming therapy—could have played a crucial part in the fiasco. Let bygones be bygones in the literal sense of the prefix *bi*. We are ready to cooperate."

"Would you turn a little? I need eye contact."

"You don't understand," we informed him patiently, as true patients do. "This is a key moment for our collaboration—establishment of trust. We can't deal with someone who takes us at the face, so to speak, value. It's too easy to take two King Lears for one Guildenkrants."

"I am afraid that without your support we can't move forward."

"What do you mean, can't? What kind of support? Maybe you

wish that right here, right on this carpet, we grabbed a scalpel and dissected ourselves into two self-sustained *semis*? The physician's life would be a paradise if every patient could self-diagnose, self-treat and self-ablate the appendix."

He switched an inkpot with a bronze pencil quiver, both empty, then, after brief contemplation, placed them back.

Shelved folios written by trickster-wisenheimers failed to intimidate us, their guns hurtful only to those who walked life in blessed ignorance. We, accustomed to reprobation, were immune to their pretense. Knowledge multiplies migraines or something like that.

"Help may come only from your understanding of our essence and our inner beauty," we uttered. "A rasp is an inept tool for fine filigree."

"All right. Face whatever you like. But do me a favor—render your story from the first person singular."

What are they? Each other's clones?

We chose to ignore his undemanding stratagem. Even if he considered himself crafty, his tricks were naïve and ineffective. Using the terms of rhetoric, our illocutionary force—something we needed to affect him with—was our desire to find Fo-Fo. In the perlocutionary act—the action following our persuasion—he was supposed to hand us the address.

Light from the window embossed our profile, smearing the shadow over the host's desk. Were he a numismatist or historian, he could have recognized a miraculous similarity to the portraits on coins, although a special commemorative medallion with two heads was yet to be minted. When we spoke, our lips moved synchronously.

"Our illness can be traced to the commencement of memory," we began, "to the zero beyond which no clock hand can reach, the mainspring making futile, unrelated-to-heartbeat clicks. Our private record started with a mythical image of Romulus and Remus suckling on a she-wolf. The loadstar pointed to the town alternately covered with slush and sand. Since that moment, we have to refer to ourselves using plural pronoun not only because of the royal hauteur but out of the accountant's diligence. . . ."

"Here is what I think . . . ," he began after we finished our excursus into times gone.

"Don't rush your judgment," we warned. "We have been staying on the other side of the looking glass for too long to accept another quack verdict. We'll be gone now. Think of us in your free time; go over our life moments before falling asleep, leaf through your useless reference books, talk to your mentors. Who knows, maybe you will find it helpful to mention us to colleague Fo-Fo. In our next visit we will provide you with advanced information—more food for thought. We are not sure now what the theme is going to be. Let's rely on inspiration. This session was extremely helpful. Thank you very much."

Visibly relieved, he cast a glance at the clock and lifted himself from the chair, ready for a farewell.

"By the way," we mused, still seated, capturing an allegedly casual thought, "we are no longer accustomed to long confessions. Our throats are parched. We prefer a *dilution* over *solution*, of course, but for now a few sips of spring water will suffice."

"One glass or two?"

We paused.

"If this is a hidden sneer, it didn't go unnoticed. If, however, your words convey compassion, we express our gratitude. One glass is sufficient. Life has taught us to share."

As soon as Phobus left the room we rushed to his desk and snatched his notebook. What letter is it under? D for Doctor, C for Colleague, FF for Fo-Fo? The steps were approaching. Not thinking four times about it, we stuffed the book into our pocket and leaned back in the chair with well-feigned indifference.

"Not sure if it's spring water," he said, handing us the glass, "but drinking—guaranteed."

We got to our feet, covering the bulging pocket with our palms—the book lay crosswise like a rebellious fetus in a womb.

"Thank you. The thirst is gone. Our body is an excellent self-tuning apparatus. The salivation has been fully restored."

Leaving him with the glass in his extended hand, we withdrew.

## The notebook

We bolted the door, two-pegged the coat and hurried to the kitchen. Strombolis have no choice but to rely on locks in the world subdued by Pinocchio's henchmen. First I then Alex took a few gulps right out of the milk carton. Then we sat down by the window—the view outside reported no suspicious commotion—whisked away the crumbs left after the hasty breakfast, and unpocketed our loot.

The leather-bound pet lay quietly, frightened by the unfamiliar setting. Our finger pads caressed its spine. We looked at each other in the mirror and blushed. Like all conscientious folk, we were embarrassed by our own immoral misdemeanor.

"Did we . . . steal it?" I mumbled. "How could we?"

"How many times did I tell you? Obey commandment eight. Thou shalt not pilfer. Thou simply shalt not do this kind of thing. Why didn't you listen to me, brother?"

"But, brother," I exclaimed, "I never broke the number eight. I did not bear false witness."

"Brother," said Alex sternly, "who cares about false witnessing? That's not even a real transgression. I am talking about *Thou shall not steal.*"

"Oh, you mean the number seven!"

"Don't try to confuse me. I know my commandments. Seven is adultery. Eight is theft."

We pulled out our memos and skipped to midway down the list. Mine said:

6. Thou shalt not commit adultery

7. Thou shalt not steal

8. Thou shalt not bear false witness

Alex's said

6. Thou shalt not murder

227

7. Thou shalt not commit adultery

8. Thou shalt not steal

What a mix-up! The two of us had memorized rules from different confessions. What was number seven for the Catholics became number eight for the Protestants!

"Next time, when you don't want me to transgress, don't hiss numbers; say words," I told Alex.

"The words are ambiguous," he objected. "Who is *Thou?* Thou-you or thou-me?"

"This story makes a nice dinner joke," we agreed. "We should mention it to Fo-Fo. He will crack up."

Gradually, the thumping bravado slowed its beat. Our desire to meet Fo-Fo must have overshadowed decency, but who can blame the famished for the desire to fill two bellies?

"We know, we know, breaking commandments is inexcusable," we assured the orphaned notebook. "We shall return you to your owner, refusing any reward, should one be offered."

"Take me back now," the mute object pleaded with our articulated assistance. "My master has already turned his office upside down."

"Don't worry, Alex and Alex will restore justice at their earliest convenience. We aren't going to violate your privacy, to forcefully peer inside, to extort evidence. You want to keep your secret? Hold on to it. Fine with us."

The metronome of the leaking faucet measured a few units of silence. Alex turned to me:

"What if he keeps his confidential information here? Something he wants to keep from us."

"What could that be?" My eyebrows rose.

We looked at two treasure troves—one on either side of the looking glass.

"Here is what I think," I announced. "Whatever we do now, it mustn't be something we may regret later."

"Sure thing," he confirmed.

". . . on the other hand. . . ," I went on after brief contemplation, and Alex concluded by reading my mind:

*Number seven for the Catholics became*
*number eight for the Protestants!*

"... on the other hand the main postulate of Hippocrates states *Do no harm*. Should the drought accidentally flip a page and reveal a line, should we peek with one, well, two eyes, nobody is going to be hurt. It's not like knocking a vase from the windowsill."

Indeed, who would suffer if nature, by the way quite apathetic to the very fact of our existence, flashed by, and all we did was spend a few moments studying its footprints?

Deliberately avoiding contact with the notebook, we got up and, copying every gesture of our reflections, opened the window. It was calm and quiet outside. The crowns of orderly, wind-abiding trees hardly swayed. No whiff from playful Zephyr; no exhale from rigorous Boreas. My mirror clone looked at Alex. His yonder twin looked at me. Our crisscross glances collided.

We weren't quite sure what happened then. Either we lost our balance, or the earth wiggled under our feet. We waved our hands and inadvertently brushed the ill-starred bookling off the table-top. Its paper wings flapped to no avail. It came crushing down like a fallen angel. The pages unfolded, feeling no shame in their nakedness. The notebook spread out flat with no resolve to slam closed. Names and numbers revealed themselves before our eyes.

"It's not your fault," we hurried to assure it, "neither is it our guilt. You didn't mean to let your master down. We'll just take a peek. It's not going to hurt at all."

Slaves of old habits, we shut the blinds. Alex rolled up my sleeves, and we turned to the captive with medical composure. Our *sang,* boiling with excitement just a second ago, turned quite *froid* (pronounced *Frou-uh,* no relation to the famous Doctor pronounced *Froid).*

"We are neither monsters nor villains," we said, disregarding our listener's lifelessness. "Any rumor in your paper world is nothing but unscrupulous fata morgana. We don't tear off pages. We don't leave marginal comments or fold corners. We don't merge second and third letters in the word *flick* or mar the first letter in *pass.*

"Would you mind opening your pages a bit wider?" I asked.

"Think of us as doctors," Alex echoed. "We have been to so many that we practically became ones ourselves."

"How about," we repeated, leaning forward and knitting our eyebrows, "some cooperation?"

No longer muffled by its leather armor, Phobus's *das buch* thrust its covers open, entrusting its bookish honor to our magnanimity. Our infatuation with anthropomorphisms proved as much fun in maturity as it had in our childhood.


What letter should we start with? Jumping to F—the first in our vital alphabet—would be like skipping the main course and going straight for dessert. We understand that spelling, especially that of last names, can play phonetic peek-a-boo and archly wink from behind another letter like in *knight* or *psyche*. The old joker may have put on a guise, concealing a decent F under pretentious Ph.

Luminous like a binary star, we went leafing through the notes, dissecting one inscription after another in search of a benign entry. Two drops of sweat—one caused by unrest, another by responsibility—slipped down our forehead grooves. Alex and I were too hunt-ridden to wipe them off. We were combing lines so that no punctuation mark could escape our omni-vision.

And what a hunt it was!

We searched under H, where unimaginative bourgeois kept their Home, the lustful hid their Hot Patootie, and the aging bumblebees provided for their Honeys. Under S we looked for the Savior, under R—for Redeemer. We found namesakes from our past—a Paul, an Anastasia, a Konstantin, misspelling notwithstanding. We saw one respectable inhabitant, his weighty status defined by two addresses, none bearing any particular thrill.

Twenty-five letters flew by like telegraph poles behind the train's windows. The only name we cared for was missing.

"What do you say?" Alex asked. "Should we?"

"We have no other choice."

Our hands trembling, we stepped into the sacred land of Fables and Fantasy, of Fibs and Fiction. We found a tiny Fairy heading a list of tutors and pediatricians. We found a no-last-name Isabella—a possible trespasser from another section. We saw. . . .

"There, there he is!" Alex screamed.

"What?" I was puzzled. "Where?"

He pointed his finger at the fugitive Fo-Fo, uneven, hasty, disguised beyond recognition by illegible handwriting.

55 WC, his line read simply.

"Are you sure?" I asked suspiciously, and Alex was only too happy to explain his brainwork.

Like in the game of hide-and-seek, Fo-Fo's negligence had let him down—his foot was sticking out from under the bed and the tree trunk he chose to freeze behind proved too slim. The entry was the only one in the whole notebook without a name. Why? Because you don't write down what you never forget. The second clue lay in its evenness. The address looked like an exercise in symmetry—two fives, vertical axis of symmetry for W and horizontal for C. Finally, the abbreviation WC offered so much ambiguity, the vagueness being the main motif of our lives. Could we overlook the hints?

"Well, well, well," we roared, addressing our future healer. "Did you seriously think that we would give up so easy? Did you think that we wouldn't recognize you under guise? We are of the same kin, you and us. That's why we have so much belief in your powers. Fo-Fo is like Nouf-Nouf and Budo Budo. It's also like Alex and Alex.

"Our names are as much twins as we ourselves are. You tried to hide under no name. How lame was that? The game is over; you can step out. How do you do, Doctor Fo-Fo? Nice to meet you in writing."

Before the next wave of shame could wash us over and evoke compassion towards the motionless, deflowered notebook, we copied his entry to a page torn off from the wasteland of uninhabited Z.

Every new address is sexless and sterile. It carries neither scent nor taste. Odd and even numbers are evenly odd. We didn't know, not yet, that is, whether Fo-Fo's house stood alone on a hill or was townhoused by the neighboring Fifty-Three and Fifty-Seven. We didn't know if the acacia blossomed in front or the façade was pitted by the ruts of renovations.

The address book no longer useful, we slammed it and unfolded the map. Our own location was marked by a red cross, the pun of our therapeutic quest coincidental. It contained neither hint nor mockery—the red pen was the only writing tool at the disposal of the friendly bus driver, who gave us the map during our ride home after the ill-fated foray to the clinic.

We slid our hands along the map's creases, flattening dells and ridges of the paper landscape. What could 55 WC mean? Fifty-five wild coyotes, a wisdom castle, a water closet? Ha-ha-ha. I was too excited to concentrate on the search when Alex slammed down his palm:

"Here it is."

Across the town, away from its busy-bee center, the tiny letters marked a West Cedar street. Crafty, we admitted. WC, indeed. Marking the godsend street with a fat circle in a firm artist's hand, I connected X and O with an arrow. Just like our father's journey that disregarded natural and man-made obstacles, our dart pierced right through and hit the bull's eye—55 West Cedar Street.

"We could have guessed the address without Mr. Wild Chance," I said.

"Could we?"

"West signifies the direction of our lives' journey, and Cedar— isn't it the most majestic plant in the orchard of genealogy? All we had to do—keep one and one undivided and put two and two together."

"Very good, Watson!" Alex shook my hand.

"*Doctor* Watson," I corrected modestly.

The town in front of us, or to be more accurate, New Wye from the bus passenger's eye view, was delusive. Abundance of greenery disguised as parks turned out to be the cartographer's euphemism for cemeteries.

We embraced ourselves, circling the kitchen in a round of polka and laughing: heartily, peacefully, not concerned that an unfriendly ear might misinterpret our joy. And what kind of impassive person could blame us for our exultation? It was no more than a game in which, for greater credibility, we frowned, expressed rage, despair, sympathy. With the same sincerity an eternity ago, dressed in identical seamen's suits and white knee-highs, we held on to the swings' chains and screamed to Mother: "Higher, stronger, faster!"

That same evening we retired to the Mint, tightly shut the door—there could be no excessive assurance of safety—and spent the night in assiduous labors. Alex-artist was copying the tiniest of traceries, not in the smallest detail deviating from the local bill. I had little to do with the process but stuck around because from the very instance of our inception we had never been apart.

We dread mockery over our clumsiness no less than we dislike jeers over our deformity. That's why we work in secrecy, keeping the process of creation from strangers. That's why we raise our collar and lower our hood, that's why we live sideways, trying to conceal the slip of nature from the eye of beholder.

I was getting restless. "How long will *In God We Trust* take?"

Alex didn't respond, copying the miniatures of a foreign banknote and extruding his tongue in an indication of utmost diligence.

We woke up late. The sullen fog outside and the last night's fatigue had kept us in bed longer than usual.

"Is it Friday? Is it the thirteenth?" Alex rubbed his eyes. "What foot are we getting up on today?"

Slapping barefoot to the kitchen, we put the kettle on. The morning routine had always been special to us. Although no microscope was capable of locating discrepancies in our genetic masonry, although our memory was one and the same, there were several issues on which we never agreed.

Alex is artistic. He filters the world through emotions. He gets excited by autumnal colors and arrangements of puffy clouds in the sky, while I don't break for this bric-a-brac. What's even worse and what causes me to double up laughing is his obsession with health. Not its aspect which we intend to bring under the clinical care of Doctor Fo-Fo and not the one that baffled his acoustic namesake Phobus. I mean Alex's concern for our mutual metabolism and dietary qualities. We don't fancy flashbacks, but some time ago he went on the morning exercise pilgrimage, cold shower crusade and totally ridiculous, considering our constitution, jogging.

He would thrust the windows open, noisily suck in the night's dampness through his nostrils, spread out arms and take a couple of squats. I had no choice but to mimic him, nurturing my irritation rather than sharing his excitement.

"Isn't life beautiful?" Alex exclaimed, coming out of bathroom, clean-shaven and deodorized.

"Let's have breakfast already. I have a sinking stir in my stomach. The headache is about to return."

"That's because you don't care about your own body. Look at your lifestyle: wake up late, smoke, eat god knows what!"

"Stop nagging. I am sick of your moralizing. My lifestyle is the same as yours."

We were not quarreling or lashing at each other. That would be nonsense—wouldn't it, Doctor?—but our gastronomic attachments do differ.

Pseudo-wholesome stench filled the kitchen. Caring little for Alex's metabolites, I smacked a generous chunk of butter in the hissing pan, added three eggs, tomatoes, salt, pepper.

"What are you doing?'

"Stop bugging me. I always wake up hungry."

"Because of you, I have heartburn!"

"Because of you, I get headaches!"

"How can you eat so much fat?"

"Don't criticize my cuisine," I parried, hacking the sausage. "Your hay brew makes me sick."

After a perfect breakfast—tasty for one and healthy for another—I rinsed my plate, and Alex, with heavy sighs, put it back in the sink, sprayed soap and rubbed until he heard squeaking. We looked at ourselves in the mirror—a crisscross handshake of truce—one more time realizing that we can't be sulky with each other for long, and said out loud, in a synchronous duet:

"Peace, brother. We are ready to visit our Wise Cracker."

It was a beautiful day. How do we define beautiful? We don't enjoy sunshine, and it didn't. We love drizzle, and it did. Dank weather forced passers-by to imitate our own anonymity. Rare figures—heads drawn in, wrapped in mackintoshes, gender and complexion irrelevant—slid over the moist asphalt. In such company we were indistinguishable from kind female- and wicked malefactors.

The bus going in the direction of WC had a random number that offered no insights of its significance in the form of digital symmetry, like our birthday or another recognizable auspice. Apparently, the cosmos reserved some room for chaos.

We took an aisle and a window seat, wiped off the misted-from-curiosity pane and watched the moving but not touching scenery outside. Protected against the grayish city maze by the bus's weather-proof crust, we felt quite comfortable. The rain smeared the visual spectrum as if the townscape in front of us was painted in watercolor.

In dotted—from stop to stop—lunges the bus crossed the river, left the town behind and rolled into the quiet suburbs.

When getting off, the two of us, too wide for the narrow passage, brushed aside a sexless figure in a monochrome raincoat but voted against apologies. We needed no witnesses. Hushed by the rain, the curse behind us died away softly like pillow sobs.

This trip had more emotional than practical value. Forethought, like thriftiness, is alien to us. Alex and I are impulsive. Our motherland—swamped in slush or peppered by sand—is notorious for the spontaneity of its alumni. Although circumstances had severed our twin umbilical twine with town M, we never acquired the business-like mannerisms of the local land, and our hearts were always ready to tremble with premonition.

The drizzle was over, but dirty colors still prevailed. Alex inhaled ozone. I exhaled carbon dioxide and looked around, trying to make out numbers concealed by the wet leafage. Behind one of these façades, protected by pilasters, porticos and two identical fives lurked our savvy savior.

In a flash of the daydream, as innocent as it was lucid, I saw his luminous figure:

*As soon as Fo-Fo places his wrinkled palms upon our temples all ailments are instantaneously alleviated. We exclaim "Cured!" and the world regains its full palette from ultra to infra. And now that we are free, we shall say, why don't you, Doctor, show us your painting collection? I prefer crafts but Alex here likes arts, so what started as a formal doctor-two-patient relationship can grow into affectionate friendship.*

This would all happen later. As to now, we probably shouldn't be as frivolous with the future as skipping notches on the axis of time. Let everything take its course. Let our Doctor sit in his leather chair with brass pinheads, reading a case record, rubbing his temples with arthritic fingers, and scribble a surefire diagnosis with his fountain pen.

Pretending to be bored, we passed Fo-Fo's Five-n-Five—a house not much different from the commonplace suburban breed. A door, a window, a roof. Did we expect something unusual? At the next intersection we stopped. There was no point in trotting farther.

"Oh, this is the *West* Cedar!" The exclamation justified our indecision before an imaginary crossing guard. "We got *occidentally* dis-*oriented*, Officer, our map must be outdated. Never mind. We'll turn back now."

During the second pass, we took a closer look at the three-story structure marked by a crooked cherry tree in the front yard. A narrow alley through rhododendrons led to the porch. The dense shrubbery separated our dear Fifty-Five from the strangers' Fifty-Seven. The creeping ivy entwined the opposite side, leaving openings for a couple of side windows. The door had no name plate that disclosed who lived behind its centered—tailor-made for a Cyclops—peephole.

"On the first floor he has a living room," I fantasized. "His bedroom is on the third."

We imagined a pillow pile over an ideally made bed with polished knobs crowning its four corner pillars.

"His study must be on the second—the same floor where he keeps his collection of paintings and curios."

If only we could take a look at the interior! Just a peek, just for a second, just one eye each. Who takes care of him—his elderly mom or his peevish spouse? Where does he keep letters from grateful patients? It wasn't idle curiosity. Very soon our own note would crown his epistolary stack.

"What if we knock?" Alex circled a puddle.

"We may scare him off." I jumped over. "Remember the disaster with Phobus?"

My admonitions missed the target. Once Alex made up his mind, it wasn't easy to dissuade him. To tell the truth, I was no less tempted to cross the street, bang on his door with my boot—not a sign of disrespect but an ancient Roman custom—wipe our feet on his *Welcome* rug and barge in.

"What if . . . ," Alex's eyes sparkled as we passed the house for the third or fifth time, the odd count defined by our direction, ". . . we peek into his window?"

"The neighbors will call the cops, who aren't going to be ceremonious with two transgressors. In the hoosegow no one cares about profiles. They prefer their mugs *en face*."

"What cops, what neighbors? In this sleepy street no one gazes into windows. I mean from inside out. Let's take a quick look from outside in. Just a one-eye, one-time glimpse?"

One-eye! I giggled. What a hilarious joke! Alex's excitement was contagious. Another rain wave passed over, making puddles bubble up with delight. The street was empty. Supporting each other, we jumped over a stream and, within an eyewink, reached the target.

Sodden humus soil squelched under our feet—a subtle reminder of our native mud. Paying no attention to the sacrificed-in-haste daffodils and to the moisture permeating our shoes, we stretched up on sinking-down tiptoes and peered into the window.

The lights were off. The pane multiplied our faces like a mirror. The dry interior was faintly seeping through the wet window. We deciphered some silhouettes: a chair, a table, a cupboard. Were it not for our tense stretch, we would shrug—nothing special. But over there, higher, on the seventh heaven of the second floor, a dim yellowish reflection of the desk light oozed through.

"You are crazy!"

It is possible—although we have no formal medical education and would value Fo-Fo's professional judgment—that our mutual harmony is based upon distinctions as much as upon similarities. My tastes are refined and my hand, when it relates to paper, is firmer. However, whenever we need to take prompt actions, I lose presence of mind and become indecisive. Alex, on the other hand, is a minute-man, determined and resolute.

"Don't yell. You will scare off the prey."

"We can't climb vertical walls."

"Rubbish. We've done it before. There is nothing easier."

His hand found a ledge—a slight defect of the masonry. His leg bent. He pulled up his body and left me no choice but to follow. He was right, of course. With plentiful toeholds and our omni-tested tenacity, we could give odds to any mountaineer. Sure, we had done it before.

That dismal day, sprawled flat on the vertical plane, in a black cloak with wet folds glistening like dragon scales, we resembled a giant Siamese simian crawling up against the Earth's gravity. Alex was my King, and I was his Kong.

In pliant accord we held on to the squares of lath that supported the ivy. Taking turns like in the old game, I circled ouths, Alex marked crosses; I ticked tacks, Alex tacked toes; so, in the end, both of us could come out winners.

The vines held tight; the yellow light on the second floor was getting closer. Our well-measured breath puffed up two weightless clouds that flew up, maneuvering between water drops. Imagination, free from physical constraints, kept on drawing the pictures we were supposed to witness only moments later:

Accompanied by the pit-a-pat of our hearts, we shall look at him through the glass, tenderly like a mother views her paired—the opposite of *impaired*—newborns. Cautiously, so the squeaks don't disrupt his thoughtfulness, we shall wipe a peephole into Fo-Fo's dry world. We shall see. . . .

Our brief flashforward was interrupted in the most prosaic fashion. One of our hands, having already reached the sill, slipped . . . no, the hand was holding on, but the foot—down there, it was impossible to see whose—the sole of the soaked muddy shoe slid off. After that, our fingers, unable to bear the quadruple load, let go. The delicate equilibrium was ruined by uncontrived betrayal. The lath cracked and our *ouths* tumbled right on top of our *crosses,* crucified and nullified at the same time. Our helpless wings flapping, we plopped down with a dull thud. Sadly, it was no fairy tale for ugly ducklings to turn into handsome princes.

Thunderous heartbeat silenced the strengthening rain. The window across revealed a shadow of an old lady, her curious oculars reflecting flashes of lightning. Alex shook his fist, I extended my middle finger. We set off up hill and down dale, champing over the flowerbed. Heavy, smudged with dirt, our cloak quivered like the banner of a dishonored army. Oblivious of puddles and decency we hobbled along deserted streets. The universe turned sideways to us, its kindness screened by the streaming waters.

## Licking the wounds

At home. . . .

How inappropriate it is to use this cozy signifier for our transient abode, but for the time being we have to call the spade a spate. So. . . .

At home, at the very bottom of our mailbox, we found a small, very personal letter. Our hearts sped up but, as it turned out in a moment, in vain. The stamp was missing, and our chopped-off name appeared drawn by an unsteady senile hand.

"Hold your donkeys, old man," we muttered, shoving his note into our pocket. "Other things are rotten outside the state of Denmark." Were he around, had he been delicate by nature or impudent by nurture, he would back away into the shadows at the very sight of our piteous condition.

Our cloak escaped the adventure unscathed, although in need of a major clean-up. We dropped it on the floor and, leaving wet footprints, rushed to the shower. Dampness in our marrows reminded us of child diseases: cold, fever, sore throat; of hated by me but loved by Alex *Kapli Datskogo Korolya,* Danish King's Drops—a cough potion heavy with anise and ever-lasting aftertaste. We remember how Mother . . . no, that was a heartwarming story for another occasion. Put it aside for a tête-à-tête with our erudite vis-à-vis, Alex. Something was rotten, indeed.

The therapeutic impact of a shower can never compare to that of a steamy bath. Lie down, relax, rest all heads on waterproof pillows, close all eyes and allow coniferous essences to cuddle body and heal soul. Regrettably, the miniscule tub could hardly accommodate a medium-built loner, let alone two lofty dolphins.

We turned the hot handle to the full. The shower heavens opened and a steamy cloud filled the room, which was only fortunate, because I am conscious of my nudity like ante-apple Adam, while Alex—like Adam after quitting Eden with dishonors—is totally casual about it. Were it not for me, he wouldn't think twice of disrobing on a public beach and, not embarrassed by our dangling loins, enter the tide in full view of sunbathers splitting before us like the waters at Moses's command.

The steam, sharing my shame, built an impenetrable border

between us and our reflections in the rusted amalgam of the bathroom looking glass. I shivered. While scrubbing with the bast whisp, I stayed mindful not to trespass my personal terrain, especially the foothills of the no-man's land, beyond which my receptors' authority waned away.

In our youth, in the old days when Mother still carried the burden of our daily tending, among other poignant garbage dragged to this day by memory, we kept *plastilin*—little bricks of colored clay. When sculpting wax Golems, we had always put together two torsos and smudged the borderline until the juncture became seamless.

Now, I tried to be watchful and not to ruin the thin coating of the bonding epidermis with my overzealous cleansing.

The shower and shivers over, we dried ourselves into redness with two rough towels. Still enveloped in steam, we threw on a robe. Alex took his time, while I hurried to outstrip the quickly demystifying mirror. Then we threw our cloak to soak in the tub, now resembling a mud bath.

Rejuvenated, we combed our hair and childishly pushed one another to get personal audience with the mirror.

I:

"I go first."

Alex:

"No, I go first."

Both of us together:

"What the. . . !"

We stared at the reflection. Apparently, during the fall, we had sustained two scratches on our foreheads. The loyal mirror immediately offered proof of their congruence. *Do svad'by zazhiviet,* Mother used to sigh. *It will* indeed *heal before the marriage day.* The folk wisdom knew well that the world was self-tuning. Things would correct themselves some time soon.

We leaned on the sink to take a closer look at the wound, and I almost screamed from an awkward touch. A splinter from the broken lath left a deep furrow in my palm, competing with the headline and making me lose my composure.

When did it happen, why didn't we . . . why didn't *I* feel anything? Was it the chill outside or the adrenalin surge inside that took the edge off our sensitivity?

"Was that instead of a princess scratching the hand of her enchanter with a rose thorn?"

Either near-sighted Fatum had blinked or its far-sighted twin Fate had taken too long to adjust the focus, for the splinter had pierced my palm only in an asymmetry that always made us helpless.

"I can pull it out," Alex offered.

Blood doesn't bother him in the least, but leaves me alone in my squeamish unease.

I turned away, shut my eyes, gritted my teeth and, as Queen Victoria's manual for modest maidens on the wedding night suggested, got ready to pray for England.

"Stop fidgeting. I haven't touched you yet."

The wound turned out to be ill-fated. Not only was my headline ruined, but the membrane between the index finger and the thumb on my right hand—the very seating upon which the quill rested firmly like a coffin on a gun-mount—was now painfully swollen. The ploughed-up groove denied any possibility of attending to our bank-bill still-life hobby any time soon. Alex wrapped the bandage; I opened my eyes.

"Give it a couple of days. You'll be as good as new."

"The letter!" I recalled. "It's still in the pocket."

"Damn it!" Alex and I slapped our knees with our healthy hands.

Pulled out of the bathtub, the letter went limp; the ink lines inflated; the words were bloated beyond recognition. The old man's message, even if legible before, lost its meaning and blurred into ineffectual blubber.

Ah, we waved our left hands, who cares? The stupid note was the least important of our problems. He could always resend it.

The recent excitement turned into exhaustion. Without saying goodnight to our precious portrait (still rolled into a tube), we went straight to bed and, before the points of an ellipsis delivered us to Morpheus, lipped a silent supplication.

Oh, Fo-Fo, Fo-Fo, why are you hiding? Why are you shielding your presence from us? Have I done wrong; has Alex angered you? We are not your usual stalkers, you know. We seek help. What kind of help? Due to our constitution—the very feature we needed to see you about—we always have two points of view. Never opposite, mind you, as nature protected us from self-confrontation, but acute enough to get around flat obstacles and afford a three-dimensional disposition. Help us, Doctor. Rid us of ambiguity.

The sun didn't shine for the second day in a row. Something must have gone wrong with the celestial furnace, and the luminary re-treated behind clouds for an interim overhaul. Drizzle was spraying the town at inconsistent intervals. My hand nagged.

"We should worm into Fo-Fo's company through a back door," Alex suggested.

"What do you mean?"

Medicine men have always been a gregarious folk, he explained. Like birds of a stethoscope, they flock together. Laymen like us are never invited to their lodge. Should we knock on the gates, the grumbling voice would redirect us to the narrow slit of reception hours. Us—yes, but not one of their own.

"Do you remember what Julius Caesar told Mark Anthony? *Chercher,* said the Augustus in foreign French, *la femme.* Phobus had a wedding ring. Fo-Fo must be his family friend. They send each other birthday cards and attend brunches together. That's just how the plot works. If Phobus refuses to usher us in, we can make friends with his *femme* and let her introduce us to Fo-Fo!"

Thus, our strategy focused on two tracks—Fo-Fo's suburban sanctuary at 55 WC and the family of Doctor Phobus. When Fo skidded, Pho should take over.

We watched Phobus from behind two oak trunks. He left his of-fice and headed home, covered by an umbrella and ignorant of re-flections, in which one—a mindful and attentive one—might see a figure blurred to the point of numeric uncertainty, pretending to be involved in casual window shopping, in tying shoelaces or in whistling a carefree serenade.

After twenty minutes of a brisk walk our unsuspecting bait brought us to his lair—an apartment building of no importance per se, but a priceless contiguity point of our quest.

The elevator rattled up to the seventh floor. Seven—we would reflect upon the significance of that number later. No subtle intricacy should remain neglected.

Phobus—our *phabulous phacilitator*—was credulous like Mother Goat (grown up and matured after her stellar cameo in *The Hunchback of Notre Dame*), who left her seven kids unattended (there you go—the sacred, no longer secret, number didn't make us wait for too long) in the famous account of *goode olde* fairytellers William and Jacob, conventional brothers.

We followed *Phather* Goat upstairs and tiptoed to the door.

"Life flies by behind doors and windows, and we are locked out on the landing," Alex remarked. "Do you have the feeling that it's Love's birthday again or that Hope's mom strokes her cat. . . ."

Not only an artist but a philosopher!

"That's not the only feeling I have," I muttered.

Our exchange was interrupted. Sounds inside the apartment intensified, the latch clicked; we barely had time to back away. From our shaded hideout we saw two figures—a woman and a young girl. While they were waiting for the elevator, we took a moment to study them.

"You," I commanded, "watch the mother, and I—"

"*You* watch the mother," Alex snapped.

With one sad sigh and one triumphant grumble we went over the plain features: middle age, medium height, short dark hair, practical suit, sturdy pumps. There was little or nothing special about the mother, but the daughter, the daughter. . . .

Slightly taller than her mother, the girl was slender, stylish and so striking that Alex and I froze in awe. She radiated innocence and, what pierced our defensive effrontery, seemed very, very fragile.

*There was nothing special about the mother,*
*but the daughter, the daughter. . . .*

High cheekbones, pale skin, soft glance. . . . Envy, Paris, her face could launch more than a thousand ships.

A full minute after the elevator took them down, we remained chapfallen.

"I wonder if she has a conjoined sister," Alex finally uttered, coming back to motion but not to sense.

"I am sure she knows Fo-Fo," I said.

"We must impress her. We should shower her with gifts."

What could we give? What was our most valuable possession?

We didn't have to verbalize it. The portrait. What else? The portrait, of course.

But first, before bearing gifts, the Greeks needed to make themselves welcome.

"If only we could rid them of danger," Alex hemmed dreamily. "Do you think they have enemies we could destroy?"

"What if we save them from drowning? You haul the mother; I do artificial respiration on the daughter. They are trembling from gratitude, celebrate their rescue, make a reception and invite dear guests: *Uncle Fo-Fo, meet Alex and Alex we told you so much about. If it weren't for—*"

"Can you swim?"

Alex had a point. Our nautical advancement stalled at the famed photo in the seamen's outfit.

"The value of salvation increases proportionally to peril," he added. "The more threatening the danger, the more generous the gratitude."

If only we could save them from fire or other means of divine wrath—frogs, locusts and death of the firstborn! Unfortunately, those didn't happen too often nowadays. The opportunity could make us wait forever.

"The surest way to evade threat is to create one first," I suggested. "It'll be like a vaccination."

"That's right. Earthquakes and tsunamis are impressive," Alex mused, "but we can't rely on nature. We need an alter ego."

Yes—we could double in brass and manage split personalities, but split personas were beyond our anatomical abilities. To keep the world in balance, God created the devil. *We* had to find a villain. Where would two decent citizens search for a ruthless accomplice? Two don't find him in waiting rooms of medical facilities or among tourists with cameras yelping at bronze monuments.

The rain stopped. The dusk slid into darkness. As opposed to the indispensable sun, the moon was replaced by a squad of street lanterns without much detriment.

"The evening is lost anyway," Alex said. "I can't work with this swollen hand."

"Let's go to a bar. I could use a shot or two."

## Costas the Villain

As soon as we found Fo-Fo, we would tell him our story, sparing no secrets, bar, so to speak, none.

"That night," we'd begin the next chapter, "still in pain after the fall and anguish after the failure, after missing you by such a narrow margin, we decided to go to a bar."

"Anchorites heading to a public abode?" Rising tone, raised eyebrows. "Aren't you contradicting yourselves?"

No contradiction, Doctor Fo-Fo or Doctor Whoever-the-feck-you-are. We do prefer seclusion, where no one takes duplicates for duplicity. A jam-packed joint is perfect to preserve a joint incognito. We are immune to Bacchus's charms since we never drink alone. As a matter of fact, we do nothing alone.

The cloak still wet, we put on the garb of the dark palette, blending well with the night, and headed down the street.

"Oh my beers and whiskeys, how late it's getting!" we hummed, looking for a rabid hole. Sure enough, it didn't make us search for too long.

Not a rabbit's—the boar's head in the window bore its tusks posthumously. A neon sign was screaming some yellowish drink with congruous semblance of *draff* and *draft*, words and liquids alike. The worse the product, the more imagination its promotion required. I pushed the door, and just like Alice we found ourselves *in the long low hall lit up by a row of lamps hanging from the roof.* If only we could enter a house under the western cedars just as easily.

"No, no." Alex brushed aside a waiter whose neck arched in obliging, swan-like grace. "We wish to deal with a female attendant. Only feminine hands should touch our dishes."

Waiters are resilient creatures, and our earnestness didn't dispirit him. We proceeded to the far corner. The light hardly reached there. Dimness and positioning provided a strategic angle of aspect from which to study the visitors. Two glances—thus, no second opinion required—confirmed their plebeian upbringing.

"Leaning on elbows is a no-no," Alex commented. "Someone should teach them etiquette."

I observed the males' tartan shirts and steel-toe shoes.

"Local fashion isn't very demanding."

We could guarantee that everybody, including those with their backs to us, had the initial stage of periodontosis, malocclusion and bad breath. Their girlfriends, also made in one image—nature didn't burden itself with variety here—had identical hairdos, with identical locks falling in identical curls.

"What kind of mothers will they make?" Alex wired in a rhetorical question. I didn't bother to reply.

"Hello, my name is Mareena. I'll be your waitress tonight. What would you like?"

Bemused by our thoughts, we hadn't noticed her coming. Dressed in black, with raven, undoubtedly dyed, hair, she kept looking at me and Alex, at Alex and me.

The contrast of her pale, almost bloodless face with the bright makeup made her look more attractive than the plain ninny she most likely was in the daylight. The pen in her hand impatiently jerked, but her eyes stayed shielded by professional amicability.

She tilted her head aside—silent for *Well?*

"Well," we began in a mandatory preamble, "a chance brought us here. We had a rough couple of days. This injury," a bandaged hand on the table constituted exhibit A, "unsettled our nightly routine. We'd like to start with two orders of the indigenous ale. Let it be bitter, as that's how we feel tonight. The choice of appetizers is yours; we are tired of making decisions."

"Something hot, spicy?"

"Whatever."

She turned around and we followed the sway of her hips, even though it hardly contributed to the advance of our storyline. She must have been somebody's Love or Hope. Had we ever watched a girl with so much melancholy? Long-gone sights of *nasha*[2] *L'ubasha* and *nasha Nad'usha,* whether retreating or approaching, used to produce expectation, anticipation and joy. Present gloom was but a side effect of youth slipping through our fingers; through the injured fingers that at the moment weren't capable of handling a paintbrush.

"How about some cherry liquor?" Alex had to say something to shatter the sad image.

No, I declined, somewhat annoyed by his damsel taste. No. We made a good choice. Tart ale was very appropriate now. It defined the inner state of the main heroes, harmonious unity of their external and internal qualities, as Mrs. Silver had taught us in her class of vernacular literature, when heart-wrecked heroines jumped off the cliff or drowned in the pond of their own tears.

"Here is your beer." She paused to watch Alex and me take two hearty sips. The drink instantly inspirited us.

"You said your name was Maria?" we asked. "It's a first-rate, cultural-laden name. We used to like two Marias—Maria Rilke and Maria Remark, two Teutonic knights of verse and prose."

"It's Mareena," she corrected. "Enjoy."

Two hearty gulps, and we smacked the emptied mugs on the table.

"Bring us more, maiden Mareena."

Where were we? Oh, yes, the pond of tears. With all those ripples in the water, no wonder the willow was weeping. There was

2. *nasha*: Russian: Our.

nothing to cry about, sister *Alyonushka*; Alex and Alex weren't going to drown like your brother *Ivanushka*. He shouldn't have sipped the porter from that brook. You lost him, *Alyonushka*. Instead, two hothead Hansels, who kept losing one Gretel after another, sat in a bar waiting for the concoction to dissolve their woes.

How could we be such romping dunces? Things were going smoothly until we committed a pair of tactical boo-boos—one per Alex. First, we made complete fools of ourselves in the clinic; then there was this unjustified and ineffectual climbing escapade.

Mareena came with more beer.

"Don't walk away," we said after supping from one tankard then from another and wiping the foam from our upper lips. "We thought about your name. Cognomens and sobriquets are our forte, you know. Our dish du jour. In a faraway land, the one that rejected our affection with affectation, your name is quite common. Here, however, in this town that knows neither sand nor slush, it sounds atypical. The connection is unequivocal—we were unwanted there, you are unwonted here. Did your parents bring you here as a child? Compatriots should help each other out, you know."

She smiled again, this time with a glimpse of sincerity.

"Sorry to disappoint you. I was born here. My parents gave me such a humdrum name. I always wanted to change it. Don't you like that sound—Mare-e-ena? It's very romantic."

We tried to hide our disappointment.

"Explain no more, Mareena, the maid from *Mare,* the merry mermaiden. We are familiar with cognominal worries. We dig you well. For a very long time we also had to make alterations until our names fit like a custom-tailored doublet. We are stereosyllabic namesakes; you can call us Alex and Alex. We need help and have nobody else to ask."

I didn't realize that Alex had been grabbing her hand until she pulled it back.

"I have to go. If you need anything, call me."

"Wait! Forgive us. Yes, we need something. We need a lot. Blame our accent. We meant *liquor,* not *lick her.*"

251

While we were internally rephrasing the question that bothered us, she was gone. Once again, both ends of the dialog were solely in our hands. Or heads.

What were we about to ask? How would we phrase it? You see, Mareena, we search for an assistant, a chap of trust and determination, to whom we, tongue-tied strangers, can disclose some sensitive facts. As appalling as it may sound, there are things that go beyond our abilities. Yes, we are two. But occasionally, not often, but once in a wild while, a need arises for us to be in different places at the same time. If Professor Tulchinsky were as much help as he believed, we would have developed this ability a long time ago. We need—*como se dice* in the local gobbledygook?—a collaborator.

"The girl is no help." Alex pushed his empty tankard that nearly tipped over the edge. "Forget her. We can read faces like Morse code. Let's take a walk, look these bastards straight in the eye and find a proper blank stare."

Emptied mugs—two, four, six?—and topfull bladders offered an excuse to get up.

"Johnny Walker meets Johnny Sitter. Pardon, pardon. Gardyloo!" Slightly unbalanced, we were hitting against human and chair backs.

A minute later Alex and I squeezed into a narrow door at the opposite corner. The stall was far from spacious, built with no consideration for abnormality, outsiders and outsizers unwelcome. Having clicked the latch, we took hygienic turns, and I poked good-natured fun at Alex's diffidence.

"Help, hold, zip?"

He rejected my assistance. The task was well within his coordination, he snapped. As you please, I shrugged. Neither of us felt offended. What's an innocent joke betwin the tweens?

While washing my hands, conscious not to splash the bandage, I asked Alex whether it was indeed *Ivanushka*, or some other dimwitted brother from a Grimms' tale, who drank from the brook?

My memory is no weaker than that of Alex. Uneven arrangement of our oddity is physically unfeasible, but, as an artist I enjoy fairy tales, while he indulges in thrillers. In need of a solution, I bring to the table a thesis; Alex counters it with antithesis, and together we achieve the union of synthesis. Isn't that how you define the summit of evolution, Doctor?

We winked at the mirror and giggled. Did we have too much to drink? Whether a side or frontal effect of ferments, the light-minded joy overwhelmed us. We kicked the restroom door wide open, nearly hitting a heading-in bruiser.

"Move, bro." Our tongues maneuvered like synchronized swimmers. "Don't sweat. Uncle Alexes aren't gonna hurt'ya."

The next confrontation was just as snappy. Freeing the way, the singleton moved his stool, drew his head into shoulders and kept quiet. Good boy!

The third dolt, however, refused to back away. Slowly, he rose from the chair and began rolling up his sleeves. Although width-wise fearless Alex and Alex held a definite advantage, height-wise he towered over us.

"Who the hell do you think you are?"

"Ha . . . ha. . . ," we burst into splatter. "We'll tell you what we think and who we are. Which name do you prefer to hear first, our *nom de plume* or our *nom de guerre*?"

The commotion attracted interest. Everyone weather-vaned towards us. The humdrum died out. A chair fell on the floor; we didn't bat an eyelid.

"Please," we heard from the black-n-white blur in the corner of our eyes—pale Mareena with dark hair, her Yin appealing to our Yangs, "please, don't make trouble."

We rotated.

"You have a *dolce voce*, dear Mar-Yin-a. Do you sing? Do you rhyme rhythms? We'd love to hear your canticles one day. Don't worry about us. This barbarian deals with noble knights!"

Alex *hicked*, I *cupped*.

The hulk roared something, but we didn't strain our hearing. Instead, we waved airily—let's take it outside. Holding an imaginary torch, we paraded towards the door.

"The exit is over there," we heard Mareena's relieved descant.

What could her real name be? Ugly, huh? Elza, Zelda, Lezlie. . . . We made two one-eighties on our heels, and switched directions like a deft sergeant.

Once outside, the breeze cooled the rouge off our cheeks. The dropping temperature caused a faint hissing sound. The Attila grinned, and we registered his pock-marked, narrowing-at-temples snout. He was delightfully hideous. Good choice, Alex, good choice.

"Over here." His phlegmatic knuckles pointed to the lawn. "It's not gonna hurt as much when you bang your head."

Alex grinned.

"Hold your knickerbockers, giant man. If you care about apologies—there, you can have them. We didn't mean to offend you. It was a test. You handled the pressure well. We needed to talk to you alone, just the three of us."

He stared at our profile. His knuckles were still white. He grumbled.

Think, Alex, if you don't want your asses whipped.

"The thing is. . . ," we had to hurry up—who knew how long it would take for his mental flywheel to slow down? ". . . we are strangers in this strange land. We are looking for an accomplice. We mean an assistant—strong and determined, someone we can rely on. The two of us, whether you can see it or not, are not enough. We need the turd man."

He made a step forward, and whatever intoxication we had left evaporated: what if his brain failed to cross over the hummocks of our accent? Did Alex harden the *th* again?

"Ah-ou-ah nai-mz a-a-a Ah-leks and Ah-leks!" We pushed the articulation lever to the top. "We have a business proposition for you. Be-e-ez-nez! What is your name, braveheart?"

"What do you care?"

"We have a proposition for you. Would you like to hear it?"

"Well," he grumbled, "I guess. I'm Costas. But be quick."

We exhaled with relief.

"How appropriate. Konstantin, Constantine, Costas." The signal was coming back—every villain in our life was properly labeled. "Your namesake was an emperor, did you know that? A very noble man. We can't give away details prematurely. That's bad luck, you know. Not that we are superstitious. Not at all. We even whistle inside at times, which is as sacrilegious for our folks as keeping an open umbrella in the house is for yours. We intend to save a girl, and we shall grandly reward our helper. For the sake of instant understanding, let's say that we are due to get an inheritance. Look at our profile. Does it remind you of a certain royal kin? You are not going to be disappointed. What do you say? Are we going to be friends?"

"I'd rather kick your butt."

We didn't lose our composure. Time had taught us patience. It also taught us that everything had its limits. For a split second we contemplated dashing for dear life. However, neither Alex nor I fell for such a risky move. Our chances in a sprint were even slimmer than in a fist fight. We resumed our verbal wiles.

"Costas." When pronounced out loud, the aggressor's name always soothes him. "Listen, Costas, we are outsiders here in both geographical and social senses. No friends, no connections. We offer a dime for a penny-worth of assistance."

His eyebrows crawled up, corrugating the coarse leather of his forehead.

"How much?"

One of our healthy hands pulled out a crisp bill prepared with love and artistic—surpassing its nominal value—care.

"This is just an advance. Keep it. Here is our address. Our local abode is modest, unbecoming to the descendants of . . . never mind now. For the time being, we have to keep low, albeit noble, profiles. We are glad that our judgment of your judgment has proved sane. Congratulations. Let's go inside and celebrate. Our treat."

He didn't move, still blocking the way. Ay-ya-ya! What a specimen! Larger than the two of us.

"There," he muttered. "No coming back. I haven't decided yet.

You should be lucky to stay in one piece."

What could he know about staying in one or two pieces?

"We should commemorate our treaty by drinking *Bruderschaft!*"

A blank stare.

He had no clue about *Bruderschaft*, we realized, that most glorious of German words. According to this tradition two males entwined hands in a lock-like tangle and drank simultaneously; after this public intimacy they switched from formal *Sie-Sie* to informal *Du-Du.*

"I'll think about the treaty. Get lost now."

The Genghis Hulk pushed us away, then made a small step towards the lawn, bent down and smacked his enormous fist against the ground, which went vibrating under our feet as if from a distant earthquake. Not looking back, Costas pulled open the door. A blinding ray split the world into light and darkness, and this time it wasn't as good.

"Wait," we pleaded in a constrained duo so that our voices would edge through. "Over there, on our table, we left some chicken wings and a barely touched bowl of curly fries. You don't have to fetch them yourself. Ask Mareena to make a doggy bag. There was also some ale, bitter, but still. . . . If she can pour it into two of something . . . paper cups will do nicely. We shall stay here, in the shadow."

He didn't wait for our ramble to finish. The door slammed. We huddled. Our internal hearth started cooling off. Just in case, Alex stepped aside, into obscure night nothingness, beyond the oval of the squeaking street lamp and the leftovers of light seeping through the windows. I followed. Of course, I did.

The cloak would be handy until the bar mermaiden brought the knapsack. She liked us, that little sea kitten, that *murr*-maid. We trotted back and forth along the façade. It was damn freezing. After five or ten minutes the door was thrust open. We rushed forward, but, instead of Mareena, a merry couple stumbled out, embracing so tightly that an unscrupulous passer-by could easily have confused us and them.

Stars above winked from behind clouds. Inside the pub, the rude clodhopper must have been washing down our chicken wings with ale from our mugs, wiping his nail-bitten fingers against his denims and showing off in front of his convives by weaving verbal cocks and bulls.

## STAGED ASSAULT

The buzz woke us up. What? What time is it? Where are we?

"What do you want, old man?" we screamed, coming to our senses. "We are not ready for you now. If this about your letter, leave the note and go away."

The door let through a few muffled syllables and trembled under a powerful bang, which our landlord could have produced only if his whole body had forcefully smacked against the gate.

"Hold it! One minute. One second."

Alex pulled the bathrobe's tippet over our heads. Still unsettled from the day-old night's escapade, we nestled close to the door.

"If you search for the portrait, we know nothing about it. It's a mistake. We've never seen it in our lives."

"It's me. You said you were gonna pay. Over there, in the bar."

A trick, a trap, a tramp? One could never be two cautious.

"What bar? How do you know where we live?"

"This is Costas. You gave me the address, remember? Needed some sort of help, you said. I didn't kick your butt."

The images gradually oozed through the thickets of sickness. That's a relief.

We straightened.

"Of course, we remember. We never forget anything we see, sew or say. We shall let you in, but beware. No irresponsible jokes. We are particularly proficient with the cane—self-defense is our life-long fancy."

The latch clicked, the hinges screeched, the staff was at call. He walked in, lowering his head dominated by a heavily armored brow. Blundering about in obscurity—we never turn the lights on in presence of strangers—he shuffled in.

"This way." Our stick pointed to the hallway. "We don't invite strangers to our living room and prefer to meet them in the kitchen with washable tiles."

We put the mirrors down to take away his manifold viewpoints, and offered a seat facing the window. He looked around while we examined him, considering whether he was a good fit for a dismal assistant. All right, Alex whispered to me, go ahead, tell him. But it was our guest who took the lead:

"Then . . . there . . . at night . . . don't hold a grudge. I am a simple man. Sometimes I get a bit agitated. I mean I don't recall beating the shit out of you. This piece of paper in my pocket . . . I sort of remember the conversation. Sure, I says, some dough wouldn't hurt. Why not, I says."

We turned the faucet on and took two gulps of tap water.

"Here is the story, Costas. Here is what we are looking for. Nothing criminal. A trifle, an artistic performance that would be rewarded royally. Or rather, with royal generosity, because we don't expect you to recognize our profile."

He nodded slowly, his brain convolving.

"We shall pay later, post, so to speak, Fatum. You have our two words."

He fidgeted on the chair, the weak wooden legs of which, unaccustomed to such burden, creaked sadly. Carefully selecting adverbs, we informed the Gargantua that his involvement was going to be purely formal. We could have easily managed the whole affair ourselves if the script didn't require the use of strangers.

". . . because we can't play the roles of a rogue and a redeemer in the same scene. That would make a farce of our poignant performance."

He agreed more from desire to get the loot at any cost rather than from understanding—his name was *Cost-us*, not *Understand-us*. We continued:

"The dramatization—its reasoning utterly irrelevant at the moment—is intended to present us, me and Alex," palms pressed to our chest, "to the best advantage. Let's say that our hearts are not indifferent to the virtues of one princess. You generate the danger, we degenerate it, she leads us to a certain famous doctor, incidentally, an art collector. As simple as that."

His lone cranium was spinning in confusion. We went down to business:

"Here is the plan. . . ."

Alex made a quick sketch: a web of streets, a riverfront of the shallow local offshoot, a boardwalk with circles marking a streetlight, a streetlamp. A windrose in the upper corner. We shall be standing here, dreaming over the rippled river amalgam. Here, pattering her heels from north-east to south-west, moves she. We should have said *she moves* but, first of all, our native tongue, the imprint of which is ever fresh, allows reordering of words, and, second, the emphasis fell on the predicate, not the verb.

Slow down, I signaled to Alex. He doesn't get it.

Here is another circle. We pointed. The full moon is essential. It welcomes premonition and creates romantic mood. There you go. Beautiful. It must have been the same full moon, supervising the first and only meeting of our parents a lifetime ago in a faraway land, which would be a nice cross-reference if it didn't go way over your head.

"What's her name?" Costas asked.

"Don't concern yourself with names," we said firmly. "Names are for the playwrights' use. Anonymous characters of the *twi*-light drama will meet here, at the X. You," we pointed at Costas, "will need two more goons."

"I can handle anybody alone."

"No one is going to handle anything without our orders. Single combat is never as impressive as the struggle against outnumbering dominance."

The question of incentives apparently bothered Costas the Profiteer, and we assured him of his allotment of thirty pieces of silver. And as a bonus, we added, Alex may paint your portrait. Full-length, noble posture, diamond order on the jerkin, a palm-tree, a column, a sailboat in the background. We are pretty good at portraits. It'll come later, as long as we are happy with your routine. How do you like that?

". . . and, by the way, before the extras participate in our . . . um, project . . . we have to approve their candidatures. We could care less about their performing skills. Our own talent will illuminate the scene twofold. Once we even captured the imagination of an audience clapping so thunderously that the fake cathedral came tumbling down."

He mumbled something impatient, and Alex cut the reminiscence short. We returned to the shambles at hand. Three little villains, Costas included, had to exude menace. Verbal tap dance the likes of *Would you be so kind?* and *Don't mind us* is banned. Sarcastic modulations are welcomed. Slang, filler words and grammatical errors are acceptable. We leaned forward:

"Your thugs should have facial imperfections—a bloth, a twitch, an eye patch."

"I am not a criminal, you know," he said. "I thought it was easy money. I don't want to break the law."

"All right," we conceded, "the scars can go. But we insist on foul miens."

"How much?" He looked about our shabby interior with the peeling plaster and a fly smashed by Alex in a minute of boredom.

Did everything in this world have to be about money? Backs to the window, we buried our faces in our palms and sighed. A wave of inspiration crashed against the utilitarian rock.

"Apparently, we can't ask too much from you. If you're in for the money and nothing else, then we are truly disappointed. We offer you an opportunity to express yourself, to find a fit for your inner artist, but if *how much* is all you can think of, then our cooperation might be severely undermined. This is fine. We are not offended. Keep in mind, though, that we won't paint you either. Let the critics rave about somebody else's portrait. We shall throw our pearls elsewhere."

"The critics?" he echoed.

Everybody has a soft spot. Cowards dream of a Purple Heart; spiritual paupers of a laurel wreath.

"Museums and critics," we confirmed. "No doubt in that. All our works are going to find proper places in art collections, making their subjects famous. But, since you decline—"

"I know two guys just like you need."

That was better, so much better.

"Very well. Have your fierce assistants handy—two grim reapers or twin *grimm* brothers. Staging and choreography are on us. We shall assign the time with cosmic precision. And remember—battery is prohibited. The assault is going to be mental and, therefore, ideal. We shall personally script your soliloquy."

Before we delved into specifics, Alex handed him the bill that I had finished a few nights before, a precise and accurate handwork, one of the best. Yet another act of mutual trust and free will, we declared.

He nodded, absorbed in his assignment. We smoothed down the table surface with our palms. Bread crumbs tickled our mounts of Mars. We pointed at the plan.

"Your goons will stay in wait. The streetlamp will sway, snatching your silhouettes from darkness. You, the leader, will grin and stretch the vowels in an ominous baritone: *There, the-ere!*"

Looking straight into his eye through the little mirror in our hand, we demanded:

"Repeat."

"The-re, the-e-ere," he mumbled, any trace of expression missing.

We jumped up, made a nervous step towards the sink and splashed our cheeks with cold water. That night in the bar he was so impressive, managing to scare us even if only for a few brief seconds. Now, his pathetic threat couldn't electrify a neurotic.

"Try again. Frighten her. Alarm her so that the world sparkles at her nerve fibers. Then, when she's desperate, enter we. We shall say *Go away, you scoundrels!* or something to that effect. A choreographed combat will chase the offenders away, like the Nutcracker chased away the Mouse King. Justice is restored; the girl is saved; you get your portrait and a little something for the best supporting role. Just don't thank the Academy."

261

He blinked. Here, we circled two more spots, your assistants will *pant* their *mimes*. Are they gap-toothed? Missing incisors create an appropriate frame of mind. Untidy attire alarms, impeccable manners terrify. We needn't go this far. *Who are you?* she exclaims, stepping back, along this dotted line. *What do you want, evil persons?*

"Instruct your blokes not to answer questions. Just smirk and bellow."

What's next? Our experience was limited to a single theatrical production, to climbing up the Notre Dame and screaming *Esmeralda, Esmeralda!*

"The-e-re," Costas rehearsed coarsely, "the-e-e-e-re! Then what?"

Then we jump onstage. We mean, onto the boardwalk. The waves crash against the concrete pier; the wind howls. The sound effects impress one no less than their famous dramatic equals—a knock at the Macbeth door and axes hacking down Chekhov's cherry orchard. Back off, bastards! we exclaim, outnumbered but valiant.

"We may have to be verbally unceremonious," we explained further. "The epithets, you see, create the scene's emotional background, like gathering clouds or wuthering heights. We don't mean to humiliate you. Authors, so that you know, love their antagonists more, because negative traits allow better demonstration of artistry."

Get up, we gestured. Time for dramatization. Alex and I shivered, pretending to be a fearful prey. Go ahead. Your turn. *Nu?*

He faltered, still uncomfortable in his role, and swayed, hitting against the cupboard. China skeletons tinkled inside. Careful! we screamed. Mirrors!

"The-ere," he said, "the-e-ere."

Ah! We pressed an imaginary handbag to our imaginary bosom. Who are you? Why are you? Please don't hurt us! We mean, don't hurt *me*, the lonely girl.

He paused, staring into the blackness under our hood. Alex and I jumped aside, showing that now we were we:

"*You three bastards! How dare you?* Wait, no. Don't you dare with three exclamation points. *Don't you dare!!! Back off. Leave Maid Marian alone. Otherwise your ass is grass.*"

Beautiful in this authentic outburst, we admired our translucent glimpse in the windowpane.

Overcome by his role, Costas grabbed and pushed us against the wall. We flapped hands. A glass fell, smashing into smashereens.

"Enough," we puffed. "Let us go. The kitchen's too small. Not bad, not bad. Now we make the end run, a loud smack; you tumble down in any fashion you fancy. Use your intuition and crawl back into non-existence. Your involvement's over. We support her and say some dignified words in compassionate tenors. Oh, she says, you are so brave! You saved me. How can I possibly repay you? Would you like me to introduce you to Doctor. . . ."

Costas rolled down his sleeves and sniffed. We handed him the plan. Study it. Learn your dumb show by heart. We'll see you in darkness. He wavered. What? we asked, still invigorated by the forthcoming victory.

"That portrait. Where do I get a jerkin?"

"Don't worry about the particulars. Entrust everything to our imagination."

# Fairy (Part 5)
## Ten Years Later

THE BOARDWALK DRAMA

"Aren't you interested in where Fairy and I went today?" Sophie asked after dinner.

Fodor leaned back as she cleaned the table, preparing to serve tea.

"Please tell me where you and Fairy went today and what the doctor said and how he looks just like Santa," he repeated obediently.

Sophie smiled like a student who knew the answer. They took a cab, she said, it was a light drizzle today, and you know how Fairy dislikes all kinds of precipitation, especially with the wind gusts, and today the wind was so strong that they had to take a cab, because it started raining, which you might not have noticed because you spent all day in the clinic and didn't even go out for lunch. . . .

"Hello, Doctor." Sophie couldn't help the slight insecurity when entering his office. "It's us again."

She let Fairy have a seat, looked around in search of another chair, found a stool in the corner and settled quietly so as not to interfere with the examination. Don't mind me, she smiled, you two go ahead; ask your questions, Doctor; say what you say every time—*What a big girl! How old are you now? Sixteen, is it?*

"Fairy is turning seventeen next month," Sophie volunteered, unable to maintain a neutral stance. "She was this tall when we came to you for the first time. Such a bright girl! Doctor didn't even have to explain to us how to put the pyramid together. Remember that, Sweetie?"

Doctor, who was supposed to be paying attention to Fairy, observed Sophie in the reflection of the wall mirror.

"My brother," he began slowly, "I mean Doctor Santer, has decided to retire. That will not affect our patients, of course. I am familiar with his cases and will continue to provide the same high level of expertise and attention. As to confusing me and him—don't apologize. Many people do. Although we aren't twins, the semblance is remarkable. You can also call me Doctor Santer."

Sophie didn't take her eyes off the well-trimmed off-white beard. This was all irrelevant. When was he going to talk about Fairy?

"Time flies, doesn't it?" he continued. "I wish someone would come up with a recipe for how to tame it. Tame time . . . hmm . . . yes. As to you and your daughter . . . Fairy, right?" An awkward *ugh-ugh* was shoved into his fist like a magician's handkerchief. Sophie eagerly nodded. "You have to stop worrying about her. Her . . . condition should no longer be a concern."

"I am very proud of her," Sophie shared happily. "Other teenagers are a nightmare for their parents. I have a friend, you see, not very close but we have known each other for a long time. She used to work in my husband's office. Her daughter and Fairy played together when they were kids. This Kate just ran away with her boyfriend. She is barely eighteen. Can you imagine? Poor Isabella. My girl would never do that to her mommy, is that right, Sweetie? My husband, that's who worries me sometimes," she whispered, then leaned back and said in a casual carefree tone, "Faye, dear, would you mind waiting outside while Doctor Santer and I have a talk?"

Sophie closed the door and returned to take the girl's seat.

"You see, Doctor, life seems to be flowing downhill now. Fodor, my husband that is, often doesn't notice Fairy, and I have to remind him to kiss her goodnight, to make her a tea, to talk to her. It's a weird sensation that he just crossed her out from our lives. Ever since Fairy's surgery—it's going to be ten years in November—I feel like we are missing something. The family is falling apart. It's either Fodor and me or me and Fairy. Instead of looking into the future, I can hardly hold on to the present."

265

Doctor Santer—or his twin, it didn't matter—closed his eyes, concentrating. A siren flashed behind the window, a phone rang on the receptionist's desk. Signs and sounds boasted a busy pulse of life as it should have been, rather than the life in which Sophie once again sat quietly in the sterile office waiting for the stern verdict.

"My brother," Doctor began, stretching the vowels, "should have had this conversation a long time ago."

Sophie's face paled, and he quickly continued:

"You don't need to come here anymore. It's not because I have a double load now. Not at all. It's just that I can't do much for you . . . or for your daughter. Let her go. Maybe your husband is right." He consulted the file. "Ten years is a long time."

"I just want Fairy to be happy, . . ." Sophie began.

"Let's talk about you for a moment. What makes *you* happy?"

In a nervous motion Sophie smoothed her skirt. This simple turn caught her by surprise. While the doctor got up, checked the waiting room and gave low-tone instructions to his secretary, Sophie stared at the pyramid assembled to perfection by one of local overachievers. She was married and, although whatever great passion Fodor and she had shared initially had become a bit time-frayed, it could be considered a plus; all hopes and frustrations of the past—a minus.

How would she tell Doctor Santer (*who may only pretend to be his own twin to get rid of me*) that her life seemed like a story told in the helpless seventh grade vocabulary? Many important subplots were ignored and what remained often lacked intensity and passion, mischievousness and imagery, adjectives and teasing. Her world was severely under-rendered. What did Sophie and Fodor look like? What was that smell in the air? Was it a mixture of city dust, sweat, perfume, flowers? Was this building made of gray brick with old gargoyles mesmerizing people, or was it a tasteless modern carbuncle numbered to avoid postal puzzlement? Did she fly here, nested in angels' wings, or had she just pulled the handle and stumbled in?

Life couldn't be only about weather and digestion. There must be love and hope and daring adventures and Prince Charming.

What else? She continued the math. Oh yes, security provided by Fodor's job was a plus. Frequent headaches—a minus. Another plus, another minus. The signs alternated, summing up to zero, but this absence of value, which constituted her life's joys and fears, wasn't as formal as the formula suggested. And, whatever anybody said, the most important part—Fairy—was a definite, unequivocal plus.

She got up from her chair.

"You can't apply impersonal logic to human life. I think Fairy is prettier than every other child. Did you know that she calls you Santa? She is sweet and warm and tender, and her hearts beat without missing a rhythm. She is my reason and my purpose. She makes me happy."

"Well. . . . When the time comes, we leave our children or our children leave us. It happens sooner or later. I wish it were as simple as commanding Lazarus to get up. Some things are beyond our control."

". . . that's what Doctor said," Sophie concluded. "He didn't even find the need to check her heartbeat, and that proves that Fairy is fine."

Fodor sat straight, rubbed his palms, then hunched and grumbled something like *m-m-m* or *uh-h-h*, reluctant to return to the sore subject. Sophie's elated disposition deflated him.

"I think," he finally said, measuring the load of each syllable and starting with weightless placeholders, "I think that you, you and Fairy that is, should reconsider those visits. Fairy was a sweet petal, but Doc's right—time to let her go. What happened to her is neither your fault nor guilt. We both knew that her two hearts were a rare condition. It's an anomaly which doesn't let life last very long. The surgery only had a marginal chance of success. The double heartbeat speeds time downhill. You can't push the truth away forever."

He got up and walked over to Sophie, who had frozen next to the sink, water falling and splashing, falling and splashing, falling and. . . .

"Do you hear me?"

She wiped her hands with precise and deliberate motions, then hung the towel onto the oven door's handle and looked at her husband.

"You give up too easily. It's our family, and we have to stand by each other. You can't choose me over Fairy or without her. What kind of a parent would look at the broken lifeline on the newborn's palm and say *I'd rather not invest in love and hope. What's the point of caring for someone who isn't going to last very long?* It was no fluke that we called her Faith, because faith conquers better-guarded fortresses than the discord of two hearts."

He hesitated for a moment; then, as if rejecting some inner unease, embraced and kissed her.

"We shall all go to bed now," Sophie said quietly like a teacher who had just skillfully circumvented a clash with rebellious youngsters. "Tomorrow will be another day."

The morning indeed brought a new day. Sophie watched closely so that Fodor wouldn't forget to say goodbye to Fairy before leaving for work, and relaxed seeing that the peace in the family was restored.

"Men are so insensitive. Don't pay attention to what your father says sometimes. He doesn't mean it. He is a dermatologist and doesn't understand much in heart matters. Come here, Flower. Let mommy kiss you. Did I tell you that I love you so much?"

She hugged her daughter.

The rest of the day took on the routine tranquility. They watched Nanny fuss around the kitchen, helped her with dishes, dusted the portrait.

"And now, let's go for a walk."

The first streetlight got stuck on red. Sophie had no destination in mind and decided to accept whatever clues the little switches came up with.

"We'll follow the lights' green brick road." She found it funny and cast a sidelong glance at Fairy. Did she get it?

"Here is the rule—we take the first green of the intersection and cross either the street or the avenue. I don't want to impose my will on you any more. Let's see where life wants to take us."

At first life seemed indecisive. Sophie, firmly grasping Fairy's hand, held on. After two blocks eastward to the art museum with a big sign for the upcoming exhibition, the streetlights bethought and brought them all the way back.

Soon, despite a few unnecessary turns, the plot—devised by winking and blinking but otherwise inanimate objects—became clear. They passed the theater district ("Last night of *Les Miserable!*" No, no, Sophie shook her head, one scare was enough) and approached the *Terra Pedestria* of the riverfront. Traffic lights retired—cars dipped into the tunnel, and for a while Sophie and Fairy needed no more illuminated supervision.

"Remember that old man who used to paint the bridge over there? No? It must have been too long ago, when you were this tall."

Fairy didn't retain small memories. Sophie herself was terrible when it came to remembering childhood. Even adult years contained mostly blank spots and preserved no continuity, disintegrating under the mind's touch like an ancient cloth. She often had to commission dreams to darn over emptiness.

"His easel stood here, and over there—" her hand pointed at an unremarkable spot "—we settled the next day with huge sketchbooks upon our knees. Yours kept sliding off. Oh, *now* you remember! I thought we'd be drawing a landscape, this hunchback bridge, the river, but you did one of your bizarre portraits instead. I confess—my sketch wasn't particularly high-class either. Watching other people paint makes it seem so easy. I am sure you had a lot of trust in me. The river is so beautiful. We should come here more often."

Sophie raked her past for something special to tell Fairy about. Something they had shared before and would cherish later. Oh, yes, once, when I was your age, an old gypsy walked over. You don't see them around nowadays. She had very kind eyes. Don't worry, she told me, everything will have a happy end. Isn't it a charming story?

The wind grew stronger and kept changing directions. The sun, troubled by swaying treetops, became concerned with its spotless reputation and dived behind promptly huddled clouds. The first overweight drop—a scout of the approaching storm—tapped Sophie on the shoulder.

The water surface below turned from a blank sheet into an endless succession of commas supplying synonyms—rain, drizzle, shower, downpour, cats and dogs. Like embittered beasts, the waves now snarled and darted into the river's stone cast. The vivid became the livid. The boardwalk emptied.

"We better hurry," Sophie mumbled just to say something—there was no need for verbal confirmation of the obvious—but, instead of picking up the pace, she halted. The darkness in front of her condensed into a monster menacing by its silent immobility among the universal trembling, zooming and howling.

"Please, let us through," Sophie said with magnified firmness and finesse. "My daughter is a delicate child. We have to avoid cold temperatures and emotional chills. We would be grateful if you'd lend us your umbrella."

The figure made no sign of retreat, keeping them naked under the skies, which started dousing the town with ice-cold splashes. Sophie's stomach tightened involuntarily. She took a step back and spread her arms, protecting Fairy. A rustle of a different kind than that of the storm and wet leaves made her look back. Two creatures crawled onto the boardwalk, blocking their escape.

"I will scream," she advised them bravely, but the wail of the wind shouted her down.

"There," muttered the monster, "there."

He grinned, and the black gap of his mouth terrified Sophie. How is Fairy? Is she all right?

"Who are you, immoral people? What do you want?"

The smirk widened and, as the villain leaned forward, the stench of his unkempt gingivitis scalded Sophie.

"There, there," he repeated.

They were surrounded—brutes in front and behind, prickly bushes and troubled waters on the sides. The two remaining directions, that of the stone-paved, impenetrable earth and soft but unattainable heavens, offered no hope. People were long gone. Only a miracle could bring salvation.

At this very moment, when Sophie shielded her daughter and shut her eyes, ready for the worst, another bidder entered the scene. Out of nowhere, a broad figure covered from top to bottom in a cape grew up between the women and the ringleader.

"*En garde!* Back away!" The cane flicked like a foil. Faster than raindrops, the staff lunged forward, and Sophie heard a muffled thump. In the twinkling of an eye the criminal diminished to a heap of tatters. His henchmen behind didn't wait for a personal invitation, but vanished as swiftly as they had materialized a minute ago.

"Milady, mademoiselle, the danger is gone."

Sophie squinted to make out the features of their savior, but the hood pulled low, and the collar pushed high, fenced in the face.

"Who are you?" she asked again, the irony of repetition, first in alarmed then in the relieved clef, unbeknownst to her.

Their rescuer turned sideways. His voice, slightly echoing in the wind, was reassuring and deep.

"Our names matter not. Not yet, that is. We understand what it is to suffer as we have often suffered ourselves. We are happy to protect two beautiful ladies and request nothing in return. Should the circumstances be fortuitous enough to bring us together again, they should elect a more auspicious setting. Until then, *au revoir, au revoir.*"

With a reverent bow towards the river—the hood's trim tipped ceremoniously like a hat's brim—the figure retreated. Sophie saw a blink of the tiny mirror. In another moment, she and Fairy were alone. Any evidence of good or evil had been washed off the blank canvas of darkness.

She barely had the strength to get home. Chilled to the marrow, she trembled with a residual shock that haunted her like a smash hit tune. Ignoring Fodor's questions, so irrelevant post factum, she entrusted Fairy to Nanny's care and locked herself in the shower. *There, there, there* kept thundering in her head, and she had to turn the faucet to full hot to drown the drum. She didn't know how much time passed. Mechanically responding to the pounding on the door, she put on her bathrobe. At the next instance of brief consciousness she cuddled under a blanket and a plaid and gestured to have something else on. A coat, a tartan, doesn't matter. I am freezing.

"Is Fairy all right?" she whispered.

"Don't worry about her now." Fodor left and returned with a steaming cup. "Drink this. You'll feel better."

"Nanny should tell her about a prince coming to the rescue. The girl is very perceptive; convince her that it's normal, that life is like a fairy tale with an inevitable happy end."

Fodor put a wet towel over Sophie's forehead. It went dry instantaneously. A terrible suspicion overcame her. They were running in circles, somewhat like a large scale clock-face. The notches on the way were marked not with dates or numbers. Instead, everybody was passing from one scene to another until the variety was exhausted and the patterns started repeating themselves. What was Directrix saying about the beginning of Fairy's life? Her mother was dead, scared by a mugger. Wasn't it precisely what they went through today? The loop closed. Physically they came out unharmed, but it didn't matter. Something more valuable was fatally damaged. Even their savior considered it unnecessary to reveal his identity. His own cycle was still unfolding while theirs came to its conclusion.

Fodor didn't understand much about her condition. He was a dermatologist for God's sake. He called a physician, a friend of his. They sat by her bed and, although her ears were deaf and her eyes shut, their words found a loophole in her armor and oozed into her mind. These words later buzzed and echoed in the hollow insides, making a lot of noise but very little sense.

The top of the bedside table filled up with vials standing not according to rank like uniformed soldiers but rather like discordant pirates. Sifted through their colored glass, the daylight blinded her with a flurry of rainbows. While Fodor was gone, Nanny with her never-finished embroidery sat in a chair by the bed and kept telling her never-ending stories in the language that only Fairy could understand. All that mattered was the sound of Nanny's voice—not the storyline, not the moral if it indeed was there, not even the meaning. For the first time Sophie realized what Fairy was so enchanted with, although, if asked, she wouldn't have been able to phrase it.

"Faye, Fairy," she called, "did Nanny tell you that story before?"

After the fever went away, she stayed in bed for another day, alarmed each time the door's lock clicked or the clock chimed.

"How about we take a walk and sit in the park for a little bit?" Fodor suggested.

"The three of us?"

"Yes. Yes, of course. If you want to. The three of us."

Sophie paused. No, you and Fairy go ahead, I'll stay home. Wait, no. Don't let Fairy go. It's not safe.

Even though Fodor assured her that there was no danger in spending a half-hour on a bench next to the pond, among other people, Sophie shook her head. She was afraid of her discovery about the full circle. He wouldn't understand. It was a woman thing.

## The House in the Suburbs

Sophie didn't feel like going outside, because . . . just because. Three women—Fairy, Nanny and she—sat by the window in full view of the portrait's eye. Crisscrossed flowers on the tambour, casual about mixing seasons, remained in eternal bloom. Sophie couldn't quite identify whether they were cow-wheats or pansies or willow herbs. The little meadow under Nanny's hand belonged to a different land, just like her tales that didn't offer much of a storyline. It was the purling voice that carried listeners away.

The clock ticked.

The lock clicked.

"I have a surprise." Fodor beamed from the doorway.

Was it all a dream? Had she fallen asleep?

"Did I fall asleep?" Sophie asked Fairy. "What time is it?"

"Let's go," Fodor said. "Right now. The cab's waiting."

As usual, Nanny expressed no interest in leaving the house. Sophie followed her husband downstairs. Before stepping outside, she
stretched her neck to look left and right, and only then, having noticed no suspicious shadows, let Fairy walk out.

She dived into the back seat and slid to the center between Fodor
and Fairy. The driver—a balding, full-mustached *muzhik* with a
coarse accent—must have been Nanny's compatriot.

Fairy had seen the city many times, but Sophie leaned over and
commented on the views all the way until they crossed the bridge—
not the cozy hunchback appropriated by pedestrians, but further
down the river, where the waters widened and the joggers' boardwalk yielded to the screeching docks. This is our park, this is the
museum, that's the concert hall, remember?

Fodor kept giving scrappy directions to the driver, relying more on
his finger than on the Cossack's familiarity with the verbal windrose.

Once the river was behind, the city's stone and glass gave way to
the low suburban shrubbery. The turns seemed to Sophie like a maze.

"Where are you taking us?"

"We are almost there." Fodor stroke her hand. "You'll like it."

The car stopped. While Fodor searched his wallet for the proper banknote, Sophie looked around. Human presence was hinted
upon visually but not audibly. Their cab was the only rattling appli-
ance on the whole street—as foreign here as its driver's mustache
and stubble were among clean-shaven city dwellers. A few cars,
quite casual about oh-so-precious parking spaces on the other side
of the river, were dozing off in front of sparsely spread houses.

"What do you say?"

The cab puffed a final farewell and was gone, leaving them next
to a crooked cherry tree. Fodor waved a friendly greeting to the
windows across the street. The narrow passage led through the rhododendrons to a three-story structure, the ivy entwining the walls
with its tenacious tentacles.

"I think it's lovely. Do you like it, Fairy? What is this place, Fodor?"

They came up the steps and, after some ineffectual wrestling with the lock, he pulled the key out and stared at it.

"I am sure this was the one. Why won't it fit?"

"Father is going to climb into the window," Sophie whispered, suppressing a merry bubble.

"There! I thought I was going crazy. Come in, come in. It's not exactly a *dacha* but for the summer much better than our hole-in-the-wall.

"One of my colleagues," he explained, "—wait, you know her— she gave you the address of that agency. I told her what happened and she offered to let us stay here as long as you wish. Very kind of her. Her daughter just got married. Did you know that? She doesn't use this house anymore."

Sophie cautiously moved through the first floor, to the kitchen in the back facing a small but welcoming backyard. So, this is Isabella's house. That's where her Kate spent summers. How could she let her go?

The floor squeaked slightly. The space was a little damp and dusty as expected after the human warmth had aired out. A fat spider stared at them from the ceiling fan. Tulle curtains turned off-white just like Santa's beard.

Three bedrooms on the second floor, Fodor indicated.

"I could use one as a study. Ever since you annexed my library I've missed it. And this room—" he pushed the next door open— "you can make Fairy's. What a beautiful view, everything's green! Some change from the city-gray, huh?"

"What about Nanny?"

"Yes, right, Nanny," Fodor grumbled. He thought that . . . well . . . a lot of time had passed and although she kept going like Scheherazade with her yarn, they didn't really need her assistance any more. "I mean, Fairy has . . . grown up and sooner or later will move on. . . ."

"No," Sophie interrupted firmly, "Nanny will stay. We needed her before, now she needs us. And where do you think Fairy is going to go? She can't leave us. That's impossible. We shall all live here. I like it."

Her voice gained commanding tones. He had found the house; now it was her job to make it cozy and keep the family together.

"In that case," Fodor said, stepping out of his future study to the small square lobby and pointing upstairs, "there is one more room." Sophie resolutely marched up.

"It's too high for Nanny. Fairy, honey, you don't mind taking the top floor, do you? See?" She kissed Fodor on the cheek. "Everything works out just fine."

She checked cabinets and wardrobes. All personal entrails were gone; bare hangers dangled like skeleton ribs. The old tenant had left only a faint unidentifiable whiff.

"I love old houses." Sophie tested the springs of the couch in the living room—the only remaining fixture. "You are not afraid of ghosts, Fairy, are you?"

"I doubt there are any here." Fodor shrugged. "This is not a medieval castle. We are only half an hour away from the city."

"That's too bad. I am sure Nanny would know how to talk to them. I'd love to hear their stories. I never imagined that I'd enjoy leaving the city. Now I realize that this is what's been missing. Look outside, Fairy, isn't it a beautiful linden?"

"I think it's a poplar," Fodor corrected.

"Since when do you know trees? As soon as we move in, I will learn all the wonderful secrets of turf and bugs and wildlife."

"I am not sure there is much of wildlife here."

"Oh, there is, there is. It's one thing if you are high above the ground in a stone cell over the tarmac streets but something else if you are here—one with nature." She switched to a low voice. "Fairy needs it even more than I do. I hope that this change will do her good. Did you see how she touched the cracked railing and that old doorpost?"

Fodor, they decided, should remain in the apartment, coming here for weekends, because the commute didn't make sense with his busy schedule. Sophie would arrange for the furniture and other necessities. The beds, of course, received the highest priority, the least importance being assigned to the study.

"You don't really need it right away."

A moving truck stopped next to the cherry tree. Two porters, tangled in straps like trained Saint Bernards, unloaded embryos of future comfort. Supported by Sophie, Nanny disembarked from the cab and watched the scene, leaning on her walking stick. A small bedside lamp in her left hand weakly wagged its cord, unattached to the life source.

Fodor, in the role of the preoccupied traffic controller, gave orders: living room, upstairs, upstairs, kitchen, that stays here for now. After the bed headboards, chairs and the dinner table, all wrapped in paper padding, found their proper places, Nanny's wrought iron chest was dragged out of the crate, causing a flurry of sparks every time it scratched asphalt. In times of pirates, of Croesus and *Open, Sesame!* such coffers contained treasures. In Nanny's case the contents were reduced to old rags, odds and ends of life in the foothills of its final exhale.

Things new and modern readily conformed to the relocation, shunning door posts and not brushing against walls. Old things resisted.

"Careful," Fodor commanded, as the heavers tried to trick the three-dimensional constraints and squeeze the chest through the narrow approach to the staircase. Sophie peeked inside and quickly stepped back.

"Let men arrange it. We shall wait here," she explained.

In a few minutes Fodor appeared, purple and perspiring.

"It doesn't fit. We'll have to leave it downstairs."

"Are you sure?" Sophie felt confident that she could solve the juxtapositional puzzle and allow the chest to take its place in Nanny's room upstairs. Fodor had never been inventive when stuffing the refrigerator with dinner leftovers.

In two hours, the entire load was relocated and arranged inside.

Wraps and straps were discarded. Apart from the coffer still settled in the corner of the living room as the winner of the combinatorial hustle, and a few scratches on the wall as evidence of human defeat, the house was ready to host life.

"I'm sure we are all going to enjoy it," Sophie announced cheerfully. "Go up to your room, Fairy, see if you feel comfortable."

The floorboards squeaked, but, contrary to the clanking of city neighbors, the sound wasn't irritating. Nanny ignored the armchair offered to her and settled on top of her indispensable treasure trove.

"Is that how you used to live in your old country, Ra-Ri? Isn't it just like a little house in the woods?"

The evening went in the unusual neglect of senses. As opposed to the city with its never fading lights and ever shrieking sirens, the new shelter enclosed all signs of existence within its four walls—after the sunset the outside went mute and blind.

# Exhibition

"You aren't going to forget Fairy's birthday *this* year?" Sophie said with feigned austerity. "It's too bad you spend so much time away. I know," and she waved him off, forestalling Fodor's protests, "work, work, work. You should see the girl's anticipation. We have to do something special this time."

Rather quickly, after the turmoil of relocation and settlement, after the helplessness of looking for the proper aisles in the local supermarket and shelves in grocery stores, life in the suburban refuge entered its cruising course. Sophie was happy to see that Fairy enjoyed fresh air and quietude as much as she herself did.

Nanny, on the other hand, seemed to give up. It was ridiculous to imagine that she could be affected by separation from her chest now anchored downstairs. Instead of offering a hand in their domestic mêlées, Nanny needed assistance herself. Some days she wouldn't leave her room, staying in bed or looking out the window from her rocking chair. As the flowers on the tambour blossomed to completion, the pace of her stories slowed down, not that Sophie was involved in the plot—rather in the flow of words, whether wise or nonsensical.

Led by Fodor, who promised a whole day of leisure and fun, Sophie and Fairy boarded a bus and arrived at the terminal with the crowd of committed commuters. The human torrent picked them up and loosened its grip only after splashing them out onto the square.

"I love the energy of the city," Fodor declared.

"This is how many people come here every day," Sophie explained to Fairy quietly as she took Fodor's arm. "So, what's the secret plan for today?"

"Let's spend the day like tourists—casual and careless. We'll wander about the curio shops and galleries; we'll ask locals for directions and stop by a chance restaurant; we'll be open for enchantment and immune to disillusionment."

Sophie happily squeezed Fairy's palm and whispered, isn't it wonderful? Isn't your father charming? "Let's buy something immediately."

"What do you want to buy?" Fodor asked, smiling.

"Doesn't matter. Here, look at this brooch, no, no, that necklace. What do you think, Fairy?"

The woman in a shawl held the mirror while Sophie tried the necklace on. She guessed citrine and quartz but then raised her eyebrows in hesitant uncertainty.

"Amethyst," suggested the woman.

"This is gorgeous. Let's pick one for you too. What stone is this? Do you like it, Fairy? Try it on. Beautiful. I love it."

"Which one would you like?" the woman asked. The mirror in her hands, once slightly turned, released Sophie's twin and sucked into its reflection the eclectic miscellany of the street.

"Both. This is going to be for me, and this one for my daughter. We all have a reason to celebrate. It's her birthday and our anniversary. Never mind the bag, we'll put them on."

Proud of her loving husband and her lovely daughter, Sophie

paused before the next window to admire their translucent trinity. I feel much better now, she thought. I am not afraid anymore. The fear is gone. Even though there might be some people who wish us harm, there are always more of those who come to our defense. Good unavoidably defeats evil.

Fodor leaned over and kissed her on the ear. And, Fairy, Fairy too!

"How could I miss that?" he laughed.

Sophie glowed. Strangers on the street and vendors in little booths were smiling at the family at the height of its bliss.

"Look!" Fodor exclaimed.

A huge poster at the Art Museum announced *Faces*—an exhibition of portraits by Leon Samorodok.

"Do you recognize the name?" he asked.

"Is he one of your colleagues?"

"The Monster. L. Samorodok is the artist who painted it. I am sure that's him."

Sophie had never liked the painting, although she had gotten used to it and stopped flinching when passing its attentive stare in the living room; but she didn't want to mar this dazzling day with objections.

"Would you like to go?" Sophie asked Fairy, then announced firmly: "Today we do everything together."

Fodor hopped up the stairs and pushed the heavy revolving door.

To reach the exhibition hall they took the staircase to the second floor, the path indicated by arrows—up, left, straight ahead—to the far wing of the building, pompous like a royal bedroom. On their way, hardly keeping up with Fodor's impatient gallop, Sophie breezed past other visitors—soft, respectful, so unlike the energized crowd out on the street.

If Fodor had any doubts about the artist, they vanished as soon as they saw the first portrait. No question. The same hand brought their monster to life. He turned to Sophie—isn't it great?—but she missed his joy, watching Fairy's eyes mesmerized by meeting the kinfolk of her favorite painting. I guess, Sophie sighed, there must be something about these works. Am I the only one who doesn't understand that art?

The life's depiction around her was driven to the extreme, stopping just short of crossing the edge of reality. Large, portrayed at the extreme close-up, the faces carried ambiguity in every trait—age, gender, morality. Like the ink blots that Dr. Santa once questioned Sophie about, the choices were too many. Fodor had mentioned that technique, some fancy word translating as *trick the eye*. It must have been this very trick. Do these eyes look *at* you or pierce *through* you? Is that a concealed sin or an overstressed virtue? Do these features radiate wisdom or reflect insanity?

The visitors whispered their way from frame to frame, bending to make out small-font inscriptions and stepping back to add a newly learned spice to the visual delicacy. Whatever the portraits were telling others, they turned mute as soon as Sophie challenged them to a dialogue. How could these inanimate, oil-on-canvas strokes compete with life? Are they looking at Fairy or at me? Do they notice that we wear new necklaces? Can they see that she is my daughter?

The questions were many, all unanswered. Sophie gave up the guessing game and simply followed Fairy—being next to her felt more important than adjusting to the twisted unreality of the art. In a world blurred and distorted around sharp-focused Fairy, the difference between visitors and portraits became obliterated, neither concerning nor bothering Sophie.

Suddenly, the sound of her name surfaced above the humdrum. Fodor was beckoning from a far corner with animated gestures. Before moving towards him, she made sure that Fairy was nearby.

"Dear, let me introduce you to Mr. and Mrs. Samorodok."

A tall man with deep grooves, marking his years like tree rings, shook her hand. His wife appeared much younger, soft and pale as if drawn in pastel.

"I was just telling Leon—or you prefer Leonid?—about his Monster, how much we love it. Now that he is famous—no sense denying it, my friend—the buzz and raving add a touch of investment appeal, which never hurts."

The artist acknowledged the flattery with confidence, picking the truth essential in the truth spoken, and tossed back his salt-and-pepper hair.

"What about you? How do *you* like these works?" the artist's wife inquired politely, setting up a woman-to-woman locution.

"I. . . ." Sophie searched for her personal azimuth, then gave up and took an easy detour: "They are very nice."

"Nice is not how you usually describe art," Fodor laughed, casting a sideways glance at the artist, and Sophie had to come up with something less elusive:

"My daughter likes them too."

"Your daughter? Is she here?"

"She is. . . ," Sophie waved her hand in the indefinite direction, "somewhere there. I am not much of an art person, you know. I am not sure what all these people see staring at the pictures for so long. I can't tell much about these faces you paint. Why are they so ambiguous, so vague? Are they real people?"

"Give it a few years, and these paintings will be more real than the people they have portrayed. And isn't life itself vague and ambiguous? I don't want to impose my views on anybody. I just reflect. You are free to take sides," Leon chuckled. "At least that's what the critics are saying, and they better know."

"I like certainty," Sophie objected. "Beauty must be good, ugliness—evil."

"That's an attitude." Leon gave no further judgment.

"The world is becoming smaller," Fodor noted philosophically to take them off the dangerous turf. "When I bought Monster I couldn't even expect that the globe's rotation would arrange for our meeting."

"It is indeed peculiar and very fortunate. Monster is my only work, I mean major work, the trace of which was lost years ago. The gallery only knew that it crossed the border. *Which border?—We don't know.—Can you find out?—We are not sure.* I had already given up. You wouldn't mind if I borrow it for my next exhibition? Not for long. It's not my desire to separate such a happy union."

Fodor beamed. He produced his business card, mewing about pleasure, about responsibility to humanity, about the arts belonging to the people. Any time, dear Leon, any time.

The crowd around them grew, all vying for the artist's attention. A stocky bearded man, undoubtedly a painter or sculptor himself, was wrinkling his forehead and clutching his chin. A reporter, her notepad atilt, was warming up her lips with mute lines, ready to jump into the conversation at the first opening. The audience granted to Fodor by the virtue of his Monster started wearing off.

"Give our regards to your daughter," Leon's wife offered as a good-bye.

I will, Sophie nodded, I will. Where is she? Fodor, do you see her?

They found Fairy in the next hall.

"Guess who we've just met! The artist who painted your Monster! Would you like to meet him? You don't have to do it now. Father gave him his card and, I am sure, we will hear from him very soon." Sophie giggled, squeezing Fairy's hand. "He wore loafers with no socks, can you imagine?"

"Should I have asked Leon about purchasing another work?" Fodor mused. "I may become a collector."

Sophie made no comment, and he didn't wait for one.

"Careful," she said to Fairy once the family was back on the street, protecting her as if she was still a little girl. "Yellow means wait even if you're late! Remember? You don't know what's on these drivers' minds."

The day was so bright, Fairy's hand so warm, and Fodor's arm so supportive that the monsters of Leon's imagination and of Sophie's own past couldn't shadow them out of the museum's halls to the riverfront. Lighting, not lightning, converted the ominous scenery of the recent incident into an innocent site.

"See the bridge?" Sophie murmured, snuggling up to Fodor. "That's where you kissed me for the first time. It was way before your time, Fairy. Remember what you said to me then?"

"Must have been something smart. Let me guess. That the pope's title pontificate means *Keeper Of Bridges*?" he ventured.

"Don't try to fool me with your smooth talk again, because *I* didn't forget. You sighed and said that you had to start some time." Sophie paused. "If I hadn't wanted that kiss so much, I'd have slapped you. I am serious." She laughed.

"My memory doesn't reach that far back. Didn't you kiss me first?" Fodor's cheeks puffed.

"Don't listen to Father, Fairy. He is too ashamed of his indecisions. Let's walk up there."

From the gently sloping hunch of the old viaduct they looked down at the streams of water below. A clot drifted underneath the bridge. It could have been a flower astray from its bunch or a letter turned into a ship for little paper Argonauts. Sophie squinted, fighting off the glare of the descending sun, then suddenly shivered. In the corner of her eye an image, fleeting like a thought, flashed by. Indistinct as one of those fuzzy ornaments from the backdrop of Leon's portraits, it had no direct affiliation with good or evil.

The unbefitting cape vanished as quickly as it had appeared, if it had appeared at all, wiping off the moment's enchantment. Approaching dusk picked a darker palette.

"Are you hungry?" she asked, prime needs always the best excuse for retreat.

"I am starving. Boy, is that a cute necklace?"

## Mount Olympus

Twilight shadows didn't paint their entry quite yet, but the street illumination had already tiptoed on. Having toyed with reflections of the happy family earlier, the shops' windows now showered no more compliments and flashed their entrails instead.

Sophie cast a quick sidelong glance. Was Fairy all right? Had she spotted the figure in the cape? Fodor with his typical male insensitivity couldn't be trusted.

"There." She pointed at the steps descending to the basement. "This seems like a cozy place."

Fodor read the name off the green awning.

"I thought you didn't like Mexican food."

"It doesn't matter. I want to sit down."

"Table *para* . . . ?" inquired a man in an ill-fitting shirt and an oversized sombrero. His fake furnishings were balanced by a thick, well-cared and quite genuine mustache.

". . . *para tres.*"

The caballero ushered them past the sparsely populated coat rack and past the steamy passage to the kitchen, dissected the hall, and stopped at a round table by the window. The restaurant's semi-submersion opened on a tangential, ground-scanning view of the street. People's top halves were non-existent. Hips swayed without torsos. Feet clanked in open defiance. Those bulky bluchers and crepe-soled boots could belong to anybody. In the shoe vanity fair, toes crunched and clutched, loafers paraded. Sophie fidgeted.

"Do you have another table?"

"What's wrong this?"

"My daughter and I, we don't like being too close to the window. The detached feet outside make me uneasy."

"This menu?"

"Not menu. We are uncomfortable here. My daughter would like to change the table."

The caballero retreated to return in the company of another man—stockier, similar mustache, tight collar, no hat.

With occasional askance looks outside, Sophie began saying that she had nothing against Mexican food or culture. She looked at her husband for support. *Carne, serveza, agava.* Fodor shook his clenched fist in a friendly *no-pasarán.* His wife, he explained, want-ed to move. How about that table over there?

The toreadors shook their facial fungus in unison. *Imposible.*—Why?—Because, you see, *Señor y Señora*, we don't serve that sec-tion now.—Serve it then.—No, no, we had a leak on the first floor, and the pipes need to be brought to order. *Señor* likes order?—*Señor* and, especially, *Señora* don't like window seats.—*Señores* celebrate something, maybe?—As a matter of fact, we do.

Outside, two pairs of twin boots exchanged a quick tap—heel-nose, nose-heel. Sophie took a step away from the window.

You see, *Señores* (the picadors broke into a smile), this is our best *celebración* table. Perhaps, *Señora* is here for the first time, but we sing serenades. *Besame, besame, mo-o-ucho.* . . . Julio has such a *dulce voz.* We strum a guitar and clasp castanets and this table has room and the sound is not hushed like in the back where pipes are hissing and the restroom door is banging. *Señora* likes music, no?

"I don't feel like fajitas any more," Sophie said. "Fairy, honey, let's find something else."

In a matter of a few awkward minutes, disastrous for diplomatic relations with Mexican food, the heavenly illumination outside had completely surrendered. Pale before, the streetlights now gained confidence and glowed like fireflies. Sophie cuddled in Fodor's embrace while not letting go of Fairy's hand.

"I remember a nice place," Fodor hummed pensively as if his statement was suspended on the question's hook. "Greek. It should be around the corner."

His memory must have shuffled the deck of images like a card sharp. They made three or four tentative turns before his triumphant *Aha!*

Sophie was no less relieved—this time they ended up above ground. Beyond the outer fluorescent shell, the hall was bathed in warm light accompanied by the clanking of china and silverware. The pianist had just collapsed after the culmination of his finger gallop, and Sophie, not yet settled, joined in the sparse applause. The gap-toothed piano keyboard was grinning with delight.

The waiter handed her a menu.

"Oh!" Her joy restored, Sophie exhaled lightly and put it down unopened. "I'm not that hungry anymore. I am just happy. You two go ahead. I'll decide later."

Another waiter with the chef's steaming specialty zoomed by.

Sophie followed him with her eyes, admiring his nimbleness, choreography and gaiety of gait. A second later, as if jinxed, he tripped. Dishes on his tray trembled and took off like a flock of turkeys scattering helter-skelter across the floor.

Sophie frowned at the giggling Fairy, but couldn't stay serious herself. The chime of shattered china made heads turn in their direction.

"Look who is here!"

Leon the Artist was waving at them from the big table half-concealed by the fake Doric column.

"Come, come," he insisted, nodding. "Join us."

After a short exchange of pings and pongs in the likes of *Are you sure?—Of course, we are sure!—We don't want to impose—You are not imposing,* they relocated, carefully stepping between smithereens.

A round of introductions ensued.

"You have already met my wife, Nadezhda." A nod, a smile, a return nod, a return smile. "This is her *cuisine.* . . ."

Her cousin, Sophie corrected automatically.

". . . Nad'usha's *cousine* L'ubov' and her husband Pyotr."

"Call me Peter." The man shook Fodor's hand. "Two hard consonants in a row are awkward." Broad shoulders, wide jaws and an old scar crossing his forehead gave away his strong character.

"And this," Sophie announced proudly, "is our Fairy."

"Your names are beautiful," Fodor courteously addressed the ladies. "They translate well. Names often give away what people really are—you must truly be Love and Hope for your men. Happy to meet you."

"We were in your country many summers ago," Sophie shared politely. "I loved the churches, nesting dolls and amber necklaces. I heard the winter was beautiful too."

"Snowdrifts and snowflakes," L'ubasha confirmed.

"Too much slush." Peter winced.

"They just oversalt the roads," Nad'usha explained.

The humdrum of food's life cycle filled the hall. The waiter orchestrated a controlled Champaign explosion.

"A toast." Leon lifted his glass. "For the day of fortunate encounters!"

"We can add to that." Fodor wrapped his arm around his wife's shoulders. "Today is our anniversary. . . ."

". . . and Fairy's birthday," Sophie added, stroking her daughter's hand.

She tried to summarize all improbable flukes chained together by a concession of chances—Fairy coming from the same place as Love and Hope, the portrait sharing Fairy's birthday, Leon and Fodor meeting each other at the exhibition. Wasn't that the climax of a story, when all the characters came together? No, she decided. . . .

No, not yet. Life isn't one of those stories that Nanny is weaving. Life often goes without a high point. It flows like a river. They are just nice people who met after a long day. No, she shook her head again, just a salad, and yes, champagne, please, I'll have some.

"We can let Fairy sip a little," she giggled, her joy sparkling.

"How come you know the meaning of names?" Peter asked. "*Vy govorite po*—?"[1]

"Unfortunately, not a word. I would love to, of course, but it's such a difficult language. My wife tried once and even bought a phrase book. That was a long time ago. Now everything but a few words is safely forgotten." Fodor used the pause to pin an olive. "L'ubasha and Nad'usha," he mused. "Love and Hope. Did you have the third cousin?"

Peter, who was rolling breadcrumbs into spheres, mentioned that their own meeting in this town was, in fact, yet another happenstance, if one cared for the complete list of coincidences. They had no idea about Leon's exhibition until passing the museum on the way to his . . . I am on a business trip, you see, and L'ubasha was kind to accompany me. . . . So, there was this huge poster, and we stopped by to look at the paintings. We haven't seen each other for years.

"A business trip," Fodor repeated politely. "What do you do?"

1. *Vy govorite po-*: Russian: You speak. . . ?

"Oh, you know, little things here and there. Nothing as exciting as the personal exhibition of mister Big Shot."

"Just a little bit," Sophie warned, lending her glass to Fairy.

"Funny you should mention it." Leon wiped his mouth with the back of his hand—a spontaneous gesture tolerated in kids and geniuses. "I never thought about ascribing any special significance to the names. Come to think of it, my art didn't get much attention until I met Nad'usha."

"What about you?" Sophie looked at L'ubasha and Peter.

They both laughed.

"Love from the first sight."

The conversation sparkled like Bengal lights—as soon as one thread burned out, another blazed up. Reddened from the food, Fodor tilted his head.

"Dear Leon, let me ask you something. You create these bizarre works. I mean, in a good sense. They are unusual. I mean, I like them, but, you have to admit, they are a tad unconventional. What do you think people see in them?"

Leon leaned to kiss his wife.

"I don't know what I would do without Nad'usha. She told me not to worry about other people and to trust my own muse. You are my muse, darling. As soon as I stopped just painting and had my brush tell stories, the luck was no longer standing sideways. It turned and looked at me face to face."

The pianist returned from his break, took a moment to saddle his bench and tried a few keys like a bather testing water with an outstretched toe. Wine vapors nourished everybody's exultation, justifying kindred etymology of spirit and spirits. Everybody was tipsy.

"What kind of story were you telling in the Monster?" Fodor reached across the table and didn't let Leon's sleeve go until the artist noisily inhaled, ready to sculpt air into an answer. The first puff was somewhat similar to the pianist's warming-up notes. Then he was on a roll.

"I am a tale-teller. My stories are made of images. Any attempt to render them with words is not going to be coherent. It's been awhile and I am not sure that I still have all the details, but the black background of the portrait represents memory, which doesn't care much about logic. It captures separate scenes or images from my own past. All of it is very subjective. I am sure that others see not what I painted but their own cupboard skeletons. Is that how you say it?"

"That makes a lot of sense," Peter quipped, raising his glass, but Leon wasn't ready to abandon the subject.

"There is always more to the story than meets the brush. Take this famous myth-turned-painting—Botticelli's Aphrodite, which literally means foam-born. She, of course, comes out of the frothy waters. But do you know why?"

"Isn't it how she was born?" L'ubasha knitted her lips while Nad'usha knitted her eyebrows.

"Such a romantic story," Sophie whispered, observing the thoroughfare of the conversation from its quiet sidewalk. "Did Nanny tell it to you, Dear?"

"Not quite certain," Fodor admitted, speaking to Leon.

"He who decreases knowledge increases joy," Peter commented matter-of-factly.

"The account is actually rather amusing," the artist continued, unfazed by the witticism. "Uranus, whose name's unfortunate acoustic incongruity may soon whither it into extinction, knew that he was going to be overthrown by his own son. That's why he never let his children leave their mother's womb. She didn't like it, of course, and gave a flint sickle to her youngest—Chronos—who waited for his father to enter the . . . help me out with a healthy euphemism. In one swoosh, Chronos castrated Uranus and threw his testicles into the sea. The waters bubbled, and from this foam sprang Aphrodite. Obstetrically, as you can see, the story is quite realistic."

"Yuck!" L'ubasha and Nad'usha winced synchronously.

"Chronos's own son, Zeus, had a similar prophecy about his children overthrowing him. Instead of keeping them inside his wife, like his father did, he swallowed her together with the fetus. When

the gestation was over, he cracked his skull wide open and produced Athena in full armor."

The cousins looked at each other with affected disgust.

"Speak about the mystery of birth!" Peter chuckled.

"Behind every appalling image there hides an eccentric story.
Speaking of Monster," Leon said as he nodded to Sophie, inviting
her into the discussion, "you must know this work quite well. Did it
confess its secrets to you?"

She kept folding and unfolding her napkin, taking the small talk
quite seriously.

"I know what it is to give birth to fully grown children. As to the
portrait, I am afraid I am not much of an expert. I don't think Mons
. . . the man favors me." She sought but failed to get help from
Fodor, who was preoccupied with chasing a piece of feta cheese
around his plate. An idea occurred to her, and Sophie brightened.
"But Fairy certainly loves the painting. When she was little, she
used to stare at it for hours. She likes fairy tales and this picture
must have been responsive to her. All those snippets—a road, a
crown, a sailor's suit—must have signified something enchanting."

"Like Prince Charming?" Peter suggested.

"Whatever my own story might have been," Leon said, "it pales
in comparison with a child's imagination."

"Fairy is an artist herself," Sophie boasted, not sure if she had
already mentioned the fact but ready to say it over and over again.

"What does she paint?"

"Fodor made a whole exhibition in his office. Her works are very
unusual."

"That's what makes art," Nad'usha and L'ubasha said at the
same time, and burst out laughing. "Sometimes we read each other's minds."

"Pardon Fairy's curiosity," Sophie said to Peter. "She keeps nagging me about your scar. She thinks you are an undercover agent
wounded in a clash with criminals."

As if he wanted to make sure they were talking about the same
thing, the man passed his hand over the old wound.

"I hate to disappoint you, but the story is very prosaic. In the third or forth grade of school we were playing hide and seek in the school yard. Somebody tripped me, and I smashed into a tree. Nothing dangerous."

"The scar makes Petya more handsome." L'ubasha placed her hand on top of his arm.

Sophie put the napkin down by her plate and got up.

"Is everything all right?" Fodor asked, raising one eyebrow.

"I need to go to the ladies' room. Fairy, dear, are you coming with me?"

Making her way through the crowded hall, Sophie extended her left hand back so that Fairy could hold on to it.

"You don't have to," she agreed once they reached the nook. "You can wait for me outside."

Alone in the spacious powder room, Sophie paused in front of the mirror. Some people, she heard, had trouble distinguishing a reflection from a real person. She didn't find it all that incredible, looking at her own face with the strand of hair promptly tucked behind her ear, with a trefoil of new wrinkles spreading out of her eye corners. I am cracking like an old painting, she thought.

So trustworthy visually, her yonder double failed a simple test of touch. Smooth cold surface stopped Sophie's hand. Was her growing-old image just a mirage? Silly question. She shrugged and hurried out, not to leave Fairy alone for too long.

The group at the table was groaning after some hearty hilarity.

"You missed it all." Peter whisked a good-natured tear away.

Sophie gestured that's fine, I don't mind.

"We had a fabulous idea," Fodor announced on the crowd's behalf once they calmed down. "Leon hasn't seen his Monster for years. I invited everybody to our house for the reunion, so to speak, and Leon agreed to explain all the little gems he had planted in the portrait. Wouldn't it be great?"

# Vera (Part 3)

THE BOARDWALK FARCE

Like a good shepherd we waited for the opportunity to separate our white sheep from the crowd. *Waiteth and thee geteth*, or something like thateth. If we rescued one, we could as well rescue both. The craft of salvation denied preferential treatment of victims.

Mother and daughter entered a boutique shop. The moment of truth was approaching.

Confined to a tight telephone booth, I kept an eye on the entrance. Alex dialed the number. He held the receiver, and I lip-synched his words to Costas.

"It's us," whispered we, the kings of conspiracy.

"What do you mean 'who'?" we snapped, unwilling to entrust proper names to the coiled wires. "The time is now and the place is here. Are your Dismas and Gestas ready?"

"They aren't. . . ." He totally missed the allusion to the two thieves—penitent Dismas and impenitent Gestas—two distal crucifees.

Hush, we barged in. Their names are expendable. Your minutemen can be called Dumachus and Titus for all we care. Mayday, mayday. Summon them Aye-Ass-Aye-Pee.

The day was humid. Wrapped in the cloak, encaped and unassuming like a medieval monk, we begged for a breeze. Our pixy princess glided by her mother's side, and neither of us could take our eyes off her figure, the aura of her hair and the glowing outline of her face—we got a glimpse of her profile every time they turned.

293

The two of them, faithfully followed by the two of us, crossed a busy street, where, if not engrossed in pursuit, we would have felt exposed and vulnerable. In their female fetish tour Mother took Daughter to a jewelry shop, then to another boutique—silk, batik, ceramic masks in the window. We made one more call to urge our sluggish accomplice and define the summit point with the greatest precision in our punctual longing for longitudes and latitudes.

". . . and don't try to spot us. We'll spot you. Have you rehearsed your part? Say it now! There, there."

The crackling connection made his barking nearly believable. That'll do, I assured Alex. His adlibbing is inessential. Our stellar soliloquy will steal the scene.

We reached the river. The boardwalk folks scurried about, irreverent and irrelevant. Joggers chased their health to be slammed by fate in mint condition. Scraps of conversations flew by like candy wraps. Mothers—generic, lowercase mothers—pushed strollers. There was only one type that could grab our interest—a double carriage for twins. Whatever we were up to, Alex and I instinctively turned our heads to study tiny commuters. Sadly, all of them were of the common, disassociated kind.

"After we rescue her from Costas," I said, "and she takes us to Fo-Fo, he won't have the heart to refuse us like that buffoon Phobus. *Dear Fo-Fo* she would beam, *please save these two persons, precious to my heart, as selflessly as they saved me.—I don't take new patients,* he would reply, *but for you, my darling . . . anything for you.*"

Mother and Daughter slowed their pace, quite leisurely as it was, and stopped by the parapet. It looked like a good spot for our circumstantial surgery, the trimming of destiny, so to speak. Engrossed in thoughts about the girl, we were startled by the stare of an old woman in colorful rags.

"Would you like to cross a fortuneteller's hand with silver?" she crackled.

"Keep away, witch," we hissed, afraid that the incident might disclose our incognito. "We don't need to learn the future, we create it."

"I feel the heart beating faster. There is an interest waiting for you."

"Of course, there is. That's why we are here. And you just failed, having confused one heartbeat with two."

In the corner of our eyes we saw a bulky figure, uncertain and hesitant, escorted by two saturnine satellites. We softened.

"Here." We put a generous banknote into her wimpled palm. It was the last one, but Alex could make plenty later. "Do you see that woman standing by the insanely attractive young princess? Walk over and tell them not to be afraid. Pretend to read their palms and say that every misfortune has a purpose, and every tale has a happy end. Can you remember that?"

We left the aged Esmeralda staring at the money, which didn't surprise us in the least. She had never owned so beautifully crafted a bill.

"Hey, you, Costas, Gestas and Dismas, the unholy trinity," we shushed through the rustle of decorative shrubs. "Don't turn your heads."

Pushing the cane through the greenery separating us, we pointed at Phobus's wife. Don't leave her out of your sight and pay attention to the skies. The clouds are gathering not only over Spain. Know thy forecast. It will downpour soon. Fear, we instructed again, intimidation, but no tactile contact.

"Did you bring the dough?"

"Ask not what we bring; ask what you can take away. Worry about your own part," we scolded. "Bake, and the dough will rise. Our pockets are full like Croesus' troves. Watch for our sign and perform to your full impotential."

The rain prophets didn't lie. Passers-by hunched over and quickened their pace. Shades enshrouded the scene of Costas-n-Co's benefice. A fat drop hit our hood. We froze in full guard, ready to command—hoick, hoicks, tally-ho!

The boardwalk emptied. The skies frowned. We fluttered from our high hideout, like Napoleon at Waterloo. Cavalry and infantry, thugs and goons—everybody at call! Rush ahead, our troops, sweep and know no remorse!

We strained our stereoscopic vision. Hand in hand, our protégés hurried to a shelter. Were they getting away? We jumped on the bench and yelled at the top of all our lungs:

"Now! Now, bastards! What are you waiting for?"

The thunder buried our command in its deafening bass, but Costas must have sensed it. His heavyset torso grew up in front of the two women. There was no way to make out words, but we moved our lips, breathing life into his mantra: "There, there."

The alarmed women drew back, and our hearts shrank. Oh, how we wished to rescue them, save them, just as soon, very soon, Doctor Fo-Fo would save us. Two creepy critters blocked their escape. With none of the five senses but compassion, we sensed the sprouting panic. There, there!

The terror of his presence blossoming, Costas lifted his hand as if attempting to slap a cheek or snatch a purse. That was too much! We cared not for the money but for female honor and safety.

"Hold it, you, scumbag!" We spread out the cape flaps, landing in front of the offender, and, after the momentous pause, included his thugs. "And you, scumbags."

A double eagle from our motherland's blazon! Twin Heracleses fighting the multiheaded Hydra! Two Perseuses battling Medusa, our mirror—a shield, our cane—a sword.

"How dare you assault these innocent damsels? Have you no heart? Not on our watch, busters. You will pay for your vile evils!" Alex raised the cane, and I hissed, prompting the supporting crew, "Drop, lie down, quick!"

Troughs of the skies split wide open. Our staff and the heaven's lightning swept over his head in simultaneous symphonies. Streams high and low joined into one turbulent surge. Alex and I were hot in the flame of passion, merging together irreconcilable elements of water and fire. Costas deflated and defeated, we swung around to face the two thieves.

"What are you waiting for?"

*Our staff and the heaven's lightning orchestrated the divine symphony.*

The raised cane—our improvised magic wand—did its trick. In the blink of an eye all three of them were reduced to a pile of rags gleaming in the rain.

We pulled the hoods low, collars high, and turned our majestic profile to the trembling victims.

"You are safe, miladies. Don't be afraid of shadows. The foe has been annihilated."

The little mirror in our hand was shaking. We had trouble capturing their faces. The women were speechless, and Alex helped them out:

". . . and if you'd like to show your gratitude, both of us would gladly accept it. You don't have to offer it this instant. We are eager but considerate. Calm down, regain your senses. We shall meet again. Until our next encounter. . . ."

Say something in French, I wired. Uvular R's make a great conclusion.

". . . until then, *au revoir.*" The two of us bowed, courteous like three musketeers, powerful like three bears, swift like three blind mice.

## Meet Isabella

We should meet them in a day or two.

"Why wait?" Alex grumbled, and I had to explain that tomorrow, the day after the incident, the fear would climax. The hottest part of fire is above the visible flame. Despite our heroic function, we risked being associated with a horrid experience, which needed to pale away, while, at the same time, the image of two gutsy saviors matured into a myth.

Nothing provides more joy than things going according to plan. Nothing annoys more than a well-planned ploy disrupted by an outlandish cartoon character. Our landlord was scratching at the door.

"You scared us, you impudent old man!" we roared, startled. "Didn't we instruct you never to appear here in insignificant person?

We accepted your ridiculous rent because privacy for us is like *Deutschland* for its subjects—it is *über alles*."

"*Schprechen sie* Roman?" I inquired.

". . . or romantic?" Alex insisted.

"Do you know what *Gott Strafe* means?" we both pressed.

He wavered, coughed out of confusion rather than indisposition, and dawdled while we tried to unlock the darn door.

"Don't walk in," we commanded, regaining our stature. "We shall converse with you through the slit. What is your business?"

He had sent a note like we asked, he mumbled, but we didn't respond and his wife had him. . . .

"Of course, we remember! We would have gotten in touch, but these last few days were extremely hectic. Your existence is not our only concern. The note was unintentionally annihilated. Remind us what it was that you wished."

The deposit, he said, the money we gave him for the apartment ("We know what a deposit is," we scoffed), it was a very large bill. He had brought it to his wife, whose existence we assumed but never verified, and according to his stuttering report, she checked the banknote from all six viewpoints, in her sick deliberation reaching as far as the attempt to tear it.

*Real* money, he said and we were offended by his emphasis on the adjective, didn't come apart as easy. She made him bring these scraps back—an envelope wiggled through the opening—and needed to ask us for a different banknote. They both, distrustful spouse and mistrustful he, were certain that the mix-up would be over and forgotten with no need to bother us again.

We grabbed the envelope. These barbarians had destroyed our best specimen as if it were a grocery list or a silly billet-doux!

"Did you have to ruin it?"

Um-m, he was sorry, he didn't even have a say, his woman just wanted. . . .

"Never ever raze money we give you. Do you think it's easy to master all these color curlicues? Look at it! Who can we foist it off to now?"

He understood, at least that's what he champed, but he had to get his rent.

We hadn't intended to initiate him in our affairs, but there was little we could do.

"We had some trouble lately," we explained. "Alex injured his hand, and we were unable to . . . m-m-m . . . proceed financially. We are artists, you see. We have a very valuable portrait, which we could show you through the crack even though it's unlikely that you appreciate art. A healthy and steady hand is essential. It still hurts a little. As much as we are disquieted by your wife's allegations, we can recover funds no sooner than. . . ." We visualized a calendar. "Now, go, old man. Pass our regards to your shrewd companion. We hope that you *are* married and your virago is not an excuse to redirect blame onto someones' innocent else."

Slam!

Annoyed more than upset, we'd forfeited the rules of the foreign lingo in favor of sincerity.

The shuffles on the landing waned away. We stepped over to the window to make sure he was gone and not setting an ambush to gun us from later.

"We could have used it to pay Costas," Alex lamented.

"I can make another," I reassured him. "The cut is almost healed."

The thunder and lightning no longer essential for the narrative, the skies cleared. Our joy, however, blurred in face of new worries, ". . . as much as we try to meet troubles sidewise." There was a pinch of sadness in our joke.

We are positive people. We try to keep the big picture in mind, not letting nuisances and nuances bother us. This time, the big picture—incidentally synonymous with the large painting—was centered at the pinnacle of our life-long journey. We had to reach Fo-Fo before Costas with his thieves and our ranting *rentlord* caught up with us. We found ourselves in a race for the noblest of prizes, the race that most of our co-*Sapienses* weren't even aware of—pursuit of redemption.

As opposed to *fine*, our *other* art didn't require daylight and was essentially nocturnal. We locked ourselves in the Mint and prepared pens and paints—tools of our trade.

"Now that they are suspicious, what should we draw?"

"We'll think of something." Alex rubbed his palms and smoothed the virgin paper, still of zip value.

With never dying astonishment over ease and perfection, I watched curls and doodles frame the center that Alex left to be filled at the end.

"How about appending another zero?" I suggested.

"Don't be gluttonous. It's a deadly sin," he replied, preoccupied with the ringlets. "Whose portrait should we place here?"

Kings and presidents as customary banknote dwellers never inspired us. As we had shouted to the old man through the crack in the door, we were artists, and true artists invented life rather than reflecting it. We'd be ashamed to pass off a fake to anybody, even if we expected little appreciation from our contra-connoisseurs and anti-aficionados.

"Who do we have faith in?" Alex hummed. "In whom do we trust?"

My cured hand was resolute, lines sure, resemblance unmistakable. After a few strokes he gasped:

"That's her! You are a genius."

The girl smiled at us from the newly born note issued by the bank of our hearts. I completed the bill with a crown, anointing our princess as the queen. We gave two kisses to our creation, wishing the Galatea story to be true, so lively and lovely had her features come out.

"I am so excited," Alex confessed, "I am going to have trouble falling asleep."

"Don't worry," I replied. "I am so tired that it will be no trouble at all."

Had he overheard this conversation—the feat we assume feasible in some superfluous dimension—Doctor Fein would surely have had a blast, praising his invaluable technique. Wrong you are again, Comrade Hippocrates! Our little argument didn't prove your point. We weren't torn apart by contradictory desires. Quite the opposite, we subdued them and made them work to our benefit. While one Alex collapsed into oblivion, the other Alex carefully observed dreams, so in the morning, refreshed and rejuvenated, we could interpret them in full accordance with Doctor Freu-Freu and his *Die Traumdeutung*—the classic guide on retrieving reveries.

That night our reveries shaped themselves into a conversation:

Let's not bother about little things, Doctor. Who cares which Alex is an artist and which is a maverick? We are both idealistic and prosaic at the same time. Ask us instead about something truly important. Ask us about the meaning of life, and let us offer you some profound imagery, which you can analyze in later seclusion during *cien anos* of your *soledad*. Ready to write it down? Here it comes.

Life, Doctor, is like a book, the word *like* here essential to announce a looming simile, because we abhor metaphors. Life has a beginning and an end. We don't care about particulars of chapters, climaxes, cliffhangers and epilogues' obituary. You can figure out the details at your leisure. What's the purpose of books, dear Fo-Fo? Fairy tales, poems, thrillers are all different genres. Likewise, it's accurate to say that everybody's life belongs to its own genre and has a distinct purpose. In a page-turner you don't care about the quality of writing or living—all the reader and the *liver* need to know is what happens next. After discovering the killer's identity, you slam the life and never return to its days again. A book read is a life forgotten.

Books of a different kind grab you by their texture, by the author's attitude, by playful pleasantness, by the sequence of syllables. This is *our* life, Doctor! Its purpose is staying with the text, living clause by clause. Will Quasimodo be able to save his girl? Will she see beauty in the beast? Will they find love? Who cares if you enjoy every sentence? And the more you read it, the more pleasure it gives.

That's all we had to say. Did you record it? Good night then.

Interpret it before our rendezvous, so we can discuss other things: ethos and pathos, heresy and hearsay, bards and bastards.

The next morning we unanimously blackballed staying home. Costas's compensation not ready, his foray here was unwelcome. Where could we go?

"Let's stop by our friend Phobus's," Alex suggested.

On the way to his office we rehearsed a sample scenario. Did you sleep well, Dr. Ph? How is your family? Are you proud of your daughter? Have you told Fo-Fo about us?

"Alex and Alex," we declared at the reception desk.

"Are you expected?"

"We are always expected. He has met us as patients, but now we are much more. Doc and we are *tres amigos*. We selflessly saved the family females from danger, although they might not be aware of our involvement yet. And soon we intend to become just as close and dear to his esteemed colleague Fo-Fo."

She pretended to be busy with case histories, and we didn't blame her. After all, this wasn't a proper social occasion. Instead of engaging in a friendly chat, she sighed and said that unfortunately. . . .

"What do you mean, not here?" we gasped. "He should have called us and said: *Alex, Alex, I am not feeling well today. Why don't you stop by some other time?* He didn't mention anything. What if it's an emergency? What if we have penetrating pangs right here or left there?"

Professional compassion twitched her features. One second, she said, let me find something out.

"Yes." My palm slammed against the countertop. "Take this second. Find. Out. We shall wait in these chairs."

What are you doing? Alex whispered. Patience, dear patient, I caroled. You never know where the next lead is coming from. Maybe Fo-Fo covers for Phobus today. That would be an ingenious twist of the therapeutic fate!

Sadly, we weren't made for free rides in the liner of Luck. Everything we had achieved came from persistence, perseverance and perspicacity. With talents like ours, we didn't need Luck's charity; we could claim and climb the Tree of Goodies ourselves.

"Doctor Phobus called in this morning with a family emergency."

"What emergency? It was an innocent incident. A dramatization. Nobody got hurt." We caught her curious gaze. "Not that we know anything about it, of course. We are just upset. Why do we have to suffer if someone," a significant glance at the inner door, "has an emotional breakdown?"

We gave her a moment to come up with a suggestion, with something like *why don't we . . .* or *why don't you . . .* but, when the silence grew awkward, stepped up.

"Can't someone else see us? A coworker, maybe? Someone we haven't met and befriended yet, but everything in due course. We need help. Our anxiety is rising. The day didn't start well—we had no dream about the queen of two hearts."

A speaker on her desk buzzed.

"Can I help you with your cloak?"

"We never take it off," we parried. "The last time that we did proved disastrous. Let's not return to this subject. We are ready. Lead us to Fo-Fo without further afore."

Not waiting for her consent, we rushed to the office, our eyes swollen with tears of which no man should be ashamed.

The room met us empty and cold.

Alex was the first to regain his composure.

"Should we sit by the window or in the shade of his desk lamp?"

"Rescued in a few minutes!" I was still a bit dreamy. "No longer ugly, no more ambiguous—proud cosmos dwellers, rightful tenants of the universe."

Our hearts played four hands like piano virtuosos. As the tempo left sixty-nine quarter notes per minute of larghetto and was nearing one hundred and eighty-two quarter notes of presto, the door opened.

It was no Fo-Fo.

"A woman?" both of us puffed in disenchantment. We stared at her, neglecting our usual cautionary stance. The unrequited mirror in our hands reflected a meaningless eclectic pattern—the trembling net of lacquered parquetry.

Middle-aged, with apparent excess of testosterone showing on her upper lip, she was packaged in a blue business wrap with a big brooch upon the white blouse. Her hair was tied in a solid bun.

"Pardon?"

"We expected to see someone else." Hiding our disappointment, we repositioned sideways, our little mirror now atilt.

"Who?"

"We visualize him as an elderly man, a noble nose bridge, understanding eyes. We are reluctant to utter his name in vain."

"My name's Isabella Fischer." She settled in the host's chair behind the desk. "I work with Doctor Phobus. 'A cute pain' you said?"

Let's go. Alex pulled my sleeve. There is no reason to cast pearls here. Insanity is a particularly male prerogative. No one named Isabella has a part in our chronicle.

"The pain is acute," he snarled.

"It's a long story," I mumbled evasively.

"You are already here. Why don't you tell it?"

Let's go, Alex insisted. I ignored him.

"Do you see these books?" We pointed at the shelves. "This one on the left is authored by one Professor Tulchinsky. We didn't read it, of course. We have no need to. He used to sit across from us, just like you do now, and, scratching his underdeveloped chin, try to adapt our misfortune to his misconceptions."

She scribbled a quick doodle.

"Don't take us wrong. We have many fond memories of this man, although he failed to explain that the world was less complex than it appeared; that two pounds of shit and two pounds of jam together produce four pounds of shit. But to his credit, while lecturing us on monozygotic and dizygotic twins, he came up with an image that we shall never forget: a dizzy Goth trying to make up his mind—to split or not to split? That, dear female Dr., was the question. Despite all his inventive mnemonics, he failed. The reasons were plenty, but one, very important, had nothing to do with his professional pretense."

"What was it?" Her lips stretched ever so slightly, but our now-steady mirror didn't overlook the scoff.

"We like that your name starts with F—the femme fatale of the alphabet—used by Chaucer, Shakespeare and King James in such important words like *Fate, Fame* and *Feign* . . . but a woman?!"

Let us make something clear, we went on. Professor Tulchinsky taught us about zygotic intricacies, about molar twins, when a viable one is endangered by the other's infirmity; or about miscarried twins, when one is miscarried early in pregnancy but the other is carried to term. We learned from him that one in eighty human births is the result of twin pregnancy; *twinology* is such a fascinating subject! The ancients were just as enamored with it. Do you know that the famous Greek hero Heracles had a twin half-brother Iphicles? One night Zeus appeared before their mother in the guise of her husband returning after a long absence. Imagine the cheesecake's shocker when the next night her human honey showed up! The rules were unambiguous—every coitus led to impregnation. The twins were born together, but conception-wise Heracles was a night older. Don't take it for a myth fancy. Your own science is aware of this phenomenon—fraternal twins with different fathers. It's called *Heteropaternal superfecundation.*

Isabella watched us in awe. She should have. We continued.

Take Romulus and Remus fathered by Mars, the god of war, or Castor and Pollux, the Gemini doubles. Romans referred to Castor as Castore, which doesn't mean that Alex is going to be Alexe, haha. You see, we have a refined sense of ridiculous, afforded by our unique viewpoint, which reminds us of two Titan brothers—Prometheus, *foresight,* and Epimetheus, *hindsight.* Jokes aside, even Jesus was believed to have a twin—Apostle Thomas.

We bent in a dramatic posture that had a stronger effect than wows and vows. Of course, the names are important! That's why noble Roman males had three—a forename *praenomen,* a clan name *gentilicium* and a personal *cognomen.*

Twins were often given similar names: Norse Freyja and Freyr, Iranian Yima and Yimeh, Aztec Xochiquetzal and Xochipilli—

none, mind you, as closely attached as Alex and Alex.

Isabella might be appropriate for the cruel queen of Spain or Spades, but not for our Holy *Healerix*. Excuse us now. You get no more paragraphs in our story. This is all we have to say.

"That was quite a performance. You are a good actor." She applauded.

"Actors," we corrected, bowing. "By the way, Actor, a common name in Greek mythology, means Prince—Prince Charming, which, should you know our genealogy, carries additional significance. One last question." We turned back in the doorway—one Alex still in the office, the other already out. "What are these peculiar drawings on the wall? We have visited Doctor Phobus before but didn't see them."

"They are Faye's, his daughter's. They've been here forever."

Faye! The second we heard the name, Alex and I appreciated its essence. We stepped back in.

"We are no strangers to art. We like to draw, we mean paint. Portraits, obviously, are our favorites. An ideal one has to depict a noble man in the cocked hat, a medal ribbon across his chest, aglets on his shoulders. A full-sailed frigate in the background is optional but desirable. Tell us more about the girl."

"The poor kid was very unfortunate," Isabella said. "A rare condition—two hearts. They hoped surgery would help but alas. . . . He loved her very much."

Alex and I shrugged. We had two hearts too. What was so unfortunate about that? But the drawings. . . . They captured our imagination. What was the meaning of the double lines? What story did they hide? Were they sea waves of Moby Dick or railroad tracks of Anna Karenina?

Leaving the office, we released a useless prisoner. If the cleaning woman is thorough, she will find Phobus's notebook under his desk.

## THE EMPTY NEST OF DR. PHOBUS

The laws of drama demand the distancing of crucial points of narration. Fo-Fo appeared to be an elusive son of a bitch, pardon the humors, and no one had invited two mad *hood*-ers to a tea party. The tension of the boardwalk pantomime had settled, ready to evolve into solemn moments of intimacy between a rescuer and his victims. What a Fo-Fo-dian slip! Daughter and Mother soaked in nightmares like a photo film in order to develop the image of their hero.

"What was that family emergency about? Have we overacted in our boardwalk benefice?" I wondered.

"There was no other choice. We needed an introduction. Two con-protagonists couldn't simply jump onto the podium." Alex shrugged. "The choreography was perfect."

The skies were perfect too—light blue and fathomless. The storm washed away the watercolors of the bygone drama. We scanned our way in the pocket mirror so that the streetlights brought the Argonauts to the Phobus fleece. The distorted world of reflections never confused us—as long as ups and downs stayed where they belonged, we could flip common lefts for our rights.

"That's the house." Alex pointed.

"Time to lift the hood and say hello?" I asked for consensus.

"A good girl like Faye shouldn't let strangers in. God knows what we look like through the mono peephole."

"Any suggestions?"

He measured the structure.

"I am not climbing any more walls!" I screamed.

He sighed.

"The princesses certainly prefer higher floors these days."

"I am not climbing up," I repeated.

He lit a cigarette.

"Quit it! This unhealthy habit has no future."

"Why is that?" He inhaled deeply. My head spun.

"Sooner or later everybody quits."

"Stop patronizing me. What am I, a school girl? If we are not climbing, we need a plan. I have to think."

"And I need to throw up."

Smoke formed into a Cheshire smile like that of Doctor Fein. Passers-by cast surprised sidelong glances at a large man wrestling his shadow. Little did they know about the inner struggle and Jacob fighting the angel. I jerked the butt out and crushed it under my heel. Alex cursed. Too late—the virtue had already beaten the vice.

A big truck, one of those that deliver furniture, pulled over, nearly blocking our view. The driver ran around to open the back gate. Still in the wrestle embrace, we stretched our necks to see the hollow container. Two porters entered the building and, in a matter of minutes, crammed the sidewalk with an armchair, a torchère and a couch, creating an oasis of domicile coziness in the midst of the street fuss. Unprotected by walls, articles of the interior looked naked. The icing on this surreal cake would have been a man in pajamas or a woman in curlers. After the last object—a ridiculously outdated, wrought-iron chest—was dragged out, the movers stuffed the truck. A puff of bluish exhaust wiped the canvas, and soon all evidence of home evisceration was gone.

The mise-en-scene was the only entertainment we got. If Fo-Fo intended to stop by to see his dear friend Phobus, he must have rescheduled his visit due to unknown-to-us excuses. The sun ducked behind the clouds. It became chilly. Our light cloak was no longer sufficient. Our homeland habit of predicting weather by slush or sand kept failing in the local sterility. Alex got up from the bench first and a split second later I followed.

Upon our return, we were stunned by the reversal of roles—someone was watching *our* entrance, although with better luck. While we hesitated whether to turn my left or Alex's right cheek to our unwelcome caller, Costas blocked our way.

"There, there."

"What are you doing here?" we demanded bravely.

"I want my money."

"Oh, you came for the retribution?" Sarcasm squeezed its way through the unemotional tone. "We should have known what kind of an opportunistic individual you were. We suppose you hauled your mob along?"

"They . . . m-m-m . . . they are waiting around the corner," he faltered.

Very well, we said. Nobody is hiding from you. We are honest folks with no intention of swindling our comrade-in-harms. We are ready to look straight at anybody's reflection.

Costas stared at us, hardly seeming to understand our words. What a *poludurok!* We refused to step down to his street-smarts level, and continued on a high note.

"You are not the first person to claim a monetary reward. Just last night we had to deal with one presumptuous old man. We are certain that you have little compassion for his senile landlordship, but, so that you know, we intend to keep our word. You are the first in line, since your services were much more valuable for *cosa nostra*, which means—in case you are clueless—*our cause* and has nothing to do with caped and hooded mafia thugs."

We frowned as if thinking.

"Not to make any assumptions about your academic pedigree, how familiar are you with arithmetic?" A pause. Before he lost his patience, we continued. "There was an opinion to increase your share by adding a zero to your bill."

"A zero?"

"Its location on the right-hand side embodies not an addition but multiplication. Ten becomes a hundred. A hundred becomes a thousand. Do you like that?"

After short hesitation he mumbled:

"It's all right, I guess. Where is it?"

Extra zero, we explained, requires extra zeal. One needs more time to etch another digit, *one* being a figure of speech, a euphemism for *two*; whereas his *zero* was quite material. "Don't worry yourself. Pacify your goons in whatever invectives they understand best. Go now, don't waste our time if you want to be rewarded soon."

Without further farewells, we marched into the building, but, instead of walking upstairs, rushed a flight down and lay doggo by the basement door. Yes, doggo like dingo. Should he decide to follow us, we'd sneak out while he was pounding at our apartment's door. Fear played no consideration in our tactics, as we were quite capable of handling him or his whole trinity. Our spirit was strong, our staff unbending, but the commandment to shun violence led like a lodestar.

Costas turned around. Alex—that must have been he, a puny artist—deflated with relief. We were safe for the moment, but a sign of the gathering storm had already marred the horizon.

On weak legs we walked up to the apartment, but our good intentions of working in the Mint were never realized—my hands were shaking.

"Com'n, paint." Somewhat annoyed, Alex pushed the palette towards me. "No one ever notices your blunders."

"I take pride in my art," I insisted. "I will not begin unless I am sure to achieve my absolute best."

We argued for awhile, but this argument resembled more of a chess riddle, when the opposites cooperate rather than compete. The game was about to end in victorious stalemate—the oxymoron making sense only in our peculiar state of affairs—when we heard a faint rustle on the landing. External interference made us forget internal discord.

"Did he change his mind?" I gasped. "Did he bring reinforce-ments?"

We tiptoed to the door. Our hearts thumped ahead. With all the anxiety of accelerating events, one of us—I am not blaming anybody, but it wasn't *my* job—forgot to hook the chain. Who knew what kind of dark talents this Costas possessed? Could he take advantage of our naiveté? He sure could. Would he pick the lock? You bet he would. Our only hope was that, hearing no signs of life, he would decide to postpone the confrontation. Hope, indeed! Didn't we lose it a long time ago?

A shy envelope corner squiggled in.

That's who you are, we hummed with relief, the persistent beggar—our lackluster land-maister with his spirited epistles! We glanced over the piece of paper. Its wobbly scribbles greatly weakening the threat, the letter demanded full and unconditional payment. Otherwise—we chuckled at his intimidating ultimatum—he would have to evict us.

"Don't worry, old man," we sang through the keyhole. "Costas can wait. We shall paint his fare later. You are the first in line."

He appealed to his wife again—a grumbling witch from his personal fairy tale.

"We don't have much time," we interrupted his *once-upon-a-time*. "Let us offer you a didactic clue, courtesy of Alex and Alex. It's about monster Kholomondumo from the creation story of the Lesotho people. It swallowed every human being apart from one woman. The woman gave birth to twins, who killed Kholomondumo and set the others free. Who do you think the monster is here and who are the courageous twins? Think about it, discuss it with your suspicious spouse and learn the morals."

Not listening to comments, we retreated to the room. One lesson we learned. Our home had lost its invincibility. No longer was it Nouf-Nouf's stronghold. Could we ever feel safe anywhere? This question, alas rhetorical, was addressed to the gods of hearth and to the portrait that shared with us all harshness of uncertainty. While the landlord was solitary and senile, Costas presented unpleasant physical complications.

"Sooner or later Dismas and Gestas will catch up with us," Alex warned. "I don't trust other duos."

We didn't leave the apartment for several days. Alex didn't approach the windows. Whenever we heard steps on the staircase, we froze, interrupting everything—chewing, breathing, thinking.

Someone kicked the door. We paused on all fours and didn't respond.

An envelope slid in. We didn't pick it up.

The lights were off even at night. Chances for the outside observers to be friendly were slim and the observers themselves slimy. Only in the Mint, having securely clicked the latch and placed a towel along the floor slit, we flipped the switch.

"You should know better than anybody that I am not a fraudster," Alex repeated. "Unless I feel challenge and pride, no picture will come out fake-perfect."

"This is not about art anymore. If we don't get them off our backs, we can kiss Fo-Fo bye-bye."

I cut a blank; he took the quill.

"I *will* draw," he replied solemnly, "but you are wrong. It is *always* about art. It is our only chance for a happy end."

Whether because of a full moon, the planet parade or any other cosmic omen, we failed to finish a single bill. Presidents jeered at us. Zeroes were the only believable jesters.

"Tomorrow," someone shrieked on the landing. "I am calling the cops tomorrow! You can't hide there forever."

By dawn, which failed to turn our gloom into glee, we dropped off exhausted. Scraps of unfinished miniatures were scattered all over the floor. Whether knocks on the door and screams at the window were nightmares or reality, they failed to wake us up.


"Get up!"

"What time is it?" I mumbled.

"I saw a panther in my dream. You know what it means? Darkness and death, lurking danger and enemies wishing harm. We better get out of here."

"You go brush your teeth. I need five more minutes."

Alex jerked the blanket.

"We have to get up on the right foot. It's your side. Up, up!"

"All right," I yawned, conciliatorily. "What's your secret plan?"

Wide-eyed, Alex looked out the window. The panther hadn't lied. Dismal Dismas and sullen Gestas stepped from around the corner, ready to cross the street.

I ran to the Mint to fetch the portrait. Alex unrolled the canvas and spread it upon the wall, holding the top corners. Oil pupils returned our stare like a mirror.

"We don't mean to alarm you," we said. "The good news is coming, but for now there is only the bad. The cream is rising. We wish we could take you along, but oil on canvas is unlikely to survive jumps off a speeding train or a swim against an ice-cold current, options to which we may have to resort. What's dangerous for people is lethal for a piece of art. You will have to stay in the apartment. When a big bad wolf bangs on the door, don't be naïve like seven kids or try to protect yourself like three piglets. The odds are long—you will fall prey like Little Red Riding Hood. Wait until we come to the rescue. It may be dark here unlike the rooms of the Louvre and dusty unlike halls at the Hermitage, but we have no other choice."

Our hearts ready to explode with sorrow, we rolled the canvas and shoved it deep under the bed. We wished we could hide under the bed as well, but many fugitives had given away their hideout by sneezing in the dust.

"Fo-Fo the Saviour, Fo-Fo the Redeemer," Alex mocked. "What if he just doesn't exist?"

"Stop this blasphemy!"

"Omniscient and compassionate Fo-Fo is too good to be true. We should stop kidding ourselves. Our quest has no meaning. The whole life with hints and promises is a hoax. We are never going to find him."

"If we don't find him," I stated firmly, "Costas's henchmen will find us."

"Time to revisit the little house under the wailing cedars," Alex agreed.

We pushed the double-hung window up and—no easy trick for two—scrambled out to the fire-escape.

Nights are custom-cut for departures. Mornings are for arrivals. It was still early and buses rolling into the terminal one after another—suburban pollen still stuck to their crust—kept delivering rested and re-dreamed commuters.

Hunched and hooded, we fought against the flow, when. . . .

"Hush!" Alex hissed, nudging me. "Look!"

At first I couldn't quite get the direction his finger was wiggling at. The mirror was too small to capture both the arrow and the target.

"A tree?" I wondered. "A dog, a pigeon?"

"Over there."

I gave up the trembling reflection in my hand and looked straight. The vast vision made me dizzy. The world in direct view was overwhelming, and it took a moment to settle. Then I saw what Alex was pointing at. I must have known it all along, because that's how we were created—identical and inseparable, sharing what others consider most private—nightmares and superstitions. However, unless both of us concentrate, we perceive objects flat and uncertain, lacking the palpable three-dimensional essence.

I recognized dear Phobus even without his smock. By his side walked a woman in a trouser suit and by her side I saw the girl whose image had been shining so brightly over our dreams that we'd put her portrait on the notes of our local bank.

Taller than her mother, she was slender and elegant, gliding among idlers and busybodies like a princess in the royal ball, with proud posture and courteous smile. The street was noisy and the family too far for us to distinguish sounds. Faye's lips moved as if she was responding to her mother's chatter with short and polite remarks.

Slowly, so as not to attract their attention by erratic moves, we ducked behind the bushes lining the alley. In another second we found that we weren't alone, not in our unique constitutional sense, but in the quite utilitarian, laymen understanding. A disheveled rascal had been playing hide-n-seek.

"What are you doing here?" We couldn't orient ourselves in space, the sideways shift not being readily available to two cornered by thorns. "Children should not play close to terminals. Off to a playground!"

"This is my spot!" the twit twitched.

"Shut up," we commanded, "shut up, whoever you are—a scamp or a hoyden. We are secret agents in the middle of a covert surveillance."

"I'm gonna tell mom. Ma, Ma!"

Alex pulled the urchin's ear, and I pushed the mirror right up to his freckles.

"Get out! You have five seconds. One, two. . . ."

He twisted his tortilla neck and bit my wrist. Alex screamed; I released the grip. The brat dashed out, nearly knocking Phobus down. Strangely, this maneuver helped more than it endangered. Amidst the commotion we backed off and regrouped.

Our framework was hardly chiseled for staying covert. We couldn't remain anonymous, let alone invisible. If only we could split up and shadow them separately, diminishing their chances of disappearing and doubling ours of staying on their tail! Nice try, Professor.

Our eyes stayed glued on the girl. She radiated so much positive energy that the magnetic attraction could only be explained by our own negative charge, moral metaphors notwithstanding. Only thunder, darkness and heat of our adamant rescue mission had made us overlook her stunning perfection.

The women dived into a jewelry shop. Beta-male Phobus remained outside, bored like a border picket.

"Call Costas," Alex suggested. "Throw him another zero. He distracts the doctor; we confront Faye."

"He'll strangle us," I hissed back. "You are mad."

"I was just pulling your leg. Don't mention insanity in vain."

Faye reappeared. We squinted. Mother threw her head back, showing off the new necklace, her palm pressed to her chest, her fingers spread out between collarbones. Doctor's lips curled, accompanied by the soundtrack of city clatters.

"Did she buy something for Faye too?" I wondered.

In what could loosely be defined as a single file, we followed them to an open square. Idle tourists already replaced purposeful commuters. Fluent like sand in an hourglass, the crowd wavered. The haystack securely sheltered our three needles. Not to lose them from sight we galloped around the corner. The grave building of the art museum rose before us.

"Let us through. Step aside. What are you staring at?" Alex pushed our way through the resistant horde. "Do you see them?"

Wide stairs led to the entrance. We caught a glimpse of Phobus's back right before he vanished like Job in the beluga's gullet.

"*Am I a sea, or a whale, that thou hast enclosed me in a prison?*"
I mumbled (The Book of Job, Chapter Seven, verify if you don't
trust us, Doctor). "Follow him."

Alex said nothing, pointing with his chin. With our chin. We
pointed at the billboard. A huge cloth hung down the portico, announcing the new exposition. If Alex thought that the day had run
out of surprises, I couldn't be more wrong. A portrait blown up to
behemoth size peered at us with its never-aging superiority. It took
no time to recognize the hand.

"So," we whispered, "Leonidas finally hatched into Leonardo."

Neither his artistic style, nor social acknowledgment, not even
his possible presence excited us, but the mere thought that somewhere behind these columns a girl of our hope could be standing by
his side made our hearts step up their duo drum.

Yes, Hope must be here. We could feel it. Our double sensitivity
never lied. We hurtled up to the entrance, skipping steps, and peeked
synchronously at the opposite directions of the spacious hall.

"Are you buying a ticket or what?"

We focused on the bespectacled guard.

"If we indeed make up our mind to get in, we will need not one
but two tickets. Unscrupulous folks could have used our spatial gift
to kill two birds with one ticket. We are not like that. Should we decide to say hello to our dear, mind you, friend Leonidas, we would
buy as many tickets as we have to. Paper money is no object."

The crowd behind pressed forward. The temptation to discard
caution and rush forward to see Hope almost thawed our natural
sang-froid. Only practical consideration stopped us. The museum
was huge and heterogeneous. Phobus could have chosen wrapped
mummies or stuffed puppies in the opposite wings.

Fine, we said, we shall come here later. Hope can't vanish twice.
We'll meet her. If not us than who? If not now, anon.

"No," we replied—Alex to the cashier, I to the herd behind, "we
are not coming in. Back off, intellectual throng, let us out."

Other people, including the medical medley of Fein, Tulchinsky
and now Phobus, viewed us as a deformity, ignoring the fact that we

were more versatile than those whom they'd like us to imitate. Separate viewpoints offered excellent judgment of the world's values. If we had expressed interests in other than the Bill Arts, we could have become a swift four-hand virtuoso or a pair of paranormal psychics cross-reading each other's minds. Incessant surveillance was our special shtick. While Alex or I watched the museum entrance, I or Alex relaxed and enjoyed the scenery of a trig town, trinket vendors and sparrows tweeting by the fountain.

What does Leonidas look like now, we wondered. Does he wash his hair? Did he learn to wear socks?

Move on, people, move on; don't stare at our royal profile.

In the middle of the swarming square, we danced like a weathervane to avoid idle pry, twisting sidewise and turning sideways to those whose gaze scanned us with aloof apathy.

An hour or so later, our protégés walked out. Phobus winced in the bright light. His wife and daughter chattered excitedly as the trio headed towards the riverfront. We watched from afar how they went up the narrow pedestrian bridge and stood looking down at the water streams.

Alex picked up a sheet of paper with someone's rejected sketch and rolled it into a telescope.

"Faye, Faye," he hummed.

"Let me see," I insisted. "Is she tender like Hope or fiery like Love?"

"She is appeasing like. . . ." He faltered, the proper parable not readily available in our vocabulary.

"Faye starts with an F," I pondered, "and that's a great sign. We can't have meaningless names in our story."

In a series of mechanical—retrieved from childhood—motions, we folded the sheet and set the paper boat afloat.

## Mount Olympus

A five-step descent and a cockroach in sombrero wiggled his mustache to welcome the family in.

Through the narrow semi-basement opening, we saw Mr., then Mrs. and finally Ms. Phobus settle right by the window. Only the transparent layer of the pane separated us. We had no fear of being recognized—all they could see was two pairs of identical footwear. The sales gimmick of *buy one pair, get one free* was shoe-made for the two of us.

"Can you hear what they are saying?" Alex whispered.

An image of fragrant burritos fogged my mind.

"I am starving," I blurted out.

"Stop being selfish. Think about your alter ego."

"If I get a headache you'll be the first to feel it."

That was solid rhetoric—we can't tolerate anything splitting.

Who knows where the discord would have led us, if the party inside hadn't gotten up from their chairs. We rushed away from the entrance.

"Did they change their mind?" Alex breathed out.

"They must dislike public places as much as we do. Food ingestion is intimate like love and prayer."

"What if they call a cab and. . . ?"

We panicked. Chance's ability to help us out had already been stretched to the limit. Fortuity, unless man made, was mostly available in singles like God and Universe.

"Halt it!" We jumped onto the street in front of a taxi and slammed three palms against its polished hood—a gutsy move, considering that our collision was mediated by a tiny pocket mirror in the forth hand. The breaks screeched. We ducked into the backseat and pressed our faces to the tinted window.

"Where are we going?"

"The man is about to come out. Follow him."

"I am sorry. I don't do that kind of thing."

"We are . . . extremely private detectives," we sputtered. "This man passes himself for a doctor. He cheats on his patients. His Hippocratic oath was hypocritical. He refused to give the address of certain Fo-Fo who is the only salvation for . . . our clients."

In another instant, Phobus emerged from the door. We drove ourselves deep into the seat cushions.

# Dmitry Zlotsky

"Don't let him spot us!" we hissed at the driver. "The *merzavets*[1] is dangerous. His friendly façade has fooled many sleuths. He can prescribe poison. He may euthanize."

Instead of looking for a ride the Phobuses strolled down the street.

"How am I supposed to go after a pedestrian?" the driver asked.

A minute ago the cab had seemed like a double margin of precaution. Now it proved to be a double jeopardy. Even our lexicon took the twofold form of double talk.

"Stop here." I tapped the padded shoulder in front while Alex twisted his neck to keep Faye in sight. "We are getting out."

"That'll be four fifty."

"Send the bill to our accountant Costas."

I slammed the door, and Alex poked his cane at the rattling bumper—go! Go, before we change our peaceful minds.

In five minutes Phobus ascended a Greek restaurant. The neon glow enveloped *Mount Olympus*. Squeezing through a narrow passage between the brick emery and the prickly shrubbery (ready for mass production of martyrs' wreaths, we quipped), Alex and I nestled by the window.

The hall seethed in the heat of consumption. People gorged, gobbled, guzzled and grasped for more with apocalyptic, approaching apoplexy, acceleration. Their eyebrows summoned waiters, their forks tinkled against glasses, they demanded bread and received circus for a side dish. A local-scale reason expanded into a large-scale disarray—the wide-angle panorama rendered little private sanity as components of the common pandemonium.

The madness became more evident in the absence of senses. The thick glass, separating us from the moving waxwork inside, excluded sound, turning the noisy feast into a mute orgy. Soundproof windows converted the pianist's twitches into the utmost absurdity. He tossed his wrists high in the air, mimed and lamented, failing to extract from his instrument even a false note. The chandelier's

---

1. *merzavets*: Russian: the scum, scab and scoundrel together.

reflection silently sparkled on the piano's lacquered surface. Waiters whisked about with steaming fare upon angular arms.

"Tref accompanied by a treble clef," Alex commented.

I wiped the glass, misted from our breath, with a sleeve. Where is our undear Phobus? To complicate our character recognition, the gluttons inside competed in making faces. They leaned over their plates and sucked in the aroma—a strong stimulus for them but fenced and nonexistent for us. Their mimic went through the stages of delight, rapture and ecstasy. All of them, brought together and observed separately, fussed and flickered, at the same time moving and vain in their communal loneliness. In the loneliness that we were never destined to perceive. What a wonderful throne speech!

Driven by the internal force and preoccupied by the external farce, we almost missed the irony of turning into doctors ourselves—Doctor Watsons.

Soon the pantomime lost its novelty. The action inside acquired the feel of a silent movie. Night cicadas chattered with the constancy of a projection device.

"There he is!"

That's why it took us so long to find him! Their table was shielded by the Ionic column. Mediterranean food ruled here, and an unsure hand had decorated the walls with antic stereotypes. Titans and athletes were painted in rigid profile stances. We felt the kindred spirit, not to mention that Homeric analogies had occurred to us before— we were two brave Jasons hunting for the Golden Flee-Flee.

Our foster doctor rose from his chair and raised his wine glass. Our eyes watered with strain, but the hissing exhale of champagne didn't reach us, just as we'd failed to discern bubbles boiling in the beaker. His lips twitched in eloquent toast.

To take a better look at the food, which now occupied sizeable real estate in our minds, we squashed our faces against the pane. Our peripheral vision (Alex's or mine—at moments of high concentration we are utterly selfless) snatched out some alarming movements. Releasing Phobus from the visual grip, we shifted our focus.

A flabby woman next to the window was staring right at us, our existence no longer covert. How improvident! Relying on darkness, we had relaxed for a moment, but this incident immediately returned us to our senses. Alex and Alex, never forget the disgust people feel at the sight of your *di-formity*!

We couldn't hear it, of course, but they must have screamed, staring at us and scaring the waiter, who tripped and smashed his tray. Oysters scattered every which way, trying to escape ravenous walruses and carpenters. The whole world was pointing in our direction.

It appeared that fate constantly auditioned us for the roles of persecuted merry-andrews in the divine comedy of boo-boos. We dashed away straight through the thorns. *Citius,* Alex! *Altius* and *fortius*—may the fittest survive!

Breathing heavily in the drum beat of our auricles and heat of our ventricles, we flattened ourselves on the ground. Now, now, now the floodlights would flare up, sirens howl and the baiting begin!

A minute ticked by, five, ten, eternity. Nothing. Gemini impassively twinkled in the black abyss above. We burst into hysterical uproar. The tapestry of our destiny had a well-defined pattern, elements of which kept repeating over and over again. Balconies, doors, windows—the domain of two-face Janus.

"We are becoming predictable," I deduced.

"Time to break the routine." Alex shook off the dirt. "Our chess set has two kings."

There, among other dwellers of Mount Olympus, in the warmth of light and aroma, having tucked a piece of feta cheese behind his cheek, Phobus must be piloting the conversation along his favorite fairway. By the way, he must be saying, hastily milling his hamster inventory, by the way, I am working with these peculiar patients now. . . .

He was going to talk about us—what other amusing story had he for Faye? Would it be a list of sterile Latin terms or a swell of sarcastic outburst? Scoff or compassion? Elegy or eulogy? Until now he had played a passive role in our drama, and we had given up hope of recruiting him as an ally despite his guild's unequivocal logo of two snakes entwining the dagger.

## THE FACE-OFF

When we walked in, the pianist was gone. His gadget was cooling off, showing its gap-toothed keys and arrogantly reflecting the chandelier. The speakers scattered sounds of the prerecorded sirtaki.

"Just you alone?" a girl in the taste of neither of us inquired. "Table for one?"

"You got it," we confirmed. "Just us alone. Table for two."

The floor had been cleaned, oysters captured; carpenters, once again, prevailed. Hand in hand, like Dante and Virgil, we entered the coil of gluttony.

Speaking of coils and vices, like any true artist, ever since our adolescence we have been enchanted by deadly sins.

"Are we subject to envy?" Alex pondered.

"Envy is shallow," I replied. "What do we care about the misery of others?"

"How about lust? Do you think it's a mortal peccadillo?"

"Lust is never creative. We should strive for art and never settle for craft."

"What about conceit?"

"Rubbish," I rejected. "We are too proud to descend into arrogance."

This conversation took place a long time ago—Mr. (or was it Doctor?) Einstein could clarify if place can take time—and, having discarded all seven sins, we burst out laughing. Several attempts to revisit Dante's canticles never reached the final rounds of paradise, where he had an appointment with Beatrice. We had always imagined her sitting motionlessly in the back light of a tall window. Her wrists were crossed over her lap like the angel's wings, her narrow ankle showed under the bell of starched crinoline.

Back from the momentous flashback, we watched Faye Phobus sitting in the very same pose.

"Anything for an appetizer?"

"As a matter of fact," we told the waiter, "we changed our minds and will now change tables. We caught sight of our friend and wish to join him. He is a famous healer. Are you suffering from any disease or disgrace yourself? We can put in a word for you."

He shrugged, pocketed his pen and trotted on. We leaned forward, ready to rise. At the same instant, in the distant corner Phobus with his wife and daughter also got up as if mirroring our move.

Are they leaving again? We sank back into our chairs, poked four holes in the description of dishes du jour and pretended to study the menu.

In another mock escape Phobus hopped away right before we honed in. We held our breaths as we watched him join someone's company. Who could that be? Who else but Fo-Fo!

So, that's what the summit of today's wanderings was! All little slips and curtseys finally summed up to a whole infinitely greater than its parts. Wake up, Lazarus, waddle across and introduce yourself.


"Doctor Fo-Fo!" we would exclaim, tears of joy warping his handheld reflection. "We are so happy to make your facial acquaintance. How fortunate that we all meet here, on Mount Olympus, of all places." And a quick nod to others: "Mes dames, mademoiselle, monsieur Phobus . . . enchanted, encharmed, ench-cited!"

We would align our profiles, giving ladies a chance to exclaim in recognition:

"Aren't you our brave boardwalk warrior?"

"Yes, yes indeed we are happy to have rid you of evil in times of storm and thunder. How appropriately it all lines up—Doctor Phobus helps us, we help his wife and daughter. . . . What a kindhearted practitioner he is! His passion for family—the flame sufficient for three bears, forty thieves and one thousand and one nights—can be an object of envy for Izolda and her Tristan, for Swan and his Leda, for Snow White and her seven dwarves."

And, before sitting down next to Fo-Fo, we would catch the menial by his menu:

"We wish to celebrate now. Make arrangements for two more chairs and a twofold of food. Hold nothing back. Bring Metaxa, moussaka, souvlaki!"

"I had a feeling that we'd meet soon," Fo-Fo would rejoice, his arms apart in pre-embrace welcome. "You came to me in a dream. I have something very important to tell you."

That's how it was supposed to happen.

As we got up and navigated between tables, the Phobuses took their seats. Which one of their neighbors is Fo-Fo—the crew-cut, broad-shouldered chap or the yellow jacket with the untidy mop of greasy hair? Wait a second! Haven't we seen the square chin of one and the hair-tossing trick of the other? How in the world do they know each other? We bent low to take a better look. Sure enough the bare ankles cuddled under the table.

When we straightened up, all doubts had cleared. We recognized the artist and his companion. It was her, of course it was her, our only and unforgettable Hope!

As stunned as we were, a bigger shock loomed ahead. Many years had passed since we had seen the woman sitting now across from Hope, but even one heart was enough to draw the connection. We thought we lost you, Love, but there you were, more vulgar and breathtaking than ever. Her crew-cut boyfriend reached for a bottle and, in the night full of revelations, we recognized him too.

The last time we saw him he was garbed in a theatrical outfit, salivating over Esmeralda's Salsa on the school stage. That's what your end of the deal was—you got our girl! And where is your devoted Paul? Oh, Peter, Peter, aren't you your Paul's keeper? We should have eliminated you then, Pyotr-Peter-Pierre—pushed you into the guillotine and pulled the rope!

With Hope's appearance, all hopes of confronting Fo-Fo were gone. He had stood us up one more time. Now, cornered by Love and Hope—our ex-Esperanza and vice-Inamorata—we needed to think quickly. Did they muster in this house of Hestia as helpresses or temptresses?

Think, Alex, think, Alex, think.

"I know!" I yelled, almost outshouting the champing humdrum. "It's us. We are the only link holding them all together."

Our abilities of reasoning and argumentation are unsurpassed. Plain people's monologue produces opinion but never wisdom. One parent fails to conceive a child. We, on the other hand, always hear each other, and the result comes out sharp and penetrating like a fish bone.

Fo-Fo or no-no, the gathering here must have something to do with us. What were they plotting here? What could they possibly want?

Phobus now our least concern, we stared at Leonidas, who stretched to get a handful of oily olives and then, in a trademark gesture, tossed his hair back without wiping his hand, oil being such an intimate part of his life. Whether he realized it or not, he was a pawn in this game. He owed his success to Hope. Before meeting her, he stagnated in anonymity.

What about Love and Peter? Which one of those two was instrumental in their appearance here? Look at his haircut and posture, Alex pointed, look at his appetite, look how this Peter Piper gobbles a peck of pickled peppers.

We backed all the way to our old table.

"Weren't you joining another party?" The waiter raised his eyebrows, his bewilderment hidden behind the professional grin.

"We have our own party to conjoin," I joked sadly. "Don't stand in the way. Bring us some bread."

"And water with lemon," Alex added. "Greek dishes are Greek to us. We need time. We can't decide between *Chtapodi Scharas* and *Soutzoukakia Smyrneika.*"

Think, Alex, think, Alex.

Isn't Peter the art-crimestigator? What if he is here on the hunt for the portrait?

That meant, we both gasped, the mishap at the museum hadn't

been resolved yet. They must still be looking for the mysterious, albeit totally innocent, double figure in a vast cloak. Peter learned the news about the skirmish at the border, about courageous strangers and their escape, put two and two together and got the two of us!

Their gathering was a conspiracy! How could we have been so naive as to take it for an opportunity! This was a trap; we had to get out. Clearing our way with the cane, the hood pulled to the tips of our noses, we attracted attention only once, when a clumsy move whisked somebody's glass off the table.

Alex and I were almost at the door, when the Maitre d' crossed our path.

"Is everything OK?"

"Yes, yes," we sputtered impatiently, "everything's perfect."

"Would you like to pay for the food now?"

"Food? We haven't ordered anything. We are still starving."

"Our policy. . . ," he started, but at this moment a flash of inspiration made it all clear.

"You thought we were running away?" we puffed. "That would be silly. We just got here. Sorry about the mess—slip of the staff, you know. Where did you say the restroom was? Is it clean? Are your stalls spacious?"

Under his distrusting stare, we marched in a double formation to the door marked with a single male dummy with spread-out extremities. The double-dealer had lied to us—the stall was tight, but as a hideout it served its purpose. Our lives went in circles. Some time ago we had found ourselves in a similar congestion, our resurrection starting in a stall just like this. We'd made the full circle. The phoenix was about to re-rise from ashes.

# Foes and Allies

From the restroom nook we peeked through the bead curtain at the table occupied by Love, Hope, Faye and other former pro- and present antagonists.

As if sensing our stares, Phobus's wife said something to Faye.

They headed in our direction. Draped into the blackest of cloaks, we pressed ourselves into the darkest of corners. The mother disappeared behind the door with the dolly, and we were left in the tiny antechamber with her daughter.

Our mimish cameo and chameleonish mimics didn't seem to trick Faye for a second. She looked us over, seeing right through the guise, right into our hearts:

"You two are funny."

People had called us wicked and weird but no one ever dubbed us funny.

"We are?"

"I saw you staring through the window, and then the waiter stumbled and the oysters scattered all over. I shouldn't have laughed, I know, poor fellow, but it was hilarious."

"We . . . hmm . . . we just peeked inside trying to decide what kind of Olympus specialty we wanted—nectar or ambrosia."

". . . and, by the way, thank you for saving me from those horrible creatures on the boardwalk. That was very brave."

Blood rushed up against gravity to our temples.

"We haven't been formally introduced. Allow us. Our names are Alex and Alex."

"I am Faith, but everybody calls me Fairy."

Faye-Faith-Fairy.

"That can't be your real name!" we exclaimed. "That's not who you are."

"We just met and you already know that I am not who I am?" Her eyes shined at both of us. She winked to me and laughed to Alex.

"Unless a proper match is found, we withhold from calling someone by name. Unfortunately, a few mistranslations from the past still haunt us. The first time we heard your name, the truth tickled us, but we didn't realize where it was hiding. Now we do. You are Vera."[2]

"That's what Nanny calls me too."

2. *Vera*: Russian: Faith

Her mother could step out any second.

"Listen, Vera, we don't have time to explain what's going on. You are our only ally, and we need your help."

The plea for assistance coming from two fit, double-able-bodied men to a frail young woman might not have sounded too convincing, but she accepted it with the utmost seriousness.

"We are on a quest to find one person. Only he can free us from oddity. For some reason, for a motive we don't fully understand, he avoids us. His name is Fo-Fo."

She burst out laughing again, and Alex's palm quickly covered her lips. "Sh-h!" I felt her breath warm the hill of Venus on his hand—no senses and sensations remained private in our tandem.

"We have to keep a low sideways profile. Our protective layer is thin and may pop if people poke fingers at us. We are prepared to reward Fo-Fo with a very precious painting, the only legacy we got . . . let's say from our father. Please take us to this man. You know him, don't you?"

"Of course, I do."

"You do?" we gasped. "Who. . . ?"

The handle turned and, not giving us a chance to finish the question, Vera's mother appeared. We covered our paled faces like phantoms of the opera. She took her daughter's hand, and the pair retreated to the main hall. As they walked by, Vera turned and silently articulated a few words.

What? We had trouble reading her lips in penumbra.

"She speaks in riddles like the Delphian oracle," I whispered. "She ended with *See you,* but what came before that?"

"She must have invited us to her home. What could that mean?"

"That's obvious, Watson. The question is—*where* could it be?"

Alex and I are excellent in di-deducing. She knew about Fo-Fo and didn't deny his existence, which was the first confirmation that he was real, as real as Vera and the two of us.

She returned to her table and, not involved in yonder mirth, stealthily waved in our direction.

Maitre d' got engaged in the farewell of gratitude and apologies

*Alex's palm quickly covered her lips. "Sh-h!"*

with the lady whose oysters had tried to flee from walruses. Unseen, we sneaked into the night.

A half-hour went by. At least we think it was a half-hour. Alex hates watches, and I don't like anything that he detests. Clocks' proximity to endlessness makes him tense. Our heartbeat, he says, is quite sufficient. We need no other ticker in or on our body. What about other people? I ask, and we laugh. All our childhood the *ad populum* was the main argument of adults—why can't you be like everybody else? We always responded *ad hominem*—just look at your *everybody else*. See how lonely they are. Do you want us to be as pathetic? Other people consulted a watch as the rhythm keeper of the heart. We didn't need that—our hearts beat in unison with one another.

When the company finally appeared on the street only one cab pulled over. Phobus got in. Wait! we were about to scream, but Peter *The Shylock* Holmes was nearby, and neither of us dared to face him. Not because we chickened out—Alex is never afraid of physical combat, and I don't get overpowered in verbal fencing.

How good am I?

Here is a little something for you, Professor:

I am as deft in the art of argumentation as both Diogenes the Dog and Aristippus. If the parable didn't lie Aristippus enjoyed luxury, while Diogenes required little for content. Once Diogenes, washing vegetables, ridiculed Aristippus: "If you had learnt to eat these vegetables, you wouldn't be a slave in the palace of a tyrant." To that Aristippus replied: "Had you known how to behave among men, you wouldn't be washing vegetables."

We knew well how to behave among men, thank you very much.

The cab blinked, carrying the Phobuses away. Vera was watching us from the back seat. As soon as Peter the Sleuth and Leonidas the Artist turned away, we dashed after the car. For a few moments the hesitant luck couldn't make up its mind whose side to take, and we almost caught up with them at the intersection. But then the light turned green, the motor roared and the question of divine affiliation never came up again.

We didn't give up easily, oh no. I panted amuck and Alex scampered like a child with scissors, but even the double lung capacity proved insufficient to compete with heartless horsepower.

During our short-lived pursuit the hood flew open, exposing our terrible deformity to the night. At that hour, however (as the last charity spared by fortune), people minded their own business and didn't focus on two men puffing heavily in the middle of the road.

"Life happens too fast. This kaleidoscope doesn't let us think clearly." I pulled Alex's sleeve. "Let's go home."

When we approached our building, the resolute and swift-to-dish-it-out Alex was about to pull the front door open. I stopped him. I am the artistic soul, sensitive and perceptive. Although both of us were exhausted—one can't be fresh while the other is weary—I caught a faint whiff of danger.

"Back away," I urged, tapping his arm.

"Enough of that nonsense," he yawned. "It's too late for playing hide-and-seek. Who would want to stalk us at bedtime?"

"Someone's up there," I warned.

The theme of observing windows took a weird twist. This time we watched our own. A dim glow, like that of a candle or a pocket flashlight, flickered behind the blinds. For a brief second, the shadow acquired anthropomorphic likeness. But, before we recognized the intruder, the light moved away, and the figure's contours smeared against drapery.

In another instant the shadow was gone. The windowpane reflected moonlight.

"I am dead," Alex said. "You must be seeing reveries from my dreams."

Oh, what the hell! I relied on my brother's judgment. I always do.

Ascending the stairs, we let our bodies keep balance on their own—the vestibular task twice as complex as that of a solo untwin.

It worked well until the last step of the last flight. Then a foot or two tripped. We flapped all our hands; the staff flew away; the cloak soared like a Jolly Roger.

Suddenly, gravitational forces got help. A heavy body—a beast or a human—saddled our backs. Blinded by the darkness, the shock and the hood swathing our faces, we stumbled. Rugged paws jammed our jerks and coarse palms gagged our mouths. After a few odd moments of uneven struggle and stagger, we came crashing down on the checkered tiles of the landing.

Crude threats plugged our ears. *Hush! Shut up!* The hooks dragged us—helpless like a whale on the shore—into our own apartment. Someone else in my shoes would surely blame Alex. Didn't I warn him against coming up? Didn't I point out that a lone flashlight promised nothing kind? But I refrained from reproofs—we were in this life together.

The switch clicked, and the light blinded us worse than darkness.

"What's going on?" we demanded, unsure which direction to deface. Our voices faltered, falling over nervous caesuras of dissonance. "Who are you? Mafia, Interpol, UNESCO?"

"Don't be ridiculous."

A hand tossed our hood open, leaving us totally self-unreliant.

"We don't understand. What do you want? You confuse us with someone elses. If you wish to kidnap us for ransom, nobody will care." We turned and twisted, seeking refuge in the nonexistent shadows.

"Stop your clownery."

"Don't hurt us. We can explain everything." Talking gave us an illusion of control. "If you are after the notebook, we didn't steal it. Somehow it got into our pocket—must be one of those mysterious cases. We returned it at the very next opportunity. We needed the address of Doctor Fo-Fo. Have you heard of him? We are disturbed, even sick, but most of all we are unhappy. Stay away from us, because dejection is contagious. Fo-Fo is the only one able to save us. We saw the notebook and thought that what if, what if his address was there? And if you were wondering about the portrait, it's a different story. We didn't steal it either. . . ."

Our eyes adjusted to light. The trembling mirror in my hand located one attacker, then the other. What a shocker!

"You? And you? We had no idea. . . . Are you in cahoots?"

The old man perched on a chair.

"Costas is my wife's nephew. What is this doctor nonsense? You swindled us. I should have known. Rose warned me and she is never wrong."

Creeps crawled down my spine. Sorry, Alex. He shuddered. Jump up, I signaled. Shake these dwarfish foes off Gulliver's shoulders. Swipe away their web of intrigues.

Alas, they had confiscated our cane, leaving us no chance against the unfair numerical equality.

As soon as Costas's pincers loosened their grip, we pulled the hood over our heads. Concealed in the fabric-afforded shade, our eyes let us see things in their true obscurity.

"Summon Fo-Fo," we stated firmly. "Let him hook us up to his gadgets and examine us with the most advanced means of his absurd science. Then you'll know that our words contain no *double entendre*, not a syllable of lies."

"I am not taking no funny money no more," the old man grumbled, choking grammar. "If I come back empty-handed, Rose will eat me alive."

"Look at this!" Costas pulled a roll from under the bed. "That's what you were mumbling about? Is it worth much?"

"Oh!" We burst into a guffaw. "It's worth more than can fit between your ears. It's priceless. Unfortunately, it's not up for a bargain."

He spread the canvas on the floor like a welcome rug or unwelcome rags and turned to the old man. "What do you think?"

"I need my rent. Real money, no candy wrappers."

Costas frowned, exhibiting some alarming thoughtfulness.

"You are pulling our leg. I am gonna hold on to the portrait. These babies—" he lovingly shook his enormous fists, which our mirror could reflect only one at a time—"these puppies will teach you a valuable lesson."

"Sheathe them back!" we squeaked. "You have no right to apply force to persons of royal descent."

"Royal, huh?"

"Yes, royal, regal, imperial! Sooner or later our awakened motherland will beg us back to take the vacant throne."

"They'll kick you out of the palace for late payments." The old grudge turned out to be quite mordant.

Costas's fist clenched again, and our internal counsel was promptly adjourned. The rhetoric of Alex the Democrat was discarded; the power politics of Alex the Autocrat triumphed—every seat in our two-chair congress voted right. In a desperate twitch we kicked Costas with all our legs, jumped up and, as he doubled over, rammed him into the wall. The thug slid down, his lips curled in imbecile bewilderment.

"Stay away from us, insatiable bourgeois! For once think not about mammon but about your fellow men. Didn't we advise you not to mess with us?"

His muscle boy in shackles, the landlord squealed some semi-comprehensible seltzer salute, spattering all over the room.

Get the portrait! Alex shrieked. I stretched my hand, but Costas grumbled, held on to the canvas and staggered to get on his feet. We had to choose between the painted dignitary and painful indignity. Without further doo-doo, we darted towards the door, knocking off the chair and sweeping the umbrella stand that escorted us for two full flights, rolling down the stairs under echoing accompaniment.

Run . . . Alex . . . run . . . Alex . . . run.

We never looked back, supporting and cheering for each other, one's breath behind the other's neck. We loped across the night until our gas tank was completely drained.

Where . . . are . . . we?

Houses gave way to trees and shrubbery. Geographical anonymity sheltered us. We were lost but not least.

When the heartbeat cacophony quelled, we balanced the accounts. Material casualties comprised the cane and the Mint supplies.

Among moral losses was the dented pride, expected to recuperate by dawn. The missing portrait severed our ties with the past. Sorry, Fo-Fo. We'll have to come to you empty-handed.

But, on the credit side, we still had each other.

*Das Mittespiel* was over—two black kings marched into the endgame hand in hand.

## Wild Fo-Fo chase

Although we had dodged Costas and stayed two half-steps ahead of Peter, sooner or later the faster of them would get on our heels and the smarter would Fo-foresee our moves. The stakes were high. We had endured Hope's disloyalty and Love's infidelity, burned the bridges and abandoned everything we held dear— Mother, motherland and moths in the wardrobe of our childhood.

By now our deck had only one ace. Vera gave us a literal *cart blanche*, a blank-address invitation to Fo-Fo. Time left us the only possible direction—ahead.

At this stage it would have been unprofessional to introduce new players and places. We knew three addresses in this town. Our Mint was now a pillaged parish, the point of no return. The old man would have to pacify his consort on his own. He should have taken better care of our bill. What a fine piece it was!

The next two addresses belonged to Phobus—his Ph-apartment and his Ph-office. We'd tried both. No trace of Fo-Fo there.

And finally, there was the house in the suburbs.

"That makes the fourth address," Alex corrected.

"Three sounds better. Dumas didn't call his book *Four Musketeers*."

The night spent in the open didn't rejuvenate us. All benches in the alley came in narrow twin sizes, the name, once again, misleading. We prefer sleeping on our backs, our arms and legs stretched. Here, in the damp inhospitality, we could only lie on our side. In the middle of the night, tossing in oblivion, we tipped the bench over and woke up in dew and undue position—rubbing our eyes and trying to make sense of our juxtaposed nightmares.

The morning brought early birds jogging by their unleashed pets—all snooping, few friendly. We got up and wandered to the little fountain, where we cupped the water, splashed, gurgled and carried out our morning routine to the best of our abilities in the worst of circumstances. Athletic idlers twisted their necks. Apparently, we failed our cautionary stance or forgot to hood our heads or took too long fishing coins out of the water. Go to hell, we muttered. We are not responsible for your sanity. We can hardly hold on to our own. With Fo-Fo awaiting us in his ivory tower, the fairy tale was approaching its frightful *ever after*.

Alex and I jumped onto the roadway and spread our hands. The bus skidded and screeched.

"Take us into your team, teamster," I exclaimed, "hightail us to the house on West Cedar Street. Put some ginger in your exhaust tube! Hey-ho!"

"Move aside."

"We pay double. Give us four tickets! Dry these coins and have them all!"

"Get off the road. It's a local route."

"What is in the route?" Alex exploded. "Are you a single-track tram? Don't you have the freedom of drive? Ye have heard that it was said by them of old time, thou shalt stick to your route, but we say unto you: follow your heart. Verily we say unto thee. . . ."

He didn't let us finish. The bus roared and jerked. Our hard-fished kopeks spilled all over the road. We had to travel to the terminal on foot like plain apostles.

"You again?" The driver turned out to be the one who had taken us to the Faux-Fo's clinic. "You paid me with this funny money the other day, remember?"

"Money," we responded gravely, "is a serious business. There is nothing funny about it. We take great pride in what we do. No, we have no idea what you are talking about."

"Get in. That was a pretty cool bill. My girlfriend got a kick out of it. Have any more of those?"

We lowered our heads.

"We are delighted that you appreciate our art, but all our possessions have been vandalized. No tools survived. It's a big game, and all who help will get rewarded. Alas, we have nothing to pay you with."

"The ticket's on the house. Get in."

There you go, Doctor, we whispered. Look how low we fell—reduced to a lone bench and a single ticket. You think it's your technique working? Are you happy now?

The town was rolling by. The novelty of the cityscape, rubbed by misadventures, wore off. We were no longer naïve newcomers but bitter fugitives. If we failed to reach Fo-Fo, we risked being apprehended by law in the hand of Peter or lawlessness in the paw of Costas.

We peered into the faces of boarding passengers. Who are they, exuberant players or plain extras in our drama?


"Stop here, good driver."

We sprang down in a well-coordinated jump, and turned the pocket mirror to the rear view.

"Drive away. It might not be safe out here."

He pulled the lever, and his bus puffed a farewell exhaust.

Number Fifty-Five lay lulled. Reflecting the blank skies, windows across the street concealed no curious eyes, no spyglass glare.

We circled the house, bending and holding our breath behind the shrubs. The flowerbed had fully recovered from debauchery. The earth's scratch was healed—the smashed stems rotted away, the injured straightened up. The rain had washed off our watercolor footsteps from the asphalt. The winds had wiped off the intrepid outline of two fearless wall-climbers, overlaying it with the new day's imprint.

Had something happened here? Was this a scene of tragedy or

travesty? There could be no certainty. Despite time's ultimate transparence, the past stayed impenetrable.

"Look!" Alex nudged. "The door's ajar."

I pulled his hood lower.

"We can't afford another mistake. Even if someone shows up on the doorstep in his dressing gown and charges at us with outstretched arms, how do we know it's Him?"

"Let's pretend to be book salesmen. It's a safe excuse—nobody falls for bibles or biblios anymore."

"Then what?"

"Then," Alex gabbled, "then, if nobody leaps at us from the darkness, we shall turn 90 degrees and, after his first shock goes away, introduce ourselves. Don't take this madness for its sideways value, we shall say. Listen to our story and what seems strange will appear rational, what seems absurd will become logical."

We cast two final glances along the quiet street like a lone first grader faltering at a dangerous intersection.

Crawling on four soft tiptoes, Alex and I reached the door and were about to push a little, testing its squeaky hinges. Instead, the door opened. Our jaws dropped.

"Vera! What are you doing here?"

"Where else should I be? I was waiting for you. Would you like to come in?"

We stepped back. I was still hesitant, and Alex couldn't let go of the image of cordial Fo-Fo.

Vera pushed the door wider so that the two of us could fit in.

"You don't mind using the conventional entrance? Unless you prefer climbing through the window, of course."

In the hallway Alex bumped into a bulky coffer. I almost tripped over it.

She switched the lights on, and we saw an ancient chest with iron corners, not unlike that in which *Koschei the Deathless*—a perennial participant of magical soaps—hid his soul to protect immortality. The soul was stashed inside a needle, which was in an egg, which was in a duck, which was in a hare, which was in an iron chest, which was buried under a green. . . .

"Did you dig it out from under an oak tree?"

"No," she laughed. "I don't know where Nanny got it."

"Who is Nanny?"

Still limping, we followed Vera into the living room, where, usually reserved and composed, we couldn't refrain from another outburst.

"What's that?"

A mischievous eye winked at us from the dark canvas. After the initial shock, we moved to the painting, almost touching it with our eyelashes, and closely studied the withered brush grooves.

"Don't take us wrong, we love pictures. We think that art is cool, but *this* is a bit excessive," we commented. "Up until last night we owned one very valuable piece. Lighter and more optimistic than this one—a long story which we, of course, are ready to unbosom before Doctor Fo-Fo."

Vera stood by our side, measuring the portrait, her head slightly atilt.

"I like that the only feature in focus is his eye," she said. "The rest is blurry and uncertain—odds of landscapes and ends of still-lives—just like memory."

"We must be seeing different things. It's too murky for our taste. We don't value ambiguity. That's exactly what we are trying to get rid of. Look here, for instance. What is it? Some kind of a town smeared by rain or snow? There is no clear distinction between the face, the background and multiple plots merging into one another. The man's eye could also be a moon over a quiet landscape, further turning into a gap-toothed grin or piano keys. The tree becomes a train's pipe, puffing out a steam cloud, which can also be a river crossed by this bridge. What did the artist have in mind? If we move closer only brush strokes remain, hiding rather than revealing details. Our shock is gone. Now that we have had a chance to examine this work, it doesn't impress as much."

Alex the Artist coughed and frowned. Alex the Adventurer raked around.

"We are ready to see Fo-Fo now."

"Follow me." Vera took our hand and led upstairs.

I told you, Alex whispered, his study was up there.

The cloak caught on the railing. The fabric crackled. Our sartorial masterpiece bulged at the seams.

"Disrobed means denounced," I moaned. "Ask Vera for a sewing machine."

"After Fo-Fo cures us, we won't have to hide."

We entered a small room, our hearts exchanging dots and dashes in the inner Morse. Here we come, Doctor. Here we are.

His study was nothing like we imagined. We expected it to be something like Fein's office with thick folios, some domesticated vegetation in a vat and a bust of this or that glazed luminary. Or, at the very least, a solid desk in fumed oak and a chart of an incised asexual dummy entwined with nerves and blood vessels. Contrary to all our guesswork, the room was almost empty. Then we heard a sigh.

Someone stirred in the tall bed, under a thick quilted blanket.

"Doctor?!"

"This is Nanny." Vera clearly enjoyed our dismay.

A head in an old-fashioned night cap emerged from under the quilt. Nanny could well be a Granny of the Little Red Riding Hoodlum, or—worse—her canine copycat.

"Who are you?" she wheezed.

"That's not him! Where is our redeemer? What have you done to Fo-Fo?" we appealed to Vera. "Is this the wrong place? We have no time for impractical jokes. Clouds are gathering. We have to beat the storm."

"Tell me a story," Nanny asked.

"Nanny is very old," Vera explained. "She used to tell me fairy tales. I am not sure whether it's my childhood or her tales that I remember better. She never asked anybody for a story. That's funny. Please, please. I'll listen too."

"But," we mumbled, demoralized by Nanny and unable to resist the girl, "we had prepared it for Fo-Fo."

Ah, why not? Alex wired. *Docster* Faux-Faux must have given up on us. I am ready to denounce him.

We had nothing else to do. We had nowhere else to hide. At least we were safe and welcome here.

Why not? I shrugged.

"We are not sure how entertaining it will be. The only story we know is the story of our lives."

We looked at one another and began in unison, never fluffing, never slipping into dissonance, always knowing ahead what the other was about to say:

"Our case history started with a dual image: Romulus and Remus suckling on a she-wolf. Kind Mother would surely excuse this lyrical embroidery. . . ."

Gradually the words grew lighter and more fluent. They enveloped us and offered the wholesome perspective of our existence from our very first days to this moment in a strange land, in the company of two women—one approaching her night time, the other just awakening. Suddenly, we had a surge of faith that everything would eventually be fine.

# Fairy (Part 6)

### THE PORTRAIT

Leon and Nad'usha were already waiting as Fodor drove up to the museum. The front tire rubbed against the curb.

"Got it last week." He tapped his palm on the steering wheel. "Now that we live in the suburbs, that's a handy toy!"

Peter and L'ubasha appeared a few minutes later, in the midst of the battle for the parking foothold by the hydrant.

"Mr. Samorodok is a great artist." Fodor pointed at the sign above the entrance.

"And I am the Tooth Fairy," the bored cop yawned.

The conflict was dissolved with Nad'usha's *Where have you been?* and L'ubasha's *Here we are!* Tallest physically and heaviest socially, Leon took the front seat. The rest squeezed in the back.

While still within the city line, Fodor ticked off landmarks with the laconic and self-explanatory *Here is this monument* or *That's the cathedral.*

"I admire how clean the streets here are," remarked Peter. "I didn't have to shine my shoes. At home they wouldn't last an hour."

"It's nice weather," Fodor agreed generously.

"In our country the soil erodes in any weather."

"And in winter—all slush. Forget about it," Leon added.

"By lunch time my hair is a disaster," Nad'usha confessed to the rear-view mirror from the backseat.

"Traffic here can be impossible," Fodor remarked as a gracious host, willing to admit minor negatives to balance out hygienic benefits of geography.

343

He stopped the car in front of the house and helped the ladies out. Peter checked the well-nurtured flowerbed, the ivy streaming up the side wall, the picturesque in its crookedness cherry tree, and nodded with appreciation.

Inside, Leon hit his foot against a huge metal-bound chest, and—after Sophie promptly lit the hallway—Fodor explained that it was supposed to be dragged up to the second floor, but the stairs here were too narrow, sorry about it, does it still hurt?

Leon stepped on his heel and pulled the injured foot out of the loafer to examine bare toes, kneading them in his hand and tuning in to subtle perceptions.

Sophie set the table in the dining hall. L'ubasha and Nad'usha exchanged a few quiet, sisterly interjections. Fodor gestured everybody to the living room and stopped in the middle like a museum guide waiting for the group to turn around.

The closed space made the portrait seem bigger. The massive frame emphasized its dominance. Limping Leon slowed down and came to a standstill. He and Fodor stared at the painting like two proud fathers.

"Not bad," Peter commented, ruining the somber reunion. Sophie was preoccupied with hosting logistics. The other two women took Peter's side, sharing his detached curiosity rather than Fodor's deifying awe.

"I am ready to hear the truth about Monster. Why such a name? What's the significance of all these background objects? Why are they here?"

Leon squinted and smiled. Not to the host or anybody else but to his own magnum opus.

"It's been so long," he whispered tenderly. "I almost forgot."

The artist moved closer to study the brush strokes, then stepped back, satisfied.

"It's all coming back to me now. Before I explain my vision, let's take turns. Tell me what you see. We shall be bystanders describing the crime scene. You would be amazed by the variety of viewpoints. Who wants to go first?"

*Leon studied brush strokes, then stepped back, satisfied.*

Sophie interrupted:

"The dinner is ready. Unless you want the fish cold, I suggest we start with the food. The portrait can wait."

That seemed like a reasonable suggestion. Accompanied by the household sounds of shuffling feet, moving chairs and fragmentary phrases, the guests settled around the table. One seat remained empty.

"You expect someone else?" Peter asked.

Fodor coughed and faltered, rolling syllables in a ball like breadcrumbs, but Sophie took it quite casually:

"Fairy always sits next to me. She must still be upstairs. What a dawdler. Excuse me for a moment."

Everybody's focus on the food, they said nothing. Sophie hurried up in a thrifty, business-like manner. Her heels marked every step with a distinct click. Tip-tap, top-tup. On the second floor the clanking paused, and in another dead-quiet instant a heart-rending scream razored the space.

Sophie slid downstairs, her foot twisting, her broken heel holding on a wing and a prayer. A gust of wind banged at the window, flapping it open. The curtain whirled up like a frigate's sail. The fruit vase flew off the sill and crashed, apples rolling all over the room.

"Nanny. . . ."

The elated gourmet humors solidified into stale stillness. Ignoring the vase and not waiting for Fodor, who like a weighty wheel took ages to gain momentum, Sophie dashed to the telephone, in her sightless haste striking the portrait's frame with a shoulder and nearly knocking down the coffee table. As she was pushing buttons—*Ambulance, ambulance!*—the hook pulled out and Monster collapsed, muffling sounds and silence alike.

# Vera (Part 4)

Vera and Nanny proved attentive listeners. The story carried us along the time stream. The day gradually grayed out. No one noticed when scraps of conversations and the tinkling of silverware started to waft from downstairs. Vera, who sat on the edge of the bed, leaned over so that her ear almost touched Nanny's lips, crackled like an old masterpiece.

"What?" We paused our almost finished story.

"She is cold," Vera translated from Oldish.

In a gesture inconceivable before, we took our cloak off and spread it on top of the blanket. Nanny's faint sigh accompanied squeaks of the floor boards outside the room. Someone was coming! We raced to the corner, nearly knocking down the floor lamp, and merged with the background shades.

"Fairy, honey," Vera's mother said, "are you still here? Everybody is waiting. Let's go say hello."

She cast a quick glance at the old woman's bed.

"Nanny, where do you find these terrible rags?" Two fastidious fingers lifted our cloak. "Is this from your chest again? I told you a thousand times, if you need a plaid or a blanket, just tell me. What? I can't hear you." She lowered her head to make out Nanny's bubbles, then gasped: "Oh, my!"

What's going on, we lipped to Vera. Was that something we said, something from our story?

I don't know, she gestured.

Phobus, panting from his speedy ascend, rushed in. Our presence unobserved, we captured a few fragments—disjoint adverbs and detached adjectives. Then he withdrew, dispirited and desperate. The three of us stayed in the room—Vera, Alex and I. Without breath, Nanny's presence became undetectable.

"Guess our story comes to the end." We stepped back into the light. "Time to get going."

We stuck our heads out the door, looked over the bannister, and recoiled hastily.

"What?" Vera asked.

"Your guests, downstairs. We know who they are. Whatever excuse they had for coming here, it's just a pretense. They are after us. We are trapped."

She didn't understand, so we took her hand and tiptoed to the door. A group of unremarkable people sat motionlessly around the table. Their plates were clean, but no one reached for the groaning board.

We pointed at each one and whispered their true names. We just told you about them, we said. They were all characters in our story with the *solo-* syllable peeking from behind their images—Nad'usha must still be coloring skies with *solid* azure. L'ubasha's thighs must still bear ballpoint imprints with outdated quiz *solutions*. They used to fill our whole mindscape, but their time was up. Absolute became obsolete.

"Figures from the past, gathered under one roof, bode ill. We have to get out before it's too late."

The conspiring chatter downstairs melted into hisses, which oozed in through the cracks like sand from a broken sandglass slipping between fingers. It grew dead quiet. Then, deafening sirens incised the sleepy suburbs. We peeked out the window. An ambulance slammed on the brakes in front of the house and dehisced, discharging two wiry figures in white robes. Alex leaned over to take a better look.

"It's them!"

"Who?" I asked.

"Who?" asked Vera.

"Costas's thugs. And he is behind the wheel. They are coming to get us."

This tiny room had enough shadows to conceal us from Vera's mom and from Phobus, but against well-trained bloodthirsty sleuths we stood no chance. If only Fo-Fo were around!

Until the very last moment we had faith that he was the one to heal our monstrosity. Instead, he betrayed us. He was nowhere. He plainly didn't exist.

Vera tucked the blanket on the still bed. Her eyes were sad, her palm covered her mouth.

"Alex, I got it!" I grabbed his sleeve. "We were blind. Fo-Fo is here, he has always been with us; not nowhere but *know*-where! The temptation of Love and the false comfort of Hope led us to Vera; that's who our cure is."

I didn't have to spell it out any more—he was quick on the uptake. How could we miss it? The girl's name, not the Latin transliteration, but its Cyrillic original, *Вера,* started with В—the fully unfolded Ф!

"Do you believe in us, Vera?" Alex turned to the girl. "Are you with us?"

"I do. I am." She looked at the bed. "My thousand and one nights here are over."

At that moment, without any external assistance, we did what Fo-Fo would have prescribed. The solution had been in front of our eyes all along. Fein and Tulchinsky failed because *we* weren't ready.

Footfalls and creaking steps of the staircase grew stronger.

The mirror images that Alex and I had been for each other all our lives separated. Seamless and indivisible before, we unclenched the embrace and slid apart without effort, without pain as if it were meant to happen from the very *Once upon a time.* We stepped aside and stared at each other. I nodded, Alex nodded. I smiled, Alex smiled. I raised my right hand, Alex raised his left.

"What are you going to do now?" he asked.

"I . . . I don't know."

For the first time I found his thoughts clouded and impenetrable. The border between us was shut down. No longer could signals freely zoom back and forth.

I took Vera's hand and led her to the window.

"Are you ready?"

She looked down, serious and determined.

"It only seems high," I reassured her. "The flowerbed is soft. We . . . I have already landed there once. Don't be afraid. Two-face Janus, the god of defenestration, is my tutelary saint."

In the final farewell I waved to Alex, squeezed Vera's hand and, right before the room's door was flung open, we leaped into the dark square. For the first time—there had to be so many first times now!—the plural pronoun signified Alex and Vera.

Alex and Vera stepped out the window and merged with the black background. As to me, I lost my interest. The room was quickly filling with fuss and anxiety. People I used to know barged in. I moved back, grabbed a random book from the shelf, sank into the armchair next to the floor lamp and pretended to be reading.

When the right moment comes, I will get up and walk away. There is no reason to fear. The hunt's on for a deformed double monster hiding under the cloak, turning sideways and observing others through the distortion of his pocket mirror. I am nothing like that. No one is going to recognize me. I will cut right through the mob; upright, stately, detached, answering their stares with an open and sympathetic smile.

What's left when the fairy tale is over?

The very same blackness that was hushed away by the promising rustle of *Once upon a time* enshrouds the stage right beyond the final slam of *Happily ever after.* Wasn't that a good story, dear?

Go to sleep now. Sweet dreams.

## От Д. к О.: Ода

От Д до О—меж нами треть
иль четверть алфавита,
что умудрилась уцелеть
до наших дней.
А что забыто,
как ять и фита,
в томах теней
не в счет,
коль речь течет
как Aqua Vita.

Теперь два слова
о том, что "время лечит."

Пусть так, но счет
времен, катящий словно
река, в которой нечет
и чет—два берега, течет
и тащит воды-годы будто
из книги буквы.

Энергия волны
в реке, как в речи—
все буквы так полны
не смысла, но
хотя б энтузиазма.
Книги вечны—
несметно их число.
И повезло:
в случайной встрече
ты выбрала меня из разных
не гласных,
но согласных.

И вот отпущен срок
средь этих строк,
что населяют времена
от оглавленья до
развязки. Чья вина
или заслуга, если на
страницах, среди глав,
несущихся стремглав,
мы птицей ряжены Додо
и нотой "до"?

## D. to O.: Ode

Oh, storyteller's art!

Aligned by alphabet,
the letters try to set,
my heart,
the two of us apart,
which matters not
as long as draught—
created by the plot
to please a reader—
is strong. *There lived an O
and D, her beau. . . .*
And, ditto,
thereupon
the tale is wending on
like Agua Vita.

The narrative of time
enshrouds whether
by rhythm or rhyme
of Lethe
that carries waters-years
like letters
to happy end. And hence
the words are rushing
if not with sense
then passion.

These words are plenty,
but, what matters,
O. chose D. of twenty
four (admit it—quite
amative) letters,
so you and I could write
lifelong romance
of consonance.

And readers of the days,
we spend in paradise
in tight embrace,
might recognize
us in the guise
of bird Dodo
and note Do.

Many thanks to my wonderful editors Michael and, tenfold, Lisa Graziano for their deferential care of my disheveled ideas.

# The Author

Dmitry Zlotsky was born in Moscow in 1960, and emigrated to the United States in 1989 with his family. He currently lives in New Jersey, where he spends time inventing puzzles, writing poetry in Russian and prose in English, and watching a cherry tree through the window of his study.

# The Illustrator

Olga Zlotsky studied both art and engineering in Moscow. Once in the United States she decided to pursue her artistic dreams. She now teaches kids art, works in New York City as a fashion designer, and illustrates books.

Dmitry and Olga have two sons, Dan and Mark.

About the Type

This book was set in Plantin, a family of text typefaces inspired by the work of Christophe Plantin (1520-1589.) In 1913, Frank Hinman Pierpont of the English Monotype Corporation directed the Plantin revival. Based on 16th century specimens from the Plantin-Moretus Museum in Antwerp, specifically a type cut by Robert Granjon and a separate cursive Italic, the Plantin typeface was conceived. Plantin was drawn for use in mechanical typesetting on the international publishing markets.

Designed by John Taylor-Convery
Composed at JTC Imagineering, Santa Maria, CA